T0344646

Deceived

Julie Anne Lindsey

MeritPress

F+W Media, Inc.

Published by Merit Press
an imprint of F+W Media, Inc.
10151 Carver Road, Suite 200
Blue Ash, Ohio 45242
www.meritpressbooks.com

ISBN 10: 1-4405-6389-6
ISBN 13: 978-1-4405-6389-8
eISBN 10: 1-4405-6390-X
eISBN 13: 978-1-4405-6390-4

Printed in the United States of America.

10   9   8   7   6   5   4   3   2   1

Library of Congress Cataloging-in-Publication Data
Lindsey, Julie Anne.
  Deceived / Julie Anne Lindsey.
      pages cm
  ISBN 978-1-4405-6389-8 (hard cover : alk. paper) -- ISBN 1-4405-6389-6 (hard
cover : alk. paper) -- ISBN 978-1-4405-6390-4 -- ISBN 1-4405-6390-X
  I. Title.
  PZ7.L66113De 2013
  [E]--dc23

2013013932

This is a work of fiction. Names, characters, corporations, institutions, organizations, events, or locales in this novel are either the product of the author's imagination or, if real, used fictitiously. The resemblance of any character to actual persons (living or dead) is entirely coincidental.

Many of the designations used by manufacturers and sellers to distinguish their product are claimed as trademarks. Where those designations appear in this book and F+W Media was aware of a trademark claim, the designations have been printed with initial capital letters.

Cover image © 123rf.com.

*This book is available at quantity discounts for bulk purchases.
For information, please call 1-800-289-0963.*

Dedication

To Bryan, my anchor

Chapter One

I shot upright, breathless and covered in a familiar sheen of sweat. The sweat I had expected, but the glass of water on my nightstand was no longer cold. That was unusual. I rubbed my eyes and peered at the soft, green glow of numbers on my clock: 4:27 A.M. I had slept for four hours, three more than I was accustomed to. Sleep hadn't been part of my routine since puberty. Before that, I couldn't really remember.

Rise and shine for the emotional misfit.

I tossed back the covers and listened. An engine revved to life outside my window. My breathing hitched. I pushed the curtain aside with one finger. The shadowy figure from my dream flashed in my memory. Outside, lampposts cast cone-shaped patterns of light onto the darkened street below. No one was there.

My heart hammered. My body felt about 500 pounds too heavy. With only a few caffeine pills left in my drawer, I made plans to get more when the sun came up. Meanwhile, coffee and the treadmill would get me moving. I had worked out the formula in eighth grade: caffeine and adrenaline. That combo shook off the fatigue.

Pills had come later, when my schedule was more than the original recipe could manage.

According to a shrink I quit visiting two moves back, I had night terrors. He was wrong. I had one recurring nightmare. One I couldn't quite remember, but I knew it was the same again and again.

I forced myself into the kitchen to prepare the coffee and shook my hands out at the wrists. They trembled as always. Not from fear but addiction. These days, they seemed to shake with or without the caffeine, but mostly without. I rubbed them hard against my thighs and took a few deep breaths before I shoved my mug under the drip and moved the pot to the counter. Two mugs later, I climbed onto the treadmill and built a steady walk into a run.

Someone in the senior dormitories must have had a friend sleeping over or a before-school job because the same engine had woken me every morning all week. A loud rumbling noise, followed by a squealing belt. I ran through a mental list of people I'd met who looked as tired as I did. It was a short list. Three miles later, I hadn't come to any conclusions, but the sun had made its ascent. All the coffee was gone, and my heart pumped from adrenaline instead of fear, a welcome trade. I turned off the treadmill and grabbed a towel and my necessities. Time to get ready for school.

Music from my roommate's alarm blared over the noise of the shower, and I moved a little faster. My time alone was about to expire. Sharing a bathroom with her put me on edge. I thought of myself as modest, but she used the word *prude*. My new roommate rocked a nose ring and leather miniskirt most days. Her name was Priscilla, but she had asked me to call her Pixie. She was exiled to Francine Frances Academy three years ago when her folks split and neither wanted full custody. I sort of knew how she felt. Until a few weeks back, Dad was the only roommate I'd ever known. Fortunately for me, Pixie knew everyone and everything about the school. Privacy issues aside, I was lucky to have her. In the three weeks since I'd arrived, I'd learned to adore her larger-than-life presence. She said I was like the sister she never had. We were completely different, and it worked. Together we were a real-life yin and yang.

"What up, Elle?" Pixie strolled into the bathroom as expected, as if I weren't trying to get dressed. Nudity was utterly inoffensive to her. Very little offended Pixie. I often pictured her wearing tie-dyed tops, rose-colored glasses, and bell-bottoms. She would've made a great hippie.

"Are you planning to call me that forever?" I knew the answer. Yes.

Gabriella Denise Smith lent itself to plenty of nicknames. I'd been called Gabrielle, Gabby, Bella, D, Dee Dee, even Neecey. Leave it to Pixie to find another name in there.

She rolled her eyes and sucked on a Blow Pop. Pixie's aversion to eating had her surviving on lollipops, breath mints, and drinks, preferably energy drinks.

I pulled my top and skirt on in a hurry, avoiding eye contact until I reached for my toothbrush and paste. I breathed easier fully dressed and with something to keep my hands busy.

"Are you ready for it? Meeting the student body? Preparing for matriculation and such?"

No. "Sure." I scrubbed my teeth a little longer, telling them to be thankful that I didn't sleep with a sucker.

"I'm so glad to be in the senior dorms." She sighed, heaving her makeup onto the counter.

"Yeah."

Being a senior came with a bonus perk at the academy. The senior dorms were the farthest from everything else on campus. A few blocks at best, but freedom no matter how you sliced it. It took a little longer to get to class, but we weren't under the same scrutiny as the underclassmen. Compared to us, they lived in a fishbowl. When Dad had expressed his disapproval, I'd reminded him that I was leaving for college in a few months, and it wouldn't be a tiny private prep school in the rural Midwest. I hoped to end up in New York or Los Angeles. I couldn't handle much more small-town America.

We stood together applying makeup, but the processes were drastically different. I had lip gloss and mascara in my makeup bag, plus concealer to cover war wounds. The rings beneath my eyes were straight out of a zombie movie. I'd left anything more complicated in a drawer somewhere back home. It'd probably rotted from disuse.

Pixie whipped electric blue liquid eyeliner from an attaché resembling an artist's palette. She prepared her face in layers. The result was breathtaking. Thirty minutes later, she looked like a life-size china doll in knee-high socks, a pleated skirt, and a cardigan. I looked like I had just woken up.

According to school propaganda, uniforms "removed the distraction of fashion and reduced competition over material things." The idea to make us look alike sounded logical on paper, but Pixie's angled black hair with blue tips made it hard to see how the uniforms mattered in practice.

Before long, my mind struggled to remember details from the dream I never talked about. I already didn't fit in. If people knew about my multitude of issues—dead mother, distant father, recurring nightmare of impending death—I'd really be sorry. The new kid yet again, I needed to blend. Blending in was self-preservation. I imagined that going to school at an obscure midwestern academy would make it more imperative, not less.

"I know what you're thinking." Pixie pulled the sucker from her lips with a clear *pop*.

"Yeah?"

"Oh yeah." Her smug tone implied a naughty reason for my reluctance to share.

I turned to look at her, and she hopped onto the counter, swinging her feet and leering back at me with a crazy, toothy smile.

"What?" I sighed, relieved that she obviously didn't know what I was thinking, and also glad for the distraction.

"You're thinking about that guy from the coffee shop in Elton."

"Ah." I blushed. Though I hadn't been thinking of him at the moment, I definitely had been thinking about him more than I should.

"Yeah." I didn't miss a beat. "He was hot." How many times a day did I lie to Pixie?

"Well, duh. I still hate you for not going home with him. You don't even know where he lives, his age, nothing. Ugh." She growled at me and dismounted the counter with unusual grace.

Honestly, I'd hoped she'd ask all the questions for me so I could sit innocently by and gather information. But she hadn't.

"His name was Brian."

"Hooray." Sarcasm dripped from the word.

On our way out, I locked the door and the deadbolt, too. Then I double-checked the knob. I'd grown up seeing Dad do the same routine. My effort was lost on my current community, which boasted a zero crime rate. Spending my early years in D.C. had made a lasting impression. Deadbolts earned their price there. Regardless of when the habit was transferred, Dad had passed the OCD on to me.

My dad, Steven Smith, a consultant for a major insurance conglomerate, supported home-security practices of all kinds. He traveled for work, examining corporations for ways to tighten security and reduce their rates (i.e., lower his company's risk in insuring them). He spent months at a time on one company, and it kept him on the road as much as home. I guess a job like his reminded him how often bad things happened.

"Gross." Pixie wrinkled her nose and kicked her toe into a pile of cigarette butts on the welcome mat outside our door. "Jeez, this is a smoke-free campus." She emphasized the final three words, raising her voice as if the perpetrator might hear her and be warned. "Do you know how bad some girl's breath smells right now?" She shook her head in distaste.

Someone in our row of apartments hung around outside our door at night for her cigarette break, and a pile of yuck sat on our mat every morning to prove it. The pile grew by the day. Our door was in front of the stairs. Whoever she was, she could've been on her way home or using the locale as a decoy. Pixie left the butts for evidence as she searched for the culprit. We were up to seven pieces of evidence for the lollipop detective. She had reported the evidence to campus security twice. They'd promised to keep an eye out, but they either weren't very good at their job or didn't care about our dirty welcome mat despite a strict campus policy against smoking. Pixie pulled out another Blow Pop. She'd already asked everyone in the building, but no one had fessed up to the deed.

I shivered and scanned the area for our audience. Tiny hairs on the back of my neck stood at attention. The sensation of being watched pulled my gaze through the spatter of shrubby trees and into nearby windows. I rubbed away the prickles on my neck, stifling an authentic set of goose bumps. Something about the sight of a smoker had always bugged me. The butts on my doorstep felt like a calling card.

Chapter Two

Pixie and I went straight to the local coffee shop, Buzz Cup. It wasn't far from our building, still on campus but near Main Street with easy access to shops. Another perk of senior housing: we were closer to the coffee. A lot of the students went to Buzz Cup for breakfast. We had tickets for meals at the cafeteria, but one meal a day from school was enough. The cafeteria served home-cooked food, a selling point to the parents but atrocious to the female patrons. No one wanted to eat mashed potatoes and homemade breads five days a week. We'd outgrow our uniforms in a month. Pixie told me the boys felt differently and most clamored to get as much sausage, biscuits, and gravy as they could before first bell. I took a pass.

Inside, we ordered coffees and a giant muffin to split. Pixie was right. There were a dozen girls to every boy in sight. The crowd parted for Pixie and then converged on us. Being the center of attention seemed to put her in her comfort zone.

"So, how was the trip?" A redhead I recognized as Aubrie noshed on an apple and smiled between bites.

"Yeah, Elle. How was the trip?" Pixie slid her eyes to me.

I promptly blushed.

"Oh?" Aubrie pulled us through the thick of the crowd to a table with her huge, green leather bag on top. "I sense a boy in this story." She flopped into a chair and anchored her elbows to the tabletop, chin in hands. "Dish."

The trip had been Pixie's idea. She'd said a road trip was the perfect summer's-end celebration because it wasn't every day that a girl became a senior. In our case, two girls. I was all moved in with nowhere to be, so she'd pressed me to get out of town with her for the day.

"I took her to the flea market in Elton." Pixie's busted old car was another bonus of having her as my roommate. Cars weren't a popular notion. Parents didn't drop us off in the middle of nowhere and then leave getaway vehicles. Pixie drove a yellow Neon from the year I was born and called it Suzy Sunshine. Her addiction to old pewter trinkets led us to a flea market about an hour away. I couldn't wait to scout out nearby towns. To my dismay, the towns were all remarkably similar, uninteresting and painfully quaint. "We were there all of five minutes before she went for coffee." Pixie tossed a thumb in my direction.

I got a few sympathetic nods.

"Yeah. She went for coffee and came back towing Abercrombie."

A round of gasps and giggles ensued.

Pixie had them eating from her palm. "He was freaking huge— black Ray-Bans, white tee, khaki cargos, flip-flops . . ." She ticked off her fingers as she went. "And he was at least nineteen or twenty. He was no high school boy." She sipped her coffee, adding a dramatic pause for anyone in the shop who had stopped to listen. Even a girl seated at a small table, previously cooing at some guy, turned in our direction. "First he bought her coffee, and then he hung with her all day."

"Details." Aubrie turned to me. "What'd he say to you? How'd you meet?"

"How can we get him enrolled here?" A little freckled girl behind her joined in.

My throat thickened, and I cleared it. "He asked if I found anything I liked."

Another round of giggles and some table slapping started.

A flea market was the last place I had expected to meet a guy. Actually, I wouldn't have expected to meet this guy anywhere. Most of the boys I attracted weren't very nice or had a third eye or something. One look at him and even the blind could see how far out of my league he was. Pixie was right. He looked like a college guy, but there weren't any colleges in the area. He was probably home for the summer.

"So, he just asked if you found anything at the flea market, then bought you coffee?" Aubrie's eyes grew wide and eager.

"He bought us both coffee."

To Pixie, we had visited a flea market. To me, it had been a portal to someplace where a guy like him would talk to me.

"He saw you in a crowd and came to find you. That's so romantic." A brunette I hadn't noticed before leaned in over Aubrie's shoulder.

"Yeah. I thanked him for the coffees, but he wanted to walk me back." All eyes on me, I started to fidget with the packets of sweetener on the table. Truthfully, his smile had hindered my concentration for the rest of our day together. Brilliant white teeth with red lips and a dimple. Swoon.

Pixie looked at my busy fingers and winked, saving me from social self-destruction. "I took one look at him and said, 'Well, all I wanted was a coffee, but I'll go for this.'"

I barked a laugh and jumped at the memory of how she'd looked at him like one of her Blow Pops. I'd laughed then, too, right before stumping my toe into the ground and splashing chai latte all over my hands. I smashed my eyes shut at the memory, hoping to keep out my immediate need to die.

He and Pixie had made introductions, shifting coffees into their left hands and shaking formally with their rights. The contrast between them had made me smile. He looked so . . . clean. She wore fishnet hose under scrubby cut-off jeans and a black, holey T-shirt for flea marketing.

One handshake and they were friends for life, to hear Pixie tell it. The world was full of potential friends for her.

Personally, I called them all the opposite until proven otherwise. I'd had my share of treacherous friendships. As a general rule, people weren't as nice as they should be. My eyes flitted over the faces closing in on us. Many were familiar, though names escaped me. The itchy feeling of being watched crept into the crowded shop, and I took another look around. There were too many eyes on me, most of them unfamiliar. I swallowed the growing lump in my throat. I'd moved a hundred times. This move was no different, just one more step toward freedom.

Something buried deep inside called me a liar.

A blond squeezed in beside Aubrie, and I blinked. I turned in the direction of the table where she had been sitting a few moments prior. A new couple sat there. The guy she'd been sitting with a few minutes before came into view two blinks later. He lounged against the counter, paying his bill and looking into my face. His expression was less than friendly. Had the crowd we drew in ruined his breakfast date? Was it his stare that had made me want to slide under the table?

"It was the strangest birthday I ever had." I gasped, faking a smile and pulling my eyes from the blond's boyfriend. "I spent an hour watching him and Pixie discuss blown glass and beer steins sold from the tailgate of a rusty pickup truck." The scene had played out like a storybook. My closest friend, a handsome stranger, tiny rural town . . . In the distance behind them a panoramic view of grass, mingled with tree-lined hills and valleys brimming with wildflowers. For one day, I had seen a life full of sleep-filled nights, a mom at home wondering who this young man was, and a dad who'd be home in time for dinner. No wonder Brian had made such an impression on me. He'd unwittingly become part of my fantasy that day. Sad evidence that I needed to get a life this year. Make senior year memorable and all that.

"He wasn't just hot. He knew all about art deco. I love to find old pieces of milk glass, jade green, not white, and anything reminiscent of Rockwell or the 1940s. It was an awesome time for emerging artists. Art deco is also a huge thrill for me. Sometimes I can hit the jackpot there."

The artists nodded in understanding. The rest looked to me. I didn't know what else to say. Being raised by an insurance man had made me cynical. My dreams had made me paranoid. Brian was cute, but Pixie had covered that already. Besides, I had a hard time making sense of his appearance, his interest in me, and then his complete disappearance. If he had liked me enough to hang all day, why just say goodbye? It didn't add up.

Another thing I'd run plenty of miles on the treadmill thinking about was the way Brian's unfathomably green eyes had roamed continually. I was impressed before he removed the shades. Once he pulled them off and hooked them into the collar of his shirt, I was done. Sunlight glistened over them, highlighting the flecks of brown and gold. As much as I wanted to marvel, my mind was distracted. What was he looking for? Did he feel he was being watched, too? All day I'd looked for something wrong in the smiling faces that greeted us at the flea market. Every shoulder nudge sent tingles down my spine. So far, Ohio had done weird things to my already-overworked imagination.

Brian also seemed to listen to all the conversations nearby. My dad did that, too. Dad called it a protective instinct. I called it nosy. He urged me to know who was nearby and what was going on around me as often as possible. The lesson had never really stuck. My mind invited distraction, which was probably why I noticed that Brian was able to carry on intricate conversations with Pixie while scanning the larger scene. Was that normal for a kid our age?

Then there was the moment when he asked what brought me to the flea market because I wasn't shopping.

"I just came for the coffee."

"It's a long way to go for coffee."

Intuition threw out red flags all over the place. A long way from where? We never said where we were from. Still, Elton was a long way from most places. I let it go, begging myself to be normal for just one day, which was, of course, impossible. My paranoia got the best of me too often, sneaking into play more and more since I had arrived on campus a few weeks back.

Dad had something going on all month, and we had managed to slip in my move a couple of weeks ahead of most everyone else's. Lucky for me, Pixie stayed year-round. She had introduced me to a few seniors in our row of dormitories as they moved back to school the previous week.

"They sat on a bench like half the day making smoosh eyes and smiling." Pixie's voice caught my attention. "He was so enormous. Even sitting he towered over her, and his shoulders . . . " She moved her arms as wide as the crowd would allow. Her eyes went glassy. I called it her artist face. "She looked like a child seated next to the Hulk. I wanted to paint them so bad." She wanted to paint everything.

"Where's he from?" the brunette asked.

"She doesn't know." Pixie tipped her coffee back. "He had nice legs, too, like a runner's."

They were nice legs. When he stretched them out in front of him, I took notice. The hair had worn thin on his calves, same as my father's. Dad blamed his military boots. He'd served for years before I was born. Maybe Brian liked to ski. All I knew for sure was that he and Dad shared too many similarities. Maybe I was more homesick than crazy. I preferred this explanation.

"He said you bartered like a master." I shifted my gaze from Pixie to Aubrie. "She always got what she wanted, and she extended her hand to seal the deal every time. Very professional."

Pixie nodded once, sharply.

Women adored her, and she caused a reaction in men, too. Even in Ohio, her gothic garb wasn't much of a turnoff. Her personality shoved everything else into the background. She could've worn anything.

"So, what happened at the end of the day?" Aubrie asked the question I had hoped would never come.

"We left." Pixie's eyes rolled, adding flair.

The blond stood and walked to the door. My story wasn't enough to keep her from her guy any longer.

I was okay with saying goodbye to Brian. It wasn't right to want more. He was a perfect memory, just the way he was. Since that day, whenever I felt really crappy about myself, I remembered the drop-dead gorgeous guy in the white T-shirt who bought me coffee. Granted, there were few other girls there under forty-five for him to talk with, but still, he didn't have to want my company either.

"Do you color your hair? It's amazing." The little freckled girl pulled it between her fingertips. My one redeeming quality. I'd inherited Dad's paranoia, but I had Mom's hair. I let it grow the way she had and only cut it when I had to for practicality.

"No." I returned her easy smile.

"Do you wash it with something special? A color rinse, maybe? I love it."

"Thank you."

Emptiness kicked in my chest, and I wiggled free from the crowd. I told Pixie I had forgotten something at the apartment, and she moved on to making plans for after school. I worked my way back to the now-empty counter and grabbed a Smartwater. I couldn't live on coffee alone. On that note, I slid out. I walked down the stairs and around the corner before sprinting the last four blocks to the pharmacy.

Adjusting my oversized shades, I shoved open the glass door and headed to the cashier, ignoring the clanging bell over the door that drew eyes my way. A small metal frame with energy supplements stood on the counter waiting for me. I grabbed a handful and paid quickly without making eye contact. I stuffed them into my bag and left before anyone could get in line behind me.

An engine roared to life as I stepped into the parking lot, and my heart stopped. Lots of cars sounded the same. *No reason to think it's the same car from outside our apartment. Squealing belts happen all the time, and it makes sense if it's the same car. This is the smallest town in the world.* I scanned the street before taking another step. The sixth sense returned, coaxing me to run back to the crowded coffee shop. A bright blue motorcycle parked on the sidewalk caught my attention mid-panic. It looked like the motorcycle Brian had rested against when we'd said goodbye in Elton. Ugh! Love struck and paranoid. A deadly combination of stupid.

Being on my own had amped up my crazy. I ground my teeth against the building internal tirade and concentrated on breathing. It was a different bike. Cute guys didn't follow me around. This town wasn't a creepy freak show. I was, and I needed to get a life.

Pulling in another full breath, I turned on my toes for Buzz Cup. I needed to really move it to fool Pixie. Our apartment was a block closer to the coffee shop than the pharmacy.

When Buzz Cup came back into view, I stopped to let my heart rate settle. Then I walked to the building. Pixie sat inside the window laughing with her mouth wide open and her head thrown back. She hadn't even noticed that I took too long. She stood the moment I walked in and linked her elbow with mine.

"Let's go!" She tossed up one arm with gusto.

I followed less enthusiastically.

In the distance, a small blue motorcycle zipped through traffic. I took a deep breath.

Chapter Three

Francine Frances Academy was beautiful. The lawns and landscaping were immaculate. Groundskeepers were plentiful. I'd scouted out a spot near a short stone wall soon after I arrived in Ohio. The wall was more aesthetic than intended for seating. That meant it was frequently vacant. Solitude was another thing I valued. In a city with a couple million people, I blended. Small-town life was too much like living under a microscope.

"I saw you looking at Davis." Pixie kept her eyes forward and bumped into me with one hip and shoulder as we walked.

Microscope.

"Who?" I knew who. He was the only boy I had made eye contact with at the coffee shop.

"Kate's crushing on him."

"The blond."

"Kate." Pixie lifted an eyebrow. "The datable seniors are in demand. They've had the upper hand for years. Kate's determined to lure him into her web."

"Web?"

"Web. Pants." She shrugged.

I blushed.

"He's the one that got away, and she has until May to lay her claim."

"So they aren't a couple? He went to breakfast with her. I figured . . ."

"Yeah, that's what everyone was talking about when we got there. He never meets anyone anywhere unless it's a party. The girls caught me up while you ran home."

The pills in my backpack felt heavier.

The closer we got to the building, the more anxiety pricked my skin. Pixie had introduced me to many of my new classmates during the last couple weeks, but I was still the new one. Outside the grand entranceway, dozens of girls chatted and gossiped near the fountain. Boys wearing khakis and ties hanging askew lounged over the wide cement stairs.

Sweat beaded on my upper lip from heat and nerves. The sun beat strong and hot against the pavement. Everyone had removed their cardigans. I tugged at the hem of mine but opted to suffer until first bell. Girls tied up the bottoms of their blouses and rolled down the waistbands of their skirts. I felt a little like a grandma. In my opinion, the skirt revealed enough. Maybe Pixie was right. Maybe I was a prude.

I smoothed my skirt, pretending I was back in my favorite jeans, and plastered a smile on my face. Thank goodness for Pixie. I'd be accepted by association. They might not like me, but they wouldn't hate me either. Or at least they wouldn't show it.

When we made it to the giant mahogany doors, Pixie and I parted ways temporarily. Our schedules differed vastly during the couple periods before lunch. After that it was standard coursework for the grade. Most of her morning classes were art related. I stuck with standard college-prep courses. She wanted to travel Europe and see the great cathedrals. I wanted to finish high school and get into a prelaw program somewhere far away from Ohio. I craved crowds and anonymity, smog and crime. I hated always knowing everyone's business and everyone wanting to know mine.

Inside the giant doors, a long hall of lockers led to an atrium with murals painted on the ceiling. A set of double doors waited on the other side. I walked through the doors to an exterior corridor with classrooms on both sides and an arching metal roof overhead. A good view of the track and lacrosse field ran down the center. Most of my classes had outside entrances, which I loved. Come winter I might change my mind.

A bell shrieked overhead and I fought the urge to duck for cover. Such a fancy campus and the bell reminded me of a fire drill. The crowd did a collective wince before dispersing to homeroom. Senior year had officially begun.

In homeroom we were assigned seats alphabetically. The teacher passed around a plastic basket with a few dozen silver combination locks and blank locker assignment forms. We took one of each and then moved into the hall to choose a locker. I chose a locker outside, beneath the covered walk. Few joined me. We worked the locks a couple times to be sure they were set correctly, according to the paper tagged on the back, and then we recorded our name, locker number, and combination for the school files. I snapped a magnetic mirror onto the inside of my door and left. Others had bags full of colorful magnets, tiny faux fur carpet for the shelves, and photographs. Kate attached a tiny chandelier to the locker ceiling as I passed her. My tiny mirror was shabby in comparison. Lockers were important. I must not have gotten the memo.

I turned in my form to the teacher and waited through an extended homeroom period while everyone managed the menial task. It took much longer than it should have, but there was some serious interior decorating going on in some of those lockers.

Everyone looked comfortable and confident. I hoped I didn't look the way I felt—ridiculous. The uniform didn't help. I tugged on the skirt. Something about the knee socks was weird. A few girls opted to wear a tie with the button-down shirt. I chose the cardigan. I wouldn't wear a tie. Girls checked their faces in small mirrors or fidgeted with their nails. The bell rang, and I pretended to write something in my empty notebook. I peeked one last time at the map in my pocket. When necessary, I planned to slip into the restroom to check it again. According to my schedule, first and second period were right next door to one another, so I wouldn't have to worry long. Once I found the first room, I'd be set. Study hall was in the cafeteria building. I could easily find that. At that point I'd be with Pixie, and I'd follow her from there.

"Hey, where ya headed?" A husky voice sounded in my ear. He smiled and stretched out a hand. "I'm Davis." The guy from the coffee shop. I lifted my chin. Up close he stood at least a head taller than me.

"Elle." I tried to keep my voice from shaking. "I have Trig now."

"I'll walk you." He kept pace beside me. People watched as they passed us in the hall. "So, I saw you with Pixie this morning. You're roommates?"

"Yeah. She's great. Are you going to Trig, too?"

"No. I have Latin first period."

"Why . . . ?" I slowed to look at him again.

His crooked smile was confident and mischievous. The morning sunlight glinted off his bright blue eyes. He looked like the boy-next-door type my dad would love. The kind of guy who was harmless and happy, and would have me home by nine.

"Just wanted to say hi." He turned on his heel and jogged off in the opposite direction, leaving me at the threshold to my next class.

I shook my head and smiled. Deep breath. Next up: Trigonometry II. What a way to start my day. The teacher was Mrs. Calhoun. She introduced me as the new student. I now had two reasons not to like first period. Worse, my assigned seat was between two girls who looked like starlets. I sank nervously into the seat and tried to blend in. It would've been easier to blend into the furniture.

Their golden-highlighted hair hung in ringlets over their ears and backs. My sandy hair was neither blond nor brown. It wasn't curly or straight. It was just sort of there, thick and wavy near the ends, stretching loosely over my shoulders. They probably paid stylists a fortune for their precision cuts. I pushed a fingerful of hair behind my ear, thankful at least that my hair held its own. Sort of. *I should consider wearing more makeup.*

My eyes ached from lack of sleep. They probably looked it, too. I should've snagged some Visine on my trip to the drugstore. There was always after school. Until then, I'd claim allergies. Other than red, my brown eyes were unremarkable, like the rest of me. They were too wide set, making me always look younger than anyone else, like a startled Disney princess. Cute shoes and big leather bags covered in logos and letters lined the floor. Acrylic nails tapped out a rhythm behind me. I deflated a bit more. These girls had brought their A game. I only had a C game. On a good day, I pulled a B-minus game. That was the best I could hope for.

An hour later, I dragged out of first period wishing I'd been able to concentrate, knowing I'd be sorry when the test came. I had no one to meet between bells and my next class was all of twenty-five feet away, so I made an unnecessary trip to my locker. No one would be there. I could hide. Anything sounded better than getting to class early and waiting for it to begin.

Second period was English, one of my best subjects. But after the titillating hour I had spent in Trig, I doubted I'd be amazed at the teaching. The tuition to Francine Frances apparently wasn't spent looking for overly zealous teachers.

I took my time getting to my locker. The lock released and fell into my hand, but the locker was stuck shut. It was middle school all over again. What senior can't open her locker? Screams built in my chest. I didn't need this drama. Being the new kid created enough stress. An approaching groundskeeper slowed and watched me wrestle the locker. If he offered to help, I'd die of humiliation on the spot.

"How was Trig?" Davis leaned casually against the locker beside mine.

"Great." I rolled my eyes and lifted the lever again. If he planned to walk me to all my classes, I could ditch my map.

I trained my eyes on the locker. Stuck. My head fell forward. Freshman humiliation for a senior.

"Where you headed?"

I puffed my cheeks out and turned. Bright blue eyes stared back at me.

"English." I couldn't trust my words further. In a school filled with starlets and about twelve boys, I was certain to make the most-hated list if he kept talking to me. The prickly sensation of being watched crept over me. My eyes automatically scanned left and right for Kate before I turned back to my locker. Irrationally, I hoped that whoever watched us was only a student. Then again, who else would it be?

"Ah. I'm going to study hall." Davis clapped me on the back gently and stepped away. Stupidly, I turned. Right on cue, he looked back in my direction. If I could've opened my locker, I would've climbed inside and stayed there.

As the second bell announced me officially late, the locker lever broke free. A sigh of relief blew across my lips. A moment later I sucked in air hard. Inside the empty locker lay a length of black satin ribbon. Turning it over in my fingers, I examined the vent on the locker door. The ribbon could easily have been fed in, but who did it belong to? A girl with a locker nearby would probably think it was stolen when she didn't find it in her locker as she expected. My thumb drew patterns over the soft fabric while I decided what to do. It looked like one of the ribbons my mom used to wear in her hair. As a child, I used to sit on her bed and watch her tie a perfect bow on top of her long sandy brown hair every morning. One gentle tug turned the bow around her head until it disappeared beneath her long, thick waves, looking like little more than an extension of her beautiful hair.

Panic beat in my head. I moved quickly to class, shoving the painful memory away. I was way beyond late.

O-for-two.

Announced as the new kid in my first class and late for the second. I hoped I could break the pattern before it went any further. I also planned to sit in the back from now on. From there, I could observe. Adapting would be trickier than predicted. I was clearly out of place, even in such a small school.

"Elle!" Pixie's voice rang out across the lawn. I turned toward her but kept moving. With any luck, this teacher wouldn't make a big deal out of me being late.

Pixie was supposed to be in gym. Her entire class was on the outdoor track in the distance, but she had apparently broken free when she saw me. She had absolutely no boundaries, and her self-control was minimal at best. This was a prime example. She waved her arms frantically overhead. I shot up one hand, smiled, and pulled myself through the classroom door. I'd see her soon enough in study hall.

"Miss Smith, I presume?" the teacher asked.

I gave Pixie one last look over my shoulder. Through the rectangular window in the door, her crazy smile made me grin. She gave up and bent over, hands on her knees to catch her breath. That was probably the farthest she'd ever run. She was so utterly bizarre.

"Miss Smith?"

I turned, guessing the other students were probably all staring at me. They weren't. They were all staring at him. I gasped and a few girls giggled.

My eyes shot around the room and landed on the first empty chair. I practically ran to go sit. The teacher motioned to Brian, who sat at a desk in the front corner, and back to me. "As I was saying, we have two new students with us this semester."

Miss Smith and Mr. Austin.

Chapter Four

"Welcome to English Lit." Mrs. Willows began pacing before the chalkboard.

I stifled a shiver. My chest constricted until it hurt. Heat rose up the back of my neck. Panic raised my heart rate to frenzy level. I didn't know where to look. Every fiber of my being refused the existence of coincidence, but my life in Ohio brimmed with it. Brian enrolling at my new school had forced my mind into overdrive. In true cowardice form, I leaned into my desk and let my hair fall over my face. The squealing engine. The blue motorcycle. I peeked through the thick wavy strands. He'd shifted in his seat and was looking at me.

Holy crap.

I held perfectly still for so long that my throat burned. *Breathe*. I managed eye contact with the teacher as often as possible but continued to check on Brian through my hair. So far he hadn't turned into the shadowy image from my nightmare. Of course not. He also hadn't vanished as part of my imagination. Confusion scrambled my brain. I had to concentrate to control my expression. My eyes had widened to the size of golf balls when I walked in, and they still tried to bulge from their sockets. I must've looked like one of those black fish they always kept in the tank with the goldfish at the pet store. I blinked and looked at the teacher again. She'd already moved on to reading from a hardbound copy of something with a well-worn cover.

All around me girls whispered and passed notes. Everyone had noticed Mr. Austin. No one seemed to notice Miss Smith. A twinge of jealousy swept through me, whether at the thought of being noticed for a change or because of some ridiculous unfounded possession over him, I wasn't sure. The "I saw him first" logic wouldn't get me far. Throughout class his demeanor remained calm, like we'd never met. He didn't look my way again. Meeting him couldn't have been a coincidence. What else could it mean? The bell screeched forty-five minutes later, and I bolted out the door.

"Miss Smith?" He was too near for me to pretend not to hear.

I slowed, and he passed me by a step before he stopped. He leaned his head downward and spoke softly.

"I'm sorry about this. I didn't know."

"It's okay." I shrugged. "No big deal, right?" I forced myself to look at him with confidence, or at least as much confidence as I could pull off.

"Listen." The word sounded urgent, but, of course, it wasn't. Why would it be?

He was too handsome to talk to me and definitely too handsome to be some random senior at this school. He belonged on billboards in L.A. His eyes were piercing. He'd probably say they were green, but they were a color without a name. The sun shone on him, reminding me how tan and muscular his arms were beneath the white dress shirt and tie. A large Indian ink tattoo played under his sleeve.

"How old are you?" *Oops.* We looked at one another.

Then there were whispers. Some girls noticed us talking and gathered to watch.

"Later." He wore a stern expression. He seemed to be trying to tell me something completely over my head. Probably "don't tell anyone about knowing me or I'll go straight to the socially nonexistent category with you."

He looked at the little crowd whispering nearby and scowled. My cheeks flamed hot. Was it so bad to be seen with me? What would the girls think of his reaction? He looked back into my eyes, held my gaze a moment too long, scoffed, and walked away.

What an ass. I couldn't believe he was so rude. So mean. What the hell?

"Elle!" Pixie flew down the long exterior corridor toward me.

"You knew," I hissed.

"Yes!" She nodded fervently like a bobble-headed china doll. Of course that news would've motivated her to try to find me earlier, to try to tell me what I was about to walk into.

Ah, she tried.

"Come on. We'll be late." I pulled her along, her head still bobbing with a grin stretched ear to ear.

We had third-period study hall together in the common area before lunch. Pixie sat on the scarlet carpeting and began to scribble notes. I dropped my bag between us and folded myself next to her with the grace of a rag doll.

I read the note she slid my way. "Did you die?"

She raised a thin, carefully sculpted eyebrow at me.

I thought a thousand things before deciding what to write. Notes got confiscated. "Yes. What on Earth?" I pushed the paper back her way.

"I knew you had a little juju in you."

"Shut up!" I stifled a giggle. The word *juju* didn't belong on the same page as me, let alone in the same sentence. "I had nothing to do with this. This is happening *to* me, not because of me." Then it hit me. "Where did he come from? Why is this happening to me? He was such a jerk out there. Did you see his face?"

"Did *you* see his face? I don't know. What did you do?" She underlined the final word six times and gave me an innocent look with her pointer finger resting against her bottom lip.

"Nothing." I scribbled. "This is weird, right? We met at a flea market and now he's one of the only guys at our little school?"

"Yes. Or maybe it's fate. You're cosmically linked or something. Like soulmates."

"He acted like he wanted to kick me."

The hairs on the back of my neck stood on end. Mindlessly, I rubbed them. Did soulmates exist? Could I believe in soulmates and not in coincidence? If someone like Brian was destined to be my soulmate, I also needed to believe in fairy tales. In a fairy tale, Brian would be the villain, wooing fair maidens and then casting them aside.

"Ladies." A firm voice cautioned us to keep to ourselves. I destroyed the paper we wrote on. I hated Francine Frances for its old-fashioned policies against cell phones during school hours.

Stupid!

Mid-pout, Pixie caught my attention from the corner of one eye. She moved her hand in a strange pattern. Her eyes were wide with excitement. Her wrist made a half circle that ended with a stabbing index finger. I followed the finger.

Brian approached the teacher with a slip of paper and then sat alone on the far side of the commons, facing us. A large, brown leather bag rested against him. He dug out a pile of notebooks and stacked them on his legs. The barrier blocked his hands from the view of the teacher, who was engrossed in *Golf Digest*. Brian pulled out a phone—injustice. His thumbs danced over the keypad, but his eyes lifted, watching me.

My heart pounded. I turned my head away before my cheeks turned the color of the carpet.

After a few short breaths, I looked up again. Maybe he wasn't used to being the new kid. I had more practice than anyone I knew. I was being unfair. He didn't need to be judged on one moment of attitude, but he'd better straighten up before acting like that again. Maybe I could find out where he came from and how he ended up in Elton and now at Francine Frances. Eliminate the "coincidence" with facts. My mind teetered between hopeful and fearful.

The rest of the day evaporated. After second period, I had too much on my mind to process anything new. The books piled up, and the assignments did, too. New teachers, new faces—they'd all have to wait for another day. I alternated between the enigma of Brian's appearance and the mystery of the misplaced ribbon. Nothing made sense, and so it went around and around inside my head until a headache started. The bonus of the drama was I hadn't ruminated over my nightmares in nearly eight hours. Anytime the shadowy figure came to mind, Brian's wide green eyes intercepted the panic.

By last period, my head swam with questions. I picked the seat nearest the door and settled in for Sociology. I recognized most of the faces from my earlier classes. Students were starting to say hi to me.

"Welcome, class!" An enthusiastic lady strode in as the final bell rang. She leaned against her desk. "I'm Susan Marks. You can call me Susan, if you'd like. I worked in the field of human services for ten years after college. I have some valuable and awkward experiences to share with you this semester. I want you to leave here with a real understanding of this science and the field. Any questions?"

We all stared.

"Then let's talk about your first assignment."

A groan rolled over the crowd.

A flash of sunlight blinded me momentarily as the door swung wide. When my eyes adjusted, I saw that Brian stood near the chalkboard handing the teacher a slip of paper. A couple of nods later, he headed my way. I'd taken the last seat in the row, leaving one empty desk between Kate and me. He slid into the seat. Kate turned around to welcome him.

"I want you to research yourselves online. Spend some time discovering what people can find out about you at the click of a button. This is the information age, ladies and gentlemen. How many of your secrets are revealed online? Find out. Then take a look at the other people who share your name. Are they similar to you? How? Talk about what's in a name. Diversity makes the world go around." She threw her arms wide like the lady in *The Sound of Music*. "We'll compare and contrast with one another on Friday."

The bell shrilled outside the closed door half an hour later.

I had my work cut out for me. With a name like Smith, there'd be plenty of people out there sharing my name.

Betrayed by my own face, I looked at Brian before I thought better of it. He and Kate were engaged in quiet conversation. Davis sat one desk over and was watching them, too. When his eyes met mine, his expression changed.

"How was your first day?" His slow, easy voice comforted me.

Before I could answer, Brian shifted in his seat. The move was subtle, but I noticed. He also stopped talking. Did he finish his conversation with Kate or stop to eavesdrop?

"Good." I focused on Davis. "Everyone's been really nice." My fake smile smoothed a little. Davis's genuine disposition made me breathe a little easier.

"Especially the guys, I bet."

My shoulders relaxed as Brian's stiffened. "No. Everyone." Though, he was right. The guys were overly welcoming. I bobbed my head. Peculiar, but nice.

"I noticed," Davis whispered.

Brian continued to imitate a statue. A few desks up, Kate and her lackeys made a big show of laughing and tossing their hair.

"Did you bring a laptop, or are you going to the library for this assignment?" He motioned toward the front board.

"I have a laptop." I doubted anyone at the academy didn't. Not that it would stop me from frequenting the library.

"Are you headed home, or do you have something going on after school?" The question felt weighted. His flat expression didn't match the polite conversation.

Tension thickened the air, constricted my throat. "I'm heading home, I guess."

Without another word, Davis swept out of his desk and around to the door, holding it wide with one arm for me to pass through. If I accepted the invitation, Kate would want me dead. If I stayed, I'd be sitting there with nothing left to do and Brian two feet away. Brian, who hadn't bothered to speak to me since he blew me off in front of all those girls earlier. I grabbed my pack and bolted. We didn't talk on the way to my locker.

"Well, I'm meeting Pixie at the fountain, so . . . "

"Sure, yeah, okay," Davis stumbled. His confidence seemed shaken since the morning. "See you tomorrow?"

I lifted my hand waist high and took off before I could start looking around for Brian. Pixie and a small army stood near the fountain looking like a school billboard. None of the girls wore a ribbon in her hair. In fact, I'd watched all day for anyone with a ribbon and found none.

"Here she is." Aubrie opened her arms and threw her head back. "Did you have a fabulous day or what?"

Or what. I had had a day made of weird and more weird. Wrapped in WTH.

"Did any of you guys lose a black hair ribbon? I found one in my locker."

A handful of nos popped up from the girls in our group. The crowd moved in unison away from the school. I joined them. No one cared about the ribbon.

"We were talking about the new kid. Did you see him?" A smaller version of Aubrie spoke in a quick, high-pitched voice that earned her a shove.

"Shh! Don't be daft."

"Elle, this is Darcy, Aubrie's little sister," Pixie explained. "She's a freshman this year. She came all the way across the pond to be with her sister."

Aubrie rolled her eyes but said nothing.

"Well, did you see him? Absolutely everyone is talking about him, and I heard he's like the son of an ambassador or something."

Pixie snickered and shot me a look. She hadn't told my secret. They didn't know he was the guy I had met in Elton. After the morning's coffee-house presentation of "I am an idiot" starring me, I was especially grateful for her discretion.

"I had Trig with him last period for like five seconds," Aubrie said. "The bell barely rang and he was already at the desk with a slip. I'd love to know where he went so I can transfer."

"I saw him in the office today before lunch and after study hall, too. I thought he might work there, but maybe he had problems with his schedule," Darcy offered.

"What? Are you stalking him or the office staff?" Aubrie stared at her little sister in disapproval.

"I applied to work there during my study hall. Then I went to check on the application later."

Eye-rolling ensued.

A chill ran over my cheeks. I knew where he had gone when he'd left her class. He'd transferred to my class. He'd been transferring to all my classes since study hall, but he hadn't spoken to me since after English. Even then he only stopped me to say we had to talk, then glared at me. I shook my head against the impending combustion. He looked like an angel, but he gave off a mean vibe. Whenever he was around, I couldn't help feeling that he was dangerous. I shook my head again to clear that thought from my mind. Paranoid. Dreams were dreams.

Life was life. Brian had eight inches and seventy-five pounds on me. In theory, he could be dangerous. No other reason to panic.

"Did you guys hear there's a serial killer on the loose?" A girl near the front of our crowd spoke in a voice better suited to a campfire than a sunny September afternoon. Darcy and a few freshmen behind me fell silent.

"Where'd you hear that?" Pixie unwrapped a Blow Pop.

The girl shrugged. "Around. Everyone's saying it."

"You think it's true?" I bit my lip to keep from saying more. My mind screamed for details.

Aubrie turned to look at her sister and the trio of freshmen tagging along. "Whatever. Don't go walking alone or I'll tell Mom you're breaking the rules."

Judging by the size of Darcy's eyes, Aubrie didn't need to worry about that anytime soon.

At the next corner, a flash of electric blue reflected off the windows of cars parked in the distance. I turned to look for the motorcycle. Nothing. I needed to get a grip.

"Darcy?" I asked. "How soon will you know if you got that position in the office?"

Never the chatty one in any pairing, I barely spoke at dinner. Pixie didn't notice. She sucked a homemade icy pop, probably concocted of organic guava juice or something equally healthy. I fought with a grilled cheese. I couldn't get used to the decrepit stove or the singed cookware. I'd made a mess of the effort, but I was hungry.

Pixie filled me in on all the day's news while I sat and stewed. She recounted personal stories of atrocious outfits and bad haircuts, whose friendships were over and, of course, the rest of the scoop on our hot new addition to the student body. She even made a few terrible jokes about his "student body."

"Everyone's going totally bonkers, Elle! Don't you want to climb up on a lunch table, pound your chest, and say, 'What's up now, ladies? The boy is M-I-N-E.'"

"Pixie."

"What? He is, right? I saw you two. Don't lie. He was following you today. I saw that, too."

"Following me? When?"

"Everywhere." She rolled her eyes. "He's in half your classes. He ought to be more discreet." Her perfect face lit up as she ran one finger down the length of her icy pop. "Ah ah ah."

He was in more than half my classes, but I didn't mention it. I didn't know what to make of the day. There was no sane way to shrug off this scenario. My gut clenched in acknowledgment. Frustration overcame me. Was I crazy? Was the dream creeping into my days, too? I rubbed my forehead. Everything in this little town creeped me out. Hearing rumors about a serial killer didn't help.

Pixie gave me a rare look of concern. "I'm glad you're here."

"Me, too. Are you okay?"

Her cheek lifted in half a smile. "You know I've been here for years, but I'm still the odd one out. I never leave the academy. Not unless the school closes. I don't run home on weekends and short holidays. My family makes itself scarce, so it's nice having a friend who gets how that feels."

I nodded. She nodded. It looked to me like Pixie had hundreds of friends. I let her words sit, unsure of how to respond. My dad wasn't around because he couldn't be, but I didn't point that out. I finished my seared-cheese sandwich and went to brush my teeth. She followed me. No boundaries.

"Let's go out!" She was going out with or without me. Her social calendar overflowed. Unlike mine.

"I'm going to the library. I missed a ton today after I saw Brian." I shrugged one shoulder and gave the palms up, head tilt. *What can I do? Out of my hands.* I hated the hold he had on me.

"Ack." She spit an exasperated throat noise at me and rolled her head around.

She planned to fix me. I wished her luck. When she left to meet friends back at the Community Center, I grabbed my laptop and backpack to walk with her. Pixie loved darts and was pretty good.

I flipped the deadbolt and checked the doorknob on our way back out.

"Good. I was going to tell you to make sure it's locked this time." Pixie tossed the stick of her Blow Pop into a trash bin as we reached the sidewalk.

"What do you mean? I always double-check."

"Not always. When I put my key in after school, it was already unlocked."

"Why didn't you say anything?" My head pounded with thoughts I couldn't voice. Images from my dream mixed with serial-killer rumors and hot boys appearing at school. My head swiveled left and right. I rubbed my neck to ease the electricity running up and down my spine.

"I was on the phone." She rolled her eyes. "It's no big deal. You were in a hurry. I still can't believe you made it here and back so fast. Impressive."

"What?"

"From Buzz Cup this morning. You came back for something." She rotated her wrist, signaling for me to keep up.

"Right. I must've forgotten to lock it after I ran home." I took one last look at the apartment over my shoulder before it disappeared into the distance. My cheeks burned with fear and humiliation. I should've told her the truth. Then I could tell her what I knew. I hadn't left the door unlocked. I'd never gone home. Someone else had unlocked the door.

Pixie chattered and texted the rest of the way until we parted. I didn't tell her. I went as far as the edge of campus and then headed to the library. There was an obvious reason she thought the door had been unlocked. She'd been on the phone, distracted. It had been locked. She was confused.

Inside the library, I read through every syllabus and outlined the papers due at semester's end. I had a solid start, which would help me secure the grades I needed. I had to stay on top of things and be focused. No more being "that" girl. So what? Some gorgeous guy entered my life and I fell apart? No. No more. Same with the dream. Goodbye.

I breathed easier inside the library. Libraries were consistent. The high wooden shelving around me showed its age. I could've been in a nineteenth-century museum if it weren't for the rows of new releases near the front desk. A man seated against the wall looked me over. I didn't recognize him from any of my classes or the hallways, but it was only my first day. He watched me, staring. I blushed. So many unusual things had transpired in one short day. I probably looked a little unstable. I chanced one last look, and he smiled. Perhaps he taught a class I didn't have this semester. Judging by his tidy appearance and approximate age, it seemed reasonable. Before he could decide to approach me, I turned back to my table.

I stayed at the library longer than I needed. My mind kept replaying Pixie's allegation that Brian had followed me, and her belief that our door had been unlocked when I remembered double-checking it. Memories of the blue bike before school and the hint of it afterward were stuck in my brain. *Don't dwell.* Usually my first day at a new school was uneventful. No one talked to me, and I wondered when they would. Life at Francine Frances was different; the whole town was different from anywhere I'd ever been. Everyone knew each other. They lived here. No parents. For the first time since Dad had agreed to let me go away for senior year, the concept dug in tight. No parents. No Dad at home. Ever. Suddenly, all I wanted in the world was to go back to my room and give him a call.

"Homework on the first day?" The man stood smiling on the other side of my table.

"Uh, yeah, some."

"Anything I can do to help?" He tilted his head. The simple act ran goose bumps over my skin.

"No." *Calm down. It's not like he's a serial killer.*

"I'll be around if you need me." He whistled his way back to where he sat.

I exhaled and pulled my bag onto my lap. The zipper on my backpack caught on the corner of an oversized text. I started unpacking to reorganize. The black ribbon, frayed and tangled, was caught by a thread in the zipper's teeth. Perhaps the ribbon belonged to a classmate, but when I looked at it, all I could think of was my mom. My throat thickened until I couldn't swallow. I ran my fingertips over the surface, fluffed the frayed edge with my thumb and forefinger, and imagined Mom tying the ribbon in her hair. After she died, Dad used to pull out her hair ribbons every year or so, take his grief to a new level, and then we moved. By the time I turned eleven, I knew what it meant when I saw the black ribbons appear: Dad would want to start over, run from what chased him. The more I thought about the ribbons, the more it scared me.

I'd had enough library time.

"Good night," the man said as I passed him on my way out. I waved.

On the walk home, my nerves were frayed worse than the ribbon. My skin snapped with anxiety. Walking through the grounds, there was a firefly near the bushes. The night air chilled my skin, and I hastened my pace. Fireflies didn't last long in September. Before I reached the main strip of apartments and shops, there was another small light. A silhouette of black against an already lonesome night. The sun had set behind the hills when I left the library, and the darkness gained momentum. The moon and stars hid behind a vast mask of gray clouds. Streetlamps cast shadows from the cones of light. The streets were quiet and the campus still.

My footsteps cracked in the night, and I cursed my choice of sandals over sneakers. Flip, flip, flip, flip. Soon my steps came faster.

Flip, flip, flip, flip. Speeding up without intent and making me more nervous. Something was wrong. Nothing was wrong. Everything was wrong.

The chill in the night air set my teeth chattering. Tension mounted, and I wrapped my arms across my chest instinctively. I tried to move faster. Blood whooshed between my ears, accompanied by my heavy breathing. A few fallen leaves rustled against the pavement. A twig cracked nearby, and bile rose in my throat. The slow thump of heavy footfalls reached my ears. I couldn't swallow anymore. For a moment I wondered if I'd ever see the coffee shop.

The desolation of the street was as frightening as the footsteps behind me. There were no sounds other than the hastening feet. My eyes darted around, making the dark walk seem more dangerous, but I couldn't stop myself. I saw nothing, just a few leaves and darkened houses.

When the light of the coffee shop window finally came into view, my heart sprinted, pulling me forward like the dash at the end of a long-distance run. My face burned. This was how it began in my dream. I didn't see what was coming. I simply knew it was there. I suddenly felt like a target, unguarded and without defense.

I reached the sidewalk and threw myself toward the building. Only a few cobblestone stairs separated me from safety. I bounded up, taking them two at a time. Pulling open the door was like reaching a refuge. Warmth comingled with scents of cocoa beans, setting my mind at ease. Physically, though, was another story.

My muscles trembled as I removed my backpack from my shoulder and concentrated on breathing. There was a way to quicken the calm. Breathe in through my mouth and out through my nose, or was it in through my nose and out through my mouth? My brain hurt. I settled on the latter because it allowed me to draw in the aromas of cocoa, vanilla, and cinnamon that encircled my head. Sugar and coffee seasoned the air. It was impossible to be afraid any longer, but it would take time to shake the adrenaline.

I collapsed into the nearest booth for several minutes before I could stand. My heartbeat was audible, and tears stung my eyes. No one seemed to notice. I wobbled to the restroom and dashed my hot face with cold water.

Shake it off, Gabriella. Shake it off. I lived in a town with a volunteer police department. Abductions didn't happen here. This odd, antiquated town probably had a neighborhood-watch group at every corner. I was fine. I was losing it, but I was fine. I dried my face with renewed purpose, as if I could somehow remove the panic with the water. Then I made my way to the counter for a vat of coffee.

Brian was seated at a corner table. He didn't look up. I ordered their largest soy vanilla latte to go but couldn't bring myself to leave. Instead, I sat down, defeated, pondering what was happening to me. I hated being afraid. This was the year I had vowed to beat this thing, not be drawn in deeper. I had promised myself a fresh start. I had come to Francine Frances with a plan. First, find out what the heck I had been dreaming about for the past twelve years. Then squash it. Instead, the dream had become reality, like in a Freddy Krueger movie.

I was stuck. I couldn't get myself to leave the coffee shop. Logically, I recognized the silliness, but my feet planted me in the booth, unwilling to move. I was living my dream, trapped, afraid to go and afraid to stay. My dream, being ever present with me, had become as real as the seat I sat on. More than a dream, this subconscious thing now affected my real life and real decisions. Maybe Krueger fit the scenario better than I thought.

Holding my phone, I pretended to text while I decided what to do. After deliberating through most of my latte, I called Pixie for a ride.

Brian watched me from his corner table without approaching, thank goodness. I prayed he hadn't seen my grand entrance. He needed to stay put until I got my head together. I didn't need another awkward situation on top of the one I was in the middle of. It crossed my mind that he'd followed me. I couldn't be sure who had arrived first, but the idea that he might be following me sent goose bumps up my arms.

"You make quite an entrance."

I slapped my chest with one hand and gasped. I hadn't seen him get up. My face burned in response. I should've known he'd walk over eventually.

"Yeah." I had no idea how to respond. *Well, you see, handsome boy, I was running from a figment of my imagination . . .* I closed my eyes to shut out the crazy and get my thoughts in order and then opened them again.

"Is everything okay?" He glanced around, probably checking to be sure no one saw us together. Not what I needed at the moment.

I tried not to look at him. Maybe he hadn't noticed that I was having a mental breakdown. He made it hard enough for me to think when I wasn't mid-freakout. His warm smile gave me pause. I bet Brian never feared anything. Never ran from his shadow. Didn't fear the dark. My eyes ran to the window beside me in remembrance. Outside, a tiny orange glow near a thick oak tree drew my eye. It reminded me of a firefly whose light lasted way too long. Then it fell and disappeared.

Brian looked outside, but only darkness stared back. I'd no sooner perceived the glow than it was gone. Only our reflections and the shine of the interior lights against the glass remained. My naturally wide eyes looked like saucers after the scare I'd had, especially compared to the narrow set of Brian's.

"I'm fine. Just in a hurry to get some coffee." I tipped my cup his way.

"At 9:00 at night." A cynical statement. "How do you sleep?"

"I don't." I answered honestly before I thought it through.

"You don't." His eyes pinched at the sides, and he sat in the chair next to mine without an invitation.

I had mentioned that I never slept when we talked at the flea market. Maybe he thought I had a fun or youthful reason. I didn't.

The coffee shop door sucked open, and I jumped in my seat. Brian followed my startled gaze. Davis ambled in. He looked at us for a long, drawn-out beat before regaining his pace to the counter. Brian continued to examine him, and Davis stole a look in our direction while waiting for his coffee. Not a friendly how-do-you-do by any stretch.

"Do you need a ride home?" Brian shifted in his chair.

My already upset stomach twisted further.

He looked torn, as if he wished he hadn't offered. His behavior today had sucked on the whole. Transferring to half my classes so he could ignore me made zero sense. Of course, in a small school like ours, it could be coincidence. The look he had given me outside of English came to mind and irked me.

"No. No thanks." I forced my mouth to betray me. Mad or not, I wouldn't mind accepting his offer. Climbing on the back of his bike and wrapping my arms around him would be a great start to a brand new me. Braver. More fun. Less spazzy. "My roommate's picking me up. It's fine. I'm good, really." *Liar.*

"If you're certain." He stood and moved back to his table but not before giving me a look that sent electricity spiraling right through to my sandals. From the moment we met, he'd been speaking to me on some other, unseen level, and it killed me. Wanting something so far out of my reach was torturous. My toes curled under the table.

Having a crush was highly underrated. The rush alone made the inevitable heartbreak worthwhile. When he turned, I couldn't resist watching him walk away. In my opinion, his existence was a bona fide phenomenon. How someone like him even existed was beyond me. Regardless of how, I was thankful for the new direction my thoughts had taken.

As much as I hated to leave the coffee shop for a second reason now, I was thrilled when Pixie pulled up.

"Hey." Davis leaned on the counter and looked me over as I passed.

"Hey."

He nodded. I pressed a shoulder into the glass door and smiled.

On my way to the car, Brian's motorcycle was nowhere to be seen. I wondered how he had gotten there. I couldn't imagine him walking around campus like the rest of us pleated-skirt doppelgangers. Hadn't he offered me a ride? I looked to the tree with the fallen firefly once more. Just a tree. A dark street. Nothing more.

The car door swung open with a loud squeak. I appreciated the ride and also the fact that Pixie didn't ask why. Instead, she seemed glad for the call. She talked too loudly. She hated to turn the stereo down, so she just talked louder.

"Don't go home. I'm going to the river. Come with. Please?" She planned to see some friends and her on-again, off-again boyfriend.

I didn't necessarily want to be alone, but it didn't interest me. "Nah. Catch me up on all the details when you get in."

"Come on, Elle. Are you kidding? The Pier is raging. I freaked when you called because I thought we were finally going to hang. We never hang." Her flawless face seemed so disappointed. I almost went with her just to see her smile.

The student body called the art studio near the river "The Pier" after the wooden pier wrapped around it. They partied there a lot. Local public-school kids met up there all the time, making it a good place to meet guys. Pixie loved the attention. So did everyone else. The Pier was crowded almost every night, and the girl-to-boy ratio had to be more than two-to-one. It was only my first day, but all the complaints about the lack of boys at Francine Frances made sense now. Of those available to date, only a few were in demand. A busy girl could quickly exhaust her resources.

"I need to get my assignments started. I barely did any work today. For like six hours straight, I tried to figure out how Brian ended up at Francine Frances." Certainly she could get behind me on that.

"I know, right? You'd think he would've mentioned the academy."

"Yes." I nodded fiercely. "Do you think he thought we were older? He never asked where we went to school."

"I guess we look too old for high school. What can we say?" She gave me one of her wild smiles. We pulled up to our place. "You know, you could meet a great guy at The Pier."

"Let me know if you see any worth meeting. Maybe I'll tag along next time."

"Fine, but it's more fun with you."

I highly doubted that, but I smiled at her ridiculous pouty face.

She bounced on her seat. "We're a team. We're Pixie and Elle. Come on. I need an anchor."

I hated letting her down. For some reason, she liked doing things with me. I didn't get it. She was fun for me, sure, but she was fun for anyone. At the few parties I had attended, I'd felt like the furniture. *Anchor* was a good word. I doubted anyone knew I'd been there. I was more like backup than the main event. I'd probably make a good designated driver in college.

"Tell me everything the minute you get home, and I promise to tether you to Earth on another night."

Pixie was as much of a loner on the inside as I was. I suspected the makeup and dramatics were mostly show. At home we wore yoga pants and herbal facemasks and watched reality television. Our apartment was a quiet, girls' drama–free zone.

I jogged from the car to our door, hoping to make it inside before she barreled away. I kicked the pile of cigarette butts aside and looked around. There were two more since the morning. I slid my key into the lock and prayed it was locked. The soft click assured me it was, but the eerie sensation I'd struggled with all day returned. One last look at the soiled welcome mat and I hustled inside to lock the door behind me. My stomach coiled inward at the smell. Deep in my mind, a memory rushed by too quickly to capture.

Chapter Five

I took a heavy breath, focusing on one thing at a time. First, the ribbon. The whole Brian fiasco had taken center stage in my mind for most of the day. I needed to think about the ribbon. I dug through my backpack. Who had lockers near mine? Who would've shoved a ribbon in through a vent instead of opening the door? Someone who had borrowed it and wanted to return it? Unlikely. Someone in a hurry? Possible. Maybe someone had found it and tried to return it to the one they thought it belonged to and got my locker instead. I pictured my dowdy, portly homeroom teacher with her frizzy hair and orthopedic sneakers. She didn't look like someone who got everything right.

At ten, I started a new pot of coffee. The phone rang.

"Well, Gabriella, how was your first day of school? Do you feel like a senior yet?" Dad sounded stoic as always. Relief washed over me.

"Yes," I tried to match his tone. "I feel one step closer to college in Fiji."

"So close? I thought you wanted to see the world."

"Well, NYU hasn't exactly come to claim me, but it's still early." I'd applied exclusively to colleges in cities without annual watermelon or apple-cider festivals: Boston, Chicago, New York, L.A. Whoever would have me.

"Anything unusual happen today?"

Could he somehow know about my day?

"Fall on the stairs? Drop your lunch? Something to make you appreciate the fact that dear old Dad sent you to a small school where your friends will feel like family?"

Of course, I was wrong. My eyes rolled in their sockets. Paranoia was so lame. "No, well, yeah. No, nothing like that, but yeah, something strange."

His voice changed. His disposition immediately tempered. I could practically see him shifting in his chair. He'd always been protective of me, of my happiness, especially after losing Mom. "What happened?"

"Well, my locker was jammed after first period. I was late because it took so long to get in." I considered ending it there. I hated to worry him unnecessarily while he was on the road, and he definitely sounded worried. I teetered.

"What else?" His voice thickened with insistence, like a television interrogator examining a criminal in custody.

I stiffened, afraid not to answer. "There was a black satin ribbon inside . . . like the ones Mom used to wear." The last part slipped out. He never talked about Mom. Ever. My voice had caught, and I was sure he'd heard it. Matter of fact, telling the story aloud made it seem sad and pathetic. What did it matter? No one had broken into my locker, I didn't think. The vent seemed the most likely way for the ribbon to have entered, though the locker did jam. It would have taken a long time to feed the ribbon in. I tapped a well-chewed nail against the phone. Black matched the uniform. Plenty of girls wore khaki pants and white polo tops. A black ribbon might look cute. I ignored the voice telling me to mention that our apartment door had been unlocked and that I thought I'd been followed. Pixie had been on the phone. Lots of people walked around the little town. I wasn't convinced, so I kept it to myself. *Liar.*

Dad didn't speak for a long beat.

"The ribbons." His voice lightened by a fraction.

Would he prefer to hear I'd been caught in an unscrupulous activity, rather than what I was about to say? I rarely connected with my emotionally detached father, but at that moment, I practically heard his thoughts. At the mention of Mom and her ribbons, his thoughts probably ran to his darker days like mine had. He remembered her with her ribbons. When they came out, we moved. Outrunning a ghost was impossible, but Dad never stopped trying.

"I almost hate to give it back. It makes me think I need to pack."

Silence.

"Dad?"

Silence.

I pulled the phone away from my face to examine it. Had he hung up on me or had a stroke or something? Tension zinged through the phone. The hairs on my arms stood on end. If he wasn't on business in Tokyo, he might've been en route to get me.

"Why?"

"Seriously? You must know we move every time you miss her too much. First, you drag out her ribbons, and then you're in a frenzy to move." Finally I'd said what I'd wanted to for years. "I know your work isn't the only reason we move so often. I know you feel chased." Dad wore his heartbreak like a neon sign. He had never gotten over losing Mom either. Her loss bonded us in complicated and permanent ways.

"Gabriella." He cleared his throat. "What?"

"I know you miss Mom. Your grief haunts you. I'm haunted, too."

"Honey, you're not hunted. I don't want you to worry about anything."

"Haunted." I enunciated. "Not hunted, Dad. Are you feeling okay? We're not moving again, are we?"

When he hesitated, I worried I'd gone too far. I blamed nerves and nightmares and gorgeous boys with magical green eyes.

"At what time did you receive your locker today?" His flattened tone frightened me. The interrogation voice was back.

"I don't know, maybe eight or a few minutes after . . . "

"When were you there?"

"Until the bell at eight-ten and then again after that class."

"When was that?" His questions came one upon another. It was as if I was in trouble again.

"What?"

"What time did you return to your locker, following your first class?" He spoke slowly, clearly. He wanted answers, facts, now.

"Ah, class is forty-five minutes long, so it was almost nine. It took a minute to get back there after the bell."

"That's when the locker was jammed? When you discovered the ribbon?"

"Yes."

"Could it have been there before your first period and you overlooked it?"

"No. The locker was empty the first time."

"Who else has access? Do you have a locker partner?"

"No. They don't do that here. Everyone has their own."

"Tell me more about the ribbon."

I described it as completely as I could. He insisted I photograph it and send the picture to his inbox while he waited. He wouldn't get off the phone until he had it in front of him. Then, after he nearly scared me to death with his questions and odd behavior, he went back to making small talk. Jekyll and Hyde much? His keyboard clicked as his fingers flew over the keys. He'd moved on. The ribbon wouldn't kill me. I rolled my eyes.

"Maybe I can come for a visit. See how things are going. I can check your apartment for safety again. Talk to the school."

"Dad, no. I'm good. Everything's good."

"We can have lunch. I can make pancakes."

The thought tempted me. I had a million memories of Dad in the kitchen tossing pancakes in the air. Of all the changes in my life, the cabin was a constant I could count on. And I did. The cabin had been in Dad's family for generations, and we all loved it. We stayed off the grid and enjoyed the peacefulness of nature. Mom had loved it. They'd always made breakfast together. She'd sliced berries and scrambled eggs. They'd sung duets and danced for me. They'd loved doing things together. I'd loved watching. After she died, he still made pancakes, but the singing ended. Her absence gonged in the silence.

I considered telling him I had been afraid to walk home from the coffee shop. I considered playing the frightened-daughter role, maybe even mention the rumor going around. I'd already spent the better part of the day telling myself I was an adult, so I skipped confessing my fears. We said goodbye after a few more feeble exchanges.

The caffeine rush ended, and I crashed. My eyes pulled shut almost before I could get my earbuds in. I set my playlist to start on my favorite song and dragged the light comforter over my body until I smelled the fabric softener. As I inhaled muted scents of powder and lavender, sleep rushed in to meet me.

The dream began immediately. This time I was at my locker. I had a strange conversation with Brian. I asked him about his age when he was about to ask me something else. He wanted to talk to me, and I knew why. He wanted me to promise silence about our previous meeting. Sun glinted off his crisp white shirt. The smell of fresh-cut grass tickled my nose. I smiled.

I wanted to reach for him, but the dream morphed in an eerie way until he was in an alley with me. He seemed at ease, though my heart raced as the scene changed. I knew to be afraid. He didn't look concerned. He didn't know we were in danger. I turned to run and ran right into him. He smiled and handed me coffee. I scanned his face for an explanation. How could he not understand that we needed to go? Something bad was near. A low noise sounded from behind me and chills rose up my spine. Frozen in place, I stifled a scream before hearing a familiar sound, the front door.

Pixie tossed her keys onto the counter.

My eyes pulled wide open. I'd slept for two hours.

"Hey, how was The Pier?" I ran a hand through messy hair and leaned into her bedroom doorjamb.

"Do you ever sleep?"

I bit my lip. Sleep and I didn't get along. "Do you?" I folded my arms over my chest.

"Not enough. I'm going to look like the bride of Frankenstein in the morning."

"As if. So, did you find me a man?"

"No one you'd look at." She gave me a sharp look and stripped out of her clothes. I turned away. "Michael stopped by and asked where I've been, like I've been avoiding him or something."

Michael, her on-again, off-again boyfriend, gave me the creeps. He dressed like her and listened to the same music, but he gave me a serious poser vibe. Hopefully Pixie knew who he was under the garb, because I recognized an act when I saw one. They told people they had met at a rave, but really it was a book signing. I knew better. I was there, and we all had matching autographed copies to prove it.

"I told him, 'give me a break. It's the first day of school.' He was all 'excuse me for caring.' I said 'yeah sure,' and he was all 'whatever.' The whole Pier saw it. I have witnesses."

"Are you going to see him again?" I wanted her to be happy, for sure, but single Pixie meant more time for her to fill, and I didn't want to become her pet project. She already looked at me like her personal social-science experiment.

"Nah. We're cool, but I hope he learned his lesson."

Sure. That lesson sounded clear as mud. Why wouldn't he have learned?

"Do you think Brian acted strange today?" Unfriendly, elusive, douchey.

"I think he was nervous and probably embarrassed to see us at his new school. I mean, he doesn't have a super-awesome roommate like you to make this place fabulous."

Who was his roommate? There weren't many guys at Francine Frances. Was he in the senior dorm, too? Davis never paid any attention to him. My mind whirled.

By the time Pixie went to bed, I was wide awake again. The fog of sleep gone. Thoughts of Brian plagued me. I walked out to check that the deadbolt and chain on the door were secure before sliding back into my bed.

What was Brian doing in Elton? Elton was an hour's drive from Francine Frances. Was he from Elton? I had so many questions. Did he register at my school before or after we met? Did he have any idea I was a student here? He looked too old for high school. I hoped Pixie was right before and he thought I looked older, too. I liked the idea that I could pass for college age. It'd make getting along next year easier if I didn't look like a child.

I combed through our conversation from the flea market. We had talked about coffee addiction and how I didn't sleep. I honestly couldn't remember him saying anything too specific about himself, and he had asked very little about me. We talked and walked and laughed. He bartered with an Amish woman over the price of her pies. He lost, but he still bought one. What would he do with an entire pie?

He rode a motorcycle. Shiny, blue, and mildly intimidating, but not a clue to his deep, dark secrets. No one had been with him at the coffee shop. I still wasn't sure if he had gotten there before or after I arrived. Though he said he saw me arrive, I hadn't seen him. He didn't talk to many people at school either. He could be shy like me, but that didn't align with the confidence he'd shown in Elton. What else did I know about Brian? He had commented on some art from Germany at the flea market. Maybe his family traveled. He had mentioned the Peace Corps, but I couldn't remember why. Very little of what he had said meant anything. I rubbed my arms as a chill slid over them. He was big enough to be dangerous. If he was following me . . . I swallowed hard. No. Brian wasn't the bad guy. There was no bad guy. I hoped.

The apartment creaked and settled around me. Pixie was sound asleep, along with everyone else in the time zone.

I booted up my laptop. If I couldn't sleep, I'd get a jump on our Sociology assignment. I was about to type *Gabriella Smith* in the search box, but instead I searched the local news site for references to a serial killer in the area. One small article reported that the FBI had contacted local police regarding a serial-killer case. The details were minimal at best, limited to names I didn't know and the date and time of the contact. Whoever had started the rumor at school had either misread the article or intended to scare the rest of us with the news. I shook my hands at the wrists, utterly tense.

I opened a new window and typed *Brian Austin* into the search engine. Pages of hits came back. I clicked on the one from D.C. first. I loved D.C. All my memories there were happy ones. We lived there until my mother died. After that, Dad avoided big cities at all costs, as if people in small towns never had car accidents.

The Brian Austin in D.C. was in his nineties. I giggled. The article was an obituary. The smile fell off my face. A small write-up in the local paper covered his lifelong career in the military and dedication to his country and community. I read a few words about his sons and grandsons who "followed in his endeavor to protect and serve our country." The article was mildly engaging but useless. It was a little interesting that someone with his name had lived in D.C. with me when I was a kid.

I looked for another Brian Austin until nearly dawn. Nothing came up matching a high school guy. Not even a Facebook profile. I expected to find a newspaper article with a photo of him on his teammates' shoulders somewhere. He looked like an athlete, a star, someone who could do anything. Another shiver passed over me. I wasn't sure if that was a good thing.

Chapter Six

I fell asleep at my desk and woke to the sound of my alarm clock for the first time in years. Sleep time: one hour and twenty-seven minutes. Didn't matter. I was amped. My heart rate spiked at the idea of intrigue. Brian could be another guy like Davis, new to the school and nothing more. He could, but, for a reason I couldn't deny, my intuition screamed otherwise. If I hadn't met him before our first day, maybe, but not now. No more ignoring my instincts.

I hadn't been exposed to anything interesting, ever. Dad's method of grieving for the past decade and all the moving could've been interesting if we had ever gone anywhere good. Instead, my lackluster life compared to the thrill of a lecture on how good kids had it today. I'd heard that one a few times. Excitement rushed through me before I had time to reach for my pills. I needed to know. Who was Brian Austin?

I popped a caffeine capsule in my mouth and swigged from the water bottle on my nightstand. Then I hit the treadmill without coffee. The belt purred underfoot. I mulled over what I knew, which admittedly wasn't much, and set out a plan to see what I could find out.

Light as a feather, I ran to expend energy, for the first time, instead of find it. The pill was part habit, part trouble-shooting the inevitable headache that came without one.

As a future attorney, I would benefit from the investigation experience, regardless of how rudimentary. So, in this case, being nosy and paranoid came second to career preparation.

I rushed through my morning routine and hated that I'd fallen asleep. I'd managed not to dream in the short snippet of time. For that I was thankful. There were too many better things to think about. I swept my hair off my shoulders and buttoned my cardigan. I shoved a journal in my backpack to write everything down. Then I left without Pixie. I wanted to get coffee and make it to the wall on campus before the crowd arrived. I hurried so I wouldn't forget anything from the night before. If Pixie saw me, she'd know something was up. I was dying to tell her my suspicions, but I didn't want to sound as unstable as I felt about my new game.

Outside, it was funny how different everything looked in the morning. Sunlight glistened off the dew, still fresh in shaded places. The blacktop sparkled. The birds sang. Squirrels were hard at work preparing for fall. Girls filled the entire shop from wall to windows. The line for coffee stretched out the door. The silent coffee shop from last night had been replaced, filled now with shoulder-to-shoulder patrons, laughing, voices blending together. Dozens of my classmates clung to one another, talking, gossiping, and smiling. I grabbed my order and ducked out.

The walk to school gave me time to think. Ideas and theories swirled in my mind. By the time I reached my wall, I already had a pen in hand. I looked over my shoulder frequently for good measure. Mowers in the distance provided the perfect amount of white noise. I tossed my bag onto the grass and got comfy.

"Good morning." One of the groundskeepers approached with a tip of his hat. I couldn't be sure, but he looked like the one who had witnessed the awesome rumble I'd had with my locker. I jumped at the sight of him, feeling inept after my attempts at vigilance. I hadn't seen anyone around or heard him approach, thanks to the mowers.

"Hi."

"Beautiful day."

"Yep."

He paused, shoving up his cap to wipe his forehead. "You picked a nice spot. Private."

Maybe too private. I considered moving. Did serial killers ever pose as janitors?

"Enjoy the stolen moments." His voice changed on the final words. His expression fell.

He walked away before I turned back to my notebook. I hated that I hadn't seen or heard him until he was right in front of me. He looked back over his shoulder twice before disappearing around the side of the school. I kept one eye on him, behind a veil of my hair, until he was gone.

I scribbled in my journal until my hand hurt, forgetting where I was, putting thoughts of the awkward exchange out of my mind. A long shadow grew over me. My muscles tensed. I hadn't heard anyone approach for the second time, and it was early. Dad would be furious. There wouldn't be students on campus for another thirty or forty minutes. I prayed I wouldn't find the same guy standing there. My tummy tightened. I turned my face upward to the shadow.

"You're here early." Brian's voice sounded concerned. His eyes narrowed, judging. "You shouldn't be here alone."

I tried to shake off the warning. How would he know what was or was not safe? Better yet, why wouldn't I be safe? Had he heard the rumor, too? The square of his shoulders and his roaming eyes made me think of my dad. His words were formal, making him sound different than he had in Elton and different from any guy my age I'd ever met. How could he be a senior in high school? I blinked my eyes to concentrate. How could he not be? The tiny school must have tons of hoops and screens to filter its applicants. Then again, how had I gotten in? I had decided to come only three months before I arrived.

"Right. All these prep-school girls can be dangerous." I smiled. I'd perfected the say-one-thing, think-another style years ago when Dad made it clear we wouldn't discuss Mom, the ribbons, his work, or anything else other than me.

Brian's fierce expression dissolved. The corners of his mouth turned up, and he squatted beside me.

I took a long, full breath as I absorbed his entirety, enjoying the return of his familiar smile.

He was unbelievable. His thighs tested his pants as they accommodated his new position. The buttons on his shirt struggled, too. His hands hung loosely between his knees, and I saw what I hadn't before. Under his jacket, peeking out from beneath the white shirt, were the unmistakable silver beads of military tags. I'd missed them that first day.

"When did you enlist?" I motioned to his chest.

His hand moved instinctively to touch the chain. "Elle."

I smiled. Everyone had picked up my nickname from Pixie.

"Forgive me. You prefer Gabriella?"

He started to stand, and, without thinking, I reached out for him.

We both looked at my hand on his. I pulled back. Shutting my eyes against the humiliation, I shook my head.

"No, Elle is fine. Please, not Gabriella. My dad is the only one who calls me that."

Forgive me. He was too young to be so formal. Could others see that?

I looked at him again, feeling nauseous but feigning bravery. "You wanted to tell me something yesterday, and I interrupted."

He searched my face for a moment. I had no idea what he expected to find, but I hoped he wanted to tell me all his secrets. To hear all his stories at once was possibly more exciting than digging them up one at a time. Frankly, I needed the excitement.

His eyes moved from my face to the distance. He looked around. "I didn't tell you I was enrolled here when we met because I didn't know I would be. I didn't intend to deceive you in any way. I know how it must seem."

He waited for me to respond, but I was busy processing the words. Did he know he had slipped? He had admitted knowing I went to school here, and I'd never said that.

When I dared look into his face again, his eyes were back on the horizon. I followed his gaze. Nothing.

When I turned back, his eyes were on me. "What?"

"Are you angry?"

"No. I understand."

"Do you?" Tension licked his words.

I nodded.

"You should study in the library, not out here in the open, and not alone." As he spoke, his eyes focused hard on mine. Again, I sensed there was something more he wanted to say. I had a rough idea of how it went, but I didn't know the specifics.

"Okay."

"Okay?" His eyebrows rose. Did he anticipate an argument? His beautiful face fell a bit. A crease appeared between his brows.

Uh-oh. I should've put up more of a fight for show. Between the creepy janitor guy and the stupid serial-killer speculation, I didn't feel much like arguing.

"Well, if you think I should study inside, then I'll study inside." Maybe he could join me, tell me about where he grew up and how he got here. We could get to know each other.

His eyes jumped back and forth between mine, examining one then the other. "What were you doing here?" He nodded toward my leather-bound journal, clearly not a schoolbook, obviously meant to be kept private.

"Journaling." I shrugged.

"Mmm. About a flirtatious guy who bought you coffee?" The muscles in his jaw relaxed. His shoulders dropped back.

"And now he's my classmate, in almost all of my classes. That'd make a good story."

"Who'd believe it?"

My tummy yanked back against my spine. "Not me." Silently, I willed him to scoop me up and carry me away. Pixie had called us soulmates. I forced the words out of my mind.

His eyes narrowed.

I would've looked away except I enjoyed him looking at me. In class, he never let his eyes land on mine for more than a second. Here, alone, beside my wall, the look felt intimate. I liked it. I returned his stare, matching his intensity.

"You're astute. I like it. That's both an admirable and necessary quality." He smiled wider. "You'll live longer, too."

I sucked in air. My heart hammered, and heat ran up my neck. Skipping breakfast had left me woozy. The tension mounted until I leaned against the wall for support. His words seemed to hold double meanings. Being alone with him tied my lungs in knots. My instincts said he was dangerous. They also said I was smitten. How was that for complicated?

"You know, if you need anything, if anyone bothers you, or if you feel . . . uncomfortable, about anything, you can come to me. I can help you." He frowned as he finished his strange statement. "New places can be a challenge."

Ah, this was his attempt to sound like a friend. Complete fail. "I've been in a dozen new places." Francine Frances wasn't my first rodeo. No need to worry about me. "I've moved nearly every year my whole life." I tried to open a line of trust between us. "Sometimes we stayed longer, but Dad would eventually be reassigned and we'd move. Anyway, aren't you new, too?" Maybe he was from here. He had never said.

"Reassigned?" His eyes narrowed further.

"My dad? Yeah, for work."

For a tiny second, his face showed surprise, but he covered it and a smirk appeared. "For work." He nodded.

"Yeah." I had caught his interest. "He travels on business, and sometimes it means we have to move. Actually, it always means we have to move."

He smiled as if we had shared a joke. His lips parted, and then his phone rang. Injustice.

He held up one finger and stepped away from me, angling himself to see me, but keeping his voice low and his words brief. I wished I could read lips. The mowers stopped, and voices danced in the distance. School would begin soon. A handful of maintenance men walked to the parking lot. I envied them. Their day was probably over. Mine hadn't started. Brian shoved the phone inside his pocket and returned to me.

I'd had just enough time to pack up my things.

"Where are you going?" He looked annoyed.

"To the library. You're not supposed to have a phone on campus, you know."

"I didn't." His tone and expression confirmed his lie as truth.

I blinked. "So, where are you from? I mean, before coming here?"

"D.C." His brows twitched. He was new, too.

I opened my mouth to speak, but the words never escaped.

He bent to tie his shoe.

I looked away, clearing my head and breathing in the spice of his cologne and a hint of shampoo or soap.

"Talk to you later." Not a question. He stood poker straight and strode away, leaving me alone, confused, bewildered, and a touch irritated.

"Good morning, gorgeous." Davis was twenty or thirty feet away, closing in on me at a racer's pace. "Coffee?"

"Yeah, thanks." Black. I had smelled it the moment he reached me.

"I missed you at the coffee shop. I figured you'd be there. I skipped hotcakes in the dining hall for you." He winked playfully. "Hey, was that Austin?"

I scanned the horizon. There was no trace of my mystery man. As nice as he'd been in private, he still didn't seem to want to be seen with me in public. My heart cracked. What was wrong with him? The fact that Davis had called him Austin and not Brian reminded me that I'd never found out whether Davis was a first or last name. Until I did, I refused to direct any name his way. If I started calling guys by their last names, where would it end? Would I be slapping them on their rears every time they walked away, too?

"Bell's going to ring. I'll walk you."

I lifted my backpack and turned in the direction of the growing crowd at the fountain.

"So, was it Austin?"

"Yeah. Do you know anything about him? Like who his roommate is or how he ended up here?"

Davis slowed. Concern covered his face as if I'd hurt his feelings.

"We're both new, so I wondered. Umm." I chewed on my lip.

His face relaxed a little.

"Where are you from?" I gave my most encouraging smile. Davis's stocky build and messy blond hair practically screamed all-American guy. If I'd ever imagined having a boy next door, he would've looked like Davis.

Davis told me about his lacrosse scholarship. His family lived in Pennsylvania, owned a small carpet company, and hoped to give him a better education than they could afford. He was in the running for a scholarship to Yale in the fall if he kept his grades up and stayed out of trouble. A very normal scenario.

I approved.

"Elle!" Pixie's voice squealed from a closing distance. The second person in ten minutes to chase me down, and the third in an hour to seek me out. Not normal. She ran full speed toward me. Smack!

She whipped my shoulder with her notebook. "Why did you leave? I had a ton of stuff to tell you this morning, and you weren't there. I love our morning routine, and you ditched me." She looked sincerely offended.

"Sorry. I don't know what I was thinking. I missed you, too." I hugged her. "I definitely won't do it again."

She looked me up and down and then pulled her mouth to one side. "Fine. I forgive you then. I hope your little escape was worth it."

Oh, it was definitely worth it, but I couldn't talk about that yet.

"Hey, Davis." She raised her coffee into the air. "Looks like you found her." Her eyes moved to mine.

"Yep." I raised my cup.

She smiled wider somehow.

Kate arrived a minute later. Our little circle grew until the bell rang. When we all moved toward the front doors, Davis fell back a step and tilted his head toward mine.

"Come on," Kate whined.

To my surprise, Davis waved her on without him.

"You want to come watch practice after school?"

"Sure." Who said that? No, I didn't want to watch practice after school. My new school would be the death of me. I sucked down the black coffee, still hot from being covered, and scalded my throat. "Thanks for the coffee," I choked.

Davis smiled like he'd won a prize and headed in the direction of his homeroom.

I didn't hear two words my Trigonometry teacher spoke. I wrote frantically in my journal the entire class period. I wrote a heading: "What stinks?" The list covered an entire page before my mind drifted to my mother. Truth be told, my mother's absence had never sat well. I had no closure and no answers. I understood Dad's heartache but not his reluctance to share her memory with me. All I had left were shreds of childish memories and whispers of her voice, long muted by years of her absence. The fact that I had no other family to ask about her made the hole in my heart bigger. Having anyone in the world who had loved her as I had and was willing to remind me of her would've helped. I had no one. When the bell rang, I anchored my feet to the floor. I had to act casual. Shake off things not worth dwelling on and focus on those I had a chance of learning.

Three minutes later, I sat in English. Three desks back, I faced my mystery man. He sat sideways in the row against the wall, leaning into it and stretching his legs into the aisle. Brian barely made eye contact. He gave no sign that he knew me. No clue he'd sought me out that morning. An infuriating hour later, class let out. The teacher and most of the class disappeared within seconds. Brian stayed seated. I fiddled with my backpack, hoping he'd look my way as he passed and headed out the door. When he finally stood, the room was empty aside from the two of us.

I waited.

"You have nowhere to be?"

"Study hall, with you." I raised my eyebrows.

His face held no expression of recognition. Surely he had noticed that we had an entire schedule together, aside from homeroom and Trig? When he made no sign of speaking again, I turned for the door, my cheeks suddenly on fire.

"Elle."

I turned back.

"I'd like it very much if we could be friends."

I gagged internally.

"I know that's probably not something you'll find acceptable. I'm not acting much like a friend, am I?"

My hands anchored to my hips. "No. You're not. In Elton, you were at least friendly, and now you're hot and cold. You won't be seen talking to me. No one knows where you came from."

He winced at the word *Elton*. His eyes definitely widened a fraction at the last accusation. He smiled. "You're asking around about me?"

"Maybe."

"Why not ask me?"

Because you're never around. Because you have a habit of taking off before I can. Because your sculpted chin and perfect, square jawline distract me.

"Fine." My eyes jumped to the clock over the door. I dared an apologetic smile before knocking twice on my desk and turning away once more. I needed to go before the next bell rang or I combusted, whichever came first.

He chuckled.

I turned.

Brian stretched, resting interlocked fingers behind his head, elbows pointing out. Beneath his shirt, his biceps bulged and the muted outline of his tattoo taunted me. Images of his bare chest and tan arms clogged my mind and throat. My head lightened. I spun on my heels and headed for the door alone, dodging the dribble of students arriving for class. I had a feeling he watched me leave. All those years spent on the treadmill just paid off.

Pixie was already seated when I got to study hall, and her knees bounced a wild rhythm. She drew patterns in the carpet with the eraser end of her pencil. When she looked up, she started and clapped her hands in a fast silent way, then patted the carpet beside her. I sat and she shoved a paper at me with words already written.

"Every girl in this school is going insane over your boy." Thank goodness she didn't name him in case of note confiscation.

"I don't blame them." I was enamored and infuriated. I had no idea how to act. Dad and I had never stayed anywhere long enough for me to get involved. The handful of dates I'd been on hadn't had half the thrill of sitting across the room from Brian. I'd walked into new territory on a number of levels. I couldn't stay mad. When he wasn't being a colossal jerk, he seemed like the guy I had met at the coffee shop. Maybe Pixie was right. Being at a new school was tough for most people, and I had Pixie.

"Have you talked to him?"

Hmm. Lie or tell the truth? Cosmically on cue, he walked in. He looked more out of place than ever. His posture was perfect, his stride confident. He walked to the table he had sat at the day before and dropped his bag before making a trip to the vending machine. His selection captured my attention as if the fate of my world depended on it. He bought a bottle of flavored water, returned to the table, and pulled an apple from his bag. I should've expected as much. He didn't look like that by eating cafeteria food and drinking coffee.

Pixie shoved the paper at me again, having underlined the previous sentence three times.

"For a minute. Nothing fun." I shrugged.

She looked at the ceiling and made a face that said "blah." She turned to look at him, and I did, too.

He watched us.

I was suddenly hypersensitive to his every move. I loved and hated the exhilaration he brought.

He raised his bottle toward her and winked.

"Agh." She looked at me, thoroughly disappointed. "Come on!" She wrote on the paper and then crumbled it into a ball.

She was done with me for now.

I looked at him one more time while I still had the nerve, but he was busy texting beside his stack of books. I went back to organizing my thoughts in my journal. When my pen died, I was forced to dig around inside my backpack for another. There was a neatly folded scrap of paper I didn't recognize. Flipping it open, a number I didn't know stared back at me.

"Pixie?" I whispered.

She glanced at the teacher, then me. He was involved in *Golf Digest*.

"Did Darcy get that job working in the office?"

Chapter Seven

After dinner, I excused myself from Pixie's company and headed back to the library under the guise of my Sociology assignment, though it wouldn't be my name I researched. I planned to find a favorite alcove there to call my own, continue my search for Brian, and maybe even look yet again into my family. I'd never found anything, but the Internet changed all the time. I couldn't guess when a site might pop up with archived data on D.C. Smiths. My dad claimed ignorance. If I cracked either case, I'd have no doubt that courtrooms were in my future.

My phone rang as I reached the library doors. I smiled at the number on my screen. "Hey, Dad."

"How's my little girl?" His voice was like balm.

"Good." I leaned against the wall, waiting to go inside.

"Listen, honey. I'm going to be in Ohio tomorrow. Can we have lunch?"

"Why will you be in Ohio?"

"Is that a no?" He chuckled. "Can't a dad check in on his little girl?"

"I mean . . . I have school tomorrow. Were you planning to come to the cafeteria?" Had he lost his mind? I sent up a prayer that he'd say no.

"Right. You're getting acclimated. Well, I'll be in the area more. If you ever have time for your old man . . . "

His work kept him away so much. I knew I should accept any time he offered, but part of me rebelled. When I had needed him in the past, he was always off working. I had a mission now and needed to stay focused. He was the one who taught me not to need him. The reasoning had holes, but whatever.

"I'll call you soon." The inflection in my voice made it sound more like a question.

"Well, I'll leave you to it then. Remember, if you need anything, I'll be nearby."

"Thanks." After a feeble exchange of affection, we disconnected.

I pulled open the door and inhaled. Somewhere inside, a table, chair, and computer port had my name on them. The library brimmed with books but very few students. I had expected at least a few study groups. Only a handful of students were sprinkled around the cavernous room. I chose an oversized table and spread out my things in an alcove. No matter where I lived, the library felt like home. The familiar smells of paper, ink, worn leather, and wood soothed me like chatting with an old friend. Every librarian I had ever met shared the understated kindness trait I appreciated, too.

I nestled into the large wooden chair and logged in. Online and in the zone, I picked up where I had fallen asleep during my first attempt. Knowing Brian was from D.C., I started digging into the papers. I looked for articles on high school sports and scholarships. When that failed miserably, I switched gears. My attempt at locating Davis's family and their carpet business turned out fruitful. The Internet still worked. When I'd searched for Brian, either the researcher or the search had been faulty. Opening a fresh window, I Googled my mom.

The lack of library patrons meant I didn't have to hide my contraband. I cracked the top off the giant coffee I had picked up on my way in and inhaled the warm sweetness. By the time the coffee ran out, my fingers ached and my wrists were numb. I stretched in the hard wooden chair, no longer feeling very nestled, and rolled my head over my shoulders.

Dead end after dead end left me more determined. I couldn't find anything more about Brian or my mom than I already knew, which was nothing. I moved on to my assignment, Googling myself, then my father. Changing my focus seemed in order, but there was nothing to find. I looked through all the papers local to D.C. and at the clerk of courts. I didn't find a birth certificate for any of us, a death certificate for my mother, or even a record of their marriage.

A click in the distance caught my attention. My mouth fell open. I was alone. Shadows of the last set of students danced along the outside of the windows. They were gone. Not a single girl or librarian in sight. The stillness sent goose bumps over my skin. Alone in the oversized room, I peered up into three empty stories above me. Thousands of volumes. No people. My skin snapped to attention. I coughed, and the sound echoed upward and out, bouncing off stone floors and sparse wooden furniture.

I turned in my seat, desperate for a sign of life. A cart loaded with books stood abandoned near a door marked "staff." What a time to take a break. Didn't the librarian know I had serious paranoia issues? I sighed and tapped my fingers against the heavy, lacquered table. I pinched my lips tight between my teeth and considered how quickly I could pack up and get out.

The week of weird had me more on edge than ever before. Brian warned me not to be alone, and the library was silent. My mind suggested some less-than-lovely possibilities. I'd spent an hour reading the awful details from article after article about some crazed serial killer who had stalked North America back when my family lived in

D.C. It seemed to be the only story of interest from the year Mom died. The killer moved from Canada to the United States and even logged a few kills in tourist areas of Mexico during his run. I shivered at the thought of that man—I used the word loosely—being free. Good to know it was over a decade ago.

Yeah. Time to leave. I turned to retrieve my backpack from the floor beside me.

"Elle?" Brian appeared out of thin air and stood less than two feet away from my chair.

"Ahhh!" I gasped for air and clutched my chest. My heart tried to escape through my mouth. Swallowing was impossible. I leaned forward and hoped to avoid passing out completely. "Are you kidding me?"

"Sorry." He sounded more amused than I liked. "What're you doing? Planning a heist?" He took a seat beside me and leaned in close to take a look. I leaned away and scrunched my brows. He took my hand and checked my pulse.

I jerked it back. My mouth fell open again. "I'm fine. You scared me."

His eyes shifted to my journal and I snapped it shut.

"One minute I'm completely alone and the next minute you're right there." I motioned with my hands for emphasis. "How long have you been here?"

"You need to be more aware of your surroundings. This is the second time I've startled you. You should've known I was here." He shook his head in disappointment.

Fire burned beneath my skin. "Why are you here?"

"Why are you?"

"I'm studying."

He looked at me skeptically. His eyes moved to the laptop and again to my journal.

He looked dubiously at the stack of closed textbooks.

One long arm dove before me and turned the laptop to face him.

I snapped the lid down. This silent conversation I understood. We both had secrets.

His eyes narrowed and he waited.

"I was researching for our Sociology assignment." I cleared my throat twice mid-sentence.

"In the D.C. paper?"

He had seen more than I thought.

"Find anything interesting?"

"No. Well, yes. I couldn't find any evidence of my existence, so I suppose I'll fail the assignment. I did learn D.C. had a serial killer while I lived there." I liked saying I had lived in D.C.

A long pause stretched between us. I wondered what he thought about us sharing a hometown.

"Well, I'm pretty sure you exist." He looked deep in thought and then refocused. "You aren't supposed to be alone. You promised."

"I wasn't alone when I got here."

"Well, how long have you been here? Do you know it's after eleven?"

"A while, and no. I was absorbed."

"Right. Good thing you don't need sleep, I suppose."

He remembered. My heart rate jumped and my mind glazed over.

"How's that coming?"

I sipped at the last cold drops of coffee, trying not to frown, thinking of the best reply. "Same." I shrugged, hoping to make the topic less interesting. He didn't need to know why.

"They never found the serial killer, you know?" I wasn't going to discuss my inability to sleep with him or delve into any personal discussion without preparation.

"Yeah, I heard that." His eyes were gentle, and they bounced around, always scanning the perimeter. He did the same thing everywhere he went, except in our classroom when the door was closed, but then again, he never had his back to it.

"How?"

"What do you mean?"

"I mean, how old are you? You never answered me, and I'm guessing you were a little young to be following that story."

"I'm seventeen, like you." He searched my face. "I'm from a family of law-enforcement officers. They still talk about it sometimes. They say he's still out there."

So, he wanted to play the partial-honesty card with me. I appreciated that. "How do you know I'm seventeen?"

"I assumed."

"You don't look seventeen. Not even close."

"Younger?"

I snorted and tipped my head.

"How old do I look?"

"Twenty. You know there's a rumor about a serial killer here?"

He straightened up in his chair. His mouth opened and closed without a sound. Had he heard? His phone buzzed and he pulled it from his pocket, only looking at it for a half second before walking into a long, high aisle of reference books. Like a true stalker, I slipped from my seat and tiptoed into the aisle next to his. He grunted and spoke in clipped words I didn't understand. Thousands of pages muffled the already quiet conversation.

"Nicholas." I caught one low word, a full octave lower than he spoke.

Nicholas. I turned back toward our table to find the man from my last library trip standing in the aisle ten feet away. The breath whooshed out of me. My eyes were glued to him. Terror gripped me. Tears welled and embarrassment pinked my cheeks. Silence stretched and I started toward the ladies' room at the opposite end of the aisle. Every sound was amplified in the silent, empty room. I dashed into the ladies' room. If there was an echo in the library, the acoustics in the ladies' room could've rivaled an amphitheater.

The white-tiled room was nondescript. I washed my hands. It would seem more authentic if I came out smelling like soap. My heart pounded against my rib cage. A torrent of emotions whirled in my chest. Fear. Mostly fear. My dream pushed in, too. Why was that man staring at me from close enough to drag me off? He looked familiar in a way that enhanced my fear. Also, he'd caught me eaves-dropping on Brian through the bookshelves. There were a lot of things I didn't know, but I knew I didn't want to be alone. Exhaling until my lungs went flat, I pulled the door open and screeched.

Brian leaned on the aisle of books less than five feet away, rubbing his face with both palms. "You want to get out of here?"

I nodded and looked around. The man was nowhere in sight. Only us. He led the way to my table. I packed my bag. The moment I finished, he reached out and tossed it over one of his shoulders. Brian moved toward the door without another word. I had to move double time to stay beside him.

A Jeep sat cocked at an angle on the cement outside the doors. Parking spots must've been too inconvenient.

"What happened to your motorcycle?" I was relieved not to be getting on it. Somehow I was certain that if I lifted one thigh toward it, my dad would materialize for a lecture on vehicle safety. Better to start my year of adventure with a seat belt.

Brian held the door for me. My last chance to decide. Was he dangerous? I stepped inside, arranging my bag at my feet before Brian shut the door behind me. Leaving with him felt wrong, risky, but walking home alone was impossible after reading all those awful newspaper articles. I glanced back toward the library one last time. A dark silhouette stood in the shadow of the building. I hoped it was just someone waiting for a friend. Brian slid in behind the wheel and I jumped. I was pretty sure he was dangerous. Something else told me I was in good hands.

The Jeep's interior was gray leather. The fragrance of cinnamon and vanilla was strong, a fragrance I could pick out anywhere. A steaming latte sat in the cup holder on the passenger's side.

"I thought if I ran into you, you'd be in the mood for coffee." He looked years younger as he spoke.

I smiled. He had come looking for me.

He rolled his eyes and turned to face the windshield. "I couldn't bring you coffee on the bike. Besides, the Jeep is safer."

I snapped my seat belt into place and bit the inside of both cheeks. Faint memories of the plain black coffee Davis had brought made the gesture sweeter. I'd ordered coffee one time in Brian's presence, and he had remembered.

The night was beautiful. It made small-town living seem nicer. The sky was clear. Deer grazed in pastures along the dark county roads. The trees showed the first signs of their fall apparel. I loved autumn in full swing. My heart fluttered. Images of swooning ladies a hundred years back crossed my mind. I understood. I couldn't speak, or breathe. Or think.

I snuck peeks at Brian as we drove. He caught me every time. On the one hand, I was completely embarrassed, but on the other . . . he was looking at me, too. I raked at my hair with my fingers. Silence with him felt heavy on my lungs. Too many secrets. Too much unsaid. I wanted to ask a hundred questions, but I had no idea what to say. I sipped the fresh coffee to keep my mouth busy.

"How did you remember what I drink?" I licked a drop from my bottom lip. I wasn't even sure Pixie would know without asking.

"I pay attention." His eyes dropped to my lips and his mouth twitched at the side.

"Astute." That's what he'd called me.

"Is there anything you want to talk about? We're finally alone. I thought we could drive for a few minutes. We can be candid, if you like." His dimple disappeared, and he looked troubled. It seemed he wanted to talk about something. Well, he wanted me to talk, but he had all the information. Shampoo mingled with the scent of new leather seats to fill the space inside the car. Cologne swirled with the cinnamon and vanilla in the air, confusing me. Anywhere I looked gave me pause. He was everywhere. Hands large enough to palm a basketball stretched around the lucky steering wheel. His knee flopped into the gearshift. An elbow rested dangerously close to mine, heat radiating from it, invading my space. Permeating my brain.

I took a deep breath. "My life is an open book. Yours is . . . "

"Not."

I supposed that meant I shouldn't ask, but if not, then what? All my questions were about him.

Too soon he angled his Jeep onto the curb outside my building. He had never asked where I lived. My muscles tensed as I thought of the car and the squeaky belt and the cigarette butts. I flipped open his ashtray and he looked at me with furrowed brows. The tray held loose coins and a pack of gum. I shut it and look at the floorboards.

"Thanks." I lifted the cup into the air and tilted my head toward my apartment.

"Of course."

I shoved open the door with my shoulder and spilled out onto the sidewalk, coffee in one hand, backpack in the other.

"Elle?" He leaned across the seat. "If you need me, you know how to reach me."

The number in my bag. I hesitated before closing the door. Walking numbly up the stairs, I fumbled for my keys and went into the kitchen. Headlights flashed over the front window as he slowly pulled onto the road and away.

Chapter Eight

Despite my increased anxiety and paranoia, or maybe because of it, time moved quickly. All things considered, I grew comfortable in this strange new town. My dream evolved, plaguing me by day more often than night. Keeping it a secret was exhausting, but I wasn't lonely.

Music blasted from Pixie's car radio as she and Aubrie screamed the lyrics to a song I'd never heard. My cheeks ached from smiling all night. Nights out with the girls were plentiful, and I enjoyed the camaraderie. Darcy drummed a beat against the back of my headrest. We pulled up to a gas station a few miles from campus.

"Who wants snackers?" Pixie bounded from the car, skipping lithely across the lot. Darcy and Aubrie followed. My ears rang. I slumped in the passenger's seat, feeling freer than I ever had. After two hours of playing darts at the rec center and laughing with Davis till my sides hurt, I was fully ready for a movie marathon with my three new besties. I peeked at the little store beyond the pumps and smiled. Pixie looked to have a handful of suckers. Of course. Pixie snackers.

Lights blinked off in the rearview mirror. A car had parked at an angle to Suzy Sunshine. Covered in shadows, a tiny flash gave way to a small glow. The glow came and went in a strange rhythm. Bright and soft, it repeated. I'd seen that glow before. I squeezed the tops of my thighs. Adrenaline shot through my veins. The same strange light had pulsed outside the coffee shop. I recognized the faint silhouette of a person inside the car. Someone was smoking a cigarette. How my brain had failed to put the glow and dim pattern together sooner was beyond me. Regardless of how hard I had tried to recognize the strange firefly outside the coffee shop, I hadn't. I couldn't put it together until this moment. Blood rushed and beat between my ears and my fuzzy brain connected dots all around me. How many cigarette butts lay outside our door? Red flags and rockets blazed inside my head.

Lots of people smoke. I gripped the door handle, waiting. I looked to the store for my friends. I needed to see them. Safety in numbers. I couldn't see them inside anymore. My chest constricted around my heart and a whimper slipped from between my teeth. I pulled my eyes back to the rearview. The glow had vanished. A tiny orange light lay on the ground outside the car.

The car hadn't moved, but the cigarette's small glow twirled in the breeze on the blacktop. Inside the car, the silhouette had vanished. I'd watched the store, so I knew the driver hadn't gone inside. I looked around the side of the car. No one. My eyes jumped and scanned the larger scene. My heart pounded painfully inside my chest. My friends were gone. The driver was gone. *I can't make out the license plate.*

I swiveled in my seat until I landed on my knees facing backward. A shadow fell over Pixie's driver-side window. Not a shadow. A person. Someone dressed in dark clothing stood beside the door. From where I sat, only his torso was visible. He was that close. I looked to the store across the lot. Could I make it before he rounded the car and grabbed me? Stupid boondocks gas stations. I needed crowds and witnesses. The steering wheel was only an arm's length away. If I sounded the horn, I might scare him away or draw the attention of my friends. Reaching for the horn meant moving closer to him. My limbs froze with indecision.

He yanked on the door handle and I yelled out. Locked. God bless Pixie. He tried again and I begged my limbs to move. Panic. Fight-or-flight kicked in. My mind and body united, demanding I choose. Now. Adrenaline coursed through my frozen limbs, ready for either. All senses heightened. A fraction of a second later, flight won. One last look out the window, and I pushed the door open wide, but not before slamming my fist against Pixie's steering wheel hard, sounding the horn. With a leap, I hit the ground running and screaming.

"Pixie!" I ran for the double glass doors. Wind blew hair across my cheeks and fueled my flight. "Pix . . . " I slammed into a wall of muscle. The too-familiar combination of spice and shampoo assaulted me. There was no mistaking him. He pulled me around the side of the building, into the shadows. He crouched to look in my face, erasing the significant height difference between us.

"What's wrong?" Brian's voice came low and level, cool and calm. He sounded as if I had nothing to worry about, yet he'd taken the time to conceal us before he asked. His green eyes seemed to glow, even in the shadows.

My hands shook. Excess adrenaline. I had much more to give for the effort of flight. I'd been cut short. I tried to explain what had sent me over the edge. The words tumbled out in a jumble of syllables and panic.

"A man. There." I lifted a trembling finger and curled it into a fist at my mouth. "He tried to get in the car." Air shuttered in and out of my chest.

Brian ran his heavy palms over the curve of my shoulders, searching my face for something more. I had nothing left to give. My legs wobbled under me. Brian clutched me to his chest, pressing his cheek against my head and cursing softly into my hair. When he stepped back, something crossed his expression that I'd never seen there before. The protective grip on me loosened and I whimpered as night air rushed over my chest where he had held me to him.

"Go inside."

He put my back against the wall and jogged toward the parking lot. I ran into the store. A rush of heat from a vent over the door burned my night-chilled skin. The girls laughed. I moved in their direction. A pimple-faced clerk played air guitar behind the counter. My friends were playing the crane game in the farthest corner. I ducked into the bathroom and lost my mind.

Tears sprang forth like a floodgate had opened. Years of repressed tension burst loose without warning and in the most inopportune place. I wiped them fervently with the backs of my hands and fingertips, but the effort didn't slow them. My legs grew limp and I slid down the inside of the door until my bottom hit the filthy checkered floor. When the tears ran dry, I pulled my knees tight to my chest and rested my cheek on them to catch my breath. This was the moment I'd been anticipating. I'd finally gone crazy. The dreams had infected my reality. No denying it. I'd cracked.

I pulled myself back up the door and splashed my face clean. Beyond the door deeper voices mixed with higher ones.

I left the safety of the bathroom, trembling and splotchy. With any luck, Brian hadn't told the others what I thought I saw. Uncertainty raged inside me. My imagination had tormented me for years, and in the moment, I didn't know what was true.

"There you are." Pixie made large air circles with her arms. "Look at all this stuff Darcy won. They're going to have to replenish the machine."

I smiled at Darcy as she maneuvered the crane down once more.

Aubrie bounced over and whispered, "Saw your boy tonight."

"Brian?" My eyes searched the store for some sign he'd been there and found none.

"Who?" Her face crumbled in confusion. "What? The new guy? Wait. Are you and the new guy a thing? I thought you were into

Davis." Her voice grew out of the whisper. Davis turned from the magazine rack and looked our way. So much for discretion.

"No. I didn't know who you meant. I mean, I thought I saw him before I came inside." Argh. My brain burned with embarrassment for a thousand things and toiled over whether I might be hallucinating. Was there a smoking shadowman outside? Had Brian come to my rescue? Lack of sleep did bad things to people. I walked over to the window. No car behind Suzy Sunshine. No Jeep anywhere.

"I thought you were into Davis." Aubrie followed me along the windows as I searched every inch of the darkened lot.

"No." I caught a glimpse of him watching from the crane machine and sighed. "He's really nice. One of the only guys here who's talked to me. I appreciate that. Being new sucks." A crazy-sounding laugh trickled out of my chest. Had I imagined it all? Was I that far gone?

"What about Brian? I've seen him talking to you. I heard you two had a date the other night?"

Jeez. Who wasn't watching me these days? I stared into the night. The empty lot mocked me.

"At Buzz Cup? No. He was there when I got there. There's nothing going on between me and anyone, as far as I know." Had someone seen us there? Or at the library? He had dropped me off after the library. I spent more time with him than I realized. Every moment we shared went twice as fast as my other moments.

Davis joined us at the window. Suddenly protective of my space, I inched back. He was cute. In an off-limits, super-intense way I didn't need in my life. I took another baby step back for good measure. Heightened emotions were dangerous.

"Where's Kate?" Pixie had warned me to stay away from Davis, but what could I do if he showed up all the time? Kate would make my life a living hell, I knew. High school was the same everywhere. Even in Crazy Town, Ohio.

"I'm not with Kate." His voice quieted. "It's impossible to date at this school. Everyone already knows everything about everyone. What's there left to learn?" Wow. That was a predicament I'd never be in. I didn't even know everything I wanted to know about me, but the guy had a point.

I leaned against the window looking into Davis's eyes. "I know what you mean."

"What they aren't told directly they assume or make up."

My lips kicked up a little at the corners. "Heard any good scoop on the new girl yet?"

"Well, all I've heard about you so far is how everyone wants to see what you sleep in."

"What?" This time the laugh burst out, gaining the attention of the entire store.

Davis lowered his head and smiled. "I was kidding, but you should laugh more. It's nice."

"Good advice." I tilted my head at him. "What are you doing all the way out here at this old gas station?"

He nodded toward the glass, where a group of guys leaned against an old SUV. "Guys night out. Rick doesn't card us for beer and it's a great night for a bonfire."

I gave the kid behind the counter another look.

"Come on, Elle. Movie time," Pixie yelled over the rows of snacks and magazines.

"You gotta go." Davis reached out and ran a fingertip over the back of my hand so lightly breath caught in my chest. The spark he left behind spread a blush up my arm and into my cheeks, especially when he followed me to the door. He held it open for our little group. His bright blue eyes looked mischievous.

The whole way across the lot I stared at the spot where the car had been. Had it ever really been there? I wondered what was real. Inside Suzy Sunshine, the girls went berserk.

"OMG. Davis freaking Stratten is crushing on you!" Darcy looked more like a freshman than I'd ever seen her. She made no attempt to control her high pitch or limit her wild bouncing on the seat behind me.

"He's not the only one." Pixie flashed me a million-dollar smile.

"Davis watches you all the time." Aubrie smiled.

I guess everyone really was watching me. If that was true . . . My eyes moved to where I'd imagined the car. Maybe I hadn't imagined anything. A tug deep inside told me I hadn't.

"You are the absolute luckiest girl to ever attend this school." Darcy threw a wrist over her forehead and feigned a swoon when I looked in the rearview mirror.

"She won't be when Kate finds out in about five seconds."

Small-town fishbowls and irony. Everyone knew everything about everyone in a small town, except I didn't know anything about the one guy I wanted to know about. Which reminded me.

"Did you guys see Brian Austin tonight?"

Pixie shot me a crazy face. They all confirmed he hadn't been there, but he had. So had the car and the smoker. They all frightened me. Or were they one and the same? Brian could've been in the car. I hadn't seen the driver's face or where he had disappeared to. I also hadn't seen where Brian had come from. Holy crap! He drove me home one night. Knew right where I lived.

"Well?" Aubrie demanded. "Earth to Elle. Are you still lost in those gorgeous baby blues or what?"

"They're super blue." I wanted to say, they're green like emeralds in a jewelry-store window, but that didn't begin to describe them and also I knew who they meant. Davis. Pixie pulled onto the street, heading back toward school, as the small group of guys climbed into an SUV by the pumps. Davis lit up a cigarette before closing the door.

The urge to vomit overtook me. I shut my eyes and begged my body to get a grip. Davis smoked. He had walked into the coffee shop the night I saw the light outside the window. Had it been him outside smoking? Did Brian smoke? What was happening? I still felt his large, warm hands on mine, where he'd drawn me into the shadows. But where did he go? Ice ran through my veins. Nausea coiled my tummy. Could the guy I was falling for be the one following me?

Was anyone following me? I wrapped my arms around my middle before a hole erupted there. I was losing myself.

No. I needed to stop blaming my dreams. Something scary was happening. The truth of the thought winded me. I needed to find out who was doing these things. Fast.

"Darcy has a freshman curfew, so we're moving movie night to her room." Pixie accelerated around a curve.

"I'm not feeling well. Can you drop me off at our place first?" I kept my eyes averted.

"Aw, no way. Don't do that because of me. Go ahead. I'll take a rain check." Darcy put her head next to the headrest beside my ear.

"It's not that. I really don't feel well. I promise to stay up all night with you next time." A promise easier to keep than they knew.

Reluctantly, Pixie allowed me to dip out on movie night. She told me not to wait up because she thought that's what I did. I doubted she'd make it home. I'd never seen anyone fall asleep in front of a movie as fast as Pixie could.

"Darcy? Did you hear back about being an office aide yet?" I twisted in my seat to look her way as much as the belt allowed.

"Yeah, right before lunch." Her voice had lost its enthusiasm. I hoped Aubrie wouldn't blame her for my going home early.

"Cool. Hey, I'm going to stop in tomorrow and say hi."

We passed a Jeep a block before arriving at our apartment, and I shuddered at the thought that it might be him, watching. When I climbed out of the car, another car shut down its engine. This car was gray and compact, like a rental. I took the stairs two at a time. Halfway to the door, my legs locked in mid-step. A tiny orange glow brightened and dimmed only a few yards away from my apartment. My mouth popped open and a choked noise rumbled out.

"You okay, man?" A guy with blond highlights and a skateboard stepped toward me. He launched the remainder of his cigarette over the railing with his thumb and first finger.

My head rotated left and right.

"Ready?" The girl from one of the other apartments on our floor, bounced out her door, kissing the guy on his cheek.

"Later." The guy passed me with a lazy look on his face. The girl trailed behind him chatting excitedly about some party. She waved. Where was campus security for that?

A huge gust of air escaped my lungs. Inside the apartment, I locked the door and used the chain. I left the lights off and moved to the window. The Jeep drove away. The driver was nothing more than a silhouette behind the wheel.

A knock on my door sent terror coursing through me again. I froze. Everything stopped. A humming in my ears warned that I should sit before I fell over. Worst night ever.

"Gabriella?" Dad's voice. Confusion swallowed the fear, and I shuffled toward the door to the tiny peephole in shock. My dad stood outside staring back at the little hole, looking agitated.

I unlocked the door. Dad pushed himself inside, closing the door behind him. He embraced me as if he hadn't seen me in a decade. His forehead pinched in the center and his lips turned down at the corners. A tremor played over my hands. Something was wrong.

"Dad, what're you doing here?" Nervous energy translated well to excitement over our reunion. My arms wound around his waist. I laid my head against his chest and fought back tears.

He pulled me back by the shoulders and looked me over. He mashed his lips together the way he did when he worried. "Looks like you've settled in nicely."

"Yeah." I locked my arm into his elbow. My breaths were shallow as I pulled him in a slow circle around the room. "I burn meals in this kitchen on a daily basis. The bedroom is covered in clothes I hardly get to wear, and the bathroom is invaded by a tiny punk girl frequently. Consider yourself warned. You've seen the grand foyer and magnificent great room." Our tiny apartment was a direct contrast to the giant old Victorian home my dad lived in now. I loved that one better than all the others before it.

"Well, it's a heck of a lot nicer than any of the dorm rooms I ever had. Wait until next year when you're sharing a room the size of your current bathroom with four other girls and sharing the actual bathroom with an entire floor full of coeds. The words *community showers* ought to help you appreciate this place." He flopped onto the sofa and pulled me down beside him.

"Coeds?"

He slid his eyes my way.

"I do like it here."

He furrowed his brow, unsure.

"What're you doing here?" I touched his sleeve to be sure he was real.

"Well, when we spoke the other night, you seemed unhappy, and I never want that for you. I worried." He rubbed a hand over his knee. "I stopped by to make sure you're okay. Like I said, I won't be that far from you again. I'm sorry. I meant what I said about working around here for a while." He looked truly heartbroken, as if he'd done me a terrible injustice by going away on business. I never thought he minded traveling.

Emotional from the night's events, hearing him sound so guilty pushed me over the edge. I threw my arms around his neck, and tears ran free again. "I really miss you, Dad. I hate when we're apart. I'm not unhappy. I was just homesick." I wiped my eyes with my sleeve and felt about ten years younger.

He kissed my head and pulled my hair away from my face until I finished crying and sat upright.

I wanted to remove any guilt I might've saddled him with. "I like it here."

"Not too much, I hope." His eyes narrowed, and I knew he wanted to know about boys. His biggest concerns next to security when he chose Francine Frances had been the boy-girl ratio and campus policies on dating. As if he thought there might be some.

"Why?" I hoped I sounded as innocent as I intended.

"Well, honey." He stalled before he rallied. "I'd like to move you to a school closer to our new home." Gentle emphasis hung on the word *new*. He didn't mean the latest new home, the one that was my favorite so far. He meant we were moving again.

"What? We're moving? Again? When? Where?"

"Well, it's a part of the job. It provides us all the comforts we're accustomed to, like food and shelter." His face gave warning. "This time we're moving west. There's a small town outside of Dallas where we can set up our homestead. You'll like it because you can drive into the city anytime you want. You want city life, right?"

I hated that he meant to please me. I didn't want to move again. "Do we have to?" The words sounded petulant.

"Honey, it's for the best. Trust me. I wouldn't ask if there was any other way." He stared at me. Authority dripped from his words.

"No."

His eyebrows crept toward his hairline. Would they stop? "No?"

I crossed my arms over my chest. "No. I want to stay this time. I just got here and I like it. It's my senior year. Next year I'm going somewhere completely different. Let me finish what I've started here." I pleaded silently with eyes I knew looked like Mom's. "You said you'd be working in this area more. If I move to Texas, then what? We're separated by a thousand miles again? Can't you wait to move until the end of the year? You travel all the time anyway. It doesn't matter where you live. Why not stay at the cabin?" He didn't jump in or push back. Hope rose in my chest. "Please, Dad."

His gaze darted over the room. Honestly, if he'd asked me to return to the cabin with him, it would've been harder. Mom was there. Every inch of the surrounding hills and forest reminded me of her. The new houses for every assignment location reminded me she was gone.

"Do we have to go now? Can't it wait until the end of the school year?"

"I have to move now."

"I don't?" Well, this was new territory for me. I didn't know how to proceed.

"You'll be going to college in a few months." He deflated. That wasn't like him.

"Gabriella, you'll be eighteen in two months. A year from now you'll live who-knows-where enjoying college life." He rubbed his chin. "I'll be working in the area for a while. You're right about me being closer to you if you don't move right away. Maybe I will visit the cabin."

"Is that a yes?"

He looked weary and older than I'd ever seen him. "If you want to stay here until graduation, you can. I won't make you leave, but I'd appreciate it if you'd take those self-defense classes the school offers and maybe carry a gun." The sparkle in his eye told me he only half-joked about the gun.

My cheeks hurt from the ridiculous smile. I could stay. *Stay.* The word had to settle in. Stay was the opposite of anything I'd ever known.

"If you're going to be . . . " He cleared his throat. "If you're going to remain here, we'll need to talk about security."

Ugh. My stomach sank. I couldn't talk about school security with Dad. If he had any inkling that I thought someone followed me around my new town, he'd pack my bags immediately and toss me in the car. I said nothing. I waited to see what he thought he knew.

"Gabriella, tell me anything that's happened since you got here. Anything at all that didn't seem right to you. The ribbon you found in your locker bothered you. I'm glad you told me, but there might be other things you blew off. Some things, by themselves, mean nothing but together are quite serious."

"Nothing." My mind ticked off a growing list—the car with the squeaky belt, the orange glow, feelings of being followed, a guy who had tried to get into Pixie's car with me, Davis's and Brian's strange appearances . . . I hated lying to my dad. As far as I knew, he had never lied to anyone a single day in his life. He valued honesty above everything else. He said honesty was a defining quality of character. Lying was low, even for me, and I was ashamed.

"Honey, anything at all that wasn't quite right. It might've been someone you encountered or a situation you found yourself in?" He searched my face.

I tried to seem surprised at the questions. "No." *Liar.* "Nothing I can think of."

"How about your dream?" Dad worried about my dream as much as I did.

I could think of no sane way to tell him that the dream had become an entity. I couldn't explain the power my dream had over me, or how desperate I was to overcome it.

In my dream it was always dark. I was on a street I didn't know, and I wasn't alone. Though I had relived the moment a thousand times, I never saw who was with me. I only knew I loved them, and we were in danger. A third person, whom I couldn't see clearly, lurked nearby and I knew he wanted to hurt us. I also knew it'd be the lethal kind of pain. From there, things happened faster than I could process, but the night felt as real as a memory or premonition.

The hardest part was trying to separate the dream from reality. Like with the invisible smoking man, the dream crept into my waking hours and messed with me long after I woke up. I barely stayed focused long enough to live in the present. Until I moved to Francine Frances, the dream had only kept me tired and preoccupied.

I'd never tell my dad any of it. Losing Mom hadn't been easy for either of us. I wouldn't add to his pain by pointing out that the loss was literally driving me crazy.

"The dream is okay. It's just a dream." I feigned a smile.

Dad shoved some bangs off my face. "Elle." He faked a smile right back at me. "We need to talk about the security here."

"Yeah?"

"Have you been watching the news?"

"No." Honestly, I hadn't even turned on the television.

"You should be keeping up with local news."

"So, campus security has something to do with local news?" He wanted to talk about it, but then I had to pull it out of him. Frustrating. *Please don't tell me the serial killer is for real. It's a misunderstanding. Kids trying to scare the freshmen. Nothing more.*

"No. I have a friend at an office in Columbus and his brother's in law enforcement. When he heard you moved here, he said there are rumors of a man stalking young women in this part of the state. You want to be sure you're vigilant. Keep an eye on the news."

Vigilant?

"You think he's right? Some guy might be stalking near campus?" I wasn't sure whether this made me feel better because I wasn't crazy or worse because he might be following me.

"I'm not sure, but I do know, with all things considered, it's better to be safe than sorry. I've let the school know what I heard and also about the issue with your locker."

Whoa. I sucked in air. Maybe Dad had taken a dip into my crazy pool. Lots of girls wore black ribbons. I mean, it was a ribbon, not a threatening letter.

Best to focus on the facts. "Do you think I'm in some kind of danger? Or Pixie?" Pixie ran around all the time. What if someone hurt her? I had to nix the cat-and-mouse with Brian. I needed straight answers. Pixie needed to know what Dad had just told me. "How reliable is your friend's brother? How do you know him?"

"He's not the sort to tell tales."

I hoped Dad's report had made its way from the school staff to the security detail. We were all being followed. How many other girls thought they were in danger and didn't know how true that was? It occurred to me I should be miffed that school administration had failed to mention we were being stalked. Seemed like an important little nugget of information.

"Shouldn't the school tell the students? The dean must know." How could we stay safe if we didn't know we were in danger? I doubted my classmates watched the news any more than I did, which was never. My heart pitched into double time.

"Not yet. The school says they have things under control. They don't want to cause a panic." He huffed. "They've beefed up security."

I chewed hard on my bottom lip. So, campus security had bigger issues than my dirty welcome mat. I was afraid, but I didn't want to leave. What was right and what my gut would allow were forces on opposite ends of the spectrum at the moment.

"Security?" I hoped to press him for more information and wondered how much the school divulged to parents.

"Yes, they've doubled the number of watchmen on campus and added additional shifts to patrols on the streets. You should notice a security car come by here hourly, if not more often. If you don't, let me know."

"Wow. Watchmen. It's like martial law," I whispered. "Will there be a curfew for everyone or something?"

"I'd like that, but there are laws. Can I see the ribbon?"

"Sure." I dug through my backpack and pulled it out. He took it with unexpected care and I wondered if he thought of Mom, too. He turned it over in his fingers and examined the frayed edge.

"It got stuck in the zipper on my backpack."

He pinched the bridge of his nose between his thumb and forefinger. "There's no reason to worry until there's a reason to worry, right?" He kissed my head.

Balling the ribbon in his fist, I thought I heard him mutter something about security doing their jobs. He looked my way. His face stayed red for a long while.

"So, you like it here?" He sighed. "Tell me everything."

He got comfortable, and I settled in beside him.

Dad and I sat and talked until he crashed on the couch. I couldn't bring myself to ask if what he really meant by *stalker* was *serial killer*. Voicing the words might make them true. I didn't want to be responsible for that. Years of worry, airline food, and jet lag looked like they had taken their toll. I pulled a quilt over him and waited for Pixie to get in. I chuckled at the thought of simply going to bed and letting her walk in to find a grown man asleep on her couch. Chances were she would've gone with it. No questions.

While I waited, I wondered about his strange arrival. When he knocked, he had seemed pretty upset. He had gotten the photo of the ribbon I sent him and gone right back to his work. I'd heard him typing. Maybe there was something else to be worried about. Of course there was. Didn't he just say there was a stalker in town? Not to mention I was followed twice in two nights. He snored softly beneath the blanket. I needed to ask him to tell me the truth about what he had heard.

I rubbed my forehead. *Get a grip, Gabriella.* Stalked by people who smoke? Don't be silly. What would a serial killer want with me in a school filled with beauty queens? Maybe someone wanted to kill me via secondhand smoke? Out of all the interesting, outgoing girls on campus, *I* caught the creeper's interest? No one else had seen him. I hadn't really *seen* anyone either. Not a face anyway. Someone had tried to get into Pixie's car, but it was a long shot to try to connect the two nights. Still, the orange glow worried me. What if it had been the same man and no coincidence? I felt it instinctually. I should be afraid.

That train of thought brought me back to Brian. Dad didn't ask me about boys. He didn't press me about the girls at school either. Though he did seem to know everything about Pixie. He told me most of what I knew about her, her family, her friends, before we met.

Pixie came in a few minutes later, complaining about the cancer agents on the mat, and my heart seized. I planned to worry about her next. Knowing our campus needed added security, it made sense to worry. Thank goodness she had come home. What if the person smoking outside our door wasn't a girl hiding a nicotine habit? Ice clogged my throat. Had he been right outside my door? Over and over.

"There's a man on our couch." Pixie pointed as she walked past.

I frowned at the lack of concern in her voice. A simple statement of fact. Oh, by the way, there's a man on our couch. "Dad stopped by to visit."

She craned her neck. They'd only met once. I wondered if she truly recognized him or if it would matter. Emotion passed over her eyes. Regret? Maybe loss. I wished desperately that her parents would call. Or just one of them. I didn't care which one. Someone should want to know she was happy.

"You missed a massive bonfire. Ah-mazing."

"What about movie night?" My voice broke and snapped on every word.

"We ran into Davis on campus, and Darcy snuck out with us. If she didn't get caught sneaking back in, we're going over for movie night Thursday."

"Oh." My mind raced to put the pieces together. I clamped my lips shut to keep from spilling all my suspicions to Pixie. I felt manic.

"First bonfire of the year. I hope you feel better 'cause you missed it."

There'd be a dozen more before the snow came. "I promise to catch the next one with you."

She rolled her eyes.

"Hey, if I'd been gone tonight, I would've missed my dad."

Her eyes roamed back over the figure on our couch. "Fine." She pointed a gas-blue fingernail in my direction. "I'm going to hold you to that. You can't hide in here forever."

"Pretty nails."

"I know, right? I'm going to do polka dots over them I think . . . in the morning."

"Do you think the girl was right the other day, about a serial killer in town?"

She raised a perfect, black-penciled eyebrow. "Why do you ask?"

I swallowed the dry lump in my throat. I'd never had a real girl-friend before. What if I was wrong? What if she thought I was crazy? What if I was?

I lifted a shoulder and let it drop. If she pressed the issue, I'd take her to my room and tell her everything.

Pixie gave me a long look and glanced at my dad. "I hope not." She moved toward her room with no fewer than two backward glances in my direction.

I pulled the scrap of paper with what I presumed to be Brian's number from my backpack and traced each digit with my finger-tip. Then, despite news of a local stalker/possible serial killer, I slept much better that night having Dad nearby.

Chapter Nine

Dad was up at a quarter till five when I headed for the treadmill.

"How'd you sleep, sweetie?" His smile warmed me.

I loved him extra for the fact that he'd made a full pot of coffee. I poured a cup and leaned against the counter. "The usual. How about you? A six-foot man on a four-foot love seat seems cozy."

"It was pure luxury after the places I've slept lately, trust me."

"Flying coach again?" I slid into a chair next to him.

"I take what's available. I can't afford to be picky." He gave me a very protective look, and I softened.

"How long can you stay?" I had to clear my throat to get the words out.

His face fell a tiny bit, and he pursed his lips. "I have to get going today. This will be the first move in some time that I have to do by myself."

"Do you have to move so far away? Texas, really?"

He shrugged and watched me. He was probably waiting for a moment of weakness to persuade me to go. "Like you said, my things will be in Texas, but I'll be on the road. My address doesn't mean much these days. Good news is, I'll be working in your area in case you need me."

Meanwhile, I wondered why I hadn't packed my bags. Someone had followed me. Possibly a serial killer, who was possibly the man I might be in love with. Denying it was futile. Whatever happened to my heart and soul and brain when Brian was near had never happened before, and every time he left, he took the air with him. I'd never been in love before, but when I dared to think of the word, my heart ached. If he was dangerous, I was in more trouble than Dad could imagine. Brian had personally warned me about my safety. A dangerous person wouldn't warn his prey. I hoped. The more I considered my choices, I should've been knocking people down to get away from Ohio, but I wasn't. I couldn't.

I was lost in my dream of espionage. I wanted to know who had followed me and why. I wanted to know everything I could about Brian. I wanted to defeat the nightmare that threatened to ruin my days, too. I wanted victory over something, and I wanted it bad. I wasn't ready to go.

Dad dropped me off at school, and I hated saying goodbye. I wanted to be strong, but I also wanted to climb into his shirt pocket and be with him, safe, wherever he went. Shutting the car door, I turned back for one last "I love you" and caught the tail end of a stiff nod and brutal scowl. I'd never figured my dad for senility, so I looked around to see who he'd threatened. I didn't see anyone.

I leaned in through the open window and gave him one more look before he drove away. Since childhood, I had always worried that every goodbye would be our last.

Dad pulled the car into the road. His taillights disappeared through the gate.

In the distance, Brian rounded a corner, moving away from me at a clip.

The classes before lunch dragged on. The moment I knew Darcy was at her new position of office aide, I made a trip to update my file.

"You came!" She beamed.

"Yeah. Sorry I bailed last night."

"You didn't miss anything. We'll do it again. So, what's up?" She leaned on her elbows on the desk, smiling.

"I wanted to add an emergency contact to my file."

"Sure." She looked excited to help me. When she turned for the filing cabinets, I followed her around the desk. Another aide watched us curiously until the phone rang. "Here you are." She plucked a slim file from the drawer marked R–Z. "What's the number?"

"Darcy?" The second aide stood at her desk. "Did anyone show you where the brochures for interested families are kept?" She put the receiver on the desk and approached us.

My eyes lifted to the drawer above mine. A–B. Brian's folder was inches away.

"I'll write the number in and leave the file on your desk. I need to get to lunch."

Darcy shrugged. She followed the other aide to search for the brochures. I began a search of my own, sliding the top drawer to the filing cabinet open with a soft click. The folders shifted easily as I thumbed through dozens of files for students whose last names began with A. Acer. Adams. Adamson. Ashton. Ayers.

No Austin. Not even an almost-empty file like mine. I checked once more. Definitely no Austin. "Thanks, Darcy!" I tossed my file on her desk and headed for lunch.

Inside the cafeteria, I bit my lip and walked over to sit with Davis. Pixie never ate, and I had too much on my mind to spend another lunch period inside the art building watching her paint. She asked a lot of really intuitive questions that I didn't want to answer.

The cafeteria bustled with activity. Laughter punctuated the chatter of a hundred voices and the clatter of plastic trays onto tabletops. The warm, buttery scents of comfort food wafted overhead. Tangy Italian sauces and salty soups thickened the air. Chicken noodle soup made me think of Grandma. I had a handful of great memories with her. Lost in my investigation, I grabbed a ready-made plate from the line and carried it toward a table.

"There you are. I thought you didn't eat." Davis moved his tray aside to make more room for my caffeinated water, soggy orange fries, and chicken nuggets. My eyes darted wistfully at the other, better-looking meals I had missed. Mental note: not everything homemade is delicious looking.

"Oh, I eat." I shoved a limp french fry into my mouth. My grimace nearly caused the mush to spill back out. I regretted skipping the soup.

Davis laughed hard like a donkey, one arm across his ribs. "Sweet-potato fries." His feet pounded the floor beneath us.

"Yuck." I gulped down my water and smiled at his apparent joy. "Thanks for the warning."

"Sorry. I thought you knew until you shook that salt on them. Then I had to watch. Oh. Classic."

"What'd I miss?" Kate bumped her elbow gently against mine and moved up against my side. I was sandwiched between Davis and Kate, who lowered herself daintily next to me and folded her hands in her lap.

"Davis let me eat sweet-potato fries." I tossed a thumb in his direction.

Davis's eyes ran over my face. "Nice to see you eating. Girls at this school seem to think anorexia is the new healthy."

I turned to Davis so as not to make eye contact with Kate, the only one at the table without a lunch.

"Thin is in." He spoke around a mouthful of meatballs.

"Where's Pixie?" Kate leaned onto the empty table before her, peering around me.

"Painting."

"Why aren't you with her?"

"I thought I'd see if the meals here were all that the brochure said they'd be."

"Plus, she wanted to check on me." It seemed unlike Davis to say that.

I peeled my eyes from Kate's.

Brian, if that was his real name, appeared across the table from us and shouldered his way in between a set of boys I hadn't been introduced to. "This seat taken?"

His green eyes smoldered and I couldn't speak. He lowered himself in front of me and I was vaguely aware of a strange triangle that had formed with me at its center.

"What's up, Austin?" The protective coating of Davis's words bothered me.

Brian narrowed his eyes. "Not much."

"What brings you to lunch today? I haven't seen you here before." Davis leaned forward.

The rest of the table had grown quiet. Their collective gaze turned to me.

Brian's eyes hadn't left mine. "Just taking care of things. Caught a break. Thought I'd grab lunch, too."

"What things?" Kate leaned farther over the table, no doubt providing a full display of her cleavage.

He didn't seem to notice. His concentrated expression started to feel like some unspoken challenge.

Tension mounted inside. "Nicholas?" I blurted. What did it mean? I sent telepathic daggers at him. *Who is Nicholas?* The one word I overheard during his private call in the library had kept me up at night wondering.

That did it. His eyebrows hit his hairline. "What?"

"What?" Kate guffawed in my direction like I was an idiot. "His name is Bri-an, honey. Not Nicholas."

His name? Was it possible that Brian wasn't his real name? Gah! I wanted to slap the table. I was just in the office with the files. I needed to visit Darcy again. Was Brian here under a fake name for some reason? Hiding from someone? Hiding a dangerous past?

"You going out for lacrosse? There's still time before the first game. I can talk to Coach," Davis challenged.

Tension brewed at my side and I excused myself. As much as I wanted to talk with Brian, Nicholas, whoever he was, lunch wasn't working.

"Hey, Elle," Davis called as I stood. "Lunch tomorrow?"

"Sure." If you can find where I'm hiding.

For once, Pixie didn't head out alone from the apartment. Being the only one in her circle with a car, she came and went alone too often, especially late at night. Everyone else got curbside service. Tonight her boyfriend picked her up for dinner at his parents' house. I breathed easier seeing her go with him for a change. Jealousy pinked my cheeks when I thought of him having a home with two parents and of her being a part of his normal family life.

I missed my dad so much that I almost called him. Sleeping proved impossible. My mind whirled with ideas of what lurked on campus, but homesickness got complicated, considering I didn't really have a home. Dad was my home, and he wasn't around.

I dug into my drawer and pulled out a box of my mom's things and lingered over a family photo from a time long gone. Any time I felt this odd-shaped hole in my chest, it helped to remember her. Things hadn't always been so complicated. My mom had kept every kind of memorabilia from her marriage and from my life, too. The first six years of it anyway. She threw crazy birthday parties with ponies and magicians. She scrapbooked, journaled, and recorded everything. She loved her life and us a lot. My fingers lingered over pressed flowers and scraps of fabric from dresses she had made me. A tear formed immediately. All the "whys" in the Universe poured over me every time I opened the box. Her life's remnants fit inside a box. My heart squeezed tight with pain. Guilt and grief never got easier. I kept her things close because they were my only proof that she had ever existed.

My actual memories of her had faded long ago, and I hated myself every day for being so weak as to lose something so precious. When all I had were memories, how could I ever let them fade? I was an awful excuse for a daughter. No wonder Dad chose to travel. It was a choice, after all. I didn't know of any other father who was gone more than he was home. He was obviously running from something. Me.

"Elle!" Pixie's voice called from the front room almost at the same moment her keys clanged onto the table.

I wiped my tears frantically and ran for the bathroom. The minute I shut the door, I cranked on the water. Hopefully, she'd assume I hadn't heard her come in. I hadn't really planned on a shower, but the water seemed like exactly what I needed, so I got in.

When I pulled the shower door open afterward to go get dressed, Pixie was standing there.

"Good grief!" I shouted. "What the heck are you doing?"

"What? I have to pee." She slouched against the wall, rolling a sucker between her lips.

"Oh." I had nothing to say. Yes, I had good reason to be paranoid, but I couldn't tell her about it, so I went to my room.

I pulled on some clean clothes and opened the door of my room. The sudden sight of Pixie on the other side scared me. "Come on!" I screamed and grabbed my chest.

Pixie bent over and grabbed her knees. She apparently enjoyed scaring the crap out of me.

"I. Am. So. Sorry. But that's hysterical. It's really, really funny, because I'm only standing here."

I squeezed past her and walked to the kitchen. She threw my purse on the counter in front of me.

"What?"

"Come on. Let's get out of here."

All I'd thought about while she was at dinner was the stalker and Brian and what the name Nicholas might mean. I'd had enough. My brain hurt. No way I wanted to stay home alone twice in one night. There wasn't much of a choice.

"Let's go." I waved an underhanded "after you" gesture toward the door.

"Squee!" Pixie grabbed my shoulders and bounced.

I frowned at her for as long as I could, but she kept going until I smiled. *What a nut.* "Come on, before I change my mind."

She rolled down the windows in her car and cranked up the music. Her head bobbed to the bass and she beat imaginary sticks against the dash at a red light.

"Where're we going?" I yelled over the music as she turned it down—which she never did. Then she roared with laughter once again. A few families out walking stared at me through the window.

"Stop!" I slapped her thigh.

She laughed harder. "The Pier, of course." She pumped her neck with the music.

"Of course."

Every kid in town must've had the same plan because not much had changed since the summer. I had assumed that with school back in session it'd be a smaller crowd, but the place pulsed with music and laughter. Fall hadn't stopped the local kids from congregating at the river.

I followed Pixie into the thick of the crowd. My first trip had been so intimidating. When I first arrived in the summer and knew only Pixie, The Pier completely overwhelmed me. Girls lounged against the railing of The Pier, looking fierce and fun in ways I never dared. My eyes bounced over the scene, scouting for danger. Lots of plastic cups in hands, several full-on bouts of PDA. Everything looked normal. Wherever I went to college, I was sure to be a loner. I hoped the fact that I didn't have a mother would be less evident after a year with Pixie. I had nothing but girl time ahead of me. I smiled.

Sitting in the dark with her and her friends was mystical. One of those bigger-than-life moments that felt more like an out-of-body experience than reality. I'd never been part of the crowd. I had had a few friends growing up, but I had learned early to be self-contained. The air around us crackled with electricity. The whole school seemed to be present. Being part of the bigger picture felt good. Kicked back, listening to the music, laughter, and gossip, it was impossible to imagine that anything bad lurked nearby.

"Whoa!" A beautiful redhead stared over my shoulder into the night. "Did you see that guy?"

We all turned. At least fifty kids gathered in more than a dozen separate knots, but one head loomed above the rest. A hoodie covered his hair and cast a shadow, hiding his features. The redhead, Macy, squealed again. She'd apparently gotten a good look at him.

When we turned back to her, she fluttered her hands over chest. "Oh. My. Goodness."

"What?" A dozen voices united.

"He's the hottest guy to ever enter this town. No, this county. It figures. He shows up when I'm leaving next week." Macy was moving home. She had no idea why, but I thought I might. Her parents probably watched our local news. A stalker seemed like enough motivation to pull your kid from any prep school. Thinking of it that way, why hadn't my dad insisted I go with him? He was the most overprotective man I knew.

We spun around again, and a few girls headed over to where he'd been. The rest of us giggled, and I learned a few things about the girls who went after him. For one thing, he was lucky to get away, or so the other girls told me. I hoped if they caught him, they wouldn't find a deranged serial killer under the hoodie. The glimpse I caught of his retreating frame felt familiar.

Waiting in line for the bathroom, some local schoolgirls complained about the academy girls. Too many girls and too few boys in one little town made for tension. I rolled my head against my shoulders and caught a glimpse of something in the trees. Familiar brilliant blue paint. Curiosity ate at me. On impulse, I worked my way out of line and left Pixie chatting up a group of kids I'd never seen before.

I crept off the edge of The Pier and onto the grass. Then I walked into the shadows. The music behind me was so loud I worried that I wouldn't be heard if I screamed for help. It took all the courage I could muster to take the last few steps. I would've bet my backpack it was Brian's bike. As I reached for the trees, I glanced back, hoping for witnesses. I was alone, and there it was.

"Ha!" I pointed. My arm swung out at the shiny blue bike. "I knew it!" I spun around, looking into the distance. Uncertainty crept in. What should I do?

Without thinking, I dug into my purse and searched for a pen and paper. The best I could come up with was a receipt from the coffee house and old eyeliner. "Gotcha!" I scribbled and wedged the note under the lip of the seat. I wanted to be sure he knew I knew he was there.

Climbing back onto The Pier, I smiled broadly and caught a glimpse of the hoodie in the distance. A head taller than the crowd, he leaned against the rail, head turned in my direction. I couldn't see his face, but I recognized his posture. A shiver ran down my arms. That was no stalker. No wonder a pack of girls went after him. He raised his right hand in the distance and saluted. I shook my head and smiled at my shoes for a minute.

Swoon.

In my mind, I did a victory dance. Outwardly, I held still, hoping he couldn't see my wild, toothy smile.

"What're you looking at?" Pixie asked when she noticed that I had wandered off.

"Nothing."

She slid into the restroom, and I pushed through the crowd. He should've been easy to spot. I stood in the parking lot alone. Where did he go? My eyes ran over the heads on The Pier. His hoodie moved away from me, toward the trees. I snuck after him.

His bike and the party were in the other direction. Careful not to step on any branches, I crept through the shadows, forcing myself to remain focused. If I thought too long about what might be out here with us, I'd lose it and run back to Pixie. A coyote called in the distance and I froze. Looking back at the distant lights of The Pier, I reconsidered my adventure. When I turned away, Brian was gone.

"Frick." Go on into the dark chasing nothing, or return to the party? I wasn't brave. Painfully curious, but not stupid. I turned around and stopped cold when something caught my eye. A man leaned against a tree trunk a few feet away.

"Haven't I warned you about staying with your friends? It's not safe to be alone." Brian stepped into the moonlight, erasing the space between us.

"Why? Because there's a serial killer in town?"

His posture stiffened. The muscle in his jaw ticked in response to my question. "Where'd you hear that?"

"Everyone says so." Embellishment. Whatever.

He covered his narrow hips with huge hands and glared at me long enough to set my hair on fire. I forced my shoulders back.

"You know there's a cold-blooded killer in town," he said. "Yet you walk off into the night. Alone. Again."

A chill slid down my spine. When he put it that way, it didn't feel so exciting to find him lurking at the party.

"Where were you going?" Subject changes were the liar's best friend. I had learned it in therapy years ago.

"Why were you following me?"

Touché.

"Where were you going?" I anchored my hands to my hips to keep them from shaking.

"I'm proving a point. You need to be more careful." He walked away, back toward the party. It took a minute for my brain to catch up. I walked double time to match pace with him.

"So, what, you're my personal security? Stalk much?"

He stopped at the edge of The Pier and nodded toward a frustrated-looking Pixie pacing outside the bathroom where I'd left her. "Yep."

I liked the notion more than I should have. I liked him more than I should have. Consistency counted for something, I hoped. "You coming?"

He shook his head. "Someone's got to keep an eye out for the killer."

I didn't like his jokes. My brain rejected the possibility that he was doing exactly what he'd said. Reluctantly, I headed off to stop Pixie from worrying. By the time I reached her, Brian was nowhere in sight.

Senior year had serious excitement potential. I attended a school with a drop-dead gorgeous boy stalking/guarding me. I could get used to being followed by him. Assuming he wasn't the killer from the news.

Chapter Ten

School went the same as every other day, except signs appeared all over campus for Harvest Festival. It was only a matter of time. Apple cider, pumpkins, acorns. All small towns had the same street-fair mentality. This particular festival would be held on campus and was closed to the public. Parents and alumni ran the show, and our sky-rocketing tuition footed the bill. No one mentioned the serial killer. Life took a turn for the normal.

At first, I didn't plan to go to the festival, but soon the fever took hold. Girls squealed and bustled about the Harvest Festival the same way girls in my past schools went on about formals or prom. They gushed over what to wear, who to ride with, and where to eat. According to Pixie, local officials attended every year, as well as some local "celebrities" and "heroes." The school buzzed with excitement that was a little infectious. I hoped Dad would come. Our cabin in the mountains was close to a small town with a similar festival. Some of my favorite memories were made there drinking cider and eating caramel apples.

The art department chose a few pieces of Pixie's art for display. Wild horses wouldn't keep her away. With all the commotion,

Brian would have to go. At the end of the day, images of meeting him at the festival filled my head. My smile fell as a flash of white caught my eye. From a distance, the tops of the lockers were visible, and something perched on top near mine. Part of me worried it might explode. I hastened my step before I lost my nerve. Stretching onto my toes, I reached for the apparition. A bulbous form slipped into my fingers and a folded strip of paper moved underneath. I recognized the item by touch. Pulling it into my trembling hands, I hoped the note was from an admirer and not the alleged evil stalker who might or might not be singling me out. Okay, so I hadn't forgotten about the maybe-killer. The small white pumpkin fit into the palm of my hand. The paper said, "The wall at five? —Nicholas."

I nearly squealed, and I wasn't a squealer. I loved it. I shoved the note into my pack and carried the pumpkin in my hand.

"What's with the cheese?" Pixie's voice almost caused me to drop my precious treasure.

"Oh!" Heat rose in my cheeks. So busted.

"Is that a tiny pumpkin?" She wrestled it from my fingers. "Cute! I want one. Where'd you get it? Let's take it home and paint it."

"Hey! What? No! Give it back, pumpkin thief. It's October in the Ohio Valley. They're a dime a dozen, literally." I narrowed my eyes. "Get your own tiny pumpkin."

She laughed and threw her arm across my shoulders. Pixie liked my pumpkin a little too much for its own good, and I considered carrying it with me for its safety. She wanted to glue sunflower seeds on it to make a Zorro mask. To Pixie, the little white pumpkin was a blank canvas in need of some pizzazz.

I shuddered at the possibilities.

"Is your boy going to the festival?" Pixie did pinky waves at masses of people heading in every direction. Her attention, however, was focused on me.

"I don't know. It's not like I get to talk to him."

Her eyes slid my way. She didn't believe a word I said. Why should she?

Sunlight sprinkled through the changing leaves. The sidewalk underfoot resembled a piece of art more than I'd ever noticed. Puddles reflected shimmery lines of amber and scarlet from above.

"Fine. You're all secretive, and I can respect your privacy."

"Thanks."

"Ha! I knew it, you hider. You do have secrets. Give me a clue. No." Her head flew left and right. "Spill. Have you kissed him?"

I fought the smirk, but a huge smile grew in its place. "Of course not."

"Then why the face?"

I shrugged and let her pass me on our steps.

"So freaking gross. I'm ready to buy one of those nanny cams and post it outside our door." The welcome mat looked like an ashtray. Pixie kicked it, and the mat sailed over the concrete, away from our door.

I pulled my eyes up, resisting the urge to chase it down and count the number of butts. The smell wafted into the air and triggered my gag reflex. A sheen of sweat covered my face and chest. The expression "like I'd just seen a ghost" came to mind, but I hadn't seen anything. I stepped carefully over the threshold and unloaded my arms. Whatever that freakout was about, I didn't have time to think about it. I needed to eat and change for my date. Meeting? Appointment?

In the kitchen, I searched for something to make with the few ingredients we had available. We needed groceries. Mac and cheese looked like my only choice until then. Pixie wouldn't eat, and I wasn't sure if I'd be able to either. I got busy boiling water and wondering what to wear. Was it a date? Did he plan to speak to me in private to tell me that we could only be friends? My fingers drummed against the counter and stress bubbled in my tummy. What if the pumpkin wasn't from Brian? What if Nicholas was someone else? I swallowed back my fear in exchange for, hopefully, getting some answers.

The mac and cheese fared better than the grilled cheese. Even this stove boiled water at a predictable temperature. My appetite faded fast as the questions piled up. Butterflies formed a mob in my stomach and tried to escape through my mouth. If I didn't eat, I'd feel woozy later, so I tried. I took a couple of hasty bites, wishing I had cuter clothes.

"What's with you and that pumpkin?" Pixie watched me eat.

I'd just run my fingertips over the little white angel. The tiny pumpkin had kept my mind on happy things instead of wallowing in my bad dream and self-pity. I loved the little thing for that. Also, I needed to protect it from her. I liked it just the way it was, plain and beautiful.

"I love fall. That's all." I shoved away from the table and took my bowl with me.

Pixie followed. "Are you going somewhere?" She stood in the doorway while I faced my closet, pouting.

"No." I was so convincing that she rolled her eyes and left.

I flopped onto the bed and shoved another forkful of dinner into my mouth. My wardrobe was junk. I owned a closet full of jeans, sneakers, and hoodies. I put the bowl on the floor and rolled over onto my back when Pixie's footsteps returned.

"Here." Annoyance gave an edge to her voice.

Thrump!

I shot upright expecting to see a hole in the floor. A giant black trunk sat at her feet.

"It's the wardrobe I came with. It's three years old but still better than anything in there." She pointed a perfect black fingernail at my closet. "Help." We heaved the giant thing onto my bed.

I was never so happy to see clothes, and I couldn't believe they were Pixie's. Scratch that. They belonged to Priscilla.

"We're practically the same size. Most of this will fit. If you're going to be outside, I'd wear the belted coat. It's cute. The designer was a friend of my mother's. He got me interested in design. It was my gateway drug. Who knew I'd love everything artsy?" She winked and began to pull things from the trunk until every square inch of my room looked like backstage at a fashion show.

I marveled at the sheer volume of couture in one place. The trunk reminded me of the enormous steamer trunks carrying supplies on the Titanic, or maybe a U-Haul without a trailer hitch. I'd seen the thing before and assumed it held more of her art supplies, not clothes.

"Your mom is friends with a clothing designer?" I might not have been the best judge, but that sounded pretty cool. Her perfect porcelain face scrunched. I immediately regretted asking. Pixie never talked about her parents. I was hungry for any scrap of information about any mom on the planet, and Pixie hated hers.

"My parents fought until I was twelve, then started their divorce when I was in middle school. It's probably still going on. They sent me here to "protect me from all the negative energy," but the truth was neither one wanted to be saddled with a kid. They were busy trying to out-date one another. Plus, dividing all their crap takes time."

I didn't know what to say. I had only six years with my mom, but the memories were treasures. My parents never fought over me. We did things together, especially the last year before her accident. We spent more time at the cabin than ever before. We always stayed a week in the summer, but that year we stayed longer. The cabin is nestled in the Blue Ridge Mountains, isolated, peaceful. After she died, Dad sold our house in D.C. and took a new position at work. He had always traveled, but we hadn't moved before. He said he couldn't pass up the opportunity. At first we visited the cabin between jobs. The cabin where Mom once wore Dad's flannel over her T-shirts and rolled up her pants to the knees. Where she made mud castles with me while Dad scouted the area or fished the stream nearby. I think Dad held on to her by keeping the memories close. I did, too. As the years passed, we visited the cabin less and less, but I thought of it every day. Thought of her every day.

Pixie's forehead smoothed. She pulled a brilliant blue silk scarf from the inside zipper section. "This is awesome with the belted coat."

Even I understood. The coat was white and the blue silk would be a crowning jewel. I tried them on immediately. Pixie had to help me with the belt. Then she slipped huge black shades onto my face. I looked like a movie star—from the waist up. I was still in my pleated skirt and knee socks. The coat flared at the hips. I sighed at my reflection, a living before-and-after photo.

A dozen combinations of Priscilla clothes later and I secretly wished I had somewhere to wear them all. I liked clothes. Who knew? I wasn't quite ready for the coat. I laid some possible outfits on my bed and considered asking Pixie about my makeup. Makeup was taking the change too far for one afternoon. I peeked at my watch for the twenty-seventh time and kept moving.

Showering happened at record speed. For the first time in my life, I couldn't wait to get ready. I slid into a pair of her dark-wash skinny jeans and a white tank before pulling a cashmere v-neck sweater over the top. The sweater was a deep shade of red, fitting for fall, and I'd been complimented when wearing a similar shade in the past. I considered painting my nails but hated to be too obvious, so I settled for a fresh clear coat. The clothes alone screamed makeover. Pixie added an oversized belt to the outside of the sweater and it showed off my waist nicely. I spun in the mirror and nodded at the me looking back. Mirror-me smiled wildly.

Pixie leaned against my door frame, looking smug.

She held a bag filled with shoes. I decided on sleek-looking boots and zipped them over the jeans to my knees. I owed her big time. What a difference an outfit could make. *Thank you, Priscilla.* I could barely look in Pixie's direction when I walked into the front room where she'd relocated. I'd kicked her out at the end so I could try not to hyperventilate in private. When I emerged from my room, she flipped through a magazine and tapped her foot. She immediately pushed to her feet and walked over to me, nodding her head. I knew the question. I was going somewhere important, somewhere that made me want to do all this, and I hadn't told her. She was the most curious person I knew, and I had no doubt the question was coming.

Then, as if she hadn't already done more than I'd ever imagined, Pixie gave me one more gift. She smiled a tight crooked smile and handed me lip gloss.

"Thanks."

"What are best friends for?"

I blinked. I hadn't had a best friend since kindergarten. Her words stung my eyes.

"Have fun not going out." She anchored her hands over her hips.

I walked the entire way to the wall in a trance, trying to take it all in. Mysterious danger aside, Ohio in the fall took my breath away. This was it. If I didn't get my questions answered tonight, I never would.

Chapter Eleven

When the wall came into view, so did Brian. He leaned against it, arms crossed over his chest, watching me. The fields behind him lit up in an orange haze as the sun set. Thick lines of purple and gray sky broke up the fiery image, making it look like a backdrop at a photography studio. I stopped walking to absorb the view.

His green eyes sparkled in the waning sun. Against the orange glow of sunset, his already-tan skin seemed to glisten. My eyes ran over his features, down the length of his neck and over his shoulders. Trying to memorize every detail, I looked back to his face once more. His eyes caught mine, and the previously stoic expression evaporated. A smile split his face, and my knees wobbled.

"You came." He sounded surprised.

"Of course." Maybe I wasn't the only crazy one. Who wouldn't come to meet him?

"What do you want to do?" He revealed the absurd little dimple in his left cheek. He was completely unfair. Just when I thought one person couldn't be any more attractive this side of reality, the dimple popped and he proved me wrong again.

I wasn't sure what to make of the question. It was his invitation that had brought me there. I assumed he had a plan.

I had nothing.

His smile stretched, and my pulse quickened. "Are you opposed to leaving town?"

Why did everyone keep asking me that? "Permanently?"

"No." He laughed. Then he motioned toward his Jeep, parked nearby in the grass. "How about for the evening?"

My eyes widened. "Someone's going to be really ticked off about this."

"Who?" His frame went rigid.

"Whoever takes care of the grass." Didn't he see the mess he had made with those off-road tires on the perfectly manicured lawn? "Look at that."

Brian made an exaggerated sigh, helped me into the passenger's seat, and shut the door behind me.

"What, no coffee?"

He shot me a sideways look. "I'm sorry. It was thoughtless."

"Completely." I'd made an effort to cut back on the pills. In just under a month, since school started, I'd managed to decrease the addiction for the first time in my life. Normally it inched up every year. This year, I'd had enough adrenaline and crazy to keep me going without it. Straight coffee kept me upright and the headaches at bay. Even the bags under my eyes looked more like carry-ons these days.

"Can we start our business after dinner?"

I wasn't positive I *could* eat, but I wasn't about to say no either. "Our business?"

We drove for about two minutes before he spoke again, which was perfect because I had no idea what to say. With a face like his, I imagined he'd been on his fair share of dates—if that was what we were doing. His ensemble mirrored mine. Dark jeans, black boots, a black concert tee pulled over a long-sleeve thermal. Casual. "Nicholas, huh?"

I licked my lips. Time for answers.

"You brought it up at lunch, remember?" He looked at me with a lifted chin waiting for my explanation. Turning the tables wasn't acceptable. I had too many questions to play games.

"Mmm hmm." I tried to sound like I knew more than I was telling. My guilty conscience hoped to hide my nosy, mildly obsessive behavior patterns.

"Care to expound?"

I squeezed my lips into a tight line and shook my head.

Despite the furrowed brow, he sounded impressed. "You surprise me. People don't normally do that. It's in my best interest not to be surprised." His lips twitched at the corners.

"About that."

"Uh-uh." He shook a finger at me. "I believe I have the floor here."

How did that happen? I might've been in trouble.

"What do you know, precisely?" Emphasis on *precisely*.

"Uh . . . " My mind scrambled in circles. I had the questions. He had nothing to question me about. I didn't know anything.

"Oh." His eyebrows reached for his hairline. "You know more than I suspected. How long did you chase your lead?"

"Well . . . "

He barked a laugh.

I looked around and chewed on my lip. Trees flew by at an alarming rate. I had no idea where we were or where we might be going. The only diner in town was long left behind.

We pulled into a driveway and stopped. An adorable little cottage on the river stared back at me. The deep blue siding and white trim looked inviting. A stained-glass window above the front door read "Welcome." Nerves tugged at my tummy. He couldn't pull into someone's drive and park. It was rude.

"I'm nosy." I admitted the obvious first. When I had to lie, I always admitted to something small and hoped the questioning party would assume I'd divulged all there was to tell. Sadly, when confronting a liar, there's always more.

"You're inquisitive. That's not exactly a criminal offense."

"You would know." I smiled through the words, and he unlocked his door.

"I would know." He slid out of the car and moved around the front toward my door. I hoped it wasn't his way of telling me he was a criminal.

"What're you doing?" My jaw dropped when he swung my door open. "I thought you said we were going to dinner? We're nowhere near anything."

"I thought you'd like to walk along the river before dinner. It's nice." He held out a hand.

I stared at him, wondering if he'd gone mad. "I'm not getting out." We weren't in D.C. Small-town people had rights, too.

"You can't park here," I said a little too loudly, and I looked around for witnesses. I didn't want to draw attention. "Where are we anyway?" We'd passed a myriad of "entering" and "leaving" corporation signs in the past few minutes alone.

"Why? No one's home." The mischievous look in his eyes taunted me.

"You live here, don't you?"

He shrugged. "Temporarily. Come on." The impish grin and concert logo were fighting with his always-too-serious presence. Not even a thermal and rock T-shirt could make me forget he was an unknown element. Dad had drilled "unknown equals run" into my brain with a hot branding iron. Still, I wanted to go with him.

I pulled in a quick breath the moment his skin met mine. His huge hand completely enveloped my smaller one. The differences between us reminded me how powerless I was. Against the dream, my imagination . . . everything. His hand was warmer and rougher than mine. The contrast sent goose bumps down my arm and heat everywhere else. My head shook a little as the shiver slid into my shoes.

"Are you cold?" He released me once my feet were planted firmly on the ground. He shut the door and ushered me along the side of the little house.

A pergola stood on a stone foundation near the river in the backyard. We stopped and he lit a small fire in a large iron pit. I watched from a wicker bench. The air chilled my cheeks, but the warmth from the fire, from his nearness, more than made up for it. Cool air swirled in from the rushing river, blowing tendrils of smoke and embers my way. Tangy, bitter scents tickled my nose, and my mom came to mind. How many backyard barbecues had I enjoyed with her?

Brian sat beside me. I bent and flexed my cold fingers. I would've gladly sat there until hypothermia set in. No fire needed. Cologne and mint mixed with the nostalgia-scented air. I felt a swoon coming on.

"Now, I know you know . . ." he slowed, " . . . my name is Nicholas."

He wanted me to lead from there. I was afraid to admit I didn't know that, not at all, despite how diligent I'd been. I didn't want him to tell me to get lost, back off, or anything else that meant it would be our last conversation.

"Do you have any questions about that?" He waited.

"No."

"No?" He wedged his elbow over the back of the bench and leaned in.

I shoved my hands under my knees to keep from reaching out to touch him again.

"How is that possible? You should be angry."

"Why?" I couldn't fathom being angry with him.

"I lied to you. That tends to irk people."

"Right. Yes." I gathered my thoughts. *I should be mad at him for lying to me.* The thought had occurred to me before, but it hadn't stuck. I sat a little straighter. All things considered, his name mattered little. "You lied to me." I narrowed my eyes.

"Yes, you seem livid." He tapped his long fingers against the back of the bench. "You don't care that I lied. I need to know why."

"Well, you have your reasons, right? I mean, you weren't trying to ditch me, or you wouldn't keep showing up everywhere I go." My face warmed at the implication. I'd accused him of following me. Saying it aloud sounded silly, but it was the truth.

"True. I've never once tried to ditch you." He turned and pressed his back to the bench and stretched his legs out before him. He had some very serious black leather boots on. Probably military issue. The boots I wore were sleek and long, quite the opposite of the chunky black leather Brian, I mean Nicholas, wore.

"Local mall?" I nodded toward the boots.

He followed my gaze and pulled his feet back underneath the bench. Trading positions, he leaned forward on his elbows.

"If you tell me what you know, or what you think you know, or even what you're assuming . . . if you tell me anything at all, it'll help me." His voice sparked and popped with sincerity.

I wanted to help him, but I didn't want him thinking me a sneak. Also, I knew nothing.

"I'd be grateful to the moon."

"Okay. Why are we here?" I traded one awkward conversation for another. At least we were in this one together. Our other conversation set me up to be busted further.

"Do you not want to be?" His lips turned down at the corners and his eyes widened by a hair.

It kind of looked as if I'd thrown something at him. Realization set in. He wanted to be here with me, too. Looking at him, I couldn't get my mind around why.

"Of course." I sounded more eager than I wanted. "I don't even know what to call you anymore, and there's a whole school full of girls, from all around the country, vying for your attention. I don't get why we're here." I motioned between us.

His eyes narrowed. He twisted on the bench until his face came an inch or two closer. "I hadn't noticed."

I envisioned my body rolling off the bench and into the river. I wouldn't have noticed if it had. My head was already swimming.

I sucked in a long breath. "I was working on a Sociology assignment, but I couldn't find any information about me online." I looked as innocent as I could manage, considering the guilt swirling in my tummy. "I tried Googling your name instead, and I found out you were either ninety years old or you gave me a bogus name. I would've stopped there and assumed you blew me off, but then you showed up and I heard you say 'Nicholas.'" I bit my bottom lip to keep from rambling further. *I thought you might be the serial killer.*

"You didn't know Nicholas was my name?" He looked out into the trees and stretched back out. Defeated.

"No. I mean, is that what I'm supposed to call you now or what? I'm so confused. This town is the absolute worst."

He nodded as if knowing exactly how I felt.

"What is your *actual* name?" I gave him a look for lying. Now that I was getting to know him, it did irk me that he had lied about his name. *Jeez.* Who did that?

He smirked and stood up. "Let's walk." His expression moved from startled to stressed.

As we walked along the river, the water roared, emphasizing the lack of words between us. He walked several inches away, and I frowned. I preferred the way he had helped me from the car. His hands were shoved deep inside his pockets. A nervous gesture, maybe, but everything else about him exuded confidence.

"My dad came to visit."

"Yeah." He averted his gaze.

I waited for him to look my way. "He said there's been something on the local news about a stalker in the area." I kept my voice breezy. "I heard from someone at school it was a serial killer. The paper had

a useless article about the FBI contacting local authorities on an un-
solved case. Have you heard anything?" I wasn't too concerned about
a stalker in the area at the moment. I had my own mystery going
on. A serial killer was another story completely. The surveillance at
Francine Frances had to take a number.

"You don't need to be afraid. He won't get near you again . . . "

Those were the last words I heard. The syllables whooshed through
my head, hazing it up like the smoke from our fire. We'd stopped
walking; Brian held me by my shoulders. The panic and terror hit. A
combination of real-life fear—fear I'd felt recently—plus the lifelong
stress of my dream. My tummy coiled.

"Elle? What is it? Please say something."

I pictured myself vomiting on his shiny black boots.

"Near me *again*?" I whispered the words. I hoped they were audible.

"Elle." His voice encouraged, as if he spoke to a child. He held my
shoulders tight, and I wondered if I might pass out. "I shouldn't have
said that." He tilted his head all the way back, looking exasperated.
"My mind is having a hard time keeping up lately."

I knew exactly what that felt like.

"Ugh! I know you know things, but I don't know what things. At
the gas station you were running and screaming and said someone
was in the parking lot with you."

"You were. Where did you come from that night anyway? No one
else saw you. Only me. Then you disappeared. Someone tried to get
into the car with me." Fire returned to my cheeks. I had so many
things to be screaming about. I couldn't pick just one. "I thought I
was crazy. Like I imagined you, him, everything!"

"I might need to transfer soon. This arrangement isn't working.
I'm not supposed to be distracted. I'm certainly not supposed to be
so out of focus every time I get you alone."

"What are you talking about? Can you please focus now, for a
minute? Answer one of my questions before you go off on your own
tangent?"

He rubbed his face with one hand and tried to hold me up with the other.

I shook my shoulders against his palm. Anger ignited, replacing fear.

"What do you mean you might transfer? You're distracted? By what? We've only been here six weeks. Where are you going? What are you concentrating on? Are you a Mensa student or something?" Betrayal burned my frosty cheeks. How dare he plan to leave over a little distraction when he was the only guy I'd ever wanted to want me? I didn't know how close he thought we were, but he was the only person I'd told about being followed and the guy at the gas station. I needed him to stay. I trusted him with my secrets. How could one person feel so strongly about another who didn't return the feeling? Life was cruel. I threw my hands into the air. I wanted to stalk off and leave him, but I had no idea where we were. I turned and headed back to the pergola.

As I traipsed along the sandy riverbank, a sixth sense tickled at my neck. I worried the predator watched me. The forest seemed scarier. Darkness had covered everything while I was engrossed in our conversation.

Could someone dangerous enough to be on the news be the same man outside the diner and gas station? Did he follow me to the coffee shop that night? The pile of ashes on our doormat flashed through my mind. Chills covered my skin. I needed to get far away from the cursed academy. Maybe it wasn't too late to go with Dad. Maybe Brian and I could pick up later, after he did his thing—whatever that was—and I secured a place at a good college. I considered all of the options. Having options made me feel less helpless.

I sighed in relief when my feet hit the stone under the pergola. From the safety of the fire, I watched Brian. He was smart enough to give me space to think. I appreciated it. I had plenty to think about.

He bided his time tossing rocks into the river and apparently talked to himself. After several minutes, he made his way back in my direction.

Evening had transitioned into night, and the fire cast eerie shadows. Of course, *romantic* didn't ever describe what he seemed to be going for, and talk of me being stalked ruined that anyway.

"Can I still make you dinner?" His tortured expression was lit by waving flames.

"You're making dinner?" Did he ever end? I burned grilled cheese.

"Come on." He reached for me, and I met him in the middle. I left the fire warmer than I'd been all night. This, I had to see.

"So what am I supposed to call you?" I stopped in my tracks. I refused to take another step without an answer. How ridiculous to be out alone with someone who wouldn't tell me his name.

"Nicholas."

What the hell? "What?"

He tugged me along behind him. "Come on. It's warmer inside."

The cute little cabin was neat as a pin. Not a lot of furniture, but the kitchen looked fully stocked. He'd already set the table. This was a date, then.

"What are you making?" I could be mad at him later. Whatever he had in the oven smelled delicious. With any luck, my stomach wouldn't roar its approval and embarrass me further.

Okay, I probably wouldn't be mad at him later either.

"I have the makings for a nice salad," he pointed to a stack of fresh-cut vegetables near the sink, "and I planned Hubbard squash, all from the garden."

Of course they were.

"And trout."

"From the river?" I joked.

He shrugged and we laughed.

"So, where are your parents?" I asked as he arranged the vegetables into a large bowl and moved it to the table.

"D.C." He watched me. "I rented the cabin to get away from the others. It helps me to . . . "

"Concentrate?"

He grabbed a dishtowel off the counter and lifted a baking dish from the oven. On quick feet he crossed the distance to the table and set dinner beside the salad. He shook his hands at the wrist and motioned for me to eat up. Dishtowels weren't the best potholders. We filled our plates in silence. I piled on the salad and fish, but I wasn't sure I could eat. No guy had ever cooked for me before.

He sighed and shoved a forkful of fish into his mouth.

"Do you miss them?"

Every minute I sat there was more than too much for my heart to handle. I wanted to explode or at least extend the night. I prayed for daylight savings to happen right then, but an extra hour wouldn't be enough either.

"My family is huge and intrusive and crazy." He smiled around a mouthful of lettuce. "For being a military family, I think half of them are legally insane."

"Shut up."

"Really. They're nuts. No one does anything without everyone knowing." Pride inflated his words. His eyes twinkled.

"Like small towns," I offered.

"We could populate a small town."

"Really?" I let that thought settle. What did a big family feel like? All those people caring about your life. Nicholas had roots. I rolled the name around in my head. It fit. "You all get along?"

"Mostly. Yeah. It takes some effort on everyone's part, though." He chewed and looked at the ceiling a minute. "We hang out a lot, go to ball games, fish, whatever." His words were aloof, but his face told the truth. He loved them, and he missed them.

"I wish I knew what it was like." I'd never admitted it out loud before. "It's always just my dad and me." I craved what he had. I wanted roots. "He taught me to fish, though. We have a cabin in the Blue

Ridge Mountains we use to get away when he's not on assignment somewhere. It's my respite."

He stopped chewing and watched me. Then he put his fork down and watched me some more.

I began to worry something might be wrong.

"What are you doing here? Why are you alone at a boarding school all of a sudden?"

I cleared my throat and wiped my hands against the napkin on my lap. "My mom died when I was six. Dad thought putting me at a private school was more practical than keeping a nanny for an eighteen-year-old. My birthday is in December. I don't need watching over anymore. Of course, Dad disagrees. I've always had some random live-in babysitter, and they weren't the English grandmotherly type either. Nothing like that. Dad always chose someone too much like himself and not much like a mother. I used to think he did it intentionally, so I'd never try to replace Mom with a nanny." I paused, wondering if there was truth to the idea. "Seriously, though, he could've done better. I think he made 'businesslike' and 'paranoid' requirements. 'Nurturing' didn't make the list. Some of them were painfully preoccupied, and from my vantage point, I felt like something to be looked over, not interacted with. I had a super childhood." In case he missed the sarcasm, I rolled my eyes. He laughed.

"I begged to lose the nanny. I'm an adult. Besides, everyone always thought having a nanny was weird." I shifted my gaze from his. "Then again, everyone else had a mom." I shrugged. I'd never spilled so much about myself to one person before.

"Are you okay? Being alone? Really?"

"I'm not alone." I supposed it seemed that way to him. "No more than ever. Dad's always traveled. We always move. It's normal to me." I looked up and my belly flopped. My life probably sounded terrible to him. "I don't love it, but it is what it is, and I'm okay with what it is." I sat a little straighter, determined not to be unhappy. I knew I was very lucky in a ton of other ways.

"You're braver than I am."

I choked. "I'm not brave. I'm Chicken Little. You have mistaken me for someone else."

"I don't think so." He looked at me way too long. It reminded me how much I needed him to be there.

"Don't go, Nicholas." I tested his name on my tongue. The words sounded like an order, and I was okay with that, too.

His throat bobbed once at the sound of his name. "I can't." He sighed and stretched his feet out beneath the table, bumping mine. His eyes moved to his plate and back to me. "I should. It's the right thing to do, but I don't think I *can* go."

"Okay."

He took and released a deep breath. His face revealed nothing. I hated making his decision more difficult, but I was deeply thankful he wanted to stay.

"So, I suppose you aren't planning to make dinner for everyone at Francine Frances."

"No." His dimple appeared. "Obviously."

"What then?"

"I don't know what I'm doing." He rested interlaced fingers on top of his head.

"Why aren't you using your real name?" I swirled the ice in my cup and waited for an answer that never came.

I put my fork down. Dinner was phenomenal, but I couldn't eat another bite. The butterflies flew back, and it felt like they brought along their friends, the hummingbirds. Maybe a swarm of bees, too. I laid a hand over my stomach under the table's edge.

I doubted I'd have another chance to figure him out. Faced with a once-in-a-lifetime opportunity, my cheeks probably glowed scarlet. I rolled my lips in over my teeth for a minute and then forged ahead.

"It's nice, being here with you. I've had a tough time wondering what you really think of me. You act so different at school."

His eyes slipped shut. They rarely did. I noticed. Nicholas lived on alert. When he opened them, he seemed to have made a decision not to talk openly any more. Whatever measure of trust he'd allowed to flow between us was clamped off. Done. "We should get you back before Pixie comes home."

"So she won't see you dropping me off."

One stern nod from him and I blew out the door to wait by the Jeep.

Chapter Twelve

"You're baaaaack." Davis smiled a wide cheesy smile as I approached the lunch table. He had a large Styrofoam cup situated in front of him on the table. "For you. I made an unauthorized trip to the teachers' lounge."

It was my first real smile since leaving Brian, or Nicholas, or whatever his real name was, the night before. I had refused to look at him all morning and prayed he'd keep his distance at lunch. Thanks to Davis's kind gesture, I now had a weapon.

"Thanks." I lifted the cup and blew over the top of the stale-smelling contents.

He walked in, took one look at my face, and moved to a small table against the wall.

"Uh-oh. You and your buddy on the outs?"

"Yeah."

"You want to talk about it?" His voice held the hope I didn't.

"No."

"You up for watching some practice tonight?"

At a loss for words, and any reason under the sun I couldn't make it, I caved. "Sure. Yeah, I can stay a while."

"Excellent."

After school, I climbed a set of metal bleachers and positioned myself in the sun. Fall had burst all over campus, lighting everything in shades from amber to crimson. Purple and gold mums lined cobblestone walkways, and pumpkins appeared with hay bales at an alarming rate.

I pulled out my journal at the first whistle and started writing. Between plays I waved at the guys and smiled, but my mind was miles away.

"Are you logging all the ways you want to kill me?"

The journal fell to my feet and nearly slipped between the bleachers to the ground below. Nicholas grabbed it and handed it to me like a peace offering. At the sound of the whistle, a cluster of players gaped upward at us. I waved a small nervous wave.

"Who are you watching?"

"Davis. I don't know anyone else."

Silence stretched between us until I turned on him. "Do you want something?"

I followed his silent gaze beyond the field, to a mass of trees on the outskirts of the general landscaping. At first I didn't see anything, and then something moved. With no rush, a man turned and disappeared into the shadows. Blending with the trees, he was gone.

"Stay."

Nicholas placed one palm on the railing beside me and hoisted himself over the edge. A second later a muffled thud preceded footfalls. Two seconds later, he ran across the field's edge and into the trees. I stood on shaky legs to peer over the edge where he'd jumped. If it had been me, I'd still be lying there eight feet below.

Stay. Jerk. I stuffed the journal into my backpack and marched with purpose down the loud metal stairs. I threw a wave and a smile in Davis's direction and swung around the corner to the library. *Stay*. Who says that to a person?

Fueled by images of his beautiful face, I Googled. I tried local sports sections in D.C. papers and combed through Deans' lists, looking through features on D.C. seniors. No Nicholas Austin.

"You okay?"

I looked up, less startled than usual. I was getting used to being snuck up on. Anger burned under my skin. The man looking down at me made me rethink my calm. He was always in the library. The last time I saw him, he didn't speak. He stood at the end of a row of books, staring. His floppy black hair hung youthfully over one eyebrow. Maybe it was a side effect of spending so much time in a high school library. He looked closer to my dad's age than mine.

"Fine."

"You're here quite a bit. Is there anything I can help with?"

"Do you work here?" I didn't see a name tag or any sort of clue that he did.

"You could say that." One cheek lifted his face into a half smile. The expression never met his eyes. The stale scent of cigarette smoke lingered on his sweater.

"I'm fine."

"If you need anything . . . " He looked over both his shoulders and pressed his palms onto the table. The sight of a pack of cigarettes stuffed into his shirt pocket sucked the air from my lungs.

I shook my head, unable to find words. People smoked. Davis smoked. I exhaled long and slow. A group of girls bustled in through the front door and set up at the next table over. He stood poker straight and walked away. No goodbye. Nothing. He walked out the way the girls had come in. Guess he wasn't working there. Freak town.

My eyes burned from lack of sleep and all the hay bales on campus. I turned back to my laptop, thankful for the girls who had saved me from a creepy old man. This time I searched for *Nicholas Austin* without first choosing a paper. I rolled my achy eyes and prepared to start again. Minors never made headlines without a nice scholastic reason.

The possibility that he was as old as he looked hadn't grown roots until then. I clicked on a link. A picture of my Nicholas lodged in the upper corner of my screen. Wearing a crisp white hat and uniform, a deluge of information washed over me. I read as fast as I could, hoping to pull the details directly into my brain like a download. I'd struck gold.

Nicholas Austin graduated from D.C. Military Academy before joining the U.S. Marine Corps. He completed a tour in Afghanistan before taking a position with the United States Marshals Service.

Holy crap. I dragged my gaze from the picture back to the article showcasing a handful of new Marshals at a fundraiser in D.C. According to the article, Nicholas had studied at the College of William and Mary in Virginia. No graduation notice. My mind reeled at the implication. Why would someone like that go back to high school? And how old was he?

Adrenaline had me shifting in my chair. I wanted to run somewhere. Nicholas had secrets bigger than a bogus name. He had an enormous flipping secret. I'd called Pixie's boyfriend, Michael, a poser. Man, Nicholas had him beat hands down. A U.S. freaking Marshal posing as a student at Francine Frances. I rubbed my eyes and reread the article.

I leaned back against the hard wooden chair and marveled. It didn't surprise me to discover he was something more than a high school student. In fact, all I'd read about him only flamed my barely hidden infatuation. This boy buying me coffee and wearing flip-flops was an all-American hero. He'd accomplished so much. Too much to be here.

A hundred searches later, I hadn't found anything new. I replayed all the clues: his dog tags, the missing hair on his calves, his continual distraction, the way he had launched himself over the railing. Dad had mentioned increased campus security.

"Things I know." I underlined it a few times. First, Nicholas took an assumed name and came here to "observe." I assumed.

Observe sounded less scary than the other night at The Pier when he said he was watching for a killer. I shivered. Second, he was a U.S. Marshal. I had no idea what that meant. I made another column and dragged my pen down the center of the paper. I needed a column for questions. Why would he use a fake name? Who knew his real name? Did the school know he wasn't a student? That's why there was no file. It took effort not to bounce my hand against my forehead. No wonder he was so bizarre. He had a lot to hide. Next question: What did Marshals do? Something was going on at this little school and Nicholas was the key. What if there was a serial killer? I swallowed long and hard, then took a careful look around. It wasn't a huge jump after all the killer talk and knowing a Marshal guarded us. The number of unpleasant things that had happened since I arrived seemed to multiply when I gave them opportunity. Considering, however lightly, that I could be the target of a serial killer hurt. The realization was like someone punching a hole through my chest.

Voices filled the library and a pack of boys with wet hair and enormous gym bags sauntered over to my table. Most stayed wrapped in their conversations, paying me little attention. Davis leaned over the table, eyes bright.

"You ready?"

I didn't fight the slow smile spreading over my face. I suddenly had a new appreciation for his straightforward personality. No games. His ready smile was real. No lies hid behind it. With Davis, what I saw was what I got. Plus, walking home with a pack of lacrosse players sounded worlds better than walking alone.

"Yeah. Where we going?" I released a cleansing breath and closed my laptop.

"Coffee?"

"Perfect." I needed a bucketful. Sleep was most definitely off my night's agenda.

Before I could push in my chair, Davis slung my backpack over his already-burdened shoulder. He winked. I took a step forward and he extended an elbow my way. A dozen eyes waited for my response under wet hair and a cloud of generic locker-room soap. Without another thought, I slipped my arm through his. A gesture of friendship older than the school.

The walk to the coffee shop passed quickly. Davis talked about practice and his little sister's enthusiasm over visiting for the fall festival. He knew his dad would embarrass him, his mom would love me, and his sister would never want to leave. The chill in the air was unmistakable autumn. A brief shower had sprinkled everything with tiny crystalized droplets. Davis guided me around masses of damp leaves and puddles formed in sidewalk crevices. His teammates hooted and barked behind us about video games and public-school girls. Only a sliver of my mind wondered who had stood in the trees and what it meant. I hoped it was another Marshal, but I doubted that was true.

Davis was comfortable walking arm in arm with me, and it put me at ease. It reminded me of Pixie when she called me an anchor. My life had been a series of moves for so long, it felt good to have people tying me to this place. Anchoring me to them. I had people. A big smile split my face. Davis was the boy next door from every sitcom ever made. And he was my friend.

"Well, well, well." Pixie and Michael stepped out of the coffee shop when Davis pulled the door open for me.

"What's up?" Michael looked at Davis and the team behind us.

"Hi." I looked at the ground before checking Davis's expression for reassurance. The smile on his face suggested they'd won a big game instead of finished a regularly scheduled practice.

"So," Pixie drew out the *o*. "What's this?" She motioned to our joined arms and I slid mine free. The carefree feeling vanished. Self-consciousness shoved its way in.

"Davis and I are getting coffee. Can you stay?" My face burned from the spotlight I imagined was trained on it. My words seemed to relax Davis, who had stiffened a bit when I untangled our arms.

She mulled it over for a minute while Michael stood there looking like I felt. "Nah. See you later?"

"Sure."

"Scoop me."

I nodded and she flitted down the stairs, pulling Michael behind her. For the first time in my life, I had a real date. My mood soured at the thought of my fake date with Nicholas. It was easy to surmise that it had been a work-related obligation, reconnaissance maybe after I'd told him about the guy at the gas station. Not real. Not like the guy across from me who didn't need me for some ulterior agenda. I shoved the bitterness aside. Brian was doing his job. He had never asked me to fall for him. That was on me. We sat at the shop until the owner turned the sign around and gave us a sympathetic look. I hated to leave. I had too many fake and ugly things to process when I got home. As long as I stayed in the booth smiling with Davis, I was safe. Snuggled in denial.

"Can I walk you home?" He retrieved our coats from where we'd tossed them on the bench beside him and passed mine to me over the table.

"I'd like that." More truth. Telling him things came easy. Could a girl have two best friends? Pixie and I had a great thing going and I loved her, but the more time I spent with Davis, the more connected I felt to him, too. Neither of them felt like anchors as much as balloons pulling me up, opening up possibilities, giving me courage. Was this what having a family felt like?

In the past couple of hours I'd told him about my mom's death and dad's travel and our moves. I didn't dig deep, but I opened up and laid the groundwork for him to know more. His lips set when I mentioned Mom's death. He loved his family. I thought he wanted to reach for me across the table, but he pulled his hands into his lap instead, which I appreciated. I hated people feeling sorry for me. Nicholas didn't even seem surprised when I told him my mother had died. Probably he didn't care or wasn't listening. It had nothing to do with the school.

We walked measurably slower from the shop to my building. At the base of the stairs, Davis softened his voice. In the dim, flickering streetlights, it seemed his cheeks darkened.

"Can I meet you for coffee in the morning?"

I pulled my lips in over my teeth. Meeting for coffee was the Francine Frances equivalent to a press conference. I doubted the lacrosse team thought twice about our coffee date, but the hoard of caffeinated girls in the morning would text the news schoolwide before the first bell.

"Okay." I might as well face it sooner rather than later. I'd made a real friend. I refused to alienate him to avoid trivial gossip.

As if my acceptance had formed another invitation altogether, Davis leaned toward me. His hands moved to my shoulders and he took the final step between us. I had to make a fast decision. I couldn't hurt his feelings. No one had ever opened up to me like he did. I wanted to keep him, but my heartstrings pulled tight against my arms, anchoring them to my sides. Like a rider steering a horse away from danger, my heart refused to accept his advance. I stepped away a baby step.

He didn't seem to notice.

Betrayed again by my stupid heart. I had fallen for Nicholas before I knew he lied. My heart didn't seem to care about the lies. Those heartstrings were irrevocably and irrationally tied to a liar. I had serious issues to deal with.

I jumped when a car revved to life nearby. A squealing belt sent me flying into Davis's arms. I buried my head in his chest and he wrapped his arms around me.

"Was that the car?"

I nodded against his shirt, thankful to have confessed my irritation to him over coffee. I hadn't even told Pixie yet.

"I'm going to go." My eyes were blurred with tears of emotional overload.

Davis ran his hand down my shoulder to my hand and squeezed before I started up the steps to my door. I ran to the top and swallowed my heart. There was a still-glowing ember on our doormat. Had someone been there while I stood a few feet away with Davis? What if I'd come home alone?

I jumped inside, locked the door, and called Pixie.

"Elle!" she squealed. "Come hang?"

"Not tonight. Can you do me a favor? Have Michael walk you to the door?"

Of course he would. They normally spent thirty minutes saying goodbye. Satisfied, I hit the treadmill to think and burn off some nerves. For five miles, the only thing I thought of was how everything fit together. Only one person could answer my questions and I doubted he would. I showered and changed into my favorite jeans and a stretchy cotton tank top. Lots of girls had stopped wearing the ultra-low-rise style, but I'd worn one pair to perfection. The strip of exposed skin above them almost managed to look tan next to the stark white tank.

On my bed, I turned on the local news and watched as the anchor covered reports of a serial killer in the area. Oh no. My nerves frayed. It was all true. On a stomach filled with coffee and nothing else, that equaled sick. I had zero chance of sleep again. Ever.

My senses heightened. Something made noise in the kitchen. I silenced the news and scooted to the edge of my bed. The sound came again. On instinct, I grabbed my bag and dug for the tiny scrap of paper. Another creak of floorboards, this time in the hallway outside my door. My thumbs danced over the keypad texting "Someone here 911" to the number on the paper. I brought up the dial pad and dialed 9-1-1, ready for the worst. Before I pressed send and brought the cavalry, I found my voice.

"The Marshals know you're here." I slipped off my bed and dropped to the floor on the side farthest from the door. My voice surprised me. Despite the tremor in my hands, I sounded confident and assured.

The footfalls stopped outside my room. I braced myself to run, even tackle him if necessary, but I would not die. Dragging a pencil from my bag as my only weapon option, I hovered my thumb over the green button.

"I called nine-one-one. You want me bad enough to risk it?" *Please don't.* I scooted along the floor to the corner and pressed my back to the wall, hoping to find leverage for an attack.

Tears stung my eyes. My knuckles turned white around the pencil.

One deep breath later, my phone vibrated in my palm. I answered but couldn't speak. I didn't have to.

"Elle, what's wrong?" In the background, a car door shut and footfalls thundered.

I would die alone in my room. Nicholas would never get here in time. I swallowed hard, thinking of my dad.

"Hello? Elle?" Nicholas barked into my ear. "Answer me, dammit!"

"I think the killer's outside my bedroom door."

Chapter Thirteen

"Elle?"

"Nicholas?"

Joy rushed over me when he pushed open the door to my room. I hated the way my heart skipped when I saw him.

Relief washed over his features. He lifted a finger to his lips and left. Through the open door, I watched him check every room before he returned.

"Are you okay?"

I nodded, not trusting my voice.

"Your front door wasn't locked. It wasn't open, but it wasn't locked. Do you remember locking it when you came home?" Bright green eyes pierced mine, begging me to think carefully.

I nodded. For a minute, we stared silently at one another. His eyes fell to the tank I had pulled on after my shower, the strip of bare tummy above my favorite jeans and then my bare feet. "Uh . . . "

A zing of anticipation sent shockwaves through me. "How'd you get here so fast?"

"I was close." He looked everywhere but at me. Sliding down to meet me on the floor, he pulled me into his side and leaned his head to mine. "You're safe now. I didn't see any signs of forced entry. I won't ever let anyone hurt you." The fury in his voice told me he meant it. "When you're ready, will you take a look around? See if anything's missing, new, or out of place."

"Okay." I sat nestled against him until I trusted my legs to hold me and then pushed myself off the floor. I inhaled deeply to steady my breathing. I needed time to put myself back together, or at least find shoes and a sweater.

"New?"

"Sometimes they leave things."

Bile rose in my throat. I didn't ask any follow-ups. My imagination filled in the blanks.

Nothing was different in the apartment. Tears sprang to my eyes. "Someone was here." I stomped my foot with indignation. "They were. I swear it." I swiped away the falling drops with the pads of my thumbs. My voice choked and cracked with effort.

"I'll wait outside." He swallowed and looked around again.

"Are you afraid to be seen here?" I crossed my arms over the ribbon of skin I knew he'd seen and didn't want to see anymore. Instant loathing began. How could I be so wrapped up in a guy who couldn't care less?

Nicholas moved through the apartment to the door. "Do you want to go back to the cottage? When will Pixie be home?"

I followed. "Whatever." At least I could try to get some information out of him, and if he was a Marshal, maybe he could use my experiences and/or paranoia as a lead. I hated the truth in that. I didn't want to be crazy even more than I didn't want to be stalked. I walked down the hall to my room and yanked a brush through my hair with shaking hands. I opened the drawer that held my caffeine pills and cringed. This wasn't the time to be addicted. This was the time to be strong. I squeezed my eyes shut for a moment and slammed the drawer closed.

Maybe the person who had been in my apartment was only a regular stalker like the guy Dad had mentioned. Stalkers followed people and what else? Were they pervy like in movies, collecting used napkins when we left restaurants? With any luck, they didn't flash, because that was not how I wanted to be first exposed to the male form. I whimpered. My hands flew to my mouth. What kind of state was I in to hope I had a stalker?

The place where my alternative was a serial killer.

"Elle. You okay in there?"

I marched back to Nicholas, who stood a complete and total two inches away from the door.

I pulled on red-and-white-striped knee socks under my jeans and shoved my feet into well-worn Chucks.

In the Jeep, my fingers worked on a thread hanging from the hem of my shirt. On the main road outside campus, we passed a group of girls I recognized and two guys I didn't. Each guy took deep drags on a cigarette. My cheeks flamed as I pictured the same scenario happening every night. The girls walked them as far as the stairs in front of our door and said their goodbyes. I was such an idiot.

"Okay," Nicholas said, as the night flew past on the windy country roads. "Tell me every detail you remember. Leave nothing out."

In my periphery, he turned to me again and again, but I had no words, no time to decide what I wanted to say and what I could never say.

"Elle, you're safe. Okay?" His voice was confident, thick with assurance. He believed the words. Why wouldn't he?

I turned. "I'm not so sure." Obviously, he had no idea I was going insane. Instead of college, I'd end up in a psychiatric ward next fall, if not sooner. All the military training in the world couldn't save me from myself.

"Talk to me."

"I have serious issues." I laughed a little at the truth of the statement.

"No doubt."

Hurt from his behavior inside my apartment resurfaced. I sighed. Dense. Stupid. He was clearly embarrassed. In keeping with his cover, he flirted with a kid. That must've been how it seemed to him anyway. Though, I wasn't a kid. Far from it. I'd celebrate my eighteenth birthday in six weeks. Chronologically and physically, I wasn't a child. Intellectually, I was already at college level, and emotionally—forget about it. I'd been through so much that I'd aged inappropriately beyond my years. Of course, he had no way of knowing any of that.

Nicholas looked young. I kept trying to make him fit the role he played, but I couldn't. He'd been through a lot, too. A tour overseas was enough to age anyone, plus his new routine as a Marshal and our protector.

"I was pretty mad at you earlier."

He slid his eyes my way and slowed to make the turn into his drive. "And now?"

He shifted the Jeep into park and cut the engine. Sounds of the river played against the glass as it steamed around the edges from our breath.

"I'm a little more understanding." I took a minute to give him an accusatory stare. "I went to the library after you left."

"With Davis." A new edge bit into his words.

"Before he got there, I had a lot of questions. Questions you wouldn't answer. I hate being lied to." My teeth gritted tight.

"You Googled my name." A statement of fact. A fact I hated to admit. It seemed too personal, like I'd hijacked his phone while he wasn't looking.

"First, you told me your name was Brian. Everyone calls you Brian. Then you said Nicholas was your name. You said to call you Nicholas. I mean, what the hell? What's that about? Are you lying to me or to five hundred students and faculty?"

He groaned a long, deep growl and jumped out the driver's-side door. He opened mine a second later and reached for my elbow. I didn't have time to complain before he hoisted me out and moved to his front door, scanning the night as we walked. He flipped on the lights and motioned to the table. I sat.

"Go on."

Rude.

"When I searched for *Nicholas Austin*, your picture came up. I realized you . . . " I didn't want to give away the fact that I'd spent nights trying to know him, or let on he'd become my own mystery man, " . . . weren't really a student."

"Not a student. This is where you want to leave it?" Skepticism dripped over the words.

"Do you? I mean, I don't know what's classified." I squinted.

He rubbed his faced roughly, then his hair, then the back of his neck. "What else?"

His expression frightened me a little. I'd never seen him less than composed. Knowing all I knew and seeing the wild look in his eyes only emphasized his size. I had no doubt he could cause some serious damage if provoked.

"That's why you called me when you thought there was an intruder. Do you want coffee?"

I didn't like the edge to his voice, or the way he said *thought*.

"No." My hands shook. I couldn't hold a cup steady.

"Oh." He flopped back against his chair, exasperated. "Am I scaring you?" He didn't wait for an answer. He tilted forward and rested his forehead in his hands for two seconds. "I'm at Francine Frances on assignment. I'm not supposed to frighten you." He raised his face to mine.

The tormented expression softened me. "There was someone in my apartment."

"What happened?"

I shrugged, unsure of what was real and what I had imagined. I'd already covered everything. I heard footsteps and then I made a threat through my bedroom door. Whoever stood on the other side of it believed my bluff because they were gone before Nicholas arrived. It only took him a minute to get there, which made me wonder how close he was when I texted. "Tell me why you're here on assignment."

"That's classified, but I'm guessing you know who I work for, so I'm willing to put that much out there if you'll help me along a little with what else you know."

"You're on assignment as a Marshal."

His missed a breath, a hiccup no one else on the planet would probably notice, and then kept pace. "Yes. Your school is believed to be in need of extra surveillance." He raised an eyebrow.

"Dad told me. I watched the news."

"I'm keeping an eye on things."

"Is there anything you don't do?"

"Apparently, I don't do undercover very well. Perhaps my mere presence is enough to alert the unsub to vacate."

"Unsub? Is that like a perp?"

"Yes." He choked out a laugh. "Do you watch crime shows?" The agony melted off his face.

"Occasionally." *Hope he never checks my TiVo.* I loved crime shows.

"I'd end up covering a budding detective." He rolled his eyes the way I did, then winked.

He was the second boy to wink at me in one day, but my physical reactions to the acts were as different as night and day. When Davis winked, stress faded and I wanted to smile. I knew I could count on him. He was my friend. When Nicholas winked, my heart stopped. My tummy rolled. My muscles tensed, and then my frozen heart leapt into a senseless sprint. When he looked at me like that, it was hard to remember why I cared if someone had been in my apartment or not.

I was intoxicated.

"Unsub is short for unknown subject."

"So you're watching the whole town?"

"The school."

"Yes, but I'm just one girl."

"Elle, you're far more than just one girl."

I blinked.

"We've suspected he was in the area for a few months." Conflict played in the line of his brow.

"Was he at the flea market?" Wow, this guy was everywhere. The other girls at school had no idea how much danger they were in. "Wait, who is he?"

He took a long time to answer. He went to the kitchen and poured two glasses of ice water, then set them in front of us. Clearly stalling. "That's classified."

He shot up a finger at me before I released one of the rude comments weighing on my tongue. "But he's dangerous. There's no mistaking that. Please understand you need to be aware all the time, of everyone and everything."

"How do I know you aren't him?" I hoped to lighten the mood before it crashed. Wondering if he could mean *every*one. Did he know anything about the guy? What was his M.O.?

He reached into his back pocket and placed a leather bifold on the table. His badge.

Ohmigosh. It was so shiny and official. I felt honored getting to look at it. "Nice."

"Right?" Pride changed his expression. He should've been proud. My chest swelled with emotion at the sight of his name etched across the metal, and I barely knew him. He should show that thing to everyone. I tried to focus on his warning. No easy task. Unsub or no unsub.

"Okay, so this man is a stalker?"

"Yes."

"Is he a serial killer?"

Pain hardened his face. The grim look was too much. I looked away before he answered. "Yes."

Breath caught in my throat and I started at my response. "It's so ironic!" It hit me and nervous laughter erupted. Another sign of my pending commitment to the loony bin.

"How is this ironic?" His brows crumbled in frustration and maybe a little anger. He shoved the badge back into his pocket.

"Well, my dad's been overprotective of me my entire life. When I didn't want to live with another nanny, he sent me here to keep me safe. How much safer can you be than in a prep school in the Ohio Valley?" I laughed. "I mean, it's hardly a crime mecca. The campus police practically *are* the police. The fire department is made up of volunteers. Oh, and there's no hospital." My laughter started sounding giddy. The whole scenario tickled me. Talk about an emotional roller coaster. "Dad sent me to the most inconsequential of towns, and it has a killer darkening its streets."

Nicholas's eyes widened. He had obviously missed the humor, but it really was ridiculous. If Dad knew things were bad enough to require undercover Marshals, he'd move me to Indonesia.

Nicholas's lips parted. He wanted to say something, but he didn't, which was fine.

I knew the facts and planned to spend as much of my free time as possible with school security.

"Elle, protecting you isn't only a part of my job. Do you get that?" His expression pleaded with me. Beautiful green eyes snapped to attention, torn somewhere between fierce and defeated. "This is important."

"Yes." I got it. The importance surged in his voice and registered in his eyes. He cared. Maybe not to the same extent I cared about him, but the words secured me to my position. When my dad got that look, I knew he'd defend me against a militia or a pack of wild animals if necessary.

"I hope you do. I hope you're okay with it." The intensity in his eyes didn't relent.

My heart picked up a bit at how much he wanted to say more and clenched when he didn't.

"I hope you're more than *okay* with it."

I was.

"Have you eaten?"

"No."

He moved through the kitchen and came back with some chips and salsa. I dug in.

"When you said goodbye at the flea market and I thought I'd never see you again, I was pretty upset." I knew my time with Nicholas had limits and we'd already pushed them. He had an entire student body to look after.

"I'm sorry for that. It wasn't my choice. I knew you'd get the wrong idea, think I didn't care. It was the worst day I've had since I got here." His hand slipped over the table between us and I felt a jolt of electricity run up my arm. The warm roughness of his calloused fingertips against my fear-frozen skin shocked me. I held still, hoping not to scare him away.

"Then you showed up again in almost every class." My eyes slipped from his to examine our hands. One of his hands could easily cover the span of my waist. Heat swirled in my chest at the thought and I swallowed.

"Not every class. It's a small school. I have to admit I never saw my life leading back to high school."

"So, where is your life heading?" I sipped at the cold water.

"To this." His shoulders rolled back an inch. "I've wanted to be a Marshal since I learned space cowboy wasn't a viable occupation. I know this is where I belong. I love what I do, and I think I'm especially equipped to do it well." He paused. "I think this is my role to play in the bigger picture."

"Are there more of you here?"

"Like, more Marshals?"

"Sure. You can't be here with me if there's no one at the school, right? What about everyone walking around town and hanging at The Pier?" *What about Pixie?*

Nicholas sat straighter and seemed to choose his words. "My team is around."

144

"Around?"

"This town has a lot of ground to cover. We keep watch on the campus all the time, in addition to the rows of housing and the main strip. I try to keep an eye on The Pier." He winked.

I pursed my lips.

"What? I'm the youngest. I blend."

"Oh, yeah. You blend." The memory of him in his hoodie passed through my mind. *Did he hear the catch in my throat?* Jeez Louise, the girls about fell over themselves chasing after him last time.

He smiled.

I let it go.

Despite the smile, tension threaded the air between us. "How old are you really?" My mind went over the information online. I added it up.

"Twenty-two."

Wow. Deep breath. "So, your age got you the job at Francine Frances?" I wanted to break the tension that had my stomach twisted and my head spinning.

"Well, that helped, and my family, plus my military training." His voice softened. Did he think he still scared me?

"Military training?"

"Yes. I spent some time in the Marines following the academy. I lived abroad. My superiors felt the experience might be applicable here."

"I know about the Marines and Afghanistan."

"You do?" His arms flopped heavily to his sides. He looked a little relieved. "Does that frighten you?"

"No. Should it?"

Something significant came and went in his expression faster than I could put a name to it. It might've been regret. My heart beat harder at the realization of things he might've seen or done defending our country.

"How is military training applicable exactly?" How his experience overseas could translate to Francine Frances, serial killer or not, hit ridiculous on the parent-paranoia scale. I smiled wildly at the silliness of the comparison between his military training and our little academy.

"It just is." Color washed from his face. "The danger here is real and significant. I'll do everything in my power to protect you." His eyes glistened with staved emotion. Beneath his breath I thought I heard him growl, "We'll find him. I'll end him."

My hands rolled into my lap. The face before me was no longer the youthful guy from five minutes prior. No, across from me sat a Marine. Coldness settled over his warm smile, setting his lips at a tight crease. Nicholas looked fierce and foreboding. My heart skipped in a faulty way. I swallowed loudly, and he remained motionless, watching. He would end him. This man, this stalker, was worse than I'd let myself imagine. *Serial killer* swirled in my mind, etching a permanent place there. I wouldn't forget again. I wouldn't play this off to avoid the reality of it. We were in danger here. Ice slid down my spine.

"Someone has to warn everyone else." Fear surged through me for Pixie and all the girls in the apartments, undefended while I monopolized their security miles away. "They should know not to be alone. We need to tell them to lock their doors and go out in pairs. What if he left my place and slid into someone else's?"

His eyes squinted. "I need to take you home now. Don't worry. Someone will be outside all night watching. We need to cut this short. I don't want to start more talk than we already have, and I want to check on Pixie. I like her."

I pushed away from the table and excused myself to use the bathroom. I liked Pixie, too, so I was in a hurry to get back. We needed to tell her everything. She went out almost every night. What if she came home alone and he was there waiting?

Chapter Fourteen

The sounds of him cleaning up the chips and running water in the sink came down the short hall. Across from the bathroom was a bedroom. Tiny hairs on my arms stood at attention. His room. The door stood slightly ajar. Two separate laptops sat on dinner trays beside the bed. The blankets were pulled tight. Not a crease or wrinkle. File boxes sat on the floor near the trays. All sorts of Boy Scout–style paraphernalia lay strewn around the room: rope, binoculars, gloves. I couldn't identify most of it. I slipped into the bathroom and pushed the door shut. A holster, with no gun in it, was hung over the hamper. It reminded me that I wasn't meant to be here. I'd called him from whatever he'd been doing to rescue me from an unseen intruder.

Washing my hands, a low murmur registered through the wall. I pulled out the lip gloss Pixie had given me and concentrated as I slid it around my lips. I couldn't make out any words. It occurred to me that I could walk in on something that might lend me a clue, and I picked up the pace. I was dying to know exactly what we faced in this small town. Hannibal Lecter came to mind and triggered my gag reflex.

My steps hastened on the way back to the kitchen. I nearly fell over when he walked around the corner. He must've disconnected when he heard me coming. I hadn't considered that he'd check up on me.

"Whoa! Are you okay?" His disposition changed. His posture relaxed.

I liked that. My cheeks burned at my plan to spy. I hoped he didn't see through me.

"Not that I mind running into you like this."

I put my hands flat against his chest to push away, but they stuck. He was close enough for me to smell the smoke from a fire on his shirt. It mingled with his cologne and my thoughts became hazy. He'd been to a bonfire. My heart danced in my chest. My feet rooted. I jerked my head back to see his face. What should I do? Fight-or-flight played again in my muscles. Half locked in tight. The other half loosened to run. Thoughts of this moment had stretched well beyond PG-13 in my mind on a daily basis. I had to do something. I needed to back away from him. I really didn't want to.

Do something.

Nicholas's head tilted downward, looking at me when I looked up. As if he'd heard my internal battle, he placed two large warm hands over mine. He held them to his chest briefly. Then he pulled them upward, over his broad shoulders, and left them dangling behind his neck. The stretch brought our bodies close, left me pulled to my tiptoes against him. We touched at our thighs and my skin heated to combustion. His eyes searched mine. I knew what came next, and anticipation rolled off me in waves. I slid my lips gently on fresh gloss, thankful for Pixie's foresight. I'd kept it in my purse since the night she gave it to me.

Buzzing drew his attention away from my face. He looked at the island, where his phone lay twisting, and gave me an apologetic glance.

I let my arms drop and walked near the window to catch my breath. Adrenaline coursed through me, and my skin tingled. I couldn't have been more amped if I'd just jumped from a plane. No amount of coffee or treadmill time had ever come close to this rush. In fact, without all the treadmill time, I might've had a stroke. Being stalked made me a nervous wreck. Worse than usual. My dreams had once been the scariest thing in my life. With a real killer lurking around, I got a face-smack of perspective.

Behind me, Nicholas spoke in fragments. I hoped whomever he spoke to understood his cryptic jargon. From my standpoint, he could've been drinking. The words amounted to gibberish in my ears—tense, sexy gibberish. I turned my focus on the view outside the window. *Get a grip, Elle. He's here to protect you, not kiss or date you.*

I hated to leave the cottage, but I needed to know Pixie was all right. I pulled my cell from my pocket, and two thick arms wound around my middle. From behind me, he gently pressed his palm over my phone.

The mere proximity softened me to the core. My heart hammered against my ribs and I held my breath, waiting. I said more silent thanks for the treadmill and prayers to pull myself together. On impulse, I turned in the small space between his body and the window. The movement sent him back a half step and spread a smirk across his face. He cleared his throat and I smiled. He squeezed the cell between his ear and shoulder before shaking a silent finger my way. I put my phone back and waited while he struggled to finish his strange call. I'd hindered his concentration for a change.

"You can call Pixie now." He lifted his hand in surrender. I supposed if he was on a work call, he might've been in trouble if they heard a girl talking in the background.

"Who was that?"

"My team. They're talking to campus security and the local sheriff. You'll need to make a report later. It's best to have everything on record."

"But there's no proof."

He cut me off with a wag of his head. "You're the proof. You heard someone inside. The door was unlocked. You remember locking it."

Relief washed through me. I wasn't crazy. He believed me.

He placed his phone on the shelf next to him.

I shook off the complicated thoughts, dialed Pixie's number, and waited. When the call connected, I heard a beep from somewhere nearby. He touched his phone lightly without looking up.

Pixie screamed into the phone over her blaring car stereo. We talked for two minutes while his eyes roamed over me. I leaned into the windowsill for support.

I disconnected. "She's going to be out late."

He nodded once and pulled keys from his pocket. We were headed back to town anyway.

I enjoyed the drive home. The air inside the Jeep smelled of Nicholas's cologne—sweet, spicy, and mouthwatering. He'd flipped on the heater to ease the evening chill, but goose bumps crawled up and down my arms anyway. More than once, he looked my way and I imagined the fervor in his eyes matched mine. Sometimes, when he reached to change gears, I suspected he wanted to take my hand. The new tension in my life defined magnificent, so much better than the kind I'd lived with for so long. With Nicholas in my life, everything else became bearable.

"You know, I need to concentrate to do a good job here." His expression was grim in the dim interior Jeep lighting.

Here it came. I braced for the "we can only be friends" speech. "Until this situation is diffused . . . " He stopped and took a breath.

"I understand. I don't want to divide your time." Lies. I wanted to monopolize all his time.

He nodded curtly and we continued in silence.

When he pulled up onto the curb outside my building, Nicholas hesitated. I looked around for the infamous orange glow, or my dad, but saw nothing but night. The typical cones of light from streetlamps cast interwoven circles over the sidewalk. Varied shades of gray against the large silhouette of our apartment building.

"What?" I whispered.

He didn't move. One hand gripped the curve of the steering wheel and the other dug into his pocket. After one long beat, he sent a text, tossed the phone into the console cup holder, and restarted his Jeep. Nicholas gave me the fierce face.

"Call Pixie. Tell her to meet you at the library after she's finished. Tell her not to go home first. Tell her you need a ride from there. She must go there first. Make sure she does." His words came slow and steady. He waited for an acknowledgment from me. The instructions were crystal clear.

My mouth fell open. Something happened that I didn't see. I turned around in my seat, looking at nothing. A full moon shone over the usual parked cars. I should've seen whatever he saw.

"Call now." Another order.

I dialed immediately.

We pulled off of the curb as Pixie's voicemail kicked on. I delivered the message as calmly as I could manage. Panic spread through me, harder to conceal with each word. I couldn't be positive, because I was talking, but it seemed like he spoke to himself as I followed orders.

I thought I heard, "Should have gone with your father."

We sped away from my street. My heart ached for Pixie to answer. I'd just spoken with her an hour earlier. I knew she was fine, but all things considered, I was terrified.

"What did she say?"

"I don't know. Nothing. I mean I got her voicemail." I looked at him for reassurance. I hoped he'd say she'd call right back, don't worry, but he didn't. I couldn't grasp why we'd fled my street or why he didn't explain.

"Try her again." Authority filled his voice.

Panic coursed through me. Pixie.

A minute later I looked back to him. "No," I whispered. "Just music and then voicemail."

A curse escaped his beautiful lips and seemed to sit there, not belonging.

"Stay here," he instructed. We were outside the main building on campus already. Several dozen assorted students, faculty, and parents stood in clusters setting things in motion for the weekend festivities. He wanted me to do what, decorate?

"There are at least two members of my team here tonight watching the crowds. You'll be safe if you stay with the crowd. Do you understand?" He waited for me to nod.

My countenance must've shown utter confusion because he leaned over me and pushed the door open.

His gun, missing from its holster, was nestled in his waistband, beneath the loosely fitting jacket.

He would end him. The words appeared in my brain. Fear grabbed me by the shoulders. I turned stiffly in my seat and got out.

Nicholas drove away too fast, drawing attention my way. I ducked into a shadow and tried to blend. In the darkness, it wasn't as difficult as I had imagined. However, I'd been warned to stay in a crowd. I joined the largest group I saw. Then, under harsh security lighting, I helped scoop goo out of pumpkins and string twinkle lights through gourds. All the while wondering which of my fellow decorators were undercover U.S. Marshals, if one might be a serial killer, and what was happening to Nicholas?

Chapter Fifteen

My mind hit overdrive and locked. I didn't know who to be more afraid for, Pixie or Nicholas. I knew Nicholas could take care of himself, but I also knew he sought danger. Something had spooked him enough to cause him to drop me off and peel out. A myriad of horrific things could be happening to the people I cared about most. Emotion threatened to overtake me.

Meandering through the crowd, I took notice of faces and interactions. Kate stood in a circle of adults and two children, smiling. Aubrie and Darcy laughed at a man old enough to be their grandfather. Lacrosse players and a mix of students from my classes shared popcorn with people I presumed to be their families. Did my dad and I look the same to others when we were together? I knew most of the teachers' faces. A handful of groundskeepers dipped and moved near the tables, filling trash bags with cast-off pumpkin parts and delivering wheelbarrows of mums. The groundskeeper from my wall stared at me through the crowd. Under the circumstances, the thought of talking with him knotted my stomach. I hid behind a tree to catch my breath. When I looked back, he was gone.

If there were hidden Marshals watching, I couldn't identify them. The tops of the buildings were clear, no sharpshooters or men with giant binoculars. The faces I didn't recognize were too young to be on assignment. Unless Nicholas's team was as young as he was. I made a second attempt to find the faces that didn't belong. They all seemed at ease, part of the picture.

Twenty minutes later, I caved. I tried Pixie's phone again. Someone answered but didn't speak. I held my breath, deciding if I should say something or hang up. I had to know if she was safe. I took a deep breath, prepared to force the word from between tight lips. "Pixie?"

"Elle? Where are you?" Nicholas answered. His voice had a sharp edge beneath the calm.

"Nicholas?" The thrill in my voice washed through me. For a moment, the killer didn't exist. Only Nicholas. Nothing else mattered. Then, for the briefest of moments, I hoped he and the stalker weren't one and the same. Silly, of course. I'd seen his badge. Unless it was a fake, or Marshals could also be killers. I chewed my lip and looked again for other "Marshals" in the crowd.

"Are you safe? Is Pixie? Can I talk to her?" I rambled through the words, not knowing what to ask first, pushing awful thoughts aside.

"She's not here, Elle." Loud rustling preceded a few thumps and the slam of his Jeep door. "I found her purse on the sofa. Her phone rang and I answered."

"Where are you now?" I looked around. Could he have her? What if he wasn't who I thought? The Internet could be wrong, couldn't it? Tears slid over my cheeks. I had no idea what was real. Pixie had had her purse an hour ago. Where was she?

"On my way. Stay with the crowd. I'll be there in three-and-a-half minutes."

The phone disconnected. I stood statue still, waiting for collapse. I stumbled back into the crowd, hoping to look natural, marveling that I stayed upright.

My fingers tingled. I clenched and released fists at my side, eyes glued to the road in search of the Jeep's headlights. Would his headlights represent my rescue party or my end? When they appeared, my muscles tensed. My feet begged to run. My brain commanded them to stay. I needed to remain in the crowd. Anchored to the ground, I waited. The Jeep seemed to move in slow motion during the longest minutes in history.

I expected him to stop along the curb. I should've known better. He came within a few feet of me. The crowd dispersed in my general area. Everyone watched as the door popped open, and I ran to get inside. He'd disabled the interior light. I doubted anyone saw Nicholas. He'd need a new car, though. If he thought no one would know whom the Jeep belonged to, he was wrong.

The door had barely closed behind me before we were in motion. I grabbed the dashboard and hoped leaving with him was the right decision. Outside the guard gate, he pulled into a field and shut down the engine.

"Are you okay?" He looked much more dramatic than before. His eyes were too wide, perhaps with relief. The subdued expressions I'd grown used to had flared into what looked like barely tamped emotion.

"Yes. I was disemboweling pumpkins with a bunch of faculty and random citizens. *You* went to hunt a killer." I suppressed the urge to laugh again. My nerves were stretched to the brink.

"I'm fine. You're safe. We're good." He leaned across me and I completely stopped breathing. Pulling my seat belt back across my torso, he smiled.

"Thank you," I whispered.

"It's my job." The words were flat. My heart fell.

"Your job."

I turned my face away from him. The car didn't move. I jumped when he touched my chin with one long finger. "Chasing murderers is my job, Elle." He narrowed his eyes when I turned to him.

"Protecting you is much more than that. I told you. You've made it personal." His voice grew tender. His expression tightened.

"Even after you've gone to school in the fall and set up a new life for yourself, I'll still be protecting you. Do you understand?" His eyes smoldered. My heart swelled at the words. He shifted into gear, and we were gone.

I cleared my head to focus on the fact that he wanted to protect me always. It wasn't his job that compelled him. That, I liked. I didn't like hearing him talk about me leaving.

He turned toward me before beginning a new line of questions. "Do you know who Pixie is with now?"

"No."

"Do you know where she is?"

"Not now. An hour ago she was headed for the coffee shop in town. She wouldn't be there now."

"She didn't say anything to you about her plans?"

"No." For as much as Pixie and I talked, I knew little about her. The trunk full of designer clothes came to mind as a perfect example.

"Where does she spend most of her time? We'll make the rounds until we find her or someone who saw her tonight." Nicholas was in business mode.

"She goes to the art studio on the river a lot."

"Right."

I wasn't sure what he meant until the Jeep spun around, throwing me into the window. He cut across two side roads and arrived on the main strip leading to the studio. He'd been there enough to know the shortcuts, or he had the small town memorized. Either struck me as possible.

We turned off the road. "There." I pointed at Suzy Sunshine.

The Jeep swerved over grass, bypassing the small parking area altogether. He leaned over me again and shoved the door wide. "Get her out here alone, all right? You have two minutes."

A combination of many things flung me from the car. The night and the urgency in his voice, for starters. His strange departure and reemergence from my apartment topped the list. I jumped out and dashed through the crowd outside the studio. "Pixie!" I pushed my way along, searching, screaming over the loud bass pounding the wide oaken planks beneath me. A bewildered freshman pointed an uncertain finger toward the ladies' room.

"Pixie!" I yelled again, pushing the door open. She stood reapplying eyeliner and fluffing her pointy hair.

When she caught sight of my reflection in the mirror, she exploded. "Elle! OMG! I'm so stoked you came." She spun and threw her arms around my neck. "So, tell. How was the not going out? Spare no details, please. Come on, give it. All of it this time. No more half stories and goofy looks. I want details. Real details." She pulled back and looked into my face.

So many things circled in my mind. Could she see my visions of a campus killer? My obsession with a gorgeous U.S. Marshal? No. Maybe the possible home invasion was written on my forehead.

Her face wrinkled. She grabbed my hand and headed for the door. "Come on. Everyone's here."

I jumped, throwing myself between Pixie and the door. I only had two minutes, and I was sure I'd already used that up trying to find her. "Wait." My voice firmed up. "You have to come with me. Now. Let's go." I took the lead and she stopped cold.

"Hey." She pulled her hand free from mine. "How'd you get here?" Her smile widened. She swung the door open and somehow I followed her again. "Ah! Is he here? The one you didn't go out with?" She stopped short, causing me to bump into her. My eyes scanned the crowd. "He totally is. I knew it. He's here and I'm dying. Where'd you put him?" She spun around, her black babydoll top spinning with her. I clearly wasn't getting across the urgency I hoped to convey.

"Let's go." I didn't need to see him to know who'd spoken.

Nicholas pressed against me from behind, forcing me into her. We moved through a crowd that barely seemed to notice him, though he towered over 80 percent of the students present.

"What?" Pixie's exclamation made my ears ring despite the powerful bass beats. "I knew it. I knew it. You tried to hide it. You faker." Her head turned left and right trying to find eye contact over her shoulder as we moved steadily ahead. "I knew it when you two met this summer. You guys have a vibe. It's completely cosmic. Destiny." She beamed at her incredible insight and threw her arms wide in the night.

"Hey," someone groaned when her hand hit his cup.

Nicholas stayed so close that I wondered if there was a danger present that I didn't see. After whatever had gone on at our apartment, I worried danger might be everywhere. I needed to stop being oblivious to it. It'd help if Nicholas told me things. I held on to Pixie with my pointer finger hooked into her belt. I didn't want to risk losing her again. Wading through the crowd took time, even with Nicholas behind us. With a little direction, Pixie led the way to the Jeep.

At the Jeep, he took her drink and tossed it into the oversized vase on The Pier before getting inside. The vase was probably supposed to be art. That night, it served as a trash can.

"Get in." His voice came deep and low. She shot me a naughty look and climbed in, probably expecting a scandalous evening with the new guy. She had no idea.

As we pulled back onto the country road, the bass in my chest weakened, until it reduced to no more than a low bumping in the distance. My mind reeled at the number of kids who, though we had literally knocked them out of our way, had no idea we'd been there. An entire sea of people hadn't seen us. Abduction seemed a lot more plausible after the experience.

"Pixie," Nicholas broke the silence.

I tensed for what he might say.

"I'm sorry I've had to lie to you. I take full responsibility for that. I was never supposed to have contact with you, not in a causal manner."

"Look, it's fine." She dismissed him before she could have had any idea what she was forgiving. Life was too short to carry a grudge. "I understand. Dating in this student body is hard to keep quiet, but you can't resist my girl's mojo. Whatever. I'm cool." She bounced along to an inaudible beat, tapping a rhythm on her thighs with silver-crackled fingernails.

He made a face. It cracked me up. All the stress had my nerves tensed to spring. Laughter bubbled in my chest. My sanity needed a release. *My mojo.* I stifled the giggles as best I could. Nervous laughter was the worst affliction ever.

Nicholas rubbed his eyes more roughly than he should while driving. "Listen to me, Pixie. I'm a U.S. Marshal on assignment at Francine Frances. You're in danger, and I'm afraid you're leaving town immediately." He glanced at me for a response. My mouth fell open.

Pixie looked down behind us, paying zero attention.

"Pixie, did you hear me?"

"Yes. I'm in danger, and we're playing some sort of Halloween role-play, who done it, mystery game. Where're we going?" She glanced up.

"This is not a game, Priscilla. There's been an intruder in your apartment, and you cannot go back there. You're going home."

She shot me a nasty look, probably for telling him her real name, but I hadn't. We both stared at him.

"You said I can't go home because of an intruder. Get your game straight, Brian. Where'd you find my purse, by the way? I lost it after Elle called before." She scrolled around in her phone. "Hey, you called again." She rolled her eyes. "I missed it."

"The bag was at your apartment. Please try to pay attention, Priscilla."

"Nicholas," I began, but Pixie interrupted.

"Is that why you're calling me Priscilla? We all have new names for this? Why Nicholas, though? Blech." She stuck her finger in her mouth and pretended to vomit.

I couldn't take it. I started to giggle again. This time it trickled out.

"Hey, and also, someone stole my bag and returned it inside my apartment? What's that about? You guys aren't very good at this game. Did you make it up?"

"Nicholas *is* my name," he growled.

I snorted. I threw a hand over my mouth and nose, cursing my awful timing.

"Brian was an alias. I'm a United States Marshal assigned to a case that brought me here." His eyes slid from the rearview to mine and back.

I had to give him credit for fortitude. I would've given up. I did give up.

Pixie sighed and put her phone in her lap. She leaned between the two front seats, one elbow on each headrest. "Okay, what'd the intruder take?"

"Nothing." His voice was low, slow, unhappy. "He wanted to show me he could get to you, to prove he's in control."

"What's this?" She pulled my tiny pumpkin from behind the seats. It had a steel kabob spear through it.

I let out a gasp. I didn't need an explanation.

Nicholas gave another sidelong glance. "A warning."

What kind of person would hurt a little pumpkin? My eyebrows gathered together for support. I didn't think it looked like a warning. It looked more like a threat to me.

"Pixie," my voice cracked when I spoke. "He's serious. This is for real."

Silence filled the car as the Jeep wound through the mountains.

"The man I'm looking for was in your apartment tonight. He's dangerous. He's a sociopath, and he knows where you live. He broke the light on your stoop and closed your blinds. He waited for you." Nicholas's eyes sought Pixie's. "When I went to drop off Elle, I noticed. I went back, but he was gone. He left the pumpkin for me."

"The bag beneath your purse is yours. I wasn't sure what you'd need. I did my best to think of everything I'd want, if I were in your position. The rest will be sent to you once you're reestablished."

My eyes widened. Could he be serious? She had to leave right now? He had tossed some random things into a duffle bag. She had to be thankful for as much and just go? My stomach fell. The same feeling I had when an elevator dropped a few feet before the door opened. I hated this for her.

"The story will be that there was a small fire in your apartment. You received minor injuries. Your parents brought you home to finish your senior year. They don't know you're coming. We aren't certain if you are or are not safe. If it's determined you're in danger, you won't be able to tell your parents where you've gone."

I shot him a horrified look. I couldn't imagine what might be going through Pixie's mind.

"There's a solid chance you'll be safe. As far as I could tell, the two of you spent very little time together outside the apartment. It's unlikely the Reaper will see you as a point of contact in the future. In which case, you'll be able to contact your parents and anyone else you choose in a few weeks." While I thought that through, he looked at me. "No one from Francine Frances."

The urge to vomit hit like someone pulling my stomach out though my belly button. The Reaper. That was the name of the man who'd killed all those women a decade back. I'd read about him at the library. Nicholas knew it. I swallowed bile and cracked the window for air. My face burned. My neck and cheeks stung. The Reaper had been in my apartment. He had watched us, followed us, and was close enough to Pixie to take her bag. He was right outside my bedroom door. I let my head fall back against the headrest and allowed the night air to wash over me. Gone went the previous images of a dorky peeping Tom on campus. My eyes sought Pixie's in the mirror.

Her pale white face looked even whiter in the dim interior glow. "You said I'm going home?"

"Back to L.A."

"You're from L.A.?" My head popped up and then fell back, sick, against the headrest. I couldn't believe she wouldn't have told me something like that. She knew how badly I wanted to go somewhere exactly like L.A. I could've asked her a thousand questions these past months.

Her lids grew heavy. "Yeah. It was great." She groaned.

I forgot.

She hated her previous life.

"Here. This will help." Nicholas tossed her an envelope from the driver's-side door.

"Ahhh!" Her squeal pierced my head.

I covered my ears against the assault. Jeez. Were hound dogs howling in the distance?

"Are you kidding?" She bounced all over the backseat and then attempted to hug him around his neck, while he drove, at night. I grabbed the wheel. He peeled her arms away.

"I'm in. When? How?"

"I applied for you this summer. I sent recommendations from your teachers at Francine Frances and samples of your work from the portfolio you keep on campus. They loved your work and offered early acceptance. It's an open invitation. You can begin immediately. Campus housing is set aside. The academy will send your transcripts and diploma in a few weeks. You must know you've had enough credits to graduate for a year."

My mouth hung open. Did I know anything about this girl? About Nicholas? "How long have you been watching us? How long before we met?"

"A while." The answer came without thought. An automated response. Our eyes met, and he cleared his throat. "You never left the apartment. I started with Pixie."

"Wait. So, you're not a student? What are you again?" Finally, she tried to catch up.

"I'm truly sorry for the deception. I mean that, but it was necessary. I'm here to monitor a threat, but it seems Elle's the only one who's actually seen him. I'm failing." He drummed his thumbs against the wheel. My heart clenched. He blamed himself for her upheaval. He should've been proud of himself for keeping her safe.

"You've seen him?" Her voice hiked a few decibels.

I rolled my head to the side and nodded her way. "He was in our apartment when I got out of the shower."

She swallowed.

"You said I might be safe in L.A.? Does that mean I might also be in danger there, all the way across the country? What kind of threat are we talking about here?"

"The worst kind." Nicholas stole a glance in the rearview and then looked at me. "And, I didn't say 'might.' I said there's a solid chance you'll be safe. That constitutes a big difference in my world."

"Oh, sure." Her tone turned to disbelief. "Why exactly would I be in danger all the way across the country? Why am I in danger here? How do the two correlate?" Her questions gained momentum.

"I'm sorry. That's classified."

I twisted in my seat to say something but couldn't find any words. She sat back and pulled her giant bag onto her lap and wrapped her arms around it like a teddy bear. "Did I do something?"

I felt another "that's classified" coming on, so I spoke up. "This person, he's barely that. He's a monster. He's crazy and evil and he tortures women. I read about him in the papers when I was doing our Sociology paper."

I glared at Nicholas.

He'd failed to point out it was the same man who hunted on our campus. That little tidbit would've been nice to know. "According to the paper, the killer was in his early thirties when I lived in D.C. Reports speculated he's an educated white male, of average build, average looking. The articles said he was probably wealthy, or grew up around money, which allowed him to not seem out of place when he approached his victims. The girls he took always came from upscale areas. He picked young, smart, good girls. He found them at prep schools, country clubs, and sports events where they competed in lacrosse, golf, tennis, and equine events. Of course, everything was based on speculation. The police hadn't caught him, but one FBI agent in D.C. claimed to be close to identifying him.

"The media nicknamed him the Reaper for the way he treated his victims, and warned women to avoid men who fit the description. The FBI promised to apprehend him. They were close, but they never got him. Instead, the agent in charge and his family were killed in a car accident. The case fell apart without him. It was something made for the big screen, one of those things that don't really happen. Except they do." I shook my head. Classified. A serial killer on campus, and they told no one. Yeah. There would've been a mass exodus. Possibly a couple hundred lawsuits.

I hadn't realized how often I'd thought of the Reaper since I read the articles. Details and facts from the stories flooded back to me.

"You'll be in witness protection until we can determine that the threat is minimal or resolved." He took a short breath. "This requires a great amount of restraint on your part. Can you understand? Your life might depend upon it."

I considered the tone in his voice, assured but soft. He seemed to hate to say the words.

When I turned again, Pixie locked eyes with me and nodded. "So, do people do this a lot?"

"You mean, are you alone? No. Absolutely not. Some people do this with no provocation. It might make it easier to think of it that way, as if it was your choice to start fresh."

I twisted my head and struggled to see her better in the dark. She lifted a finger in my direction. "Processing."

I understood. Until recently, I'd spent a large portion of my days processing. Lately, I'd dropped it cold turkey. I replaced the bulk of my obsessive thoughts of failure and remorse with ones of Nicholas. Hopeful thoughts. Now this.

The Jeep slowed and he hit the blinker. We waited for a logging truck to pass then made a left onto a small asphalt road. A metal chainlink fence stood on either side of the road leading to a small lot. Lights illuminated the white-lined asphalt and revealed the nature of our location. We were at a small airport I didn't know existed. The lot was tiny, reminding me of a flight school more than a functioning airport.

"This plane will take you to Hopkins International where you'll be briefed on anything else you need to know." He pointed out the window at an aircraft the size of a shoebox. Then he reached across me to open the glove box. He handed her an envelope filled with money and some other documents I couldn't make out.

With one hand on the wheel, he angled the Jeep into a space near the building and shifted into park. Nicholas stepped out of the car and made an arm circle. A minute later a man approached. He wore a suit and nodded to Nicholas, who looked like any jock at my old high school.

"Take your time," he said. The two men moved out of earshot.

I opened my door and walked on wobbly knees to the back of the Jeep. Nothing made sense anymore.

"I can't believe this," Pixie whispered, closing her door and joining me behind the Jeep.

"I know what you mean. I would've liked to stay with you this year. You're the closest thing to a friend I've had in years, probably the best friend I'll ever have." I laughed nervously as a tear spilled over one lid. She threw her tiny arms around me and pulled me close.

"You're the best friend anyone ever had. I'll write you the minute they say I can. Promise." She sniffled in my ear. "You can visit. You'd love L.A. It's amazing and warm and noisy, all your favorite things." Pixie wiped her eyes and vibrated in place.

"I promise. I'll come the minute I'm allowed." I blinked back tears.

Her whole existence evaporated from under her.

What would I do? In the past half-hour she'd learned a murderer had stalked her, stolen her bag, and let himself into our apartment. Something like that had to require therapy. At the drop of a hat, boom, off to start a new life, possibly without telling her parents. It was more than I could process. Too fast. This man, the Reaper, had followed me looking for her. Good thing I hadn't spent more time with her outside of school. It might've been what kept her safe for so long.

"I'm going to UCLA." Shock flashed under the awe. "I'm going to college, like now, right now!" She started to bounce again. I let her go. She had no attachment to her family. Art was her life. She hated the Midwest. Now, she'd live her dream. A fresh start. No parents. I guess there was an upside, for her. Plus, she loved the drama, the change. She embraced things that scared everyone else. I hoped she'd find an anchor in L.A.

Nicholas stood a few feet away, waiting. She released me and moved to him. A moment later, Pixie boarded the plane. The guard drew the stairs in behind them. I waved goodbye to a tiny oval window behind the pilot and hoped she saw me. Just like that, she was gone.

Nicholas's arm wound through mine. He pulled me to him and we watched the plane disappear across the sky. I turned instinctively and buried my face against his broad chest. The gun beneath his jacket bulged.

He patted my hair softly and brushed it away from my eyes. "Elle, I'll protect you." The sincerity in his voice stung my eyes.

The confusion in my heart killed me. I believed, now, that he wasn't the one stalking our school. His signals left a lot to be desired, though.

We walked back to his Jeep. He took everything out of it before heading toward the building. I followed silently. I had no words, so I went through the motions. I'd catch on when things became evident. No more investigating for me.

Inside, he traded in the Jeep keys for others. We walked back into the lot, and he loaded everything into a small SUV while I followed along in a vegetative state. "Are you wondering what happens now?"

I nodded.

"You'll finish your senior year as planned. You'll go along with the story about the fire. Tell people you're staying with a relative off campus."

"What?" I gasped. "No witness protection for me?" My joke flopped.

He froze, and it reminded me of another question. One that had come to mind earlier, when I had been too nauseated to speak.

"Do all Marshals relocate people? You already had a new life ready for her, just in case?" It didn't make sense. Did he have a new life ready for every girl at our school? Impossible. I reasoned the danger was specific to Pixie and probably classified.

The look he gave me sent chills over my skin. I couldn't fathom what it meant, but I knew it was bad. My eyes darted away from his face, from the look. There was a long silence.

"You'll be protected by me. Unless . . . " He puffed his cheeks out. "Are you morally opposed to cohabitation?"

Chapter Sixteen

"I'm sorry, but I don't have a better plan."

Driving away from the airport made it official. I'd never see Pixie again.

"What?" A tear slipped from my eye. I wanted to stamp my foot. What would Pixie's parents think when they called to check in on her and found her in California? I tried to remember her taking a call from her mom and couldn't. I knew, without a doubt, my father would blow a gasket.

"You have to stay with me until I can make better arrangements. I'm sorry about that. My team's working on it. It won't be forever. They know . . . "

Wait. My brain reversed through his words. What did he say? The alarm on his face frightened me. I breathed on the cool glass window inside the vehicle and watched it blush in response. Aimlessly, I doodled swirls and patterns in the steam. My mind wanted to reject the entire evening, from start to finish. It simply wasn't real. I didn't want to look at him.

"I know it's nothing like home, but since you don't sleep anyway."

"I miss my mom."

Silence.

"She was in some kind of accident on her way home from work one night. Dad's never been willing to give me any details. He pretty much forbade me to ask years ago." I was unable to stop. "It never sat right with me. All this craziness with the Reaper and a stalker and you has me dwelling on things I don't understand. I get these feelings I can't explain. Like déjà vu but obviously not." I blinked out a tear and scrubbed it off my cheek.

Something about the anxiety of the night, and losing Pixie, made me feel raw, exposed. A geyser built in my heart. "It was probably a good thing I didn't have more ammunition." I stroked my fingertips again through the steam on the window. "I know myself well enough to know I'd have used every detail to punish myself. I'd try to picture it, her death, if I had details. I'm a master at self-imposed torture."

Something tugged at me. A tear slid down my cheek. I rubbed it off with my sleeve.

We pulled into his driveway sometime after midnight. He went ahead of me, into the house, turning on lights and securing the area. He had a large black duffle over his shoulder. One he'd moved from the back of his Jeep at the airport. Inside, he took me from room to room, showing me the details, the light switches, where to find the land line, and then instructed me never to use the land line. He gave me a new cell phone and disassembled mine. I went to the kitchen to make coffee. When I got back, he was hauling blankets and pillows from the bedroom.

I followed after him to thank him for doing that for me. When I got to his room, the bed was still made. I did a double take. My pillow was on top of the bed. My toiletries were on the nightstand and a duffle of my things sat on the dresser.

"Are you making coffee?" The scent made its way through the house.

My hands trembled. I needed it. Shame heated my cheeks. I'd helped myself. Faced with the decision, I'd rather be a rude coffee snatcher than have him know how much I needed it. Plus, the absence had given him time to make up his room for me.

"Yeah, but you can go to bed. I won't keep you up. I just . . . I don't sleep well."

"Why is that? You've never said." The look on his face was so full of concern that I folded. Even with a serial killer on the loose, he wasn't on his laptop working. He was worried about my rest.

"Um, I have nightmares. Well, one nightmare, every night, or most nights." I looked up to see how he'd react.

He sat on the bed.

I sat, too.

"What about?"

"I don't know. I'm afraid. Whatever is happening isn't totally clear. I know I'm in danger or someone I love is in danger. The panic's there, but the reasoning isn't. It's like in a scary movie when the maniacal music begins, but you don't see the danger yet. You just know something's wrong, and you're afraid for the girl. In my dream, I'm the girl."

Without saying a word, he reached out for me and pulled me sideways under his arm. He held me without speaking, and I was at ease. After too short a time, he released me. "Come on, let's get some coffee."

He led me back to the living room. "Keep talking."

I took one very deep breath and blew it out slowly. This was it. "I can't really say when the dream started. It feels like it's always been a part of life for me, but I know that's not true. I lost my mom when I was young. That's what triggered the dream, I think. A child really isn't equipped to deal with that sort of loss, you know?"

I looked up. Nicholas retrieved some mugs from the cupboards in the kitchen. I snuggled into the soft cushions of the couch.

"It's the most tragic kind, I think, losing your mother. I was too small to really understand."

Nicholas had his back to me.

"That's actually just a theory of mine. The argument I have against my theory is I'm no longer a child. I'm more than able to understand the loss, but it doesn't stop the dream."

"What are you doing about it?"

"Well, I've adjusted."

He chuckled.

"No amount of therapy seemed to be effective in remedying the problem, and I've had my fair share of therapy. So, I took a new approach."

His eyes widened.

"I decided if I couldn't exorcise the thing, then I'd have to live with it. In about ninth grade, I started to treat the dream like a disease, a treatable illness. Dreams can't kill me, so I chose to endure. I accepted the fact I'll never get the recommended eight hours of rest. My nerves will forever be on edge from caffeine and sleep deprivation. I ditched counseling and picked up an expensive coffee habit."

"Cheers." He handed me a large green mug.

"I think if I knew what has me running for my life every night, maybe I could confront it." I shrugged, sipping the coffee. "I'm not a confrontational person, but I'm willing to do anything for a little sleep. The dream is my nemesis. Other people my age sleep." I made a face.

Nicholas smiled. The effort didn't make it to his eyes.

"My phone. My dad," I gasped. The light bulb in my head must've been on a delay switch.

"All calls to your old number will ring on this phone. I added a few dozen songs, so you have some to start with. Add anything you like." He twisted my new phone in his hands. He'd anticipated my reaction before it hit me. "My number's in there." He set the phone on the coffee table. That nugget helped sell me on the phone a little more than the first explanation.

"Oh."

"That's my mother." He looked at the frame I held in my hands. "As if it's not obvious."

He was right. They looked alike. I looked nothing like my dad.

"Are you worried about your father?"

"Yeah."

No, I was thinking about how much I missed my mother, though I didn't remember her. Change the subject. "So, you always wanted to be a Marshal?"

"No. I didn't know what I wanted to do for a long time. I knew it would be something like this because of my legacy."

He had a legacy? I didn't know any of my relatives, other than Dad. I didn't really know him either. In a way, being in witness protection would be an easy transition for me. I already had nothing to leave behind.

"When I turned eighteen, I followed the path of every other Austin man and went into the military. Unfortunately for me, it was war time."

"When you got out, you became a Marshal?"

"Yeah. Being a veteran helped a lot. Plus, it's always good to know people."

"Your family."

"Yeah."

"What about you, Elle. What do you want to do?"

"I'd like to go to law school." It was my standard answer. Truthfully, I'd like to be a mother. If I couldn't have one, I thought I'd appreciate being a mom more than most women did.

"Have you always wanted to be a lawyer?"

"No."

I squeezed my eyes shut, but the tears fell anyway. How many times had he seen me cry this week? *Ugh.*

"Hey, listen, it's okay to be afraid. That's normal. This is all new to you. It's scary. I get that, but it will be okay."

I blinked away a few tears.

"This guy is elusive, but he's not unattainable."

I rolled my eyes. "It's been fourteen years. That has to count for something."

"It's made him overconfident. He's bound to trip up." Something was off in his expression. He continued a little too quickly. "He began fourteen years ago, but from the best we can tell, he hasn't murdered anyone in a decade, so he's out of practice, too."

"Or he's really improved. What was he doing all those years?"

Nicholas walked back to the kitchen for a refill, but I'd hardly seen him take two sips from his mug. He appeared to be hiding something.

"Nicholas? Do you know what he was doing?"

"Yes."

He turned at the waist. His eyes avoided mine. He *was* hiding something. My pulse picked up speed. I followed after him. I laid a hand on his arm.

"Stalking." His voice came in a hoarse whisper. His breath reached my face and my knees went weak.

I closed the small distance between us and stretched up onto my tiptoes. Nicholas leaned into the counter. I faced all six-and-a-half feet of him. Timidly, I trailed my hands up his chest, over his soft tee, and beyond his shoulders. I wasn't positive what I expected to happen next. Boldness and I weren't close. What I wanted and what I expected rarely lined up. More than anything, I wanted to be safe. Nicholas was safety. If he held me, nothing could hurt me. I stretched further.

"Who?" I let the warmth of my breath coat his skin.

He lifted his chin high, looking over the top of my head. Defeat fell into the pit of my stomach. He rejected me, until all at once, he didn't. His face turned downward without warning, and our lips connected like two magnets drawn together. Whatever held us apart before had snapped without warning. Nicholas had let go.

I felt small in his arms. He towered over me, his shoulders twice as wide as mine. The contrast of us sent chills down my back, and the smallest sound I ever heard escaped my lips. He tightened his hold on me in response, pulling me closer still, kissing me with a passion I'd never imagined. I'd seen a thousand kisses, in life, on television, but they hadn't prepared me. Blood boiled and raced beneath my skin. I was fevered and frenzied. His hands moved over my back, into my hair and clutched softly. I did the same in response. I held on for fear he'd disappear.

As my fingers wound tightly in his soft brown hair, he pulled his lips away, kissing me softly once on the cheek and then resting his head against the top of mine. His scent enveloped me—soap, musky cologne, minty breath. A deep sigh blew free from his chest. His heart beat hard beneath my ear. His hands splayed over my lower back and they covered the width of me. All the tiptoeing had pulled my sweater away from my jeans enough for his fingers to land on bare skin.

With caution, I raised my face, seeking his. I had to know his reaction. How had he responded to the kiss that overshadowed every single experience I'd ever had?

"I'm sorry." His eyes were closed.

"I'm not."

"I'm supposed to protect you. I can't seem to get that right. I'm failing at this assignment, and your life depends on me." He tightened his hold of me.

"I'm making this harder." What began as an attraction to his incredible face had morphed entirely. I wanted to be with him, near him. He was suddenly my best friend, my confidant, and my makeshift family.

I loved that he had a family he appreciated. I loved the respect he showed them, me, and everyone I'd ever seen him come in contact with. He was a guardian, my protector. His kindness contrasted strangely with his military training and the gun wedged in his waistband.

"Yes, infinitely, yes."

I frowned.

When his eyes opened, they sparkled. "Ugh, Elle. I'm losing it. You can't imagine the struggle I'm having, the struggle I've been having." His eyes looked wild, like Pixie's when she got really amped up about something.

"I need to turn this case over to someone who's not in . . . " he trailed off for a moment, " . . . volved with the subject, but I can't. I can't trust your safety to anyone else because I need to know you're safe, every minute, and I need to be with you for that. It's wrong to stay, but I can't leave." He stroked my hair behind my ear. "I won't leave you, Elle."

"There are a number of reasons why I need to keep my hands to myself." He used his business voice. "It's unprofessional, extremely distracting, and *illegal*. Would you forgive me if I kept a distance until we capture the bad guy? I have to try to focus." His lopsided smile sent a shiver over my arms.

"I make no promises." That was the best I could do. "Living here will make things more complicated." I liked the way it played out in my head.

"Slightly." He raised his hands from me. I took one baby step away. He rubbed his face, and I smiled.

"I won't leave you, Elle, and it'll be okay."

"You can't know that." I hoped somehow he could.

"I believe it." He snapped back up beside me.

"How?" My heart spiked. Life was not a fairy tale. I found it hard to believe in happy endings.

Nicholas looked adorably mischievous. His deep green eyes sparkled. His enthusiasm was contagious. He made everything seem easier.

"I need to keep my head straight and you'll be safe." Then he nodded and winked.

I blushed.

He rubbed his face some more.

I reached for his hand. With all the bravery I could muster, I let my fingertips trace the lines of Indian ink peeking from beneath the sleeve of his T-shirt. He lifted the sleeve with his free hand and hooked it over his shoulder, allowing me to explore one of his secrets.

"An armband of barbed wire."

"Yeah."

"What's the number mean?" The lines coiled and twisted over one another, most ending in sharp points, while a few morphed carefully into dangerous-looking numbers.

"My men." He pulled me to him and told me things I longed to hear. He wanted me to know him.

"How do you do this?"

"What?"

"How do you date? How can you get close to anyone when you're always moving, changing names, keeping secrets?"

"How do you?" He posed the question back to me, though it only partially applied.

I still got it. "I don't."

"Same here."

"I've never met anyone I wanted to be with, though."

"Neither have I."

"Come on. You can tell me. It ends in a train wreck, right?" No way the man standing in front of me had never been in a relationship. Women must throw themselves at him. I was pretty sure that was what I was doing.

He leaned back against the counter and looked at the ceiling. "Let's see. I attended an all-boys military academy, followed by the Marines, where I was in a war zone . . . "

"There are women in the Marines. You've had enough time to be involved with someone."

He ran one huge hand up my arm and back. The sight of the sinewy muscles in his forearm gave me goose bumps.

"I'm not saying I've dated as little as you," he looked at me strangely, "but I am saying nothing ever went anywhere. I never met anyone who could distract me from my focus. Girls were the side note to my life. Work was my life."

"I dated."

"I know." He appeased me.

"I did. I dated."

"No one worth documenting."

That was true enough, although it was an odd expression.

"Do you have any other questions before I turn in for the night?"

"You're going to bed already?"

"Elle, it's late. We have school in the morning."

I guffawed. School seemed a relatively stupid thing to bother with. I couldn't see the point.

"We have a façade to maintain. Brian." He flattened his hand against his chest. He nodded to me. "You'll need to play along with the story about the fire and stay in crowds. We'll meet at the wall after school, and we'll ride together. You're not going to have any privacy. Not for a while." He posed it carefully, as a warning. It sounded good to me.

"What about the fire? The Reaper knows there wasn't a fire."

He laughed. "Oh, there was a fire. You'll read all about it in the morning paper."

Chapter Seventeen

Reluctantly, I made my way to my new bedroom. Nicholas needed rest, and he wouldn't sleep if I stayed in the living room. It took me about three minutes of tossing and turning before I gave up and opened my laptop. I needed to know everything about the Reaper. I needed to know how much danger Nicholas was in and what he'd be facing every time he went out because his phone buzzed.

From what I could gather, the Reaper was barely human. Profilers assumed he'd probably had a normal upbringing with a sudden trauma that caused him to snap. I didn't buy it. I'd had a childhood trauma and I didn't murder people. Though, I suppose, I did snap. I didn't sleep. I had a nightmare come to life and haunt my days. The Reaper didn't internalize it like I did. He brimmed and overflowed with hate. His murders were too brutal to be fueled by anything else. Something triggered them, too.

Investigators didn't see the murders as random, though the girls had no connection to one another. There was a common theme. The girls were all like me. They were like everyone at the academy.

In some ways, the girls were likened to Holocaust victims because in addition to denying them food, he removed their identities. Their heads were always shaved. Their clothes were replaced with gunnysacks that he crudely cut arm and neck holes into. The media speculated but couldn't confirm allegations of other abuse. When the girl was barely recognizable, he removed her fingerprints by burning them off. He strangled them with surgical glove–covered hands. Then he dumped her body somewhere. I shuddered thinking of the tiny orange glow. I could almost hear the sounds of the cigarettes against their fingers, one by one. The screams of terrified girls. My stomach flipped, and I held it down with one hand while I scrolled on with the other.

The process from abduction to death took some time. When a girl fitting his preference went missing, investigators knew they had about ten days to find her. They never found her, not in time. I couldn't imagine what those girls went through. I thought of all those mothers at their homes, mourning their daughters. My chest literally ached from the pain.

I rubbed my shoulders, my throat, my head, to hold myself together. Sobs welled up. I began to shake violently. Panic fed the fire as my mind demanded that my body settle down. My room was only twenty feet from Nicholas. I couldn't have a mental breakdown. I buried my face in my pillow and wept.

I might have passed out from lack of oxygen, or maybe my body shut down to stop the attack. Either way, I woke six hours later to the smell of coffee. My hands trembled more than usual. It'd been hours since I'd had any coffee. *Hours.* I hadn't slept that long, ever.

Everything had changed.

It didn't take me any time to remember where I was and what was happening. That used to happen after a move. I'd wake up in a new bedroom and feel completely disoriented. I'd grown accustomed to new rooms over time.

I sat on the edge of the bed and ran my fingers through my hair. My hands trembled. I rubbed them heavily against my thighs. It didn't help. Hopefully the addiction could be eradicated if I started sleeping again.

I stood and shook my wrists at my sides before heading toward the kitchen. The bedroom door creaked. Scents of deliciousness drifted down the little hallway. Plates and cups clanked in the kitchen.

"I didn't know what you ate." He looked uncomfortable.

The island was covered in food: fruits, scrambled eggs, and giant muffins. I walked past them to the coffee. I had to stop trembling before he noticed.

"Elle, are you okay? Did something upset you?" He was beside me in an instant, easily reaching the mug I stretched toward. Nicholas took my hands in his and looked at them. He rubbed them vigorously between his, folded them, and pulled them to his chest. The look on his face disarmed me. He was afraid of something.

"I'm fine." I pulled my hands free and turned to hide my embarrassment.

"Your hands." He popped back into view, waiting.

"I have a caffeine addiction. You know that." I couldn't bring myself to look at him. I sipped the coffee and took a seat at the island.

"Caffeine?"

"I told you," my voice was soft, "I don't sleep well. I haven't for . . . I don't know. Forever. I consume way too much caffeine to stay awake all day. That has its own consequences. At home, I had pills to help, and a treadmill." I slid off the stool and headed away from him. I was mad that I had to have this conversation. He was perfect and I was a freak. He might as well know up front.

"Where're you going?" He spun on his heels and moved behind me.

"To change. I'm going to run before I get ready for school. Running helps." I shut the door in his face and pressed my back against it. Then I dressed quickly and sucked the rest of the coffee down, burning my throat as it went. I stopped in the bathroom to brush my teeth and pull my hair into a ponytail. I pressed a cold rag against my eyes to help with the puffiness. This was my new start. No more playing the victim. Time to take control of my life.

Back in my room, I grabbed my phone and set up my playlist. Then I walked straight out the front door without a word. I was sure he was watching, wherever he was.

Around back, I crossed the yard under the pergola and stopped to stretch on the riverbank. I locked my fingers under the toes of my shoes and felt the burn in my legs and back. I moved from side to side, recreating the stretch for each leg. Then, from a topsy-turvy vantage, I saw him appear.

Nicholas was dressed similar to myself, standing near the fire pit, waiting. I stopped mid-stretch. His body looked even more athletic in running pants and an oversized *Marines* hoodie. He had a black knit cap pulled over both ears and his nose was red.

The blood pooled in my forehead. Remembering I wasn't in a very favorable position, I stood upright too quickly. The movement caused me to falter backwards and land against the grassy hill behind me.

"Whoa!" He closed the distance in three long strides. "Are you okay?"

"No." My ego was fatally wounded. First, I had spent an eternity with my bottom in the air staring at him. Then I fell down. I was nothing but sexy. *Ugh.*

He pulled me up by my elbow. He smiled.

I grimaced. "Why's your face red?"

"You said you were going running." He looked confused.

"So?"

"I ran ahead about a half mile to check things out. It's fine. You're good."

"You ran a mile while I changed clothes?"

Jeez.

He smiled that smile that knocked the wind out of me.

"Shut up."

He'd heard the awe in my voice and gloated. I calculated his time. It couldn't have been more than ten minutes.

I ran along the riverbank until he stopped me. I'd been focused on the music, trying to ignore the articles about the Reaper I'd read the night before. Trying not to think about him jogging along behind me. At the half-mile point, he insisted I head back. My run was abbreviated, but my blood pumped hard. I turned like he asked, rejuvenated, ready to face the day.

The morning air beat cool and crisp off the river. Fall in Ohio was like being stuck inside a painting. The leaves left hanging in the trees were every shade from gold to purple. The fallen ones crunched under my shoes as I ran. The smell of autumn in the air made me smile. Fall had always been my favorite. I had a hard time accepting danger in such a beautiful world. My immediate surroundings resembled a storybook. With a monster lurking nearby, maybe I was Little Red Riding Hood.

Two bottles of water waited on the pergola. I grabbed one and pulled out my earbuds, ready to talk. It looked as if he'd been waiting for that.

"You slept last night. Did you dream?"

"No."

"No?" He looked relieved. "Good. I thought I'd have to hide your laptop."

A giggle burst from my lips.

His face was stern.

"I wanted to know who was after her. Do you blame me? Anyway, the research didn't give me nightmares." I sipped the cool water. The contrast caused a new burn in my throat. It took a few minutes to get my body temperature back to normal after the run.

"Well, now you know, but you can't dwell and make yourself unhappy. She's already gone. You have to focus on getting yourself through this emotionally."

I'd never seen him look so vulnerable, sad.

"I'll do everything else."

"We need to get this guy."

Nicholas smiled. "Yes."

"I searched for hours and I'm no clearer about one thing. I don't understand. Why her?"

His eyebrows crunched together. Clearly he didn't understand my question, but I didn't have a better way to articulate it.

I tried repetition for clarity. "Why her? Why Pixie?"

"Pixie?" He let out a whole chestful of air. He'd apparently stopped breathing at some point.

"Yes, Pixie. Who do you think I'm talking about? Is this a game? What's happening? I swear, sometimes I feel like we're having two separate conversations. This isn't the first time."

"This isn't a game. I'm sorry. You confused me for a second. This situation has moved beyond complicated to insane. I promise you, I'm not trying to be coy or difficult."

I softened for a moment at his sincerity. It didn't last.

"The answer to what you asked is classified."

I threw my arms into the air and jogged up to the house. *Classified.* Pft. I stomped through the house then took my time in the shower so he'd have to rush to get ready on time. I refused to care that he'd have to take a short shower. Maybe a cold one. Soaking under the streaming hot water loosened the knotted frustration in my back and shoulders. I stepped out in a better mood than when I got in. Steam hung thick in the air. I wrung the water from my hair and rubbed a strip on the mirror so I could see.

I took my time combing out my tangles and brushing my teeth, but even I couldn't put on makeup in the steamy conditions. I headed back to my room wrapped in a giant white towel made in heaven. Nicholas waited in the hall.

"Elle!" He threw his hand up to cover his face. "What took you so long?" His fingers widened over his eyes. "You were in there forever. I expected you to come out ready to leave. Where's your uniform?"

"In my room. I see you peeking." I wanted to stay mad at him, but disarming the tough guy was fun. Before he got past the towel to see I had no makeup on and my hair sopped over my shoulders, I moved on. "Excuse me." I brushed past him and headed down the tiny hallway. When I grabbed the bedroom doorknob, I spun around.

His eyes widened and his cheeks darkened. Let him think about that in the shower.

My uniform took two minutes to put on and so did my makeup. My hair was another story. He hadn't thought to grab my blow dryer, and he didn't have one. I twisted my hair up and secured it with pins I fished out of the bottom of my bag. Then I packed up and waited on my bed until the bathroom door opened.

"Clothes." He motioned with his hands to his ensemble. He shook his head and walked toward the kitchen. When I got there, he handed me an apple and took my bag. He slung the bag over his shoulder and put a bottle of water in my free hand. He poured himself a mug of coffee.

I made a point of staring at the coffee. I imagined he thought coffee wasn't good for me. "I had a cold shower." He held the cup near his cheek as if it could warm him. I poured my own to-go cup.

We walked to the SUV in silence. The interior felt strange. I'd accepted a Jeep as his vehicle. It fit. The SUV reminded me of the reason for the Jeep's replacement. I played around with the inside temperature while we drove.

"Are you ready for this?" It was the same thing Pixie had asked me on my first day at Francine Frances. It seemed like years ago instead of a couple of months.

"Absolutely, Brian." I nodded, looking straight ahead. Remembering to call him that worried me. Truth be told, remembering my own name might prove difficult. Not the senior year I had expected.

"Do you want to talk about anything you read last night?"

"No. All the things I want to know are classified. Everything else was in the old papers. The only thing that matters now is that he's stopped." I should've expected he'd monitor the Internet. I knew the new phone monitored my calls, too. He didn't have to say it. I watched prime time. Without Pixie, I'd only call my dad. Nothing scandalous there. Phone surveillance would put him to sleep.

He bit his lip and looked at me. "What're you doing for Thanksgiving?"

"I don't know what I'm doing this weekend, let alone in three weeks."

"Well, this weekend you're attending the fall festival at school. For Thanksgiving, I thought we'd go see your father."

Chapter Eighteen

There were no words for this insanity. First of all, being stalked by a killer seemed like a solid reason not to go to a festival. They needed to cancel that thing. Secondly, I didn't plan to go home for Thanksgiving. I didn't even know how to find our new home, and if I had to go, I certainly wasn't bringing a guy with me.

"Elle."

"You're joking, right? I'm not going to some festival. No one should go to that festival."

"They're reasonably safe. There's no reason to cancel the festival."

"Reasonably safe. Why? Because of the crowd? You're wrong. You'll see today."

The vehicle slowed. "What do you mean?"

"Well, we went to a party last night. We moved right through the center of a huge crowd, and no one saw us. If they did, and I'm wrong, then everyone will be gossiping about it today, but they didn't. I think a crowd is actually worse than having only one or two witnesses."

His mouth turned down at the corners. "Elle, in a crowd you have more people within an arm's length to grab onto. Get their attention.

If you're in danger, do whatever it takes to get someone's help. That's the point of a crowd. There are more opportunities for you." He shut his eyes then, though the SUV continued to move. He opened them. "We'll work on this. We'll start this afternoon."

"Nicholas." I'd been dying to ask him since he had dropped me off to decorate.

He glanced in my direction. The muscles in his arms clenched and his fingers tightened around the steering wheel. *A major overreaction.*

"Tell me about our apartment." I kept my eyes on the road, unsure of how much I wanted to hear.

"On the way to Ohio, I worried myself sick over how well I could protect you. Since the plane landed, I've done everything wrong. I had a strict no-contact order, which I've completely violated." He rubbed the back of his neck with one hand. "Now, circumstances have changed and I'm . . . "

"Involved."

He cleared his throat. "Nothing in my training says it's acceptable to have a personal relationship with the witness."

"The what?" I eyed him and watched for a response. I'd told him more than once that I hadn't seen the guy, only the glow. He usually dealt with witness-protection people. The slip reminded me how hard this assignment must be for him. He was forced out of his element. Not to mention returning to high school.

"Your curtains were closed."

"What?" How much of our conversation had I missed?

"You never close your curtains. Also, the stoop light was out. You always leave that on."

"Okay."

"I knew something had happened. I hoped I wouldn't find Pixie in there."

"What if the light had just burnt out?" I forced images of Pixie in a gunnysack from my mind.

"I had just changed it." He looked sideways at me. "Anyway, the curtains."

"Oh, right, the curtains." Did we leave the curtains open? Weird. I hadn't noticed.

"Glass was all over your stoop when I got there. Broken light. That's good for cover and a good way to let him know when you've made it up to the door. Stepping on glass is louder than you think."

I shivered and swallowed hard.

"I cleared every room. He wasn't there, but he'd killed your pumpkin."

"Thank you for the pumpkin." I'd never thanked him. "Then what?"

"I called my team and told them to set up a perimeter. We knew roughly where to start looking. They came and swept the apartment for any kind of clue or note or anything and staged the fire."

He looked my way and took a deep breath. "I gathered some things for you and Pixie, and I left. Well, you called Pixie's phone, we talked, and then I left. You know the rest from there."

"Okay. What else?" I wanted to be cool like him, but curiosity and I never got along. Besides, he already knew everything. I'd probably be more relaxed if I had the same details. "You knew he was in town."

"We suspected as much but needed confirmation."

"Tell me how you ended up here without confirmation. You must've had some reason to come. I have a theory."

Nicholas looked at his watch. The SUV coasted to the side of the road. A few yards into a random field, he shut down the engine and unlocked his seat belt. I followed his lead. He cocked his knee up on the seat between us.

"I was back home in D.C., shooting hoops in my mom's driveway with my brothers and a cousin, when I got assigned to this case. I'd just gotten home from a mission in Chicago, where I removed a threat to a family in witness protection. I relocated them again for the sake of due diligence."

I bit my tongue. I wanted these details.

"I celebrate with my family after every mission because they're crazy. Everyone gets together at my parents' house for a barbecue. Honestly, they're always on the lookout for a reason to throw a party. Anyway, the house brimmed with guests, and the street out front resembled a parking lot." He rolled his eyes and smiled. "I try not to take it for granted, but it can be nuts."

"We call ourselves a team." He laughed lightly. "Everyone plays their part, each one strengthens the whole. My great-grandparents started the team mentality when they arrived in New York after leaving Europe. They were in a new place and barely spoke the language. The way they got by was to be united with one another. It worked. They set a precedence that has been honored in every generation that followed."

"So, you'd gotten home from Chicago . . . "

"Protocol mandates a standard three-to-five-day break between assignments. This time, I guess, someone fudged the protocol because my phone rang before lunch.

"I never expected it to be anyone other than my partner wondering what he and his wife should bring to the cookout. Headquarters called me in, said I was reassigned—immediately."

I couldn't help notice he looked sad. He loved his family so much. I felt awful. He'd just gotten home and was sent out again. He'd been stuck in Ohio alone for months. How rotten.

"There were so many people. People on the lawn, on the deck, in the driveway. My parents like a crowd. Essentially, I missed my party because 'immediately' means 'right now.' I couldn't even dip home to shower and change. Everything had to wait until I got the details and went to pack. I handed the ball to my youngest brother and went inside to tell Mom." He raised an eyebrow.

I pictured what he described and pined for it. I needed to hear more. My eyes widened, telling him to go on.

He sighed. "I had to go to the station, wearing an 'I'm in Witness Protection' T-shirt Mom had bought me as a joke." He laughed. "I had on jeans with holes in the knees and back pocket. I didn't even pull on a pair of socks before I left. Let me tell you, I regretted the flip-flops every step of the way. They cracked hard against the marble steps on my way up to the office, and everyone heard me coming."

I had had my own experience with loud flip-flops. I nodded.

"My superior officer hates me. He glared at my outfit. He wore a perfectly pressed suit, properly shined shoes, the whole bit. He had never approved of me as a Marshal. It took him years to get into the program while I seemed to slide in on namesake, which isn't true. I'm qualified on paper. I have the credentials and the military training. I was born to do this. I know it, and I plan to prove it.

"Anyway, he led me into a big empty conference room and gave me the details of another break on the Reaper case. They wanted me on it, which is funny because they think of me as too young and inexperienced. This time, they needed someone who could blend. Youth came in handy. This case is their pet project. All the older guys were in my shoes back when the Reaper made his way across America. Now those agents are in positions of authority. There are new leads again, and they're bent on getting him this time. I think they think it'll validate them somehow if we catch him. They want to make up for the mess he caused."

"What's so special about this guy? I mean, I'm sure you see lots of similar lunatics. More criminals than the Reaper have gotten away."

"Well," he worked for the words. "My superiors witnessed the effects he had on one of the Bureau's agents and his family." He stopped short and worked his jaw. "The Reaper's the Bureau's equivalent of 'the one who got away.' Being assigned to this case is an honor.

"My grandfather ran the department when it all came to a head. He retired after, but he still talks about the Reaper. I couldn't wait to tell him about my assignment. I knew he'd be proud."

Another smile graced his face.

I smiled, too.

"For my briefing, they played a slide show. They showed me kids in uniforms in what looked like the Midwest. Cobblestone streets, small shops, pretty typical stuff for a safe location. Small towns are often chosen for families to begin again. I spend a lot of time in small-town America. Then I saw a shot of a girl inside a coffee shop."

"Was she cute?"

"Beautiful," he corrected.

"If you like the highly caffeinated and deeply crazy kind."

"The deeper the better."

I shook my head. "Go on."

"I had orders to maintain a safe distance. I was sworn to a strict no-contact order."

"Fail," I muttered, smiling widely out my side window.

"Uh, huge, epic fail. So much for vigilant and unseen."

"My dad just told me to be vigilant."

"He's a wise man."

"Hmph."

"I left three hours later. Here I am."

"You started what? Tailing all of us?"

"I started with Pixie, which led me to you." He chuckled. "The day you two went to the flea market I nearly ran out of gas. I started to think you were running away or something. You headed out of town and kept on going. It took you all of five minutes to separate. I realized then that my job would be harder than I imagined."

"Yeah, you used to buy me coffee." I eyed the travel mug in his holder.

"I used to have hot showers."

"Right."

"I didn't plan on talking to you, but when I got close, I couldn't help myself. I followed you to the coffee place, threw out my grandfather's name as mine, and promised myself it'd be the last time we spoke."

He shook his head and put his hands neatly in his lap.

"Fine. What else?"

"I felt like a major jerk for a long time after because I let you leave. I knew I'd be seeing you again, but you couldn't see me. I was forced to be 'that weird guy from the flea market who followed you around all day but didn't ask for your number,' in order to protect you. Of course, you didn't know why."

"Then you showed up at my new school."

His eyes lit up. "What a nightmare. When they gave me those orders, I nearly died. How was I supposed to pull that off casually? I couldn't tell them, 'Sorry, I went against orders already and spent the day talking to Gabriella Smith.' So, I sucked it up and hoped you wouldn't label me a predator and file a formal complaint with your school."

"Nice."

"Right?"

"You thought being a jerk to me would help things how?"

Nicholas pulled back onto the road and headed for Francine Frances. "I thought you'd be pissed and ignore me back. That didn't work."

"Not when you kept talking to me."

"You complicate my life." He slid an impish look my way.

I knew the rest of the story.

"Where's your partner now?"

He turned to me and smiled. "On assignment without me, I'm guessing. We relocate families together. The Reaper case is something else entirely. For this I have an entire team, and everything is classified."

The guard booth appeared from nowhere. The time had come to let go of Nicholas, my only friend, my guardian. I had to replace him with Brian, an oversized Ken doll with no personality.

I climbed out of the new vehicle near the fountain and walked directly through the front doors. From inside I watched Nicholas take the SUV around the building, to the lot.

I got started on my new normal immediately. First, to my locker to get ready. Then I took my things to the cafeteria. I bought a pop and sat down to study. I hadn't opened one of my texts all week. I'd pay for it soon enough. No prelaw program in the country would accept a student whose grades plummeted during her senior year.

Students trickled into the large room a few minutes later. One more thing to distract me from my grades. They laughed, oblivious and happy. A small circle of girls I recognized from The Pier formed nearby. I listened hard. They talked about music, boys, and their clothes, nothing more. When their voices dropped without warning, I shifted nervously. I was sure they'd seen me staring. I forced my eyes up, expecting them to glare at me for my poor manners, but they were focused on someone beyond my table. I felt sorry for the brunt of their gossip.

Carefully, I turned to retrieve a book from my bag. I hoped to steal a peek at the unfortunate soul. A giggle passed through my lips. I kept my head down until I'd recovered. Nicholas squatted before the large vending machine, pretending to make a tough decision. The girls enjoyed their view. His khakis stretched to accommodate the position, but the resulting fit was droolworthy. If he guarded the school, I had nothing to worry about. I went back to studying.

"Hey! Weren't you at The Pier last night?" an unfamiliar voice spoke. I jumped. From a few feet away, Nicholas's head snapped to look my way as well.

"Um, no. I haven't actually been out there in weeks." I was thankful for the lifetime of little lies like that one.

"Oh." The girl looked confused. She'd seen me. "You're Pixie's roommate, right?"

"Yes."

Several others made their way over to me. They carried copies of the school paper with them. They'd read the official report. There'd been a fire. Pixie had gone home to heal from minor injuries. I had moved in with family.

All the lie rehearsals were suddenly worth my effort. Student interest kept me recounting the story. I never knew how much they all loved Pixie. Nicholas even gave me bogus addresses for them to send e-mails and get-well letters. The student body cared about her. It was touching.

I missed Pixie, too, in a severe way. I wondered how she was doing and where she was. Her empty seat haunted me. I sat alone at lunch and during study hall. Wherever she was, she'd probably already made a dozen friends. Imagining her in the sun comforted me. Knowing she came from L.A. made a lot of sense really. She'd be great there.

Nicholas's team had been thorough with the charade. One girl said our apartment had crime tape draped over the door, and the curtains were charred. I found relief in knowing the only fire behind the crime tape came from my culinary attempts on the crappy old stove. I could've gone back there to stay. No one would've been any wiser, but Nicholas insisted the Reaper might return. He didn't think the fire would stop him from looking there for me.

I missed my things, but it could've been much worse. I pictured Pixie, bald and hungry, frightened and alone. At least she was safe and far away from the danger. Hopefully. The idea that this monster might've somehow followed her hollowed out my insides. She *had* to be okay.

Classes dragged on. Watching Nicholas pretend to be someone else annoyed me. I pictured him in his hoodie and knit cap earlier and compared the image to him near the chalkboard. He wore standard khaki pants and a white dress shirt and tie. His blazer hung over his chair and the white shirt teased beneath the lights. If he turned at the right angle, his tattoo was visible beneath the sleeves. Nicholas had said his friends had inked a barbed-wire armband when he left the service. An act of camaraderie and remembrance for one another and for those who didn't come home. He talked about them like they were frat buddies instead of men he'd guarded with his life. I knew it wrapped his ridiculous bicep at the fullest point, and I knew he was both proud and saddened to have it. Accepting the dual roles he played gave me a headache.

Again, I heard nothing my teachers said. I spent the day wondering what it was like to be one of his witnesses under protection. They lived an entire life of pretend. It disturbed me. How confusing, changing yourself again and again. They must struggle with who they really are beneath all the lies. I would.

After English, I tarried, allowing him time to come to me, if he needed. He did.

"Heard anything?"

"No, you?"

"Nothing out of place. They've seen the apartment and read the paper. They're taking it in stride. Life marches on." He sighed and looked at me more seriously. "You doing okay?"

"Yeah."

"She's fine, Elle. You don't need to worry about Pixie. She's setting up in a new place and she's embraced it. She'll handle this better than most people. She's strong, like you." He walked out of the room without me.

Davis knocked shoulders with him on his way around the corner. "I was worried when you didn't show up for coffee this morning." His face crumbled with relief.

"Oh, I'm so sorry. I completely forgot. I had no idea . . . " How to finish that sentence.

"No." His eyes widened. "I thought you ditched me for sure. Then I noticed Pixie was missing, too. I went over to your place to see if you guys had overslept or were sick or something. When I saw the fire, I almost hurled."

Then he hugged me like a child grabbing onto a beloved teddy. My arms mashed to my sides.

I laughed. "I'm fine."

"I can't believe you're at school. How's Pixie? I heard she was burnt pretty bad trying to put out the fire."

I hadn't heard that, but I liked the heroic legend she had left behind. In a couple of decades, kids might tell ghost stories about the ghost of the girl who died saving a hundred kids from the fire of the century.

"She's going to be okay." I knew it was true.

"Tell me everything." He whirled me away from his grip, leaving only one arm slung over my shoulders. We headed to my locker. Then he dropped me off for study hall. "Hey, I'll buy you lunch today." I'd never known a happier person in my life. Maybe Pixie.

"Deal."

Sitting alone on the carpet in study hall, I worked my way through the time since I arrived at Francine Frances. One thing grabbed me again and again.

"Why Pixie?" I scribbled. My pen doodled around the words on autopilot. When I snapped out of my confusion, I'd written "why" a dozen more times. From all I'd read about the Reaper, he chose girls in our situation, but never girls like Pixie. He picked ones like Priscilla, like every other face here. Pixie stood out. His girls didn't. They came from money like her, and the academy met his M.O., but he never picked wild art students, not even close.

My eyes moved around the room. Any of the other girls fit the description better than Pixie. I'd watched enough crime dramas to know killers didn't change their routines. I tried a bunch of scenarios. None fit. He might've followed her from her previous life, but she'd been at the academy for three years. He never took kids that young. Even as Priscilla, she wouldn't have caught his attention because she was only fifteen when she came to Francine Frances.

The other problem I had was his long-term disappearance. Why stop for so long then begin again? Killers had triggers. That's what they always said. This guy wasn't much younger than my dad, so I doubted he had problems with girls anymore. I couldn't picture him being normal for a decade and then one day thinking, "I'll go to Ohio and find a girl to kill." Dozens of schools like mine existed in better locations. For Pixie's sake, I hoped this wasn't personal.

I was no detective, but the facts didn't add up.

Chapter Nineteen

After school, I met Nicholas in the lot. I made it to the SUV before him and waited.

When he came into view, his phone was pressed to his cheek. A scowl ruined his beautiful features. When he saw me, he smiled.

My heart jumped in my chest. The problem with our situation was I had no idea which parts were real. How much was his job? How much was his heart?

He slid the phone into his pocket and came to me, leaning a little too close as he unlocked my door. The moment stole my breath. He pulled open the door and barely moved away. I had to slide inside. As I did, he whispered, "Let's go home."

The seat enveloped me. Time alone with him put me at ease. I dozed all the way back to our little house on the river.

When we pulled into the drive, he just sat there. He shut down the engine but made no move to leave.

When I woke up, he was poking at his phone, Bluetooth in ear, seat rolled back, one foot on the dash. The clock read 4:45.

I sat straight up and rubbed my eyes. "What're you doing?" His behavior was so illogical that I wondered if I might be dreaming.

"You fell asleep." He put his phone and Bluetooth inside his bag and turned in his seat. He wedged his knee between us and managed to look comfortable.

"So?"

"So, you never sleep. You crashed sitting straight up during a ten-minute drive. I let you rest."

"That's nuts." I needed the rest, but he shouldn't have sat there working from an uncomfortable driver's seat. Not because of me.

"I had plenty to work on from right here." His low voice relaxed me. "This must feel safer to you than a big empty room." He got out and walked around to my side of the car.

I climbed out awkwardly and stamped my foot that had fallen asleep. He took my bags from me and led the way inside. I flopped onto the couch. He headed to the kitchen. Pots and pans clanged. The refrigerator opened and closed.

"You don't have to take care of me like this." I felt like a baby again. "You're supposed to keep me safe, not monitor my happiness, my sleep, my nutrition . . . "

"I like to." He hummed along to an old rock anthem while he worked. Then he came to sit with me and offered me a tall glass of water. "I've always had family doing everything for me. I like being able to do things for someone else, for you."

With that all cleared up, he leaned in as if we were about to share a great secret. "Now, what's been on your mind all day? Something's rolling around in there. Every time I saw you today, you were contemplating, planning, diagnosing . . . I don't know what, and it's driving me insane. Please share."

I turned and faced him on the couch, deciding what to say. I wanted to talk with him as a friend. I wanted to sift through the things that didn't sit right with me, but I knew he couldn't do that. He wasn't my friend, not like that, and not when it came to this.

"Talk to me, Elle. I want to know what's going on with you. You keep so much hidden."

"Why Pixie?" I couldn't talk about this with him the way I wanted, and it upset me. I'd heard the word *classified* more than I could stand. *Classified* meant he knew more and wasn't telling. He had the information I wanted, but he wouldn't give it to me. We weren't in this together.

He slid against the back of the couch. The slouch made him look like a brooding teen. I honestly didn't feel so protected at the moment. He rubbed his face, elbows pointed to the ceiling.

"Well?"

"I don't know."

"She isn't like anyone else he ever took, and after all these years, why?"

"She isn't like the others. You're right. How much did you read about him?"

"I read enough to know that none of this makes any sense. Enough to know that he wouldn't have chosen someone as outstanding as Pixie. Why would he come here, to Nowhereland, to pick up where he left off?"

His lids grew heavy, as if he carried some great burden but refused to let me help with it. "Have you talked to your father yet about Thanksgiving?"

"Don't do that. Don't change the subject." I groaned. "You asked me to tell you what I'm thinking, and I did. Now help me understand."

He paused, apparently deciding if and how to handle my eruption. "What exactly are you saying?"

"I'm saying I don't think he was after Pixie. I'm saying I think you're wrong."

"Hey." He stood and took my hand. "We have work to do. We'll finish this later."

Just like I expected.

He stood facing me. "I need to think." He backed up a few steps so he didn't tower over me.

I looked up with my best mean face. I hated being treated like an outsider when I obviously wasn't.

"Ready?" Nicholas sounded chipper.

"Ready for what?" I had no clue what he meant. I wanted him to agree with me. It didn't make sense for the Reaper to want Pixie. If he agreed, then I could say maybe it wasn't the Reaper after all. Maybe Pixie wasn't really in danger and could have her life back.

He walked toward me slowly.

I stopped breathing.

An extremely mischievous look appeared on his face. "Run."

I ran.

He'd warned me about this. That morning he'd said we'd work on self-defense after school. Plus, when I'm told to run by someone that big, I run. He caught me before I made it past the couch. He had his arms wrapped tightly around my chest. It wasn't as nice as I had imagined.

"Now what?" Nicholas expected me to have some kind of answer.

"Uh . . . "

"Stomp on my foot." His voice was carefree, as if he'd asked me to pass him the ketchup.

"Okay." I stomped. "You moved!"

"I knew it was coming. Someone else wouldn't. Now, when the assailant is yelling because you just broke his foot, hit him hard with your elbow, like this." He moved my arm slowly, showing me how the motion would feel in progress.

"If you're lucky, he'll be shorter than I am. You'll hit him in the gut. That hurts worse than the chest, normally. Now, try the combo. Go easy on my foot."

We repeated the same combination a dozen times. I didn't go easy on him. After dinner he added some additional steps. We worked on the "fist to the forehead" and then "my foot to his shin as I sprinted away" move. I assumed I could outrun a man with a broken foot.

We tried a few other moves before calling it a night. He called them self-defense. They weren't. The moves he taught were more like self-preservation. Every move was swift, followed by stern instructions to run. He'd say, "Do this and then run." "Give him one of these and then run."

The biggest lesson I got from our practice was whatever I did, I needed to get free. Get free and run. We practiced every night, anytime I wasn't doing homework. I hated being so close to him and knowing I couldn't touch him, not the way I wanted. I suspected he felt the same, though he never said a word. Tension seasoned our every conversation. Enough electricity ran up my arms when we touched to light a city. I sensed the unnecessary beats before he released me during practice, but I didn't want to make things more difficult. I kept what distance I could. The theme remained day after day. I grew comfortable with it. I even saw myself performing his moves in my dream. Under Nicholas's tenacious supervision, I learned to crush knees and break ribs. And I wasn't afraid to do it.

The nightmares began to pale in comparison to my real and present danger. Nicholas and his team continued to communicate in cryptic phone calls. They believed the Reaper was near. It relieved a lot of pressure knowing that meant Pixie was safe. My dream faded a bit, despite this information. The focus and direction changed, too. I dreamed of escaping an assailant, a murderer, the Reaper. I found comfort waking up and knowing what it was I feared. Giving a name to the enemy was great consolation. Sleeping better and spending next to no time alone helped, too.

At school, everyone chatted about the upcoming festival. It was the first Friday in November, and the following night was the big event. The school and all of its supporters had spent days in preparation. I was surprisingly thankful to have something to do outside of lockdown.

I grabbed my bag and a few other things on my way to the door.

"Ready?" Nicholas called from the kitchen.

"Not even remotely." I swung myself out the door right behind him.

Since surveillance was his job, I had to stay under his thumb. He assigned me to a job that would keep me in one place and easily trackable for him. I would serve punch.

Nicholas pulled onto the grass and parked near a large stack of hay bales. I slid out and moved across the lawn with him. We walked silently, together but not, to the refreshment stand. I stopped there for instructions from an elderly lady in a "Francine Frances Academy 1951-1954" sweatshirt. Nicholas stopped several feet away and folded his hands in front of him. He looked like Secret Service.

The festival was elegant. The speakers were good, too. It came as no surprise when we ran out of cups. I'd handed out at least two hundred personally. The old lady who trained me told me where to find supplies in the cafeteria in case this happened. She'd also assured me that she'd be with me all night. She said I wouldn't have to leave my post. I hadn't seen her in an hour.

I turned away several people while I waited for a chance to tell Nicholas I was in need of supplies. Though he kept a close eye on me, we hadn't been able to talk. The girls at my school, and their mothers, had held him captive, incessantly so, since we arrived.

I admitted defeat around nine and left my station. Twinkle lights wrapped trees in a magical look no one could deny. I told the nearest person I could that I was going in for cups if anyone asked. I moved quickly into the building and down the hall to the kitchen. It wasn't a far walk from the front door, where I'd been stationed.

Inside the room, emergency lighting illuminated the space. No need to look for the switches. I doubted I'd find the right one, and I was in a hurry. The lighting made it possible to see clearly through the center of the room. It was actually lighter there than outside. I moved along the countertop looking for a box of cups. The huge, unmarked boxes gave no indication, so I began opening them. One at a time, I pulled the tops up and shoved them aside. I found plates, napkins, everything but the cups.

I tossed the last box onto the counter and prepared to rip into it when my hands froze. My heart spluttered erratically. A picture of me hung on the outside of the box. The same picture I'd had taped to my mirror inside my apartment. I hadn't seen it in over a week. Now it was stuck to the box with a large serving fork stabbed through my chest. My father's face was rubbed out, probably with the fork that impaled me. The rough outline of a heart shape snaked around my head.

My breathing was loud against the silence. The room suddenly seemed darker. Fear gripped my feet, rooting them in place. Time slowed. An ache in my chest spread out over my skin. Pricked my eyes. Stung my nose. I visualized the hallway separating me from the outside. It looked longer in my mind than it had on the way in. I'd never make it. With my head tilted toward the box, I scanned the room. Blood rushed and pounded between my ears. Breath whooshed in and out of my lungs. Then, it appeared. In the corner of the room where I stood, in a darkened slip of space between a wall and a commercial-sized refrigerator, a tiny orange glow began to shine.

Chapter Twenty

I couldn't swallow. My throat was thick with fear. I choked out a soft sound as my eyes tried in desperation to see the glow. To identify it as anything other than what it surely was. I thought of my dad losing me this way after he'd already lost Mom.

Only a thin metal island stood between us. The week's training played on my mind's recorder. Nicholas's voice demanded, "Run." I spun and threw myself into the doorjamb. I hit it with force. Pushing off with both hands, I propelled myself around the edge and into the hallway. The corridor stretched out for miles before me, yet I heard voices beyond the outside door. My strides came quicker. I knew Nicholas waited on the other side of the door to save me. If I could only reach the door. My feet slid on freshly waxed marble. My arms swung and my knees pumped, forcing space between the glow and me. I visualized slamming my palms against the cool metal door frame. Only twenty-five more feet to Nicholas. Blood surged through my veins.

A heavy arm crashed down over my shoulder stopping my escape. Another grabbed me from behind. Forcing me to a stop. Pulling me backward. Momentum urged me on. My body jerked and fell into the unreasonable grip of the monster. I screamed in torment over what would happen next. I knew too much. I'd read all about this thing that hunted at my school. It was worse for me than the others. I knew what would happen to me in ten short days.

His hot hand clamped over my mouth, stopping the screams. I tried to bite him. My teeth were muzzled securely behind my lips. The monster dragged me back toward the kitchen. The grip of rubber soles on marble proved worthless. My ankles turned and slid helplessly against the smooth floor. Pain shot up from my neck into my head from his grip. My chest burned and ached, as I struggled to pull in enough air. A wheeze fought its way through my windpipe. I knew exactly why he wanted me in the kitchen. So he could plunge an enormous fork into my chest. He planned to bring his fantasy home.

Please, no.

Adrenaline coursed through my veins, tightening my muscles, fueling my weakened body into action. This time flight was out of the question. I prepared to fight. Willed myself to be brave the way I'd planned. The time had come to face my fear. It was my moment. I would not die. I would not be held prisoner by yet another terror. My resolution firmed and hardened into stone. As thoughts moved through my mind, my shoulders squared from their slump. My struggling body became rigid against his grip.

I slammed my previously floundering heel into his foot. He stopped moving for a fraction of a second. The large hand over my mouth loosened infinitesimally. Our backwards propulsion hesitated. Not for long, but enough for me to connect my elbow with his gut and my fist with his forehead. I kicked back one last time with gusto, raising a growl from his chest. I smashed his shin with precision and ran. My shoes slid with every step, but I kept going. The sounds that began to erupt from my throat were unlike anything I'd ever heard. I would not be his victim.

The great metal door before me swung wide. Nicholas flew to my side, gun in hand, protective stance in place. He looked me over in the blink of an eye, embraced me for less than a heartbeat, and then shoved me outside. Through the door. Onto the great stairs. Behind me, a thousand voices mixed with music and laughter. Before me, darkness and danger. I stood frozen outside the enormous door. Through the window in the door, I stared as Nicholas approached every interior threshold with his back to the wall. He spun, kicked, and turned in two directions before moving on. It was methodical, calculated, and precise.

He would end him.

I stumbled back to my concessions assignment, rubbing my shoulder and ribs. My skin was ice over stone. His hands had burned impressions on me that would never wash away. A heartbeat before my legs gave way, the folding chair at the refreshment table hit the backs of my legs and I sat. My muscles turned to stew and oozed over the seat. Scents of candied apples and popcorn wafted overhead. People spoke to me, but their words were muted, blurred, and distant. My photograph was stabbed into the box. This man hadn't simply waited for a girl to wander off tonight. It was not a photograph of any girl. *My* father's face was erased. *My* chest had been skewered. He had waited for *me*.

I had no idea how much time had passed when the woman who was supposed to help me finally returned. She scolded me for sitting and not getting more cups then turned to enter the building.

"No!" my rough voice choked out. I sounded awful.

She examined me. "Are you ill, dear? You look pale." Her keen grandmotherly eyes searched my face. Her cold hand brushed my cheek. My skin burned from fear, and her cool touch stung.

I jumped. "No." On my feet and prepared to take the lady down if she insisted on entering the building, I leered. "Someone went in for me so I wouldn't have to leave."

"Oh, well did you explain it as I did? There are so many boxes in there." She looked at the doors again as if she thought she could help him somehow. No one could help him.

I took a sidestep, placing my body between her and the building. The tears began to fall. I allowed the panic to sway and the fear to swell.

She immediately forgot the cups. "Sit down, dear. Are you sure you're well? You might need to go home and rest. Let me see." She picked up my wrist and looked at her watch.

"I was a nurse for thirty-five years. Did you know? I often fill in here when the school nurse is away." Her thin lips and small blue eyes comforted me. I'd never had a grandmother.

"Oh dear," she said softly, as if she hadn't meant me to hear. "Your heart is racing. Are you fevered?" She pressed her hand against my forehead, and her brows pulled together. An enormity of wrinkles gathered across her face.

"Let's get you into the office so I can take a better look." She glanced up at the moon as if to point out the obvious. It was dark. She was old.

Again with the building. Did she have a death wish?

"Is everything okay here?" Nicholas's voice startled me. I turned to wrap my arms around him. He caught them mid-flight before pulling me awkwardly against him.

"What's this about?" His voice was strange, distant and cold.

The woman appraised us. "She's not feeling well."

"I'll get her home."

"Mmm." She considered him again. He was hard to resist even at her age, I suppose. "She's not well. She's flushed. Her heart is racing and she might have a fever. I'd prefer to get her inside to the nurse's station before sending her home."

"I ran into the dean inside. He sent me out. The building is to remain vacant tonight. No one's allowed access."

"But," she tried to argue, "we're out of cups. How can I serve punch with no cups?"

His face remained blank and stern. He bent over and lifted a box onto the table beside her. "I was coming from the kitchen when I ran into him." A painful smile changed his lips but not his eyes. Those were clearly troubled. I followed the gaze to two large holes in the side of the box, where the fork had been.

The woman was stunned and apparently confused.

He took advantage. "Ma'am, if you can handle the refreshments on your own, I'll take Elle to her parents." He nodded into the crowd as if my parents roamed together among the guests.

I tried to stay on top of their exchange, but my eyes adhered to the holes.

"Yes, well, that's fine . . ." she stammered. "I do think she needs to be looked at properly."

We were already walking away into the night before she finished her weak protest.

Inside the SUV, Nicholas apologized. "Elle . . ." There was fierce emotion behind the words. "I'm so sorry. We shouldn't have been here. I should never have allowed myself to become distracted. I wanted to make your life more normal, with one less sacrifice."

Did he think I'd feel deprived in some way if I missed the festival?

I looked at him but saw only darkness, the little orange glow, and my father's face scratched from the photograph. My mind couldn't formulate anything worth saying, nothing coherent, for that matter.

"You know this, but I need to say it any way. I didn't find him. He's either still hiding in there, or he's gone. I've called my team and they'll search the entire area for anything that might lead us to him." His voice deepened. "We had to wait, to know for sure . . ."

"Wait for him to kill me?" The words flew from my mouth. I'd been used like bait for a predator. I didn't appreciate it.

"Of course not!"

Oh sure. I offended him. He had things backwards. I contemplated getting out of the SUV, but my chances were better with Nicholas. So, I fumed and pouted as long as I could manage.

"We had to maintain surveillance, nothing else. We had nothing solid. Even the times you believed you were followed . . . nothing concrete arose. Now we can be more proactive. We can assign more resources. We can act now, stop waiting." He looked at me for something, but I kept my eyes on the road. "Elle, we don't even know who he is . . .

"I need to take you in. We can't go back to the house because he might've seen me while I looked for him inside the school. If he did, then he's surely put two and two together. He's been watching here. He likely knows we're together, and if he saw my response protocol, he knows I'm not a student."

"Take me in where?" Steam must've coiled from my ears. I'd never been so angry. "Where are we going?"

"To my local rendezvous. You'll be questioned. We'll call in a sketch artist. No one has any idea what the Reaper looks like. You're the first to see him . . . "

"And live." I was completely disturbed.

"I'm so sorry, Elle. I should've been there." His voice broke. "You did real good, okay? You did great."

I zoned out for the rest of the trip. I couldn't deal with any of it. I let myself shut down.

Nicholas let me, too. He glanced my way every few minutes, but he never spoke.

I concentrated on the scenery, the road signs. To busy my mind, I tried to decipher where we were headed. Where was his "local rendezvous"?

Chapter Twenty-One

Two hours later we arrived at a small office complex in suburbia. I had no idea if we'd left Ohio. Every window on the first floor of one building shined in the night. Nicholas swung the SUV onto the walk out front and led me inside. Several people stopped to watch our entrance. Steaming mugs paused at lips. Phone calls disconnected. Talking ceased. Keyboards stilled.

All eyes fixed on me. Nicholas directed me to a conference room where the group of strangers followed and began to question me. They sought every detail of the events leading up to, during, and after the attack. One person took notes. Others asked questions. Someone cleaned under my fingernails and took my vitals as I spoke. Nicholas brought me coffee, but he wasn't permitted to stay. A tall man in dress pants and Reeboks took him into another room. I assumed he had his own questions to answer.

The night's details rolled off my tongue. Each event replayed in my mind like a movie clip on a loop. Being attacked by the Reaper definitely gave my current nightmare some healthy competition. When the sketch artist arrived, I failed. I hadn't seen his face. I'd never heard his voice. Based on my description of the way he'd held me, they guessed his height was roughly six feet, but only roughly. He was thin. I knew from the feel of his arm across my chest. Nicholas's arms were double the width of his. When I'd kicked his shin, it felt small against my foot. I hoped I'd snapped it.

Of all I'd been able to tell them, the cigarette, which had become his calling card to me, was the biggest lead. They went back to look for a butt. If he'd been smoking when I saw him, and not smoking a minute later when he chased me, then he must have dropped the butt. The answers were in that cigarette. His DNA would be on the tiny, filthy piece of trash. If they could find it and put a name to it, the Reaper would no longer be able to hide. They radioed over to the crew clearing the scene and all were put on the lookout for one priceless piece of evidence.

I answered the same questions a dozen times. So many, in fact, I began to wonder if I answered incorrectly. Reeboks scolded Nicholas for letting me out of his sight and also for moving me in with him. He seemed especially concerned about what my father would say. I bit my cheeks to keep from yelling, "I'm almost eighteen!" On the whole, it was lose-lose for Nicholas. I felt horrible, but I didn't want to stick up for him. Our relationship needed to stay hidden or he'd be in more trouble. I didn't want him taken away from me.

When everyone had had their turn questioning me, a woman in a gray suit led me into a dimly lit room with a couch made up like a bed. She told me to make myself comfortable. It was going to be an all-nighter for their team. They agreed I needed to sleep. As if I could. Sleep sounded great to my body, but my mind refused to relent.

I didn't know what my dreams might bring. I could handle the humdrum, impending-death dream that had plagued me before. What I couldn't handle was falling helpless to the imagery in my head. Nothing I did pushed it away. During the questioning, I was relieved to spill it all out. After I finished, I shoved it into the mental lockbox that had reached capacity long ago.

I shuffled closer to the couch and sat. I sank into the faux-leather, overstuffed cushions with relief. A glass end table stood beside it adorned with a Tiffany-style lamp and some pads of paper. The blanket and pillow looked like they had come from a hotel, and were definitely new. Giant square-shaped creases from packaging covered the blanket. Pixie would've commented on how the cream color looked against the dark brown faux leather. She would've said something about the contrast. The word *inviting* rose in my mind, and my feet curled up beneath me. Torn between the rest I needed and the fear of what would come from sleep, I looked back to the lady who'd brought me.

"Is everything okay?" Genuine concern covered her face. I could only imagine what I looked like to her.

"Is there anywhere to get a good latte around here?" I was half joking, half desperate. I shook for too many reasons. I felt sick.

"Yeah, come on. I'll take you." She smiled.

"Really?" I perked up instantly. "Can you do that?"

She shifted her eyes left and then right. "I'm from the school of thought where it's better to ask for forgiveness than permission."

I liked her already. When I smiled, she motioned for me to come to the doorway. She pointed down the hall to a storage area. I went ahead. Then she made a big play of turning off the light in the room and shutting the door.

"Back in ten," she announced into the air and ran toward me on her tiptoes, stopping her pumps from clicking away as she went.

We made our way through a mostly empty storage room to a rear door. She held one perfect finger to her lips in warning. The sensible brown polish on her nail matched her well-tailored suit. By her youthful face, I assumed she wanted to look older, be taken seriously. Me, too.

She punched a code into a lighted keypad and swung the door open with one arm, allowing me to pass. I walked out into a small parking area and looked around. The night air chilled me. I had no idea what time it was by then. A swift breeze tousled my hair. I rubbed my arms while I waited for her to catch up. I appreciated the slap the night air gave me.

Several cars slept in ordered rows. The SUV we had arrived in looked like a drunken monkey had parked it. Nicholas must've brought it around while I told my story over and over to his colleagues. It occurred to me then that aside from Reeboks, his team was pretty young. Only two of the seven I met looked as if they could be in their forties. They were all younger than my father. Most looked closer to Nicholas's age than I would've thought possible. The lady who had helped me escape looked a lot like half the girls in my senior class. Watching her, though, she was no teenager.

She approached a car. I followed. Her car was small, black, and sleek. It looked fast. I sank inside and strapped in. We'd barely left the business park before the giant green glow of my favorite coffee shop came into view. We pulled up to the drive-thru window, and I ordered my usual with an extra shot of espresso. She got tea. When she paid for the order, I realized I hadn't brought my purse in from the SUV. I wasn't even sure I'd brought it from the festival.

"So," she mused, having softened me up with coffee. "You've been living with Nicholas for a week?"

I choked and coughed for what seemed like ten minutes. "Yeah," I croaked. I didn't know what to say, or what she was listening for.

"What's that like for you, exactly?"

Ah, she wasn't immune to him either. If they'd worked together long, she probably hated me for the time I got with him—not working. A sense of smugness filled my chest. I tucked my nose into the cup. If she was the catty type, she'd look for a way to separate us.

"I don't know." I drew on the poor-girl-in-danger persona. "It's been overwhelming and a little scary this week. I'm not sure what to think about anything." I watched her for a response.

She smiled. She was gorgeous.

I couldn't compete with a woman in his profession who looked like her. They had way more in common than he and I ever would. She was all legs and heels, with a cool car and a dimple like his. Their wedding photos would be adorable. I leaned my head against the glass and wished I'd stayed in the couch room.

"He likes you, you know?" Her voice took on a little singsong quality.

I turned to look at her. "What?"

"He likes you. We can all see it. The others think he's too attached to be careful. They think it has to do with the family history of the case, but I know him. He likes you."

"I don't understand."

"He calls you Elle," she said, as if that meant something or like it should've meant something.

"That's my name." *What was he supposed to call me?*

She swung her cup in the air over the console. "No, you're not 'the subject' or 'the girl,' or some code name. He gives code names a lot. Terrible ones, too. He sucks with names." She shook her head and pulled onto the road back toward the office. "With you, it's always 'Elle did this. Elle did that.'"

My eyes popped. I turned my face back to the window, grateful for a short ride. The car bounced over speed bumps reentering the lot. I balanced my precious cargo in both hands, prepared to make a run for the couch. I couldn't have this conversation, not with her, whoever she was. I reached for the door, ready to make a break for it. Nicholas waited outside in the dark next to the door we had escaped through. His arms were crossed over his chest. There was menace on his face.

As she shut down the engine, he strode into the lot and approached the car on the driver's side. I worried for a minute that she was about to lose a car door. He knocked hard on her window with one knuckle. She smiled at me and held up one finger. I dropped my hand from the door. Then she cracked the power window a millimeter.

"Get out here, Sara, now," he growled.

"Wait here a second, sweetie," she whispered to me and let her eyes run up to the tiny crack in the window. I looked there with her. She winked and slid out.

"Are you insane!" he barked in a hush. I saw only their torsos from my seat, but thanks to the tiny crack, I could hear them loud and clear.

"She wanted coffee. You should know the girl needs her coffee."

"That's not funny. Do you know what you did to me? I went to check on her and she was gone!"

"Were you worried I was gone?"

She sounded jealous.

"No, actually, once I realized you were gone, it all made sense. Who else would take her without telling me? You always have to pull this crap. We're not twelve anymore."

Then I was lost.

"No, that's true, Nicholas. You're actually acting more like you're sixteen than twelve." Her voice was light, teasing.

His tone dropped. He leaned in closer to her. "Who have you told? Did you tell Mom?"

Did he say Mom?

No way. My mind searched for any other explanation. *It couldn't be.*

"Mom and I might've talked about it on Sunday afternoon." She pushed his chest playfully.

His hand shot up. I guessed he was rubbing his neck. "Who else was there for your weekly luncheon? I suppose Nikki and Lily were there? And Olivia? Oh, you're killing me, Sara. What about the guys? Tell me what I need to know. I don't want to be ambushed. You owe me that much."

"No, I know how they get. Matter of fact, little brother, you might want to tone it down before you announce it yourself."

She reached behind her back to open her door and leaned inside. "Be good to him."

Before I could speak, Nicholas went around the car and pulled open my door. He hauled me out, held me against his chest, and spoke over my head. "Thanks for buying her coffee."

I turned in time to see the door close against the building.

"Your sister works on your team?" I spoke into his chest. I didn't want to let go an inch.

"She's here being nosy. Sara works as an intern with the Marshal service in D.C., but she grew up on this story. She's a senior at William & Mary. We're a real dynamic duo."

"She's your big sister? She looks pretty young."

"Right. She calls me little brother because she knows it gets on my nerves. That's what sisters do, right?"

I wouldn't know.

"So she's not your older sister? I'm confused."

"No. Well, she is by like a minute." He bobbed his head. "Seven minutes. If you ask her, she'll be specific. Seven minutes."

"She's your twin!" Well, that explained the dimple. Scratch the crude thought about their wedding pictures. *Ick*. "Why's she still in college?"

"I went to school every summer. She went to Key West."

"Nice." I smiled. He scoffed.

"I about had a coronary when I went into that room and you were gone. Actually, I knew you were gone when I saw the light off. You'd never lie down and sleep, especially here, like this."

I ignored him. I had bigger things to address. "She said you like me."

He pulled my chin away from his chest and bent at the knees until he was in my face. "*Like* does not begin to describe what I feel for you. I'm trying hard to make that clear without getting fired. You're a slow learner." His dimple caved in.

I melted into the hug, where my cheeks threatened to catch fire.

"The office, though, they have to wait."

I smiled like a ninny. "Who are Lily, Nikki, and Lisa?"

"Olivia," he corrected. "Lily, Nikki, and Olivia. Olivia is our big sis. Nikki and Lily are our cousins. We're all nearly the same age. We grew up like siblings. We're always together. The guys, too. Andrew and Jacob, both younger. They're our little brothers."

"Good night! How many kids are in your family?" What he described sounded like a small village. I couldn't imagine having all those kids in my family.

"Five at our house, but there are eleven cousins and six aunts and uncles that go with them."

I looked at him.

"Does that scare you?" He looked sad. "You like solitude. My family is intense. Your worst nightmare, I think."

Au contraire. It was my dream come true. A life filled with people who really knew me, people who shared my inside jokes and humiliating stories. I desperately wanted what he had. "It sounds wonderful."

Evidently he liked my answer because he smiled and hugged me tighter. "Ah, don't say I didn't warn you."

I wondered if I'd ever meet his family. I didn't know where my dad was. My boring, predictable life suddenly resembled a puzzle thrown into the air.

"You know, you and your father are always welcome. 'The more the merrier' is branded on my mom's forehead."

I considered adding *mind reader* to his lengthy list of attributes. *Crazy* topped the list because that was an insane thing to say.

"We'll invite him for a visit when we're out there for Thanksgiving."

Chapter Twenty-Two

Nicholas took me to the couch room and left me there with the light on and door open. I finished my coffee. My mind wandered over everything from my first day in Ohio until that night.

There were several holes in the Reaper story. Pacing around the room, I worked over the pieces, but something didn't fit. The notepads on the end table caught my eye. I grabbed one and picked up my purse off the floor. Nice to know all of my personal information and my phone weren't lost or in the possession of the man who had attacked me. I dug through my purse, fruitlessly. Pens always disappeared in an emergency. I stuck my head out of the doorway to see if I could borrow one. No one was there.

I walked into the open area near the door we had arrived through, but the cubicles were empty. Voices filtered through the conference room wall where I'd been questioned. Seven heads nodded in unison from the chairs inside. Their backs faced the glass wall separating us.

Facing me, against the far wall, stood a giant corkboard on wheels. Women's faces covered the board, along with crime-scene photographs and other things I couldn't read. They'd arranged the pieces on some sort of timeline. Near the bottom right a photograph of me stared back. I was six. My father's and my mother's photos were pinned up beside me, surrounded by newspaper clippings and current photos of Dad and me as well. My heart stopped.

Sara turned and saw me. I couldn't run or hide. I didn't care if I was being nosy. I wanted to know why my mother was on that board. At my core, I hoped I didn't already know the answer. My mother wasn't in a car accident.

"Elle." Sara moved to my side. Her words were muffled. I saw my kindergarten photo, my dad's photo, and my poor mother. It didn't make sense. He wouldn't have abducted my mother, a then thirty-year-old woman, a mother. He wouldn't have chosen her any more than he would've chosen Pixie.

"Sweetie, let's go talk." She pulled me along, back into the couch room. I stumbled awkwardly beside her. She didn't have to ask me to sit. My legs were near collapse. I wondered how much my heart could take before it gave out.

Heartbeats played the score to the slide show of oddities running through my mind. Some made sense. Others floated without purpose outside the screen. They belonged, but I didn't understand how. Pixie and Mom, for example. *My mom.* Tears flowed. I remembered Nicholas's face on the day we met, not by accident, assigned to my school, to me, not Pixie. The man had stalked me, followed me, entered my apartment, and taken the photo he later stabbed a fork through. It was always about me. It made perfect sense. *Now.* Nicholas spent his time with me, no one else. He'd warned me repeatedly not to be alone. How had I been so ignorant?

The irony set off a rumble of nervous laughter in my chest. I sounded like the villain in a cartoon. How many times had I thought myself ordinary? I'd imagined my life to be boring. Making a retired serial killer's hit list wasn't boring. What about me was messed up enough to bring him out of a decade-long retirement? For the briefest moment, I was thankful that my dad's job had kept us moving. If it hadn't, I might not have been so lucky. Then again, if he'd chosen the school first and me second, it wouldn't have mattered.

Answers stared me in the face. I only moved them in circles. Someone had left a ribbon in my locker on my first day at the academy. Was it an accident? Could the killer have followed me from my last home? Did he know my mother had worn one like it? I pictured her face beside mine on the corkboard. I thought of my dad's photo, feeling relieved he'd moved far away.

The picture of my mom popped back into my mind's eye. Mom's picture and the ribbon. The Reaper wouldn't have taken her. I needed that to be true. For the first time in my life, a car accident seemed like a great way to die. I couldn't handle thinking that the Reaper had starved, tortured, and beaten her. Then thrown her away as if she wasn't even human.

"What you saw in there wasn't meant for you to see. Not now. We planned to tell you everything in the morning, after our meeting. We're here to put together what we can. Now that you're in imminent danger, you have to be debriefed, with or without your father's approval." Sara looked over her shoulder to the doorway where Nicholas stood. His expression was unreadable, a blank stare. His soldier face.

Sara patted my knee gently and moved toward the door. "I'll keep them at bay." She closed the blinds on the window behind her.

Nicholas stayed against the wall. I wished he'd come to me, but he kept his distance, and my heart ached. I couldn't look up when he began to talk. My body was locked in a coma. My mind was numbed with frustration. Tears formed and dropped in pointless rhythm, landing on the rug beneath my feet in tiny crystal piles.

"I was assigned to the Reaper case, and to you, in the spring. The agency knew the Reaper had found you again. We knew he was likely to follow you first. We believe he wants to make it more painful for Special Agent Smith."

My eyes shot upwards and my cheeks were on fire. I waited.

"Your mother did die in a car, that part wasn't a lie." His eyes moved to the floor then. "It wasn't an accident, though. The Reaper shot her."

My hands grabbed at my neck and chest knowing the information would kill me. I stood to run like a chicken that had lost its head. I bolted forward, but a wall of muscle stopped me short. Nicholas didn't let me anywhere near the door. He pulled me back to the couch.

"Shot?" Tears and distress blazed hot in my throat. "A serial killer shot my mother." There was nothing more horrific. Any hate I had toward the Reaper based on some old newspaper articles and the idea that he had stalked me and Pixie looked like rainbows and unicorns compared to the fire burning in my heart. He killed my mother.

"Your father saved her, in a manner of speaking. The Reaper was escaping with her. Your father managed to stop their car. If not, you know she would've been through so much worse."

"Special Agent Smith."

My father, the insurance adjuster who moved at the drop of a hat, was some kind of federal agent. Had I slipped into the looking glass? My life was an extended two-hour crime drama set for prime time.

"Special Agent Smith was very close to naming him, Elle. We believe the Reaper planned to kill all of you that night, as punishment for your father's interference." He looked proud of my dad.

"Your father blames himself for not being able to save her. He chose this life to protect you. We had no way of knowing how dedicated the Reaper would become. Leaving everyone behind to keep you safe only caused you a messed-up childhood, and it never really kept him away. He was never more than a year or two behind you guys."

"That's why we moved?" I had a small epiphany. "Not because Dad's been chasing him but because he's been chasing us?" The room began to brighten around my periphery. I worried I was about to black out. I fought against it, needing to stay alert and collect information. I needed to process. I covered my heart with one hand as it beat against my rib cage.

"The cabin. He didn't have downtime between assignments. We were going off-grid." A barrage of memories knocked the wind from my lungs. The cabin had no address. We got mail from a post office box in the next town. No Internet. My cell never worked there. He scouted for firewood every morning and evening, probably checking for signs of a killer, or calling the freaking FBI for updates from his phone, which always worked.

"In theory, separating you from your father this year should've slowed his progress. It was supposed to buy enough time for you to leave for a large college and disappear."

"The agent and his family who died before naming The Reaper?"

Nicholas nodded once to my question. "Your family."

"So, I'm what? In witness protection? I've been in witness protection for my entire life and no one bothered to tell me?" My voice pitched into a series of squeaks. Hysteria. I rubbed my chest against the pounding. My periphery twinkled once more.

In the bigger scheme of things, witness protection seemed insignificant, but I was mad. My voice grew louder as I explored that truth. "Stupid! Stupid! Stupid!" I pounded my feet against the soft carpet. "I was followed twice before he got a hold of me. I thought it was my *imagination*! Didn't anyone 'in the know' think maybe, just maybe, it would've behooved me to actually know I was being stalked by a murderer? For crying out loud! I almost forced myself to walk home from the coffee shop that first night because I wanted to face my fears. I thought I was way too old to be afraid of the dark! *Ugh*! And that ribbon! And those cigarette butts! The *car*!"

I was on my feet again, shaking out my wrists.

Nicholas joined me. "I wouldn't have let you walk home."

"Oh. Yes, that's right." The words came in a flood. They sounded like gibberish to me, running together. "I've been spied on every day of my entire existence. Tell me, Nick, who followed me around before you did? I've been stalked by one good guy and one bad guy all my life. Super. Wonderful. Lovely." My every adolescent faux pas had been documented somewhere. Anger ripped through my muscles. I wanted to hurt somebody.

"I want to talk to my dad. Now."

I marched to the next room with Nicholas on my heels. The room emptied. I dialed Dad and waited for the inevitable voicemail.

"Gabriella." Dad's voice was low and troubled. "I'm very sorry for what's happening here. I owe you an explanation. I know. A few explanations."

Bad things built on my tongue and I clamped my teeth tight to keep them there. I settled on the obvious. "You lied to me. About everything." I sniffled and shoved images of my mother at the hands of the Reaper from my mind. "Why? Didn't I deserve to know?"

"No." One angry word stood alone between us.

I crumbled.

"You deserved none of this. None," he growled. "What was I to do? Tell my six-year-old daughter whose mother was murdered in cold blood that I should've been more careful? Should I have explained to a kindergartener that her daddy should've been less certain he had everything in control? That I was the reason her mother was gone?"

"This isn't your fault. Don't start that. I need answers. I need to know why you lied to me every day after I was six. In case you didn't notice, I'm not six anymore. You've had years to tell me instead of running away."

"You've never been a parent. You can't understand. It's impossible. I made the decision to hide us, to cut ties and run. For years, every day was about you and your nightmare. Counselors barely gained your trust and it was time to move again. I've stayed on the case. I've seen him. I wanted to be the one to make him pay, but I couldn't find him again. I turned around a few times, and I was gray and you were in middle school. I couldn't tell you I'd lied for six years waiting for you to be old enough to understand. Hell, I don't understand. You were happy, or as happy as I could expect you to be. How could I tell you the truth? Time disappeared, Gabriella. Before I knew it, you were applying to colleges and asking about boarding school. I couldn't tell you I'd lied, and I couldn't tell you the truth. Not if I wanted to keep you safe."

The obvious irony hung in the air. I wasn't safe, and, thanks to the lies, I didn't even know to be afraid. My biceps burned where his fingers had been. Invisible brands from the monster who'd taken Mom away. The sobbing racked my chest until I found myself back on the couch, curled onto my side. The phone long forgotten.

My every personal travesty ran over my conscience. I was *never* alone! Nicholas had said my dating life wasn't worth documenting. My cheeks flamed with embarrassment and total humiliation. What else did Nicholas know about me? The questions and memories overwhelmed me. *My mom.* A fissure in my heart widened until I doubted it would ever heal.

"It was my dad." Nicholas stood over me. He folded himself onto the floor.

"My dad was assigned to the Reaper case after your dad stepped down from leading the investigation. They were colleagues for many years. Your dad worked for the Federal Bureau of Investigation. My dad worked here. The two branches aren't big on cooperation. Nobody likes to share. Everyone wants to win, but those two knew each other outside the office."

"My dad came home from Japan to see me." I raised an eyebrow, realizing he hadn't been in Japan at all. He'd been somewhere looking for the man who watched me. No wonder he came back when I told him about the ribbon. He told me he'd be working nearby now. Pft. Of course he would. This was where the psychopathic killer was.

"I saw him the night he came to check on you. I received a stern warning about proximity." Nicholas looked puzzled. "He was home from D.C."

"Has anyone in my life not lied to me?" Something else came to mind. "The nannies?"

"Field agents, Bureau employees, miscellaneous secretaries."

"Of course." I felt like a balloon with a pin in it. "The agents were the unfriendly, all-business ones, and the secretaries were the paranoid and antsy ones," I guessed.

"Probably." He laughed.

"They were all crappy nannies."

"Yeah, they would be." He smiled a sad smile. Then his eyebrows rose. "Earlier, what did you say about a car and cigarette butts?"

I reached for the box of tissues he'd placed on the floor near my head. "I told you about it. Every morning at the apartment I woke from my dream to a loud engine with a squealing belt." I waited for his light bulb to go on. "We'd leave for school with new cigarette butts piled on the mat outside our door.

"Also, there was a ribbon in my locker." I described it to him completely and remembered he was right again. I hadn't told him about it. I'd told my dad. Nicholas listened intently as I described it and told him about telling Dad.

"I was at your apartment recently. I didn't see any butts."

"Pixie got mad and kicked the mat full of them down the walkway."

"I need to see that ribbon. It could have prints on it. How much did you handle it?"

"Tons. I kept pulling it out of my bag, plus I looked at it a lot when I first got it, trying to figure out how it had gotten into a locker I'd only just received." I didn't want to think of the way it made me remember my mom. A precious memory had been planted to taunt me. My hands fisted in my lap.

"May I see it?"

"I gave it to Dad when he visited."

"Okay. You took a picture for your dad with your phone? Can I see your phone?"

"Uh, you took that phone, remember? Now I have this." I twisted the new phone in the air.

Nicholas groaned. "Gah. I'll run back and get it. I need to talk to cleanup anyway, see if they dusted your locker. I'll send them to look for your mat and maybe locate some butts from there. Forensics is amazing. You never know about those guys." He jumped to his feet and stuck his head through the door. "Is Agent Smith still on the line?" Only then did I realize I'd never said goodbye.

Nicholas caught my panic. "He's on the line now with the team. You can talk to him anytime you're ready."

He took a step across the threshold.

I jumped up. "You can't leave!"

"I won't be long."

"You won't be right back." I'd climb onto his back if I had to. No way was he leaving me. "We drove for at least two hours to get here. That means four hours of travel time alone. I'm coming." I picked up my purse and turned for the door.

"Elle." His voice was stern. "You're not going anywhere near that town. The answer is no. Do you hear me? No." The Marine stood before me, towering over me, shoulders squared, commanding his men.

Not this one.

I shoved past him and called for Sara before he could stop me. He had better reflexes than that. I supposed he wasn't used to being ignored when he put his mind to something.

At the sound of his sister's name, he flopped his giant body onto the couch. "Now you've done it."

"Everything okay?" Sara smiled warmly.

"Peachy," Nicholas grumbled.

Sara's smile broadened. "What're we up to?" She shut the door behind her.

"Elle has something back in the valley that might provide a clue. I want to go and get it."

"Excellent." She had a twinkle in her eye.

I recognized that look.

"But . . . " Nicholas stopped her, mid-twinkle. "She won't stay here." Heavy emphasis on *she*. It sounded like a dirty word. Their eyes focused in on me, appraising, maybe wondering what it would take to sway me.

I had no price. Sara started by trying to comfort me into staying. She played on my need for security, my desire not to be alone or in danger for once. "I'll be right here the whole time."

Nicholas shook his head at her. His look said, *amateur*.

"What if I come with?" she suggested, more bubbly.

"No."

"I can wait with her in the car and . . . "

"No."

"Jim," she called out of nowhere.

Nicholas rubbed his eyes again and gave me a nasty look.

I didn't care. He wasn't leaving me.

"What about the pumpkin?" I tried to think of anything else that could help, since he was going back.

"I dusted the pumpkin," he mumbled underneath his hand.

"What's this about a pumpkin?" Sara chimed in, and Nicholas let out a long, throaty sound.

"Of course, the pumpkin," I whispered. He'd seen me with it. Knew it was mine. "That threat was meant for me."

Chapter
Twenty-Three

"Yeah, you guys got something?" Reeboks appeared. "Have you remembered something else, Elle?"

"No." I'd barely spoken and Sara was already delivering the entire situation to him.

"Road trip?" He looked younger then. They obviously loved what they did. It wasn't a chore. It was a passion. They grabbed folders, coffee, and keys. Ten minutes later, we pulled out of the parking lot.

Two more agents joined us. All four of them seemed jazzed to get out of the office. Three stayed behind. Someone had to wait for forensics to report back when the school was cleared. Nicholas, Sara, and I rode in the SUV. I sat in back. Reeboks, whose name I learned was Jim, and his partner, Mason, rode together in a large town car behind us.

Darkness engulfed the country roads. Moonlight filtered through treetops hanging overhead. The forests weren't as beautiful as I remembered. Instead, the trees seemed like a foreboding killer's playground. Inside the forest there were a million places to hide and watch. My skin tightened down my arms, raising the hairs on end. The tears had dried. Shock gave way to numbness. I'd mentally checked out of that horror.

It was funny how I'd once compared my life to witness protection, back when Pixie left. I'd considered how I had nothing to leave or to lose. It was ironic, and yet, not at all. So as not to wallow, I searched for a silver lining. The Reaper had been too busy following us to kill in over a decade. Saving all the other potential victims made running worthwhile. The much smaller consolation was that my dad had been able to keep my mom from becoming one of his captives.

"When was the last update from Special Agent Smith?" Sara adjusted her seat belt.

Nicholas glanced in the mirror at me and then rolled his eyes toward his sister. "You call. He's not speaking to me."

"What?" I leaned forward from the backseat.

Nicholas sighed.

I had no words.

Sara snickered and curled one tiny hand around her nose and mouth to hide her pretty lips.

"You talked to my dad today?" I gasped.

"Uh, the way I remember it, he mostly talked to me, loudly."

"Good grief." I leaned my head against the window at my side. "Hey!" I shot up again. "Your dad looked after me when I was small?"

Sara nodded fervently. "Yep. He talked about you a lot. I kind of feel like I know you. For a while, I actually thought I had another cousin, Gabby, out there."

"Sure. What's one more cousin?"

My heart didn't miss the fact that I was tied to this family long before I ever met them. All these years, I did have a family. My heart swelled at the thought. I hid in the shadow of the backseat while I beamed at the idea of being a part of Nicholas's family. I wished my mom was part of mine.

I dozed off and on throughout the drive, comforted by the sound of Nicholas and Sara talking in the front. They were serious sometimes, discussing the case, and playful other times. Working together suited them. I struggled with how much of their conversation seeped into my dreams and how much was my mind's adaptation.

My dreams ran wild as we drove.

I thought of Pixie in the California sun, seated on a beach, drawing a sunrise. I'd never been there, but I thought she'd love someplace like Venice Beach. There would be so much diversity to entertain her. In my dream, she was happy and not as gothic as she was in Ohio. I'd never bought that anyway. Her personality was more pink and yellow than black and gray. Like the way she always listened to music while hanging over the edge of her bed. She wore tiny pigtails and polka-dotted toe socks during movie nights in.

Nicholas and Sara stood in the background keeping watch. Their voices came and went with the tide. I heard my name often. Occasionally, Pixie stopped to listen to them, too. I never took my eyes off her. My heart ached knowing she'd been in danger because of me. If I'd had any idea I would've lived in a cave across the sea where no one could find me.

"I love her," Nicholas said.

"I love her, too. She's perfect for you. Finally, a woman to balance you out. You know, our family hasn't grown in at least two years."

"No, I mean it. I love her. The minute I saw the first photo of her, she had me captivated. I thought of a million ways to meet her. I needed to know her. I've never even heard of anything like that."

"Love at first surveillance photo? Sure, that happens all the time."

My dad appeared carrying a turkey on a white oval platter, moving in slow motion. He slammed the platter onto the table and drew his gun. I jumped and ran, looking for the danger and wondering what had caused his reaction. My dad wasn't fierce. Dad was a marshmallow. I followed his gaze to Nicholas, seated in the chair beside the one from which I'd fled. *Thanksgiving*.

"How much farther is this place?" Sara asked. A fog covered her words. "We passed the academy miles ago."

As far as I could tell, her question got no response. I imagined a dozen duplications of the Reaper, hidden behind the large trees near the road. They disappeared and reappeared as the SUV raced forward.

"This must be the opposite of how Dorothy felt." Sara didn't seem ruffled at having to hold a one-sided conversation. "She arrived in an other-worldly place, right out of Kansas. Coming from D.C., I think I might've accidently arrived in Kansas."

A long line of curse words spilled from Nicholas. They seemed wrong. It wasn't an appropriate response to Sara. Something had happened that I couldn't see. Phones rang. They spoke.

I drifted back into the dream. This time, I wasn't at the beach, and Pixie was gone.

I walked beside the river as it roared. The water burned. I needed to get through it to find Nicholas. I could hear him, but I couldn't see him past the flames glowing all around me. Sirens raged in the distance. I hoped they'd hurry. I hoped they could see the inferno from wherever they were. Flames licked upward into the trees. My eyes fought to see through the incredible heat and light.

"Elle."

My heart raced as I thought of all the things that might be happening to Nicholas just beyond my reach. I was going to lose him.

My mind told me to keep trying. *Keep looking.*

"Please," I screamed. Then a breeze intermingled with the heat.

Impossibly cold air blew against my cheek. A cool breeze couldn't exist amidst the heat that engulfed me. It should've consumed me, not chilled me. I sat abruptly, willing my eyes to see, taking a moment to understand. It had been a dream. I was so thankful for that truth.

Before me, a fire raged against the sky.

"Elle. I'm sorry. It looks like we're going to be camping here for a while." Sara gave me notice of our change in plans. The team had to improvise.

Two policemen approached us.

I began to put things together. Both of the cars in our tiny caravan were parked on the side of the road about 300 feet from the little cottage on the river. Between us and the house stood two fire trucks, an ambulance, and several police cars. The cottage burned, completely destroyed, taking any hope of finding my phone along with it.

I couldn't hear the exchange between the policemen and the Marshals. Their words drowned in the roaring fire and the raging river. The sky was lit with embers. Gray and black smoke ghosted into the night. The smell was acrid. The upside, if there was one, was hope that the Reaper had accidently left another lead in the fire.

The little cottage by the river was no more than a memory. My few belongings gone with it. I was devastated by the loss of photographs Nicholas had inside. There were so many of his family. I sank back, defeated, into the seat and closed my eyes against fear and anger.

As it turned out, it truly was an all-nighter, just like Sara predicted. The sun was rising when a knock landed on my window, scaring me senseless. Jim held up one arm in surrender and the other held a carrier filled with coffee, balanced on a bakery box. I sat up and shoved the large black coat down onto my legs. The coat belonged to Nicholas. He stood beyond the door, rubbing his hands against his arms. He must've been freezing.

I opened the door and got out to stretch. It was cold. I handed Nicholas his coat and grabbed a coffee from Jim. Jim patted the area next to him on some large rocks beside the road. I sat and watched my breath in the air as it wound around the pillar of steam from my cup.

"Some night." Jim made nice with me. We'd never had a conversation before, unless I counted the interrogation twelve hours earlier.

"Thanks for the coffee." I tried to feel less awkward. I wrapped my arms around my knees and held my cup near my face for warmth.

"I hear you're somewhat of a connoisseur." He smiled a half smile, tipping his cup. He reminded me of my dad.

"Bad luck is another thing I am." I rolled my eyes toward the charred remains near the river.

"Not everyone thinks so." He faced the cottage, smiling at the ground. For a minute I wondered if he was somehow related to Nicholas, too.

"Well, what now?" I was prepared for anything.

"Now we wait for forensics. We try to put a name to this guy. We keep you safe. I'll liaison with your father."

"Tell him I'm sorry I lost it last night."

"We'll make a pit stop at your old apartment." Nicholas's voice was like music to my ears. I smiled before I even looked at him. My eyes moved over his unbuttoned dress shirt. He hadn't had a chance to change since the festival either. I saved his face for last. The crease between his brows showed pure determination, no sign of stress, agitation, or fear. He gave Jim an odd look. Jim left.

"Are you ready?" His voice was smooth and confident.

"Now?"

"This is the best time we have until tomorrow when the students leave for school. No one will be up and about at this hour on a Sunday morning."

The man had a point. I slid into the passenger's seat, and we set off for the scene of yet another crime. It only took a few minutes to arrive at my old place. It seemed like ages since I'd last been inside. On the ride over, I mentally tallied up a list of things I wanted to bring with me. Also a list of things I thought Pixie would appreciate having back. I was surprised to see the curtains were all burnt and the yellow tape was pulled off the stoop.

When Nicholas opened my car door, I sucked in a few lungfuls of fresh air. At the river, the air stunk of burnt plastic and other unpleasant things. Outside the apartment, on the quaint cobblestone street, it smelled as pure and right as I remembered. The air tasted almost as refreshing as the coffee.

We walked side by side to the door. Nicholas gave me a look. His eyes narrowed and he pumped one hand slowly, palm down. I thought it meant to stay put while he went inside first. So, I waited. I knew the fallen tape wasn't something he'd take lightly. After a few short minutes, he pulled me inside. I had time to get what I needed while he moved more slowly, looking for anything he'd missed before.

The leather journal I'd used to keep tabs on Nicholas was lying on my desk. "I think I know how he found you at the river." Nicholas appeared in my doorway. I held up the journal and waved it around.

"Where was that?"

"Here." I pointed to my desk.

"Is that where you left it?" His gorgeous face was pinched between the brows.

"No, I kept it in my dresser." I turned toward the mirror where my photos had been pulled off and reordered. The one that'd been forked was missing. All my things were neatly arranged in some strange pattern. By size? Age?

"It wasn't there when I came back that night. I know that book. I would've brought it to you. You write in it all the time. Sometimes even in class." He gave me a disapproving look.

Really? This is important now? Come on.

"So, he's been here again? Since the fire?" I pondered the question. "He took this, read it, and brought it back? Do you think he came here after he attacked me?" The questions mounted up. "Did he really think I'd come home? Why did he do that?" I pointed to the things on my dresser.

"I don't pretend to know how he thinks, but it seems he's spent a lot of time here. Probably waiting for you."

He snuck a peek at me.

I tried to look as if I was hearing the details of a case instead of my life.

"You stayed away. I think that's when he began to try to locate you. He wanted to know you so you'd be easier for him to find. Also, we made him mad. We faked a fire here when he hadn't made one. We think that's why he set the fire at my place."

I gathered up the suitcases I'd come with and put everything back in them, all the while considering Nicholas's theories. I traded some of my blue jeans and hoodies for Priscilla's designer things. I didn't think she'd mind. I also filled a bag with Pixie's art supplies and some things she had kept on display. I knew Nicholas could get them to her. I stacked the bags on top of one another and then looked for Nicholas.

He was propped up on my bed reading the brown journal.

I wanted to die, but I sucked it up. That thing was probably state's evidence or something. Now everyone would read it, including my father.

When I walked in, he sat upright and dropped the journal into a freezer bag. Then he removed a pair of plastic gloves I hadn't noticed before.

"Everything looks the same except in here. I went around all the rooms. Nothing," I said.

"He was interested in you, learning about you. Studying."

I suppressed a gag. "You could've told me to be careful about what I touched." I felt silly that I hadn't thought of it.

"Your fingerprints are already everywhere. This is your place, re-member?" He walked over to me and rubbed my shoulders gently. "Are you ready?"

"Sure." I needed a hospital stay to recuperate from the humilia-tion, but that was a luxury I didn't have.

Nicholas loaded himself down with bags and still managed to take me by my hand as we left the apartment. He stacked everything in the back of the SUV before helping me back into the passenger's seat. I thought of Pixie and was thankful she'd gotten out when she had. Eternally grateful to Nicholas for insisting she go and for having a plan in place before she needed it. I hoped to send a note along with her things, if they'd allow it.

The engine hummed to life. I gave my apartment a final look over one shoulder as we drove away. My time at Francine Frances had been brief, but I'd miss it. Life changes always made me a little sad.

Nicholas had spoken with his team while I looked around the apartment. They were on their way. Once he knew the Reaper had spent so much time there, he knew there would be some clue left behind. Hanging around the way he had demonstrated the intensity of his obsession. He'd been literally waiting to kill me. The pretend fire didn't stop him from thinking I'd be back. He just pulled down the crime tape and waited inside. I was all he'd thought about for years and now, he was so close. He was going all out to make his point. The Reaper wanted me dead. I wished I understood why.

He wanted to punish my father, but I didn't know why he wasn't stalking him. Yes, hurting me would be much worse for Dad. My dad would die for me, without a doubt, without a thought. No questions. There had been plenty of times over the years when the look on Dad's face matched Nicholas's. The memory sent a shiver over my skin. What had he seen that I hadn't?

Did he know that the Reaper had gotten close a few times? Had the Reaper really planned to murder me as a child? That didn't sound right. I was only six when it began. He couldn't have been this angry with me then. I wondered what it was I had done recently that had pushed him off of the precipice he dangled from.

The next few days were a blur. I slept in offices and cars most nights. We ate takeout from cartons and hamburgers wrapped in paper sleeves. My muscles itched to run. My neck cramped from flat hotel pillows and duffle-bag headrests on the road. I didn't feel mistreated. No one near me slept at all. Sara stayed with us in utter discomfort when she could have gone home. Nicholas lectured her about missing classes.

I worked through the conversation with Dad, angry from the lies and burdened by guilt. As much as I wanted to hate him, I didn't think I would've acted differently in his shoes. His hands were tied. His load was far too much for anyone to carry. Still, I wished I'd been able to say goodbye to her. The gaping trench in my heart widened whenever I thought about what had happened.

Nicholas and his team worked around the clock tracking every possibility of a lead. Sara made the waiting easier. She taught me to play Spades, painted my nails, and complained about how hard it was for the women in her family to date. Guys freaked out when her dad gave them a tour of the house and included his medals for valor and gun closet. She said her brothers had it easy because no one worried about their safety. I wondered if my dad would behave the same way if things were different.

The group Sara called the Clean Team found dozens of cigarette butts on campus, but the pile that had been growing outside my apartment had disappeared. Our welcome mat was left with nothing more than ashes and stink. The butts they found in the bushes were being processed in a lab for DNA. The first few had already come back as matches for students. Other results were pending. Luckily it wasn't all happening in the 70s or there would've been a lot more butts to go through. Since girls learned that smoking causes premature aging and wrinkles, the smokers in my generation were numbered. Still, I'd seen my share of smokers around campus. Davis came to mind.

By Wednesday, the team had done all they could for a while. Nicholas would've loved to join the ones who were tracking the Reaper, no doubt, but he was loyal to his assignment. He never left my side. That afternoon over lunch a new drama unrolled.

"I picked up your midterms from the school. Well, I had them faxed. You finish them and I'll return them for you." Nicholas avoided eye contact. "This isn't your fault. We won't let your grades suffer."

He handed me a huge stack of papers, notes, and my texts. I'd conveniently left those at the apartment.

"I'm supposed to study?"

"Yes. You're supposed to go on behaving as normally as you can. It makes it easier long-term." He winked at me and added, "Witness protection can really mess a person up."

"Don't I know it." I sighed and took the stack. Mom wouldn't have wanted this monster to keep me from graduating. I'd put my life on hold too long.

"Have you talked to your dad yet about Thanksgiving?" He was still serious.

"I haven't talked to my dad in over a week. We traded e-mails on Thursday and Friday, before all this started Saturday night. Normally we talk on the phone." Whenever he asked for me, I refused to take his calls. I wanted to, but I wasn't ready.

"Call him." Nicholas flipped open his phone.

I gave him my best crazy face. "Uh, no way. Not on that thing." I pulled my new phone from my jacket pocket. "Will this say my number when it comes up? Will he know it's a new phone?"

He shook his head. "He knows everything, Elle. You're under some serious surveillance. Like lockdown mode." Right. I dialed. I waited for the ringing and teetered between being livid and being afraid. Special Agent Steven Smith had lied to me my entire life. He had left me wrestling an emotional mudslide on an hourly basis. The last time we talked was the same night I was attacked. Yet another thought I had trouble reconciling with reality.

Eventually, I was relieved of the debate. I got his voicemail. I left him a lengthy message about being sorry and needing to talk. I said he could reach me by phone or e-mail. The whole thing probably sounded a lot like "I'm doing swell, ramble, ramble, click." I wiped my forehead with the back of my arm. Nicholas hid a laugh behind the sleeve of his shirt.

"Well, let's go home!" Sara chirped.

Nicholas slapped the table and agreed. "Elle, is it too soon for you to meet my parents?"

Chapter
Twenty-Four

We arrived in Bethesda, Maryland, at midnight. Nicholas's entire family lived in Montgomery County, most of them in the same community. Sara had called ahead while Nicholas and I secured tickets at the airport. They knew we were coming—all of us. I'd have paid good money to listen in on that conversation. I was terrified of bringing Nicholas with me for two days at Thanksgiving. He and Sara acted as if it was no big deal to bring me home for an undetermined amount of time.

Headlights glistened on the rain-spattered streets. From the backseat of the new rental car they looked like the streets back in Ohio, except the houses were bigger. They were all homes the size of the old Victorian I'd loved in South Bend, but these homes were much newer. Most were made of stone and were mildly intimidating. The Victorian I'd loved had been colorful and inviting. It was like living at a bed and breakfast where you made your own breakfast.

I expected the commute to be much longer, but we pulled into one of the drives on the street with big houses. I got out and shut the car door gently, hoping not to awaken anyone inside.

"Nicky! Sara!" A woman ran at us in her robe and slippers across the wetted drive. Her arms opened wide. The twins came together and embraced her. I took a step backward.

"Come on, come on." She pushed them toward the door and reached for me with her free arm. My eyes widened. The word *bewildered* came to mind.

She caught hold of my jacket and pulled me up to meet her. Nicholas managed to slip from her death grip and maneuver his way to my side. He smiled down at me before he kissed the top of my head. I sucked in a chestful of night air, and Sara giggled.

"Mama, this is Elle. I'm not sure what Sara hasn't told you, but here she is." He squeezed me against his side. He sounded proud. Proud of what exactly, I wasn't sure. I thought I probably looked like a puppy might if it were adopted from the pound—just before execution. I was frightened, confused, and desperately grateful. I wanted to hide.

The woman was his mother. The word sank through the layers of my mind. I'd seen her in the dozens of pictures at the cottage. I didn't know why she'd wait up for two Marshals. Of all people, they were prepared to get in safely. Later, I learned they all waited up every time "Nicky" came home. That night was twice the party because Sara had been away, too.

She pulled me to her chest. "Of course she is. Welcome to our home. You may stay here for as long as you'd like." Then she pulled me back to get a better look. She squinted against the night. "Consider yourself part of the family." The words stung my eyes, making me glad to be in the dark.

"Well, get in out of the cold, for crying out loud!" A man's voice called from the front door. He held it wide to let two guys pass. They appeared to be my age.

"Jake, Drew, this is Elle," Nicholas announced as they approached. They took turns lifting and twirling Sara before they made it over to me. Thankfully, they just shook my hand. The boys grabbed all the bags from the car, and the six of us moved toward the front door.

It was like a pajama party inside. In addition to his parents, two brothers, and the three of us, their older sister Olivia was there with her husband and two kids. Olivia and her husband were the only ones who weren't in their pajamas, probably because they weren't sleeping over. They had their own house ten minutes away.

The Austin home was brightly lit and fully decorated for fall. Garlands of silk leaves adorned the fireplace mantle, and pumpkins of every size sat on the hearth. The pillows on the couch and window treatments were brilliant hues of burnt orange. The centerpiece on the dining room table was a cornucopia of fall harvest. Three small white pumpkins finished the perfect look.

Thanksgiving at their house must've been phenomenal. I pictured my dad and me sharing a turkey breast and a few sides. It seemed pitiful in comparison. I loved my Thanksgiving memories anyway, small as they were. I appreciated my life, now more than ever, even if it was a lengthy series of lies.

"So, this is the one who stole your heart?" Olivia approached me and then embraced me without notice.

"This is Olivia," Nicholas said. "My very nosy sister."

"I'm your very observant sister, sweetie." She patted his cheek.

"Would anyone like coffee?" his mother asked from behind me. "You guys must be hungry, too." She stood in the kitchen on the other side of an island filled with food. "Help yourself, kids."

"What can I get you?" Nicholas whispered to me, turning us toward the kitchen. He pulled out a chair at the island. I sat.

"Nothing." I was busy freaking out inside. No time to eat.

"Yeah?" He picked up a plate and filled it with a croissant, a muffin, and a tiny bowl of fruit. He set down the plate in front of me and winked.

A smile crept over me. Everyone watched.

Nicholas sat beside me with a heaping plate of food and two cups of coffee. He set one next to my plate and began to chat with me as if we weren't in a fishbowl.

"I warned you. Our family is crazy."

I couldn't speak. I fought back a lump in my throat. Serial killer or no serial killer, I was as happy as I'd ever been. My eyes scanned the scene, taking in the rooms, the people, and the family. It was perfect.

"Nicky," his mom interrupted our low conversation. "Be sure to show her around the house before you show her to your room. Make sure she's comfortable. Don't just leave her."

I remembered the first night I stayed with him at the cottage. He had walked me into every room, showing me all the switches and detailing everything for me. He was a complete gentleman. I was by far the luckiest girl in America.

After a few minutes, he led me around their home. It was even bigger than it seemed from the driveway. I'd thought it was a one-story home, but it was two stories. Because the house was seated on a hill, the rear of the house was twice as tall as the front. The fully finished basement let out to a large yard and some water. We were on Fenwick Island. A stack of black inner tubes leaned against the patio doors and a dock sliced into the dark water.

I'd spent countless hours imagining myself in movies and sitcoms where there were siblings and two parents. However, until that moment, I'd never truly longed for it. I'd never seen it up close and personal.

My things were already in Nicholas's old room. The room had a shared Jack and Jill bathroom that connected it with Sara's old room. I decided to freshen up from the trip before I went back out to say my good nights.

"Don't look at any of these pictures," Nicholas warned. "Do not touch my yearbooks, and please don't ask my mother about any of these awards." He looked almost like a kid, humbled and embarrassed. Inside those walls, he was just his mother's son. I nodded in confirmation, and he closed the door behind him.

Inside the bathroom, I cried before I showered. I wasn't even sure why. I tried to hurry, but despite the coffee, I was dragging. After my shower, I discovered I hadn't packed any pajamas nice enough to be seen in. Tatty sweats and Dad's old tees weren't how I wanted the Austins to remember me. I knocked on Sara's door.

"Come in." Her voice sounded like my body felt. Exhausted.

"Hey, Elle. Everything okay?"

"Um, yeah, everything's great, except . . . "

"No pajamas?"

My standing in a towel might have given me away.

She dug into a drawer and tossed me something to put on.

I ducked out to change.

After a few minutes, there was a knock on my door.

"Elle?" Sara waited.

I let out a sigh of relief and opened the door.

"Thanks for the pajamas." They were cute. The top looked like a football jersey and the pants were plain gray, made of the softest cotton I'd ever felt. I'd been in my last outfit for two days.

"I'm glad they fit. I hope you're not uncomfortable here." She seemed troubled. "I was in here thinking of how much quiet and privacy you've always had. We must seem like a circus to you."

"No, I'm glad to be here. I'm . . . adjusting." I felt a little bashful talking to her so candidly.

"Hey, you two." Nicholas appeared in the hall behind her. "I made up my bed in the game room. I think the guys are going to stay with me. They're gaming. I need to borrow a plastic guitar."

"Borrow Mom's." Sara smiled.

"It's pink."

Nicholas took my hand and led me out to the great room where his parents sat talking. "The girls are going to turn in," he announced. "I'm going to go rock."

"Do you need my little guitar?" his mom asked genuinely. Sara giggled and elbowed him in the ribs. Mrs. Austin went to get the guitar.

"Well, good night, kids. We're awfully glad you decided to stay here." His father packed up his glasses and reading material. "It's not the same without you." Mr. Austin's voice was another version of Nicholas's, authoritative by trade but softened by age.

Back in the room, I thought about him some more. Nicholas's father had watched me for years. I didn't know how long exactly, but I was definitely a child when it began. To a man who valued family, I thought he might've considered me to be already a part of his. He had protected me like I was his own, and he had watched me grow up until he retired.

I fell asleep that night thinking of my father, Special Agent Smith, and all he'd given up to protect me. I thought Mom would've approved. I did, too. Somehow, I would help make this right.

Chapter Twenty-Five

Nicholas's dad greeted me at the breakfast table with a ready smile. I schlepped to the coffee pot and sat in the chair across from him. "Hi."

"Not a morning person?" His smile grew. I stared. My brain idled.

"I spoke to your dad late last night. He's eager to talk with you."

"Really?" I sat straighter, forcing my mind to attention. "He's safe? Is he coming here?"

"He's working a solid lead. His team's got him covered, but they think it's wise to keep you two apart for the moment."

My shoulders drooped. I pressed the steaming mug to my lips and sipped. I had so much to say to Dad.

The front door swung open, setting a blast of cold air loose through the room. I nearly dropped under the table with a heart attack. Nicholas pushed the door shut and rubbed his palms together. Dressed in running gear and a beanie, his cheeks and nose were red from brisk morning air. Nothing like a sudden blast of icy air to wake me up in the morning. I rubbed my palms against the gooseflesh on my arms.

He winked at me and clapped his dad on the back.

"How'd you sleep?"

I shivered. My fingers wrapped around the mug for warmth as the cold air settled around us. "Dad called last night. He's calling for me today."

"When?" Nicholas's mom spoke nearby. Mrs. Austin smiled in the hallway off the kitchen. "Sara and I are going shopping. We hoped you'd come along."

I shook my head. "I think I should stay here." Dad had given up everything trying to keep me safe. I needed to get back to him in one piece, no matter how good gourmet coffee and a hot pretzel from the food court sounded.

"You can spend the day with me." Nicholas sat beside me with a bottle of water.

Awkwardness settled on my shoulders. I pressed the mug against my lips.

I dressed in jeans and a hoodie after breakfast, but Nicholas zipped his parka over me too, insisting that the wind off the bay was ruthless. Sun shone over the water behind the Austin home, twinkling on the surface and blinding me temporarily.

"I love the water," he said. "I grew up tubing on this water. Jet Skis, kayaks, you name it. I love it."

"I grew up loving our cabin in the woods. I'm more of a tree climber, four-wheeler girl."

Nicholas took my hand in his, warming me from head to toe. We walked along the water and onto a short private dock. He lifted my hand to his lips and kissed it. Quick and gentle. No big deal, like he did it all the time. Then he dropped it and handed me a rock.

I scrunched my nose. "Thanks?" A giggle slipped out. Weird guy.

"Okay, Outdoor Barbie, can you do this?"

I lifted an eyebrow. No one had ever called me a Barbie before.

Nicholas made a big show of winding his arm back and rocking on his heel like a professional baseball pitcher, then came forward in slow motion, whipping his wrist at the last moment and tossing his rock against the water. It skipped and spun several times before disappearing. I clapped and whistled through my teeth and two fingers.

"You want to see that again?" He tossed another smooth, flat stone in the air before us. A stack of stones sat at our feet on the wide wooden planks.

While he wound up, I lifted a rock from the pile.

"What? No cheering this time? One cheer is all I get?" He popped one hip in a what-gives pose.

"Can I try?"

He smirked and bent down to choose a rock.

"Oh, no I'm ready." I held my rock between my fingers.

Nicholas gave me an underhand wave and I let it loose. My rock glided over the water like it had an engine, touching and jumping endlessly until it disappeared in the distance. Unable to hide the smug look on my face, I looked at my feet, enjoying the burn of my cheeks.

A round of applause broke out from the lawn behind us. His brothers and their friends clapped, some with footballs tucked under their arms.

The youngest wrapped fingers around his lips and yelled, "She schooled you, son."

That was it. I laughed. My world went topsy-turvy as Nicholas tossed me over one shoulder and took off toward his house. The crowd of boys came running after us. I laughed until my sides ached from lack of oxygen and sheer joy.

"Nicholas?" Our run stopped short when his mother opened the rear deck door. "Elle's phone's ringing."

Nicholas set me on the tile inside the back door. I jumped and stumbled over my feet getting to my bag and pulled half the contents out with the phone.

"Dad! Is that you? Oh my goodness, I've been so freaked out." I didn't care that all of the Austins probably listened. I also didn't care about the lies or any of it. Dad was safe and that was all I needed to know. As long as he was safe, I had hope for a different future with him. We could make sure the Reaper never tore another family apart.

Having all the lies stripped away made it so much easier for me to really know my dad. For once, we were in cahoots instead of avoiding one another. Dad had kept his distance in the past. He didn't need to anymore. We'd reached a turning point.

"Elle, can I come and get you? I can be there in a few hours. We have a lot to talk about."

I shook my head and struggled for a full breath. "No, don't, Dad. I'm doing fine here." He sounded so eager to be with me. My heart warmed. "I'd like to see our new house. Maybe I can come to Texas for Thanksgiving?"

"It's not safe to travel. You need to take this more seriously. Let me come to you."

"I am." I bit into the thick of my lips. Maybe he didn't get the whole story. I was taking it very seriously. "I'll bring my Marshal with me."

I heard a few coughs from the next room, and I smiled.

After a few minutes of begging, he agreed. Then he requested to speak with Nicholas.

"Your turn," I whispered to Nicholas, extending the phone in his direction.

His family backed away.

Nicholas smiled a charming smile and took the call on the front porch.

I paced around the kitchen island for an eternity. When the latch on the door sounded, I jumped. "What'd he say?"

"He'll see us for Thanksgiving."

I nodded and pushed the thought from my mind before heading to take a shower. I did a double take when I opened the bedroom door. The room looked different. White eyelet lace had replaced the blue comforter. There were several outfits strewn across the bed. I looked around for evidence that another Austin might be staying there.

"We went shopping." His mom's voice startled me. She stood in the doorway smiling. "We got you a few new things. Olivia joined us at the mall. The girls had fun picking it all out. The bedspread is one of mine. It's been in my family for years. I thought it suited you better than that old blue thing."

"The clothes are . . . "

"Gifts. We wanted to do something nice. You don't like them? They're probably all the wrong size, but you're so small, we went with those. Will they work?"

"No. I mean yes. I love them. Thank you. I . . . I don't have anything for you, and you've done so much already." I sat on the bed feeling small like she said but not in the way she meant.

"You've done more than you know." Her voice was soft before she closed the door, leaving me to my shower.

I lived the next few days in a fairy tale, my fairy tale. I blended with Nicholas's family. His dad was just like mine. His mother was more than I could've hoped for, and all the siblings made chaos enjoyable. The boys attended high school like me, and they had a continuous parade of friends coming through the house. They were all welcomed, all known by name, and they all called Nicholas's parents Mom and Dad.

I hated to leave them, but I missed my dad.

Chapter Twenty-Six

Nicholas and I packed our bags and headed to Dallas. If I thought about it too long, terror seized my chest. I'd promised to bring my Marshal for protection. I hadn't told Dad I'd fallen in love with him. Nicholas's dad, Daniel, warned us. If we had any personal stories to tell, they'd have to be told by us. In other words, he wasn't getting involved. That shot of awkward was on us. Telling Dad how I felt about Nicholas would be more difficult than telling him about being attacked.

I waited for my luggage at the carrousel, bouncing in place a mile a minute. Nicholas stayed close to capture each bag as it came riding by. Once he had them all, he reached out and pulled me to him.

"Hey, it's going to be fine. I promise. We're going to have a great Thanksgiving. You're surrounded by security. There will be one military-trained professional with you at all times. You have nothing to fear." He leaned in close enough to kiss me, and my heart fluttered. He pressed his forehead to mine instead. It was hard to be upset with Nicholas so close.

I never knew how to take his gentleness. Sometimes it felt like he was coddling a child. Before he straightened, he pushed the hair from my shoulders and planted a feathery kiss below my right ear. My temperature rose ten degrees. The moment was brief but intimate. Hope rose through my chest. I took his hand, and we turned together to meet Dad outside of the terminal.

Before I'd taken my first step I saw him. He must've used his badge to get past security because he stood, frozen, not twenty feet from us, staring. I had no defense for what came next. The look on his purple face told me the exchange between Nicholas and me hadn't gone unseen. Incapable of bravado, I shut my eyes to hide. It never worked. Nicholas dragged me toward him.

"Mr. Smith, it's nice to see you again, sir." Nicholas stretched his arm out to shake my father's hand. "It's an honor to be here and to work the Reaper case with you. We've made some real headway these past few months. I'd love to talk to you about it."

My father stared at me, waiting. I smiled, hoping I looked innocent.

Dad ran a hand through his graying hair. "Nicholas." He shook his hand and the pain in my chest eased slightly. "Gabby." He pulled me to his chest and held me tight. Dad rested his cheek on my head and made no effort to release me. "I missed you, baby girl," he said, his voice thick with emotion. He stroked my hair against my back.

"I missed you too, Dad."

"I've been worried sick. I'm so sorry."

"It's okay. I'm in good hands." I smiled at the memories I'd collected in Maryland.

Dad straightened, took one of my hands, and pulled me away from the baggage claim.

Nicholas kept pace, pulling our things along with him.

I couldn't form a complete sentence the whole way to our new house.

That didn't stop Nicholas. "Being assigned to Elle has changed my life, Agent Smith," Nicholas said in the car.

My mouth popped open, and Dad glared at him in the rearview mirror.

Nicholas had thick skin. He just kept going. He told Dad all about his family and what they'd been up to for the past few years. Some of it seemed to entertain Dad, but mostly, it all led back to the glaring.

Once Dad started speaking, he and Nicholas had a long discussion regarding the details of my attack and what had gone on since then. They communicated in that same odd code Nicholas had used on the phone at the cottage. This time, I was more familiar with the lingo and acronyms. Mr. Austin had given Dad the framework. Now Nicholas filled in the details.

We pulled into the driveway of a large one-story home. An inviting front porch adorned an otherwise standard red-brick construction. My new home looked abandoned. I followed Dad to the door. Nicholas carried in the bags behind me. The heat was unreal, and I'd run out of layers to remove. I needed another shower.

Inside the front door, the entranceway led into the family room. The dining area and kitchen flowed together. Bedrooms were nestled on the other side of the house. Boxes lined the walls in every direction. None of them had any labels in Sharpie like I told him. Some had been torn open and stuffed shut again. I sighed. Welcome to my new home.

"Dad, how long have you been here?"

He rolled his eyes. "Honestly, most of these boxes have spent more time here than I have. I've been on a plane headed to Dallas from Indiana, then back to Illinois, then back to Dallas, oh, and I stopped for a day in Branson. It's been a runaround." He looked defeated.

"I'll help. You guys talk, and I'll see what I can do."

They left together for Dad's home office. I opened the boxes one at a time. I moved them to the appropriate rooms and unpacked them. Three hours later the men emerged. I'd ordered delivery. The aroma must've been enough to break their concentration.

"Holy smokes, Elle! How long were we in there?" Nicholas looked at the door to the office and back to me. I'd managed to clear the family room and dining area, as well as put out some décor. It wasn't my first rodeo. The boxes were flattened and tied for recycling. Overall, the house looked more like a home and less like a makeshift distribution center.

I didn't miss the contrast between Nicholas's easy disposition and Dad's stiff posture. I shoved my hands into my pockets and looked back at Nicholas.

"Enjoy the takeout tonight, because tomorrow I cook." I considered them warned.

Chapter
Twenty-Seven

"Dad, I have a list of foods, and I need to get to the grocery store," I announced as soon as Nicholas walked into the kitchen.

He let us out of his sight after a staring contest with Nicholas. He imposed a time limit and gave us a specific store to shop at not five miles away. We were to shop and return, nothing more. Dad had never been so protective. I wondered if it was the killer or the Marshal who had him worried.

"I'm so sorry he's freaking out," I said in the car. "I told you this was a bad idea. I'm so embarrassed."

"Don't be."

"Right. Easy for you to say. Your parents welcomed me, no questions."

"You're comparing apples to circus people. I expected much worse than this. It's been only the two of you for years. He's right to be protective. What would he have without you?"

I snuck a peek at him and smiled.

"My family's so big, what's one more? Besides, you should've seen Dad when Olivia first brought Allen home. It wasn't much better."

"Yeah?" I didn't care if it was true. I enjoyed the comparison. He must not have thought of me as a pound puppy. Perhaps, if things were much different, I'd be a love interest.

"Yeah." He squeezed my hand for reassurance. "It's not the same for girls. You're more vulnerable." He hitched an eyebrow and braced himself for the hit he deserved. Totally sexist remark, yes, but true anyway. I wasn't as strong as Nicholas, and I hoped the Reaper wasn't either.

We made it to the store in ten minutes. I could've run it if there wouldn't have been so many bags to bring back. I hadn't been able to run in two weeks. My hands shook, but not like before. Despite everything, I slept better, and in my dream, I fought back. There was comfort in not playing the sitting-duck role. I missed running, though, and I wondered what it would be like to run in the Texas heat. Running in the midwestern summer didn't compare. The heat in Texas was different. Even in November the air was stifling, unless that was symptomatic of my state of mind.

Icy air belted us in the face as we walked through the automatic sliding doors of the store. I headed to the butcher for the main dish first. Nicholas's phone rang before I had time to choose a small turkey for three. He stepped away to answer the call, leaving me to select a bird. It wasn't easy. Most of them were frozen, but considering we planned to eat ours in a few hours, I had to go with fresh. The choices were daunting. A lady in a white smock tried to help me from behind a four-foot counter. I looked to Nicholas for help, but the expression on his face was blank, fathomless, as he listened. The Marine. A zing jumped through my heart at what the face might mean. I pointed at a random turkey, and the counter lady wrapped it.

I picked up the pace and headed to the checkout. Something had happened. I knew Nicholas couldn't talk to me about it in public. I couldn't get to the car fast enough. One hundred and twenty-two dollars later, we headed home. Nicholas hadn't spoken since the phone rang. We loaded the car in silence, too. The minute I shut my car door, I exploded, "Who was on the phone?"

"That was the team."

Nicholas and I spoke at the same time. He smiled at me, and my concentration failed for a minute.

"Go," I said, pointing at him. I needed to know what he knew.

"They have a hit on the cigarette." He smiled. I knew he thought I should be thanked for the lead. I couldn't tell them anything other than that he smoked. Who knew that would be useful?

"Okay."

"It's not a match for any member of the student body, teaching staff, groundskeepers, alumni, or the guest speakers from the festival. It's an anomaly. They were unable to make any viable connection between it and anyone who actually belonged at Francine Frances. The butt matched those they found on the ground outside your apartment building. Your tip about the mat was pure gold. The team had to sift through the bushes, but they got what they needed."

My heart pounded and flipped in my chest. I was about to hear what I'd been waiting for.

"Elle, we've got him. His name is Miles Thomas Wade."

The name rolled around in my mind, trying to sound lethal. It was disappointing on some level. I wasn't sure what I'd expected. It's not like his parents named him "homicidal maniac." I knew he'd have a name just like everyone else, but it didn't fit. *Miles Thomas Wade* sounded like a spoiled rich kid, or a character in a made-for-TV movie.

"You said groundskeepers?"

"They checked anyone who might've been on campus for a good reason."

"There was a guy. He wore tan overalls and approached me at the wall." Images of the stranger came vividly to mind. "I saw him when

I was decorating for the festival, too." Could he have taken me then? I was so stupid to be alone.

"Mack Harris. He's fine. A little pervy, according to staff, but harmless. No record. I saw him talk to you and checked him out."

"You saw that?"

"I see everything." The serious set of his brow worried me. Emotion flashed over his face and was buried before I could name it. "I didn't know he was decorating."

"He was helping clean up the mess we were making. There were a few groundskeepers there that night."

Nicholas drove back to the house at warp speed. I barely saw him or my dad for the rest of the afternoon. When dinner was almost ready, I snuck up on them. I had a few minutes of downtime while the turkey sat, before the rolls needed to go in the oven, so I peeked in on them.

I wasn't surprised to see my dad's office fully set up. He was on the phone and online at the same time. Nicholas watched over Dad's shoulder as he worked. The files lying everywhere looked a lot different to me through enlightened eyes. The whole room looked more like the Batcave than an old guy's office. Knowing what I knew, it was hard to imagine how I hadn't seen it for what it was sooner.

He hung up and glared at Nicholas. "We're all set on my end."

"Yes, sir. We'll head home. I'll keep her there until you call."

"What's going on between you and my daughter?" Dad's tone was harsh. I stepped back farther into the hall. "Your family's always been professional. How is it you've become involved with Gabriella? What's your family have to say about this? Your dad seemed to think you'd have all the answers. Then I came to meet you at the airport and found you kissing her."

The edge in his voice made me sweat. It was unimaginably hot in Texas.

There was a very long pause. So long, in fact, that I had to peek back to see if Nicholas had climbed out the window. The two men were having another stare-down.

"I love her, sir."

My head swam. I'm pretty sure my heart stopped. I quit breathing.

"Excuse me?"

I peeked again.

Dad gripped his desk. "How do you expect to protect her if you're involved like this?"

I pulled my head back, and he pounded a fist against his desk. I shuddered.

"Are you crazy or just suffering from an extremely low IQ? That's my daughter out there." His voice rose, and suddenly I had no idea how I had ever believed my dad was an insurance adjuster.

"My only daughter, my only family, my only reason to get up every morning, and you're risking her life. You do realize that. You're going to get her killed because every single minute you spend thinking about your feelings is a moment you aren't guarding her. In case you haven't noticed, son, she needs a protector, not a boyfriend."

"Yes, sir."

My heart dissolved at his agreement. Ice filled my veins. My cheeks burned.

"I know this, sir. I've discussed it at length with my father and grandfather. It's a difficult position, one I know you're well acquainted with, but I cannot reassign her because I cannot leave her."

There was a tiny crash, like a pencil hitting the wall, and then some low murmuring.

"If you put her in danger . . . " Dad's voice choked off mid-threat.

Nicholas cut in. "I will not fail her, sir. I will not." The conviction in his voice was so strong that he could have promised anything and I would've believed him.

Dad huffed and swore. I bit my lip, waiting. My heartbeat pounded in my throat.

"I love her, too." Dad's voice was barely a whisper.

"I know, sir."

I held my breath during the long pause, afraid I'd miss what he said next.

"When you're attached, everything's more complicated. Your thoughts are divided. Your reaction time's hindered while you weigh the added possibilities and wonder how your response will impact her. How will your attachment impact her? How do you know this isn't your undoing? How can *I* know you'll keep her safe?"

"Because I would give my life for hers."

Dad sighed. His desk chair squeaked. "Don't let her down, Austin."

"No, sir."

My mouth fell open. My eyes filled with tears. Nicholas noticed me looking and slipped out.

"Can I help you for a while?" He motioned toward the kitchen.

"I'm okay," I lied, unless *okay* meant terrified and thrilled and crazy.

"Come on. I know my way around a kitchen. Let me help. Your dad won't mind."

I smiled because I'd heard it all firsthand. "You can go back in there, you know."

"Uh-uh." He waved a finger at me. "You're my responsibility. There's nothing I can do in there that they aren't already doing. This sweet-potato casserole isn't going to bake itself."

I appreciated the company. I'd adjusted quickly to not being alone. Any excuse to be with Nicholas was a good one.

We worked on the trimmings for a while and then it was finally time. Thanksgiving in Dallas. I took a mental snapshot for later.

My dad closed his eyes for the standard Thanksgiving prayer, but it wasn't the same. Normally, the prayer was dry and predictable. *"Thank you for the food, for the time off work to be with Gabriella, etc."* Thanksgiving in Dallas was full of surprises.

"Father," Dad began in a small voice. "Thank you for my daughter. Thank you for keeping her safe all of these years and for the marvelous future I know You have planned for her. I should've done many things differently."

My dad wiped his face. "Thank you," he choked, "for her precious mother and every single day I had with her."

There was a long pause. My eyes stung with emotion. *My dad was praying, for me.*

"Thank you for the Austin family. You put them in place long ago, long before I could've known the role they'd play today. But, You knew. Give this young man the wisdom and strength he needs to protect my little girl." One more pause had me choking back a decade of tears. "For today, bless this food and the hands that prepared it. Amen."

That prayer contained more emotion than I'd heard from my father in years. Being so guarded and feeling so guilty must've been difficult for him. Maybe guarded and guilty was another level we could connect on. I dabbed my napkin at my eyes and looked to see what effect the words had had on Nicholas.

Nicholas only winked at me and added a hearty, "Amen."

They must've agreed to separate the case from Thanksgiving because no one mentioned the Reaper. He didn't belong at our dinner table. Everything I needed sat in front of me. After dinner, Dad helped with the dishes.

"Well," I said. "Spill."

Dad looked at Nicholas first and then me. Dinner was over. Time to get down to business.

"They've linked him to the Wade family in Grosse Pointe, Michigan."

They told me this was an affluent community in the Snow Belt.

Using his name, Nicholas's team found the house near Francine Frances where Miles Thomas Wade had stayed. They couldn't find any evidence to suggest he remained. To the contrary, they were certain he'd gone. They just didn't know where. They guessed Miles had left abruptly because the apartment was in disarray. According to

Jim, he had an ashtray full of cigarette butts to match the one found on the school grounds, and his fingerprints were everywhere.

The next morning, while everyone else in America brawled for bargains, I rode to the airport. These past few weeks had given me a better idea of what my dad's life had been like. I had always assumed he liked to travel. There was no way that was possible. He had it rough, especially during the holidays. While we headed back to Maryland, Dad and a few agents went up to Michigan for a visit. Traffic, air or otherwise, was horrendous.

"Take care of my baby." Dad squeezed my cheeks in his hands. "You're guarding my heart, son."

"Yes, sir."

Dad kissed my head and shook Nicholas's hand. They exchanged a long, meaningful look before breaking apart. Dad let me go with the only man to ever proclaim his love for me. A twenty-two-year-old U.S. Marshal. How had I ever believed my life was boring?

Chapter
Twenty-Eight

I was back in my room in Maryland when we got the next update.

"Elle, are you up?" Nicholas's voice came on the heels of a knock against my door.

"Come in." I stood to let him in, but he met me halfway. He had his hand extended before him. Phone in one hand, he sat on the bed.

"Okay, go ahead, Jim. Elle's here now."

Jim's voice came through the little speaker loud and clear. "Federal agents met with Mr. Thomas Wade in Michigan this afternoon. No sign of his son. I thought you might like an update."

"Yes, thank you." I was desperate to hear that my father was okay and we were closer to finding this monster.

"Well, Thomas Wade is in his late seventies, seventy-seven to be exact. He's the retired dean of a prep school in Grosse Pointe. He's not in great health, and he's in agreement that his son is a likely candidate for this behavior. The story he told your father went like this . . . "

263

Jim began at the beginning, when Miles was young. "Thomas Wade had an affair with a student from his school. His wife died the same year this information came to light. Mr. Wade married the girl after his wife's death. She later went missing. He refused to date again, certain that Miles had had a hand in his second wife's disappearance. He and Miles spent some very uncomfortable years together until Miles left for college."

"Wow. So, there's a link to a private school? That's where Dad thought that I should spend my senior year." Astonished, I looked at Nicholas. Irony at its finest.

Nicholas looked aggravated. "Yeah, and assuming he saw you with me, if he knew I wasn't a student, no wonder he had another snap." Nicholas pointed out the elephant I'd missed.

Dumb luck. He must've seen the whole thing replaying—his mother's death, his father's indiscretion, and the girl ruining his life. There I was running from him, never knowing who he was, and I had still managed to play out the exact worst scenario right before his sick, watchful eyes.

"Mr. Wade insisted that his son seek counseling after his mother's death. There were extensive notes at the practice where he was seen. We've sent them to you."

Nicholas logged into his e-mail and turned the screen between us so we could read together. The notes painted an ominous picture.

"Until he was twelve, he lived with both his parents. His parents were from well-to-do backgrounds, and his mother stayed at home while his father acted as dean at a local private school.

"His mother rarely remained at their home, however. She spent her days at social engagements or the spa. In his perception, Mrs. Wade had rare need of Miles's company and spoke to him only as was required by etiquette.

"On the other hand, Mrs. Wade expressed concern over her son's behavior while he was very young. She described his proclivity for dissecting things found on their property. Her husband dismissed her, saying boys were curious. She brought Miles to a counselor for a handful of sessions with no results. Miles was young. The counselor didn't get much response from him.

"A few years later his mother found him with her missing cat. She'd sought the cat for several days before confronting her son directly. The cat, once a treasured pet, was slit up the abdomen. Still alive. Miles claimed he had found him that way, but his mother believed he held the cat for several days before carving into it. After that, she pulled away from Miles completely. When Mr. Wade continued to make excuses for their son's behavior, she spent as much time as possible in their summer home, traveling, or otherwise avoiding the child.

"Miles's father was another story. He was dean of the private high school, where Miles later enrolled. Miles openly begrudged his father's long hours, claiming he spent barely three hours annually in his father's presence, and he hated him for that.

"He and his father had a turbulent relationship at best. Miles was perpetually in trouble, and Mr. Wade stayed busy brooming it under the rug. While Miles was enrolled in Mr. Wade's high school, there were a number of complaints by his classmates about Miles's behavior outside of class. He was known for his sexual aggression. The reports were stanched because the incidents didn't happen on school property. The students didn't file reports with local authorities.

"Miles's mother became ill during his freshman year and moved home for the duration of her illness.

"A few months later, his father asked his mother for a divorce despite her dwindling health. He professed his love for a student from Miles's school, as if it were a thing to be proud of instead of the final nail in his wife's coffin. He announced that the affair with the girl had gone on for more than a year. She'd finally reached her eighteenth birthday, and he wanted to leave his wife and marry the girl. Miles's new stepmother would be barely more than four years his senior.

"Following his mother's funeral, his father married the girl, but she went missing during Miles's senior year of high school. Police investigated Mr. Wade and searched the home and the couple's other properties. Her body wasn't recovered, but they confirmed her pregnancy through medical records. A pregnancy that the family tennis pro, Tim Echolls, claimed was the result of their relationship. A journal found with the missing woman's things outlined a penchant for multiple lovers, included rants about her husband's preoccupation with work, and detailed her numerous sexual exploits and rebellions, including a sexual relationship with Miles."

My eyes stretched wide as I finished reading. My cheeks burned with this information. Despite the disturbing images floating in my mind, I wanted more, wished there was a page to turn to hear how it ended, but we all knew.

I jumped at the voice on the other side of the phone. I forgot he waited while we read. Now we were caught up.

"We believe the stepmother was Miles's first murder, though the body has never been recovered. It's not uncommon for someone like him to hone his M.O. After graduation Miles bounced from college to college, enrolling and dropping out until Mr. Wade got tired of his son's shenanigans and stopped paying for his lifestyle. Unfortunately, Miles had a trust fund. His father's position didn't change Miles's ability to move around the country. Father and son are estranged. Miles hasn't been home in over a decade."

"Did his mom's death push him over the edge?" Disbelief colored my words. I had lost my mom. She was torn from my life at a much younger age than fourteen, and I never hurt anyone.

"No. We have multiple complaints from childhood neighbors about pets going missing. Accusations from a schoolmate that a young Miles fed antifreeze to a local puppy. Records show that the fire department made a number of trips to the Wade home in Miles's formative years as well. The details surrounding the cases weren't available, but I think if we find a fireman from that ladder, we'll hear that the fires weren't all accidents."

"So, do we know his whereabouts during all that time?" Nicholas asked.

"Yes." Jim's voice dropped a bit. "His father gave us a list of all the schools he attended. We called the schools and got his academic records. That helped us set up a timeline for him. I don't think any of us was surprised to see that each of the Reaper murders happened in cities where he attended college, during the same time he was there. When the prosecution adds that information to the DNA on the cigarettes, found on the school grounds and at his apartment, it'll be easy to bring him in. We expect his fingerprints will match some partial prints found in the first victims' apartments. We're building our case around the clock. After fourteen years, Elle, we have what we need to find him. Thank you."

Me? I did nothing, unless being oblivious counted.

"What about Elle?" Nicholas asked.

How could I be the first question he had after everything Jim had told us? I had a dozen questions.

"We think she should stay in D.C. Pick a safe location. Change her name. Change her look. Stay with her. We need to pull her deep under cover. She needs to disappear. He's already mad, and we're about to tip him over."

"What about you guys and my dad?" I didn't want to think about what my new look would be.

"We're preparing to hold a press conference tomorrow. Agent Smith's planning to do it exactly as he did twelve years ago. Only this time, we have a name and a face to broadcast."

"What will he do?" Hadn't the last press conference infuriated him, sent him straight for my family and resulted in my mother's death? Nicholas stifled a laugh, probably because I had monopolized the exchange. I'd lost all self-control. The questions fell out of me.

"We fully expect to provoke him," Jim stated with zeal. "For that reason, we want to move you immediately. Your dad will be under twenty-four-hour surveillance as well. We're hoping Miles will slip up, see red, and get caught. Now, we wait."

The look on my face must've been priceless. Nicholas took Jim off of speaker. They spoke privately for a few minutes while I processed.

He hung up. "They're setting up a tip line, and they'll keep us posted."

"What did he mean about the fingerprints? I thought he never left any evidence?"

"He killed for years Elle. The early murders were farther apart. He spent time in their apartments instead of taking them directly to a second location, and he didn't remove their nails or fingerprints. By the time the FBI linked the newer, fast-coming murders with the older, sparser ones, evidence was lost or damaged. However, there were some partial prints on a bedroom door they never matched with anyone they could link to the victim. Same thing in two other early cases. It's small, but it's something. You'd be surprised what our team can pull together from a thread left on the carpet." He squeezed my hand.

"He'll be enraged after the press conference." I didn't want to lose my dad. My chest tightened with fear, even while seated on the crisp white lace of my fairy tale. Everything in sight was lovely. Everything beyond my sight was death.

Chapter
Twenty-Nine

Sunlight swirled in through the aromas of vanilla and cinnamon overhead. The clock on the nightstand read 7:00. Last time I'd peeked, it was after six. Mr. Austin knocked at my door.

"Care if I come in?"

"No. Of course not. Come in." I sat up, pulling the comforter around me.

"So, I hear today's the big day. Nicholas and his mother are out preparing for your makeover." He carried a tray in one hand with coffee service for two. I lifted one cup to my lips.

"Ugh." I rolled my eyes and sucked down the coffee. "Thank you."

"We'd do it for anyone." He caught my eye.

"I believe that. That wasn't what I meant, though."

"What *do* you mean, Elle?"

My lips rolled in over my teeth. "For protecting us all those years. For getting Dad and me this far." I pulled in a long breath. "For Nicholas. You've done so much more than I could ever really thank you for, I suppose." To me, Nicholas represented his family. Some had to overcome their family issues. His wasn't one of those. This family produced incredible, kind, loving, honorable people like Nicholas. I would be forever indebted.

Without another word, he pulled me to his shoulder and squeezed.

"What's this?" Nicholas's voice broke up our exchange.

"Oh, I just love coffee." I blinked back the emotions that threatened my composure.

"What's the new look?" Mr. Austin cleared his throat.

"How about a tribute to Pixie?" Nicholas hitched up one side of his mouth and winked.

"You wouldn't!" I nearly pulled the covers over my head.

"Who's Pixie? Isn't that one of those bands from the game your brothers play?"

"You're thinking of the Pixies."

Mr. Austin looked incredulous, and it broke the tension. Surely that was what Nicholas was going for, breaking the tension. He couldn't be serious. I had something else in mind, like a dark wig and glasses á la Clark Kent. The point being, it'd be easy to remove.

Nicholas held out an enormous bag full of things from a preferred goth store at one of the larger malls. I held my breath. Sara entered the room behind him with a large makeup case and bottle of black hair dye. Crap. They weren't kidding. I gulped down the coffee and pretended it was another Priscilla-style makeover.

Two-and-a-half hours later, the transformation felt a lot like an overdone Halloween to me. I had no idea how to recreate the effect despite the fact that Sara explained it to me slowly, twice. I cringed as she dyed my hair black, cut it to an inch above my shoulders, and straightened it with a straightening iron. She painted my face white and added a few faux piercings to my basically unrecognizable face. Even my fake eyelashes had rhinestones at the tips.

"That's hot," Andrew stated on his way past. Jacob lounged behind him. They stared at me for a moment, then exchanged a quick glance and moved on. Neither of them said another word.

"What do you think?" Sara asked me.

"I think the skirt is too short, the heels are too high, and the piercings are scary." Those were my top three complaints. I had more.

"I like the skirt." Nicholas strode into the room, taking my breath away. His expression grew sober.

"You said it yourself, Elle. The Reaper wouldn't look twice at someone like Pixie. I believe you're right. I think he'll look right past this person in a crowd." He pointed to my reflection in the mirror.

"There's no crowd here. I stick out like a sore thumb." Complaining fit the ensemble. "So, where are we going this time?"

"D.C. There are a number of federal safe locations there. Sometimes a large metropolis is better than a small town. You follow?"

"Gotcha."

He was hiding me in plain sight. They said it all the time on television. I remembered the crowd at The Pier. Emotion lodged in my throat. Moving back to the town from which we'd fled brought emotion. I'd lived there with my mom. Mom had *lived* there.

Back to where it all started. Wow.

"Here, you'll need these." Nicholas handed me an envelope like the one he'd given Pixie. Money and some documents lay inside. I thumbed over a birth certificate, social security number, and a metro pass.

"Sloan McQuewick?" I raised a freshly plucked brow. "I sound like a real-estate agent."

"Making up girl names isn't my strongest job skill." He smiled.

I frowned. "Sloan?" I shook my head.

He pulled me to him, smiling. "I'm not great at names. I can still call you Elle. You don't have to get used to answering to Sloan or anything."

"Unless I talk to anyone else."

"Right."

Fine. I had no intention of speaking to anyone. For all I knew, I'd chat up the Reaper. "What's with all the documentation? Why bother?" Overkill, especially if he believed they were on the verge of catching the Reaper. I'd be back to Francine Frances after winter break.

He avoided eye contact. "Due diligence." He pretended to pack up my new wardrobe. "You might decide to come back when you graduate. A metro pass is good to have."

I couldn't speak. Two things hit me. First, the idea that this could be over soon. Second, did he want me to move out here? Live near him for college? I let myself get excited. There was an amazing pre-law program in D.C., less than an hour from the Austins. I would finally live in a thriving metropolis. A place filled with people, smog, and crime. I'd be close to my new family. My ultimate collegiate goal. Nicholas had made it feel possible.

Tears threatened to ruin my new makeup.

"You have to keep up with your studies while you're away. Your school understands there are extenuating circumstances, but you can't quit working toward graduation. You've worked your whole life to have options like law school, and you can probably have your pick. You have plenty of essays to write and applications to fill out. Even if this drags on, stay on top of your studies. Have you seen your grades and test scores? Crazy good. The amount of volunteer work you've done? Incredible. A little mind-boggling, to be honest."

"We never stayed in one place long enough for me to join a team or school club, but every town needs volunteers. I made do."

"Six months till graduation."

"Yep."

"And I can do the work from D.C.?"

"Yes." He smiled a dashing "you're welcome" smile.

I stared at him, utterly speechless. Then I kissed him. I threw myself at him. I didn't care if his family stood nearby. I breathed in his cologne and cherry ChapStick, memorizing the feeling of him holding me. His lips were soft and full. His hands were warm against my back. He didn't push me away as I expected. He pulled me closer, held me tight, and kissed me back.

The sensation of two magnets pulled together overcame me once more. It was the kind of feeling I wished wouldn't end. My heart pounded for a new reason. My head fell away from his too soon. I held my eyes shut tight. His family was gone when I opened them.

"Sorry," I breathed, half afraid I'd crossed a line. My lips were full and tingly from the kiss, hot and sweet like his ChapStick.

He smiled a very cat-that-ate-the-canary smile, seemingly unaffected by my attack. "I feel the need to remind you. You're a witness in my care, and also a minor." The last word intentionally broken in half.

I crossed my arms behind my back to assure him I'd control myself. I didn't deserve this man, but I wouldn't let that stop me from reveling in my good fortune.

We spent the next day choosing a safe location in the city. Nicholas managed to get a place two blocks from the Marshals' offices. We went to get acclimated after dinner. The city was busier than I'd remembered. The highways seemed to morph into one surging entity as they merged and converged in every direction. A far cry from small-town America.

Keeping in line with the new me, Nicholas wore camouflaged cargo pants and a black hooded sweatshirt with army boots. He still managed to look hot. Together he and Sloan were quite a sight. We spent the day like any normal goth tourists. In our case, Nicholas also served as tour guide. The crowd was thick and diverse. I had no problem melding into the mix.

The setting sun backlit lit the monuments. My heart swelled. The architecture was amazing. All these years later, I saw it with new, grown-up eyes and appreciated what the city represented.

After dinner, we went to the safe house. It was a two-story townhome in an old stone building on the corner of Fifth and Bechtel.

Inside, the refrigerator brimmed, and the bed looked inviting. Someone had beaten us there and set up everything I'd need.

I stood before the bay window, trying to count the number of times I'd moved since I first lived in D.C., or even since May.

Nicholas's phone rang.

My heart stopped mid-beat. Thoughts of my dad shoved their way in. I twisted the curtains around my fingers. Creases and wrinkles raced up the length of the fabric. The call sounded bad. Nicholas no longer smiled. I worked my fingers free from the crinkled fabric and listened for some clue as to what had happened. This wasn't news about a lead.

"Mr. Wade's not talking." He placed the phone inside his back pocket. "They're interviewing others from Miles's past, but his dad's refusing to get involved."

"You think he's afraid of his son?" I frowned.

"From what we know, I assume his dad wants to keep his family name out of the paper. He's a staple in the community. This could ruin what he's worked so hard to ignore all these years. I'm sure Miles has heard about the press conference by now. We named him. With any luck, he's not thinking clearly. He's not scheming and plotting anymore. He'll lose control. If so, that's good news for us. So long as we keep you hidden."

Without thinking, I wound my arms around his waist. I was safe, but what would the Reaper do to my father if he got the opportunity? Small tremors began in my hands and spread over my limbs. I let them have me. Tears fell. I didn't feel guilty. Nicholas pulled me in tighter. I rubbed my hands together behind his back. Pulling my hands back in, I tried to wipe my tears away. A mess of wet makeup stained his sweatshirt. "I hate this guy."

Nicholas handed me a wad of tissues. "Me, too." He kept an eye on me. If I kept clinging to him, I risked rejection. He risked a ruined shirt. I sat on the couch and flipped on the television. Deep breath. I didn't understand why things like this happened. Why did people like the Reaper exist?

Nicholas flipped through the channels. I hoped he'd find a nice game show to take my mind off reality. He scooted onto the floor and sat against the couch by my legs. I started to move them, but he pulled my feet onto his lap. He tugged off my boots and rubbed my feet. He handed me the remote.

I stopped flipping at the first channel I recognized. The news seemed like a good enough choice. All the bad things in the world would help put my issues in perspective. It worked for a few minutes.

Right after the weather, the station featured a clip from my father's press conference. I was drawn in like a moth to a light. I hadn't seen Dad's face since the morning after Thanksgiving in Texas, and I missed him. I scooted closer to the edge of the couch to listen. I wanted to absorb every word, but all I saw was the photograph.

In the top-left corner of the screen was a photo of Miles Thomas Wade, the Reaper. Someone gasped. Maybe me. I pulled my feet onto the sofa, jerking them out of Nicholas's hands. It was the face in my dream. I'd never seen it until now. In my dreams it wasn't a face, it was a feeling, a fear. Seeing it on the television, my life snapped into place. *My dream was as real as if it were a premonition or a memory.* I'd written that in a dozen journals a hundred times.

It was a memory.

"Elle?" Nicholas sounded frightened.

I didn't know how I looked to him, but my mind pulsed with a decade of thoughts and tears and sleepless nights. This man looking back from the television was the thing in my dream that wanted to kill me. I'd been running from him my entire life.

"Elle, can you hear me?" Nicholas's voice persisted, but I couldn't see him.

"Open your eyes, Elle. Tell me what you saw. What's happening?" Panic edged his voice.

I tried to pull my eyes open. I couldn't. He might be there with us. What if we weren't alone?

My trembling lips refused to move for an eternity. When my brain found a way to explain what my heart had known all along, I whimpered, "I was there," wanting it not to be true.

In the next instant, I was falling. Nicholas had me in his lap before I'd even finished my revelation.

"Yes," he said.

Sobs came again, shaking my frame until my teeth chattered. Shock settled into my system. Coldness covered me. I felt raw and exposed. With every scrap of power I could find, I pried my body out of Nicholas's grip and went to hide.

I stumbled to the bathroom and shut the door behind me. Hysterics took over. Leaning into the door, I slid down to meet the rug. I cried until my body hurt from shaking. My head pounded. My eyes burned. Eventually, I had nothing left. The tears ran dry. Numbness replaced the cold. My body was a shell, and everything inside had oozed out. I faced the mirror, not quite ready to assess the damage. Thankfully, Nicholas had missed my grand finale.

I had to clean up before I faced him. Hopefully he was far enough away to have missed the wailing.

We were in for the night. It was safe to wash the remnants of makeup off my face. I pulled the fake piercings from my nose and lip. I looked like the Joker. I needed more water than the sink could give.

With barely enough energy to stand, I turned the shower knob and climbed in. When I stepped out, I was never so happy to put on pajamas. I left my new black ensemble in the hamper against the wall. The dark garb suddenly seemed much more appropriate than I wanted to accept. I opened the door.

Nicholas sat on the floor outside. He hopped to his feet, probably wondering if I should be admitted somewhere for insanity. I wanted to care, but I didn't. I wasn't sure where I was going, so I stood there.

The Reaper killed my mother, *and I was there.*

Nicholas took me to my room and sat me on the bed. "Here." He handed me a series of thick accordion folders. They each said "Smith" along the flap. Then, he left to stand guard outside the door. Who knew what he thought I might do. The truth was I couldn't do anything.

I stared at the files for a long time before I reached for them. Eventually, curiosity won me over. Opening the first file, I held my breath. Time to unlock my actual life, the one derailed and abandoned long ago.

The details were horrifying.

Chapter Thirty

According to the files, the Reaper had eluded officials for close to fourteen years. He had stalked girls at schools exactly like Francine Frances. A decade ago, my father, Special Agent Smith, came close to naming him. Close enough to hold a press conference. The images of the Reaper's shorn head and smirking face haunted me. The memory was overlaid with haze, whether from how young I was when I saw him, the terror of that day, or my mind trying to protect itself, I wasn't sure.

Almost two dozen girls had been taken, tortured, and murdered at the Reaper's hands. Their pictures and reports were in the files. I cried over ever name, every photo, every death. The Reaper wasn't happy to end his run. A few days after the press conference, the Reaper met my family as we left a downtown restaurant and were walking to our car. The folder shook in my hands. Papers rattled. I laid the folder on the bed, unsure of how much more I could read.

Dad protected me, but we lost Mom. Back then I'd answered to Stella. I let it sit for a minute. *Stella.* Named after a grandmother I didn't remember. Her name was burned in my memory. It had appeared on cards sent to the hospital when I was born. Dad had kept a few with Mom's things. Tears blurred my vision. I had a grandmother.

How many other family members thought I died all those years ago? I pulled the folder back to my face and blinked the tears loose. One report stated that Mom pulled me from the Reaper's reach and passed me off to Dad. I pictured the horrible scene. Or did I remember it? I growled. The monster forced Dad to choose between us, the two people who meant the world to him. He couldn't leave me, and he couldn't protect my mom if he didn't.

According to Dad's statement, when he shoved me behind him, I fell. He lunged for Mom and managed to separate her from the Reaper. It only lasted a moment before the Reaper hit Dad with a stun gun. He fell to the ground, completely immobile but thoroughly awake.

I wiped my nose and mouth with one sleeve, forcing myself to read on.

Dad was face to face on the ground beside me. He wrote, "She was terrified, confused, and crying. I couldn't move to defend her or my wife." I rubbed my heart. What began as a fissure had cracked open wide. If it was possible to die of a broken heart, I'd be gone. Dad hadn't been able to protect us. I pulled in a deep breath and finished his statement.

"I begged her, 'Run, Stella, please, for Daddy. Stella, run.'"

I shook my head hard against the memory fighting to resurface. "Oh no." I threw a hand over my mouth and tried not to vomit. I remembered.

I remembered scooting on my backside a few feet, pleading for Dad to get up, begging the Reaper to let Mom go. I remembered my eyes making the circuit between the three of them until Dad's words penetrated my tiny heart. Even at six, I knew, and I fled. Turning over until my knees scraped against concrete, I ran into the darkness. Away from the killer. Away from my parents.

Sobs racked my body again, and it hurt. When Nicholas appeared beside my bed, I stood and fell into him. He held me until sleep took me away.

The next day, I planned to ignore the folders. I couldn't. I read about how the Reaper held Mom by her hair. How he taunted Dad for his weakness, for the way his love disabled him. Dad had written in his barely legible script all the details I didn't want to see but needed to know. He watched the Reaper shake Mom and whisper horrific things into her ear before pulling her to a waiting car. Electric shocks ravaged Dad's body as he watched the Reaper open the door, stuff Mom inside, and pull away. Dad forced his limbs to cooperate, freed his sidearm, and fired at the car. The single wild shot hit a tire, and the car rolled to a stop.

Dad hoped the shot would get attention. His head hit the pavement, his will no longer enough to hold it upright. Then he heard a second shot. I imagined silent tears rolling from the corners of his eyes as he lay there lost in despair, listening for the sirens in the distance. He woke in the ambulance to news of his wife's death and his daughter's disappearance. The Reaper was gone.

For three days, he lived believing the Reaper had found me, imagined what he'd done to me. Blamed himself for all that had transpired. The search for me ended on the morning of my mother's funeral. No wonder I didn't remember being there. We missed her funeral. Reports said Dad received news of my location hours before Mom's service. For the second time that week, he was forced to choose. My throat constricted. I retched into the small plastic can at my bedside.

From the stacks of newspaper clippings and internal memorandums, I gathered the rest of the details. After Dad's statement, the paperwork on us grew thin. The focus shifted to Dad's work in naming the Reaper. Local media announced the loss of our family to the public. A funeral was fabricated in our memory. Three caskets were buried. Hundreds of people came to pay their respects. Just like that, my life ended.

Gabriella Denise Smith was born.

A knock against the wall caught my attention. Nicholas stood in the doorway with a tray. My stomach groaned at the sight. "I brought coffee and a bagel. I figured anything more and you'd send me away."

"Thanks."

"May I?"

I nodded. He moved to place the tray on the stand. I cleared enough papers to make space on the bed where he could sit with me.

"How're you doing?"

"According to initial psychiatric reviews, I adjusted well." I smiled. No joy fueled the act. "It sounds like the nightmares started when we left D.C." They also noted I had trouble accepting my mother's death. No kidding. I'd blocked the event completely. "I have no recollection of how I spent the days that I was missing."

"One day, an officer found you wandering and took you in. He didn't realize who you were." Nicholas handed me the coffee.

"I read the files on the Reaper, too." My hand trembled. The coffee inside edged toward the rim. I wrapped both palms around the mug. "Something in there should tell us where he's hiding, shouldn't it?"

He shrugged and patted my hand. It wasn't a hopeful gesture.

We spent the next few days in silence. I holed up in my room with the files, not eating, not talking. Learning. Processing. Determined to gain insight into the monster. Nicholas puttered around the door to my room. He brought me food and coffee. Other than "thank you," I never knew what to say. He'd lied to me, too. He had always known all the gory details of my life and death. I knew he was forbidden from telling me. He did bring me the files eventually. My mind was numbed from the weight of it. All of it.

I memorized the names and faces of his victims. They shouldn't be forgotten while he was remembered. Feared. The first, Amber Laney, was taken to her apartment and starved for days. The partial print was there. He dumped her along the Towpath Trail outside of D.C. A year passed before victim two, Alicia McFarland, went on a date and never returned. These victims both had steady boyfriends. He cut the women's hair crudely with scissors. I wondered if had he asked them out and punished them for accepting. Was this about the cheating stepmom? Was he intrinsically evil? How many others like him were out there? As the murders piled up, he tightened his process to a predictable ten days, starved them, removed their fingerprints, shaved their heads, swapped their clothes for burlap or some other makeshift scraps. Rape was consistent in every case. Would a ten-year-old rape kit hold up in court as evidence?

Tears fell in a salty deluge onto the papers. My mom was the lucky one. A gag caught in my throat.

There were a couple of guards outside of the apartment 24/7. Nicholas's team checked in regularly. Most nights Marshals from the local office played cards in the kitchen. It was a repetitive existence. My view never changed, but I was safe and unafraid. Mostly.

"How are you holding up?" Nicholas leaned against the doorjamb to my room.

"Awesome." I rolled my eyes and smiled.

"Have you spoken to your dad?"

I waved him over to the bed where I sat with my head on my knees and my back against the wall. "Last night. He's chasing another lead."

Nicholas nodded. He scooted against the wall beside me and tucked me against his side. He reached into his jacket and produced a pack of letters.

"What's that?" I curled my fingers around the envelopes as he tilted them toward me.

"You've got mail."

"From who?" Excitement shot through me. I checked every return address for an L.A. zip code. They all said Ohio. "Francine Frances Academy?"

"Half the school sent you cards. According to the team, word around school is that after the fire you wanted to go home. Losing your place freaked you out and you didn't want to stay without Pixie, so you left. They want you back."

"Aw. They miss me." I leaned into Nicholas as I flipped through the letters. They missed me. I loved it.

"Some miss you more than others." Nicholas's cop voice was in place. He used it with the other agents. It annoyed me.

The same address appeared on several envelopes. "Davis." I opened one of the cards and skimmed over the text.

"I don't like that kid." Nicholas bumped me with his arm.

I leaned forward, smiling widely at Nicholas's flat expression.

"What's there not to like? Says here he got a lacrosse scholarship." I feigned interest in the card, holding it over my face.

"That kid's a marshmallow."

"And yet amazingly age appropriate." I peeked around the card.

Nicholas's mouth twitched. Deep green eyes bore into mine. "Which would matter if you weren't already in a highly inappropriate relationship."

I pulled my lips to one side. "A relationship, huh?" My tummy knotted with the thrill and possibilities loaded into that statement.

"Come here." Nicholas flipped me onto the mattress and hovered over me, one hand poised at my ribs. "Do you have a problem with that? You can call it whatever you want, but the bottom line is I saw you first."

I laughed. "That's right. You were stalking me."

"True, but Davis is still a marshmallow." Nicholas kissed my nose but didn't move away.

I slapped his hand away from my ribs. "If you tickle me, I'll scream for help."

He smiled.

"I mean it. Do not tickle me." I rolled toward the edge of the bed, but he caught me at the waist and tickled me. My body convulsed like a complete freak show. I kicked my feet and squealed, but no one came to my rescue. "Stop."

When I pried my eyes open again, Nicholas looked proud of himself.

"Some protective custody I have out there," I panted.

"I'm your protective custody."

A witty comeback dissolved on my tongue as his lips pressed against mine. Nicholas never let his guard down, so I took advantage. I wrapped my hands around his neck and pulled him into the kiss. He planted his palms against the bed, holding himself in check over me, but didn't break the kiss. I arched my back, bringing our chests together. Maybe he needed the release as much as I did because he let me. His lips moved with meaning over mine in a series of slow and life-changing kisses. Enveloped in Nicholas's kiss, the weeks of stress and anxiety fell away. None of it mattered. I was safe. I was loved. All was well.

When he broke the kiss, I reached for his cheeks and traced the shape of his lips with my fingertips. He moaned against my skin.

"Kiss me," I whispered.

"Elle."

"Please." I batted my eyelids as a tear slipped away.

Nicholas wavered. The heat in his eyes overwhelmed me. He obviously didn't want to say no, but he was the guy who did the right thing. He straightened his arms further, inching away from me. Rejection pooled in my gut.

"Please."

When I turned my face away, ashamed at my plea, he kissed my cheek.

"Don't. It's fine. I understand." I scooted up on the bed, unable to look him in the eye.

"Soon." He stroked the tear from my cheek. I nodded. Listening to a familiar sound in the distance.

"I hear your phone."

Nicholas jumped off the bed like he'd been electrocuted and ran for the other room. His deep voice rumbled down the hall. Another lead. Another night filled with worry for nothing. I couldn't believe I'd asked him to kiss me. *And he'd said no.*

I pulled a pillow over my face. I should tattoo *loser* on my forehead.

"Elle," Nicholas called from the kitchen.

I didn't answer. Calling back required more enthusiasm than I could manage.

I'd fallen asleep the night before from utter mental exhaustion. Kissing him was the most physical effort I'd expended in days and look at how that had ended. I slept twelve hours straight every night and woke feeling weaker and more desperate than the day before. I wasn't even thankful for the rest. I felt hollow. Didn't care. Didn't know what to make of my life, or what I thought about my revelations. I liked the kissing. I could pass all my time that way. Not thinking, just drowning in his touch.

"Elle," his voice called again. He said we were in a relationship. He'd claimed me the way my heart had claimed him weeks ago.

"Elle." He was closer this time. Urgency colored my name.

Curiosity bloomed in my stomach, and I rose to look for Nicholas.

He appeared at my door with his coat on. He held my coat in his hand. "We've got to move."

"What's happening?"

Nicholas was in soldier mode, his expression locked. He'd detached from himself in a way I envied.

"I need to take you to headquarters." He handed me my coat and packed a duffle of my things. "You'll be safer there." He slung the bag over one shoulder and reached for my hand.

I slipped into my coat and followed him, lifelessly, down the stairs. I wished I knew how he so easily slipped in and out of his personality. When things were at their worst, he faced them. I hid.

Maybe that was his secret. My hand slid along the railing in the stairwell, around the corner, and down another flight. He held the door for me. I stepped out onto the busy street, surrounded by faces oblivious to my life. It seemed right. I'd been oblivious for so long.

Nicholas opened a car door for me. I slid inside. He shut the door and moved quickly around the front. I never took my eyes off him. I didn't know what I thought I might see, but it seemed important to watch him.

He looked me over before shifting into drive. When I was strapped in to his satisfaction, we were off.

"The Reaper has Sara. Your father's on his way to the airport now. My dad is meeting him there. They'll be in D.C. as soon as they can, but it's a long flight from Dallas."

"How?" *How had Sara ended up in my nightmare?*

"She was at the office entering the reports we've been throwing at her. Reports we're too irresponsible to do ourselves. She's been doing all the stuff we don't want to do. We all abuse the interns, but she's my sister. She's not some kid using the Marshals' office as a line on a resume. This is our life. With our family connections, she could've interned anywhere in town, but she wanted to be there." He choked on the final word.

"He took her from your office?"

"We think he got her when she stepped out for lunch."

"Does he know where you are now?" How many people might I lose before he finished?

"He was at your dad's house in Dallas while your dad trailed him in Michigan. He saw a photo of my dad."

"A photo?" I'd never seen a photo of Mr. Austin at our house. "How do you know?"

"He called my dad."

"The Reaper?" My eyes widened to a full stretch.

"Yes." Nicholas saw where I was heading and interrupted me. "I guess Dad had sent him an old fishing picture. They were rebuilding a friendship." He snorted.

"How'd he find your dad based on a picture or even know who he was?"

"How did you nail me back in September? The Internet is a tool as well as a nuisance."

"You think he knew your dad was assigned to my case?" It was the only explanation for involving Sara. I no longer believed in co-incidences.

"I don't know if he did. I'm sure he does now. He wants to trade my sister for you. One daughter for another."

We pulled into an underground parking garage. The change in lighting hurt my sore eyes. The garage made me shiver. I was still trying to unbuckle my seat belt when Nicholas opened my door. We rushed inside. I wished I looked more like myself. My new look made me uncomfortable. I hadn't kept up the makeup because I wasn't expecting to leave, but the hair and clothes were still there. Among all the people in suits, I felt like I should be questioned instead of protected.

Inside the atrium, we climbed two enormous sets of marble stairs. The interior was grand and pristine, bustling with activity. People rushed down halls. Elevators carried full loads of workers. Every conference room we passed appeared full.

My boots clunked hard against the marble, drawing too much attention our way. A knot of men came to meet us. They barely looked at me, despite my goofy appearance. They all looked remarkably alike. Everyone had the same face, the same composed, driven look. Questions came at us from all directions.

"Where's your father?" they asked Nicholas.

"Your mother and the boys?" I listened for the answers.

"Mom and the boys are going to Canada."

Canadian border patrol had been given Miles Thomas Wade's photograph and description. That made Canada a good destination for the Austin family.

Rounding a corner, Nicholas simultaneously gave and received information. He tugged me along behind him. We entered a large conference room where half a dozen machines were hooked up. One replayed a call between the Reaper and Mr. Austin.

"He sounds familiar," I whispered.

Eyes glanced from me to Nicholas. No one stopped working. A man nodded at Nicholas and we took two seats at the enormous, file-covered table.

"Do you think you've heard him recently, or could it be a memory taking shape?" The look on Nicholas's face unnerved me.

"I'm not sure. I don't know."

He waited.

"What're they doing?" I nodded to the desk where they replayed the message in increments.

"They're trying to trace the call." Nicholas leaned in toward my ear. "They're analyzing the recording for any background noise or clues to help narrow down his whereabouts. He couldn't have taken her far."

"Sara's last text was sent at nine twelve this morning. The call placed by the Reaper came in at ten forty. That means it took him an hour and a half to get somewhere he felt comfortable making a call."

"He could've been on the road." A man whom I'd met in the hall spoke.

"They could be anywhere," I said in a low tone, mostly to myself.

"Not anywhere," Nicholas answered. "He has a plan. This is important to him. He took one daughter to exchange for another. That's not his playing style. It's much more personal."

"He's not playing anymore," I mumbled, remembering the press conference. "He's got nothing to lose. Dad named him. What's his incentive to hide?"

"We don't think he's hiding, necessarily. Your father seems to think he's staying in D.C."

"D.C.?" I shrieked. "What if he comes for you?" My heart hitched and then stopped. I couldn't lose Nicholas. The Reaper must want to take out the entire Austin family since he was unable to get mine.

Several men and women coughed and giggled at my conclusion. Nicholas's head hung back over the top of his chair. When he pulled it up he had a sarcastic look on his face. "Not me, Elle."

Right. Me. He wanted to kill me.

"We've got something." A man with headphones pulled one side off his ear and waved us over to him. He had isolated a voice yelling in the background.

"Cumberland." A man I recognized spoke to Nicholas, who stood protectively at my side.

"Is that near here?" My voice startled me. I hadn't planned to ask it out loud.

Before he could answer, my father's voice sounded through a speaker nearby, a phone call I presumed. He was safe. Nicholas covertly slipped his hand over mine and squeezed.

"We think they were in Cumberland when the call was placed."

"I know where he's going." My dad's voice became official. It was low and rough but certain.

"He's taking her back to the beginning. We're headed there now." Instead of "goodbye," he commanded, "Get there."

The crowd dispersed. Most scurried around right outside the door. Nicholas stood and told the few who remained that he was going. He instructed a giant, bald man to keep an eye on me, and then he left, but not before giving me an appraising look.

I stood there, frozen. I'd read the files a hundred times. I knew where the beginning was. Unfortunately, a giant, bald man stood near the door with his hands folded in front of him. I wasn't getting out that way, and he wasn't talking.

I knew what I needed to do.

"I think I'm going to be sick." Real tears needed few summons. "I need to use the ladies' room."

He stepped aside and waved an arm toward the hallway beside us. I threw one hand over my lips and bolted for the front door.

I hailed a cab and jumped in, hoping no one followed me. "Take me to the Towpath Trail in Cumberland."

"Cumberland?" The driver didn't look thrilled. I handed him a wad of the cash that had come with my new identity. He pulled away from the building looking slightly more interested.

The drive away from town was surreal. Traffic moved like game pieces along a crowded board. Forward two spaces. Wait. Forward three spaces. Wait. It continued that way until the cab pulled onto one finger of the twisted freeway. Then we were free. If the killer wanted to make a trade, there was still hope. I could save Sara the way her family had already saved me. My dad and Nicholas wouldn't be far behind me. I hoped I'd beat them there. If they arrived without me, Sara might end up like my mom.

Cumberland was closer than I was prepared for.

At the Towpath gateway, I paid a fee for entrance. I doubted Miles had walked up, with Sara in his grip, and paid the man his fee. I had no idea where I was going. In retrospect, I should've paid more attention to the crime-scene photos in the file. Not that it would've helped. The forest looked like the forest. I turned in a weary circle. No green leaves in sight. He had dumped his first victim in the spring. What little I remembered of her photos was green, not gray, brown, and barren like the space around me.

All I had was the small pamphlet I'd received with my admission ticket. According to the pamphlet, the trail wound on for miles. I pulled my jacket tight and moved forward. Fresh snow dusted the ground beneath my feet. I tugged at my hair, too short to keep my neck warm. I hadn't brought a scarf or gloves. We'd left the apartment in a hurry.

As I crunched through the frozen grass, the canal came into view ahead of me. The trail wound along it in both directions. My map indicated I was close to the beginning, so I went the other way. I walked and walked, every moment expecting to run into Nicholas. I could've been miles from where Amber Laney was found, for all I knew. I was looking for a needle in a haystack, and I didn't have a plan.

What would I do if I found them?

According to my watch, it was a few minutes after four. The sun had already begun its descent. Once it set, I'd have no way to see. Lighting along the trail was sporadic at best. I hastened, remembering a report of coyote attacks in the metro parks. The exposed gray bark of the trees was a reflection of me. Their stark winding branches reached into the white sky like gnarled fingertips of warning. The forest wasn't enchanted. I didn't live in a storybook. What awaited me in the dimming winter light was a very real monster.

A twig snapped.

"Hello?" A chuckle echoed through the growing darkness. "Hello?" Only the sound of leaves in the wind answered.

I took a step off the trail, creeping forward in the direction of the laughter. My stomach retched. My heart hit the frozen ground with a coiling thump. Not twenty feet from the trail, Sara lay on the ground near a tree. Her hands and feet were pulled back in an unnatural posture. She didn't move. I slipped on snow-covered leaves in my hurry to reach her. I fell twice, pulling myself up the small incline toward my friend. She was tied up. My stomach rolled into my spine. I ran the final steps to her side and pulled at the rope that bound her. She still didn't move.

Low chuckles echoed around me, edging closer. I hastened my attempt to wake or free Sara. Her cold skin scared me. I didn't want to think of what it meant. "Sara," I urged. "Sara." No response. I fought to keep my head clear. *It is supposed to be me. It should've been me.* I yanked on the ropes, working my frozen fingers into the knots, begging Sara to wake up.

A branch snapped behind me, and he appeared.

Chapter Thirty-One

"You," I whispered.

Directly before me stood Miles Thomas Wade. He wore a brown leather coat and khaki slacks. His loafers seemed inappropriate for a woodland murder.

"It's nice to meet you. Officially." The voice. I squinted hard at his face. My heartbeat crashed in my chest. "I'm Miles. I've wanted to introduce myself to you for so long." He stepped closer, outstretching his hand.

The man from the Francine Frances library stood as close as ever. My head worked to match his voice with the picture on the television. He was older than he was in the photo. His hair was darker and moppy, hanging in his eyes. No longer worn close to his head. He was clean-shaven. No longer blond or bearded. I never would've known. He'd made me so uncomfortable that I'd avoided eye contact. Look where that had gotten me.

"I suppose that was rude of me. Of course, we've met before." The look in his eye added fear to my physical pain. "Unofficially."

"I don't understand." I wanted to keep him talking. Adrenaline surged, bringing clarity to my situation. My skin heated from the inside.

"Uh." He sighed, indicating that he had a long story to catch me up on. A long story was good. In a few more minutes, I might be able to call out for help or be discovered by the Marshals. Maybe even run.

"I made a promise. You for her."

I looked back at Sara lying motionless on the icy ground. I didn't know if she was dead or alive. I hadn't had a chance to check for a heartbeat. What would happen if I left her? I couldn't take her with me. We needed help.

"Come with me, and the Austins can go on. Your entourage will be here soon. Choose."

I teetered. Could I stall long enough?

"You're a clever girl. I counted on that, too. Here you are. Now, what will it be? You or her?" He moved to Sara's side, squatted beside her, and pulled a giant hunting knife from his inside coat pocket.

"Where will we go?" My eyes scanned the area. Could I leave a trail? I didn't have time or materials.

"Someplace you love." He lifted Sara's limp torso by her hair. She didn't flinch. Her arms hung loosely at her sides. Nicholas would blame me if she died. I would, too. This was my chance to be someone's hero. My turn to look out for someone else. After a lifetime of others protecting me, I owed the Austins this much.

"Don't hurt her."

He released her hair and she flopped to the snowy ground. "Off we go then." He motioned for me to walk. A helicopter chopped the air above us, swaying evergreens and leafless trees alike.

"No place to land." He didn't sound upset. At least the Marshals were close. Sara wouldn't freeze to death, and I had a chance.

"Through the thicket." He pressed his body against my back, and a sick feeling washed over me. He forced me through dense, thorny vines and low-hanging branches that clung to my clothes and stung my cheeks. His breath filled the air around me, and his knife punctured my jacket when I stopped to move a batch of brush.

"Ah." I whimpered. His knife had broken the skin on my back.

"Keep moving or it goes deeper."

I wrapped one arm around my waist, pinching my side where the skin burned. Beyond the thicket was an abandoned lot, overgrown with weeds and filled with tents and lean-tos. Two dozen homeless men and women huddled, warming their hands over fires in brown rusty barrels. Miles directed me to a beat-up Chevy and unlocked the trunk.

"Get in."

The trunk reeked of gasoline and motor oil. Tears blurred my vision. Another helicopter beat in the distance. None of the men and women made eye contact with us. Surrounded by people and no one helped. I climbed over the crumbling bumper and lowered myself into the filthy space.

He nodded in approval.

"I'm claustrophobic. I can ride in the car. I won't be any trouble," I pleaded, using the calmest voice I had. He hadn't bound me. I could get away if I was vigilant. Careful. Fast. Seated in the trunk, I wished I'd made a run for it instead of complying. I could've run into the crowd and begged them to take notice. He couldn't kill them all and at least then someone would have seen me. Instead, I was a ghost, the whisper of a girl passing through and then gone.

"This will help with the ride." He pressed a cloth to my face, and I fought against the tide of sweetly scented material until my mind floated away from my body and the world went black.

"Your dad's not the leave-a-key-under-the-mat kind." Miles leaned me against his body and closed the trunk. My muscles ached like I'd been beaten or in a terrible car accident. My head hurt. How much damage had the chemical on the cloth done to my brain cells, not to mention inhaling gasoline and oil fumes for who knew how long? The sun had just set when I climbed into the trunk. The world around me was near black now.

"Move, or I'll carry you," he whispered against my cheek before planting a kiss in my hair.

My dead feet shuffled forward. We stopped at a too-familiar door and Miles jammed his elbow through the window. "No key," he added by way of explanation. He reached into the window and the knob turned.

The door swung wide, revealing a thousand bittersweet memories. My tummy coiled and my heart clenched. "Our cabin."

"Poetic, I think. He brought you here to keep you safe. I did not." Miles shut the door and shoved me onto the couch, barely a silhouette in the night-darkened room. "My turn to make some memories with you."

He powered up the lantern near the door and returned to me. He tied my right arm and leg to the wooden framework of the couch that my great granddad had made. My mother's afghan lay across the back.

His fingers worked over the twine around my wrists. I recognized the knot he made. My dad had used it when we camped.

"Time for a fire. Where do you keep the matches?"

"Kitchen." He would've found them anyway. I wanted him to trust me. See me as a person, not a conquest he had chased for a decade. I struggled against the ties, blinking through tears. Why did he have to bring me here? This was my place. My safe place. Mom had been here.

The fire started with some coaxing. Orange and blue flames licked into the chimney, casting an evil glow over everything in sight, soiling my sweet memories. I couldn't die here. Absently, I wondered if I did, would I be with her again?

Another thought shot through me like gunfire. He had known about this place all along. No one would look here for me. Hope died in my chest. At least Sara was safe.

"I waited a very long time for you to grow up." Miles slid into the seat beside me and placed my free hand in his lap. I swallowed back vomit that filled my mouth. "You were a sweet girl. What happened to you? You hold hands with lacrosse players and kiss federal agents." He tsked with his tongue. "That's the way it starts. A little hand holding." He laced his fingers with mine. "A kiss." He leaned toward me, pressing his mouth to mine.

I cried out, whipping my head away from his.

"Why are you doing this?"

"Your father interrupted my work. There's so much work to do, Stella, and he messed that up for me. That's your name, by the way. Stella, not Gabby or Elle or whatever it is they all call you these days. Your name is Stella." He fiddled with the cushion between us like it was just another day in the life of crazy.

"You look like your mother. Did he ever tell you that?"

The mention of my mother stirred something else in me. *He killed her. He robbed me of a life with her. He robbed her of life.* Fire burned beneath the searing pain in my head. My vision sharpened, adjusting to the dim light. A large pair of scissors lay in his right hand. The scissors were for me. I blinked, unable to figure out where they had come from. My thoughts were muted in my head.

"I like to take my time. He's ruined that, too. I had special plans for you." He shifted in his seat, tugging at his pant legs and weighing the scissors in his grip.

"I spent days with my first, trying to teach her how wrong her life was. I erased all the things that defined her. No one wants to be a whore, Stella. I shaved her head. Dressed her in bags. Withheld food so she'd understand that labels don't make someone a better person. They just emphasized what a total abomination she really was. She resisted. The mission failed.

"The only thing left to do was to get rid of her before she ruined another home. I tossed her into a ravine. I like to make a point." He tapped his temple with one finger.

"She was no one. The best part of the entire week was tossing her body. An enormous weight was lifted. I did something good. I wanted to do it again."

I closed my eyes, praying for a clear thought. He dragged the point of his scissors down my chest, pressing the material of my jacket between my breasts. I sucked in a breath.

"You like that." He unzipped the jacket, watching his hands instead of my face. Nicholas always watched my face. Nicholas loved me. He was kind and good, everything the monster beside me was not, and yet it was this beast who touched me. Desperation filled my chest and I sobbed against the pressure of his hands. The rape came next. I knew. I'd read. I'd rather die than live through that. How do women live past something so evil?

Miles pressed the scissors against the inside of one knee and dragged them up my thigh.

I squeezed my eyes shut again.

"You look like a filthy whore in that getup. What would your mother have said? All dressed in black like that obnoxious roommate of yours. Is that where you learned to whore?" He spat at me. Then he leaned in close, arranging the scissors in his right hand. "Let's get you out of those clothes."

My mind worked at a frantic pace, unwilling to give up, rejecting this as my future or my end.

He worked my jacket off one arm and looked at me with disgust. Carefully, he removed all he could from half my body, tossing my boots near the fire. Leaving me exposed and shaking despite the fire before us. "Will I be your first, Stella?"

Yes. "Please, don't." I squeezed my eyes shut, praying for clarity. My tongue thickened in my desert-dry mouth.

He rolled my shoulder away from him, forcing my arms together and my back to him. His fingers wound into my too-short hair and the scissors chopped and pulled at my new style. I slipped my left hand under the sleeve bunched up on my right arm and worked the ties as he worked on my hair. I wiggled the binding until my hand could slip through.

He pulled me back for a look at his handiwork. A length of black bangs fell into my eyes.

"I wanted your mother, too, but he ruined that. Your father ruins everything. He's ruining my life!" His eyes went wild. "Your mom was old for my taste, but you look like her. Feels like I get a second chance." My skin tightened with goose bumps in the icy winter air. The fire struggled in the hearth, fighting against the chill clinging to the walls and air around us. Fear and understanding froze me to the core.

Miles never took his eyes off my body. He dipped his face toward my breasts, and I shoved him away. When he raised his eyes to mine, I smashed my head against his nose with all the force I could muster. A sickening crunch led to a guttural roar.

"You broke my nose, you bitch."

His fist whipped forward, punching me in the mouth. My head whipped back, and the world shimmered. Miles grabbed a poker from the fireplace and swung it at my head.

I woke some time later to piercing pain. My head ached. I pressed a palm to my hair. It came back warm and wet. Blood. I moved to rub my hand against my clothes. They were gone, hacked off roughly, leaving only my sleeve where he hadn't bothered to untie me. My clothes had been replaced by a black trash bag cut open at the bottom like a dress and cinched under my arms. I tested my right ankle. He hadn't retied it.

The fire was almost out. My skin burned from the cold. Shards of yellow light streamed in through the front window. A new day. I had lived through the night and escaped my impending rape for one more day. My tummy knotted with hunger. Through squinted eyes, I watched Miles toss the last scraps of kindling into the fire. The scissors poked out of his back pocket. He hadn't finished my hair. Of course not. He'd wait for me to wake up and participate as his victim. Where was the fun of torment without a good fight?

He shoved the poker around the fire, cursing. Dad and I hadn't been to the cabin since the summer. We didn't stock firewood inside. Dad kept a seasoned pile outside. Miles turned to me and let out a slew of vulgarities and curses. I feigned unconsciousness.

"When I get back, we'll get started." He crushed my jaw in his iron grip and my eyes opened. "Thanks to all the trouble you gave me and the posse out looking for us, we'll have to start right away." He released my face, and blood rushed under my skin to the dents left behind by his cruel fingers. "Hair, nails, fingerprints."

"You don't have to rush. I won't cause more trouble. I promise." My voice cracked on every word. Fear encased my heart in ice.

Miles grinned. He grabbed my thighs in his hands and locked his eyes on mine. I wished he hadn't. Suddenly I prayed he'd turn his gaze back to my body instead. Squeezing my bare skin in his hands, he stared into my eyes. A slow, easy smile spread over his face and I realized I'd given him what he wanted. He wanted the fear. The submission.

"I'll be the Reaper of that." *The Reaper.*

My chest heaved with stuttered breaths.

"I promise to take the important things nice and slow."

He pressed my legs apart and I trembled. My teeth chattered until my limbs rocked with cold and sheer terror.

"The best things are worth waiting for." He licked his lips and walked away, holding my gaze. I shut my eyes.

The door sucked shut behind him and he ambled off the porch. When I no longer saw him through the window, I yanked my wrist free of the loosened strap and forced my body upright. I hobbled to the back door and unlocked it with shaking hands. Wind whipped through my hair, pasting the plastic bag to my skin. Snow flurries added sting to the air.

Confusion darted and skipped in my mind. I'd been in these woods a thousand times, but sunlight blinded my eyes. My brain beat inside my skull. My lips ached from his punch. My head throbbed from the blast he had given me with the poker. It hurt to open my eyes wider than a squint. I scurried into the trees behind the cabin and fell. My feet slid on wet, frigid leaves. Resting on my knees in the blowing snow, I cried silently. This was how it would end for me. The Reaper had taken my clothes, touched my body, *seen* me. Vomit pressed its way up my throat. Tears formed as I pictured my father finding me outside our cabin dressed like the other victims. The Reaper would finish me off and go into town for breakfast. He was dressed for polite company.

I was dressed for disposal.

I pulled myself up with the help of a nearby tree. I had no shoes or clothes. I was bleeding and dressed in plastic.

"Stella." His voice echoed through the trees.

To stay was to die, brutally. To go was unknown. Agents were looking for Miles. They were out there somewhere, nowhere near here, but if I made it to town, I could call for help. Heavy footfalls thumped behind me, cracking branches and shuffling leaves.

"No one can help you," he taunted, drawing nearer.

I jogged, forcing my body forward.

My eyes adjusted to the light and I looked through the bare trees. I had nowhere to go. My head jerked back. His fingers were in my shorn hair, curled into the few swaths he had left.

"I'm building a fire. Where are you going?" He screamed into my face.

"I'm sorry."

"It's okay." He stroked my head. "Don't be in such a hurry. I'll bring you back out here later. When I'm done."

He released my hair, and I ran. He caught me around the waist and threw me on the ground. "Why are you trying to ruin this for me?" he snarled.

He pulled the scissors from his back pocket and shifted them from one of his neatly manicured hands to the other. My life was a game to him. My shoulder ached from having landed on an exposed root. The expression of victory glowed on his face. He was dragging out my death on purpose, savoring each moment. Fine by me. Every minute he extended my life was another moment I'd try to live. Adrenaline heated my torso. My fingers and toes were numb, but my heart was pumping hard, sending much-needed blood and oxygen to my appendages, clearing my thoughts.

Miles had a protocol to adhere to. He took his victims' identities. He'd already taken my clothes. Now, he'd finish my hair.

"You're all the same," he barked. "You're all in a hurry. You don't want to change. You won't listen. All across the country, girls like you are ruining marriages, killing mothers. It's up to me to stop you." He stopped to wipe some spittle from his chin.

I moaned and rubbed my head, luring him into reach. Nicholas's commanding voice exploded in my head. All the lessons he'd taught me by the river flooded back. Stern and determined, his voice said, "Run."

The Reaper leaned forward and placed his fingers into the thick of my bangs. I jerked my head upward with all I had in me. His face crunched again as my head connected with it. His hand loosened by a degree. He stumbled backward and dragged me with him. "Fucking bitch!"

I wrapped my frozen fingers around a large branch lying beside me and stabbed it into the air behind me. The branch connected briefly with his flesh. I turned to see. I'd caught him in his neck. His grip loosened again. Hate and fear flung my body upward. Away from the man. Into the forest. Leaving a large portion of my hair behind. I knew his plans. I'd read the files. He wouldn't be my first. I wouldn't be his next.

Barefoot, naked, and almost blind from pain, I ran. My feet slipped and ached as they pounded the icy ground. Branches cracked and snapped as I leapt and landed again and again through the woods. My heart clenched with fear. My body was at home, trained to run. Muscle memory. I barely needed to think. The cold forest floor didn't compare to my treadmill, but it mattered little, considering the circumstances.

I ran confidently for several minutes before it all went south. There was no way a man twice my age would've caught me if I'd been wearing shoes. Cresting the top of the hill, away from the cabin, my left foot landed on a sharp stick and I collapsed. The branch jammed deeply into my sole. I screamed and fell. Blood oozed around it. I knew enough not to remove the stick. The blood would rush out. I'd die. I couldn't run, or walk, with the branch wedged into my skin. A main artery ran through the arch of the foot. Severing it meant death. Trickles of blood ran out from around the branch, coating my skin in a sticky burn.

The space I'd put between us would be lost if I didn't move. My name echoed through the trees in his creepy voice. My eyes darted frantically for a wide tree or thicket of brush within crawling distance. I had nowhere to hide, and he was pissed. Pain seized my body. He cursed and swore as he approached, taking his time. The monster stood over me like a hunter over prey. Then he yanked the stick from my foot and tossed it into the woods.

"Gah!" Instinctively I folded into myself and applied pressure to the wound. Blood soaked my hands. Tears fell freely into the snow. I didn't want to die at his hands, not like my mother.

Not like this, my heart screamed. *Not like this. Please.*

"You useless little whore!" he roared, interrupting any feeble measure of hope. A huge cold hand slammed into my cheek. My head flung sideways into the snow. "You're supposed to be in the cabin! Steven's supposed to watch you die. You two keep ruining my plans!" He enunciated every syllable. Spittle flew from his lips and hit my burning cheeks. "I know all about his security cameras. Why do you think I brought you here? When I'm finished, I'll tell him to watch his footage. I'll be long gone by then, but so will you, Stella."

He knelt next to me with the scissors and began to chop at my already too-short hair. My loss of blood was tremendous, especially the way my heart pumped from the run. I slumped over, forehead to the ground, trying to think. I'd had no idea about the cameras. Of course, it seemed reasonable now. My tummy flopped and my face burned. If I passed out, I was dead. My ears rang. A sick burn crept over me. Nausea. Terror. Loss. Black spots floated in my vision. I bawled into the freezing dirt. A thrumming began in the sky.

The Reaper's voice drawled on. I couldn't hold the words in my head. Concentration became harder. Like falling asleep and waking only to realize I was still asleep. I slipped to and from my dream, adding confusion to the pain and panic. His voice added a new dimension to the nightmare. My memory. He was in the alley. My mother cried in his arms. My father was sprawled on the ground near me. He spoke to me.

The voices mingled together. Dream and reality. Miles whispered against my ear, all the demented thoughts of a man like him. My father's voice whispered in my mind more simply, "Run, Elle, please. For Daddy, Elle, run, please . . . " On another level altogether, I knew I could. A final push of fury and determination coursed through my system, and I was lucid.

The steady beating in the air above me was a beacon to my soul.

The next time the Reaper raised his scissors to cut the hair from my head, I rallied. Pulling every ounce of adrenaline and hate and rage, thinking only of what he'd done to my mother, stealing her from us, killing her, I attacked. I locked my fingers together the way Nicholas had taught me. When the Reaper rolled me onto my back to chop another chunk of my hair, I swung with everything I had. Like serving a volleyball. My suddenly powerful arms landed squarely against his scissors.

The scissors and his arms flew backwards away from me. Shock shown on his face. He thought he'd won. He thought I'd given up. To everyone not present in my mind, I was all but dead. The scissors twisted in his wrist. He didn't know me. I was not a victim. They barreled toward him as he moved toward me. No time to change their course. His head turned in confusion. The moment was done. Two metal points lodged deep into his face. Sharp ringing filled the air around me. Blood flowed out of his eyes in deep crimson rivers onto snow-white leaves. Echoes filled the forest. His angry, crazy body fell flat onto mine. I fell down into the snow. The points of his scissors dove deeper into him as the handles met the ground beside my head. The sick, tearing crunch elicited vomit from my churning gut. Echoes of the ringing vibrated through my head.

The crush of my body against the leaves seemed to ring out through the forest. My face was frozen in snow. I couldn't breathe. His weight flattened my already-weakened lungs. The heaving of my stomach stopped and I struggled instead for air. His weight suffocated me. My mind grew limp. I couldn't process. Scents of wet earth and decay filled my nostrils. Muffled voices tickled my ears. Perhaps angels had been dispatched to meet me in my death. I'd miss my father and my new family, but I'd finally be with my mother. I'd been saved, in a way. Like her, I hadn't suffered the way the others had. My cheek grew numb against the earth. I had nothing left to give.

The rumble of plummeting boulders shook the earth. My eyes wouldn't open, but the sounds roused my thoughts from a distant place. I was flying, floating, moving toward the sounds.

The dark quiet enveloped me. My heart rate slowed. My muscles relaxed. I found warmth, peace. Relaxing into the ether, I drifted peacefully away.

Chapter Thirty-Two

Whoosh. Whoosh. Beep. Whoosh. Whoosh. Beep.

The pattern repeated until I could anticipate it. My mind joined in on the song. *Whoosh. Whoosh. Beep.* With heavy lids and limbs of jelly, I focused on the reliable chorus. My hand moved, levitated, reached. Then, the voice of the angel.

"Elle." The angel's voice was burdened, sad and low.

Angels shouldn't be sad. I hated the sound.

I felt wetness and heat in my palm. I forced my lids to open and see what my mind couldn't understand.

Weakly, my eyelids parted, taking in the peculiar scene around me. Nicholas sat at my bedside, head bowed. His forehead was pressed against my pillow, and he murmured in my sweet angel's voice. He pressed my hand against his wet cheek.

"You're going to come out of this, Elle. I made you a promise. I won't leave. I won't . . . "

Sounds disappeared. My vision cleared, as if only one sense could function at a time. The room around us brimmed with flowers of every kind. Helium balloons hovered at half-mast. Cards were stuck to the far wall from floor to ceiling. *Sports Center* was on the TV.

"Nicholas," I rasped, barely audible over the cacophony of machinery.

The television snapped off.

"Elle?" My ears worked again. Nicholas hovered over me.

My lids slipped shut.

"Nurse?"

"Yes?" The intercom responded near my head.

"She's moving. I think she spoke."

A draft of air moved over my arms. Several bodies filed in. More voices and shuffling feet. The only voice I understood was his.

"Elle." Nicholas moved opposite the crowd, shoved away by people in white and green coats. He positioned himself on my other side. "I knew it. You're strong. So strong." He sniffed and chuckled low in his throat. "Strong and stupid. I can't decide whether to kiss you or yell at you."

"Nicholas."

A hush came over the room.

"Yes. I'm here. Your dad's here, too, and Sara, and my folks." He was still naming my guests.

I didn't care about any of that. "I love you." The words arrived weak and soft, but my heart spoke them with ferocity. It was all that mattered.

Warm tears ran down my cheeks.

He kissed my hand and pressed it to his face once more.

A man cleared his throat. The ugly sound broke through my bliss. I blinked my tired eyes open again, squinting against the harsh fluorescent lighting.

"Gabriella." My father's voice. "How do you feel?"

"Like my head is wrapped in a blanket."

"It is." A strange accented voice answered. A nurse or a doctor maybe.

"You suffered from hypothermia, a concussion, massive blood loss, and a myriad of less threatening injuries." Dad lifted a weary look at Nicholas and ran his hands through unruly hair. Stubble darkened his cheeks. His hair stood on end from the rubbing. His shirt and pants looked like they'd been tied in a knot instead of folded when he picked them out.

I tossed his words around in my mind. How had I been injured? I was with Nicholas. I was with his family. I was in the woods. The images began to fall into place, like a puzzle thrown into the wind and coming together as it landed.

Terror filled my heart. My breaths were suddenly shallow. Machinery beeped louder behind me. I examined each face inside my small room. They looked joyful. I turned to Nicholas. Why hadn't he told them?

"He's out there. He's in the woods. He . . . " My voice cracked under the emotion. Unable to hide from the eyes that surrounded me, I rolled my head to the side and sobbed against my pillow. *He touched me.*

"No. He's gone, Elle. He's not in the woods. I promise." Nicholas kissed my knuckles softly. He pressed his lips against my temple. The nurse ushered everyone away. Nicholas didn't even flinch. Her words were lost on him. He squeezed my hand. A silent promise. He wouldn't leave. My father lodged himself in the doorway, unwilling to be escorted any farther.

"Sara?" As I said it, I remembered her lying dead on the ground with us.

"She's fine. She's good, really." His voice became a whisper. "Much better than you. You've been asleep for a week. You lost a lot of blood. Your body was shutting down. The hypothermia was bad, and your head . . . " He swallowed long and hard. His eyelids closed and reopened slowly. Pain carved a deep crease between his eyebrows.

I moved my free hand to touch my head. He'd hacked off my new black hair. I couldn't feel it. My head was wrapped in something soft and cushiony.

"You have a concussion. You've been through a huge trauma. I should've been there."

Memories came again, this time in the vivid hues of the forest. Blinding white and deep, punctuating black. An empty expanse of trees and hopelessness around me. Sara on the ground. The Reaper and his scissors. The garbage bag.

"Where is he?" I was afraid to say his name aloud. My hands moved over the blankets. A tear blurred my vision. He had dressed me for disposal. Kissed me. A whimper escaped.

"He's dead, Elle. It's over."

"How?" I cleared my throat, forcing down the wave of panic in my chest.

"Well, the autopsy will make the final determination." Nicholas squinted his sparkling green eyes. "For starters, your dad shot him a half-dozen times." He held back a smirk. I had to admit, it wasn't *bad* news.

"That seems pretty clear." *Where was the need for an autopsy?*

He nodded, as if to say "Yes, but . . . "

"When they got to him, he was face down in the leaves . . . on top of you." His voice seethed on the last words. "When they moved him, they saw the scissors."

Scissors. "I did that." It was both a statement and a question.

"Unless it was a ghastly suicide. Yes. We assumed."

Nicholas leaned forward to kiss my cheek. His smile grew until his dimple broke free, sinking into his beautiful face and pulling a bunch of stubble with it. Then, in an act that couldn't be put at bay, regardless of bed rails and hospital sheets and IVs, the kisses continued. His warm breath brushed across my cheek. His lips grazed the tip of my nose, my forehead, my chin. They kept coming until I felt a surge inside me. I pulled him to my lips with my free hand. My fingers locked behind his wide neck. He was warm and strong, and I loved him.

He tried to protest, but it was a halfhearted attempt. I knew I'd win. I pulled softly against his lower lip until he made a distinct sound of defeat. His mouth moved against mine. My head swam, not from injury or medication but from joy, from completion. My heart brimmed and flew. His lips parted gently, and I deepened the kiss, reveling in the taste of him.

My father's voice boomed in the distance. "Nicholas, I'd like a moment, please."

Nicholas released me slowly, pressing his lips to my forehead, lingering there before pulling away. His eyes smoldered inches from mine. "Happy birthday." A wide wolfish grin exposed two rows of straight white teeth under lips made for kissing.

My birthday. I was eighteen.

"Get well so we can go home." He squeezed my hand.

Home.

Chapter
Thirty-Three

Dad warned me. Going back to Francine Frances wouldn't be a great idea for the wallflower he knew. But it turned out, I'd changed a lot in a short amount of time. The truth and a life-altering experience could do that to a girl. I had some things I needed to do, like finish what I had started. Senior year in a quirky little town with my friends.

The town bustled and clamored in a new way since the crazy serial killer was reported to have stayed there. Added security patrolled the streets, heavy with new faces. Cameras snapped and flashed in the snowy air. Tourists took pictures of the street signs and storefronts. The quaint town had an influx of interest. A few stores added signs saying things like "The Reaper ate here," or shopped here, or some other infuriating attempt to cash in on the monster. I ignored it all and focused on my agenda.

I nodded to Dad as he loaded the last of my things into the rental car. A wistful mix of emotion encased me as I locked my apartment door for the last time. I was voluntarily moving to another dorm.

Dad had arranged a typical cramped room in Aubrie's building, closer to the main buildings. The welcome mat and ashes were long gone, removed by the Clean Team or covered in snow. I didn't search for them. He'd stolen enough of my time, monopolized too many of my thoughts in one form or another.

School would let out in half an hour. I hoped to get settled before then.

"Meet you at the coffee shop in an hour?"

Dad nodded, pushing large mirrored Aviators over his broad, smiling face. The trench in my heart had pulled together, if still ragged on the edges. I had a dad who wanted me. He hadn't left my side since the accident. A Smith family miracle in more ways than one. Nicholas's constant presence had probably fueled Dad's need to stay close, but I didn't care about the reason.

"You sure about this?"

"Absolutely."

Dad slid behind the wheel and drove me to Francine Frances through sloshy, muck-covered streets. I'd been right in September. An outside locker was not a smart choice. I smiled and shivered as I popped it open. An outdoor locker was my biggest problem and I was okay with that. The campus was silent as I loaded my personal things into my arms and made a trip to the office with the rest.

As I reached for the doorknob, the bell screamed over my head. My shoulders shot up to guard my ears. My hands were full.

"Elle!" Darcy barreled through the office doors with a dozen freshmen in tow.

I left my pile of textbooks on the large administration desk and hugged her to me.

"OMG! I can't even believe you're here! You've been on the news like every night for weeks! This town is going complete bat sh—"

"I'm fine."

Over the sea of freshman, I locked eyes with Aubrie in the crowded hall. Her eyes popped wide at the sight of me. I pushed my way in her direction.

"Is Pixie . . . ?" She stopped mid-sentence. I could only imagine why. Here? Dead? Who knew what the latest rumors were.

"No. She's good. I talked to her last night. She's in California, and she's supposed to send you an e-mail later. She'll tell you everything."

Aubrie hugged me tight around my chest and started bouncing. Darcy and the group of freshmen joined in. A few lockers down, Davis and Kate stood talking, pretending to be oblivious of the commotion twenty feet away.

Then my reason for coming back to school strolled over to meet me. Davis left Kate's side, cutting through the crowd like butter. My feet were in the air, knocking into everything in my small space as I spun around and into his arms.

"You're okay." He rested me onto my feet and stared down. Surprise and disbelief colored his face. "I can't believe I talked about my stupid family drama and you were going through all that. I've felt so stupid. I had no idea. Then you were gone. I worried, you know?"

I knew. That's why I was there.

The crowd dissipated a little. I patted Aubrie's shoulder. I spoke to Davis but looked at the eager faces nearby. "I received early admission to the prelaw program in D.C. I'm going to go." Aubrie embraced me softer this time. Davis's mouth fell open. "But I'm finishing senior year here. With you." My smile grew until my face hurt. "Pixie will be in touch. She misses everyone, but she's staying put." I rolled my eyes, feeling a little like Pixie in the center of this crowd. "She apparently thinks L.A. is more awesome than Ohio." They laughed and told a hundred Pixie stories at once.

I faced Davis directly then. "I wanted to tell you in person. You know, aside from Pixie, you're my best friend here."

He pulled his lips to the side. "Ah. The old 'let's just be friends' line." The words were so full of truth. Only his face hinted at the flopping joke. "Can I buy you coffee?"

I locked my arm in his with my chin held high. Together, we left behind the school I barely knew.

My feet froze inside my favorite canvas sneakers, but I laughed and smiled every step of the way to Buzz Cup.

"So, Pixie's okay? You've talked to her?"

"She's not okay. She's a nut, and all that sunshine is making her crazier. I'll know more soon." I peeked at him. I hadn't told anyone this yet. "Dad's sending me out to see her for spring break. I've never been to California, let alone any place like Los Angeles."

"Yeah, I bet you're terribly disappointed to be making that trip."

"I can't wait. Dad's worried I won't come back."

"Prelaw, huh?"

"Yes, I'll be living on the frozen side of the country next year."

"Can I ask you something?" He stopped short of opening the door to the coffee shop.

Dad sat inside reading the paper.

"Austin disappeared when you did."

Interesting. Somehow I'd become the poster child for campus security and urban folklore fodder. Nicholas had turned to smoke and disappeared. No one had prepped me on what to say about him. I doubted it was an oversight. In fact, since he'd announced his plans to study criminal justice at the school where I had earned an acceptance, he'd changed to a desk job with the Marshals. Dad said very little about him. His response to our dates and phone calls came down to sighs and eye-rolling, broken occasionally with comments about how young I was and how long forever could be.

He didn't protest, though I knew he wanted to. He and his old friends, the Austins, had reunited. Not to mention, Nicholas was perfect. Everyone loved him. I supposed that was half the problem.

"He's good. Enrolled at a new school this semester." I followed Davis through the door into the warm, coffee-scented air.

"Are you two," he fumbled for words, "like a long-distance thing now?"

"Yeah. Something like that." Were there words for what we had? I doubted any would do it justice, so I didn't try.

"Well, hey, the good news is I have you to myself a few more months."

I smiled when Dad saw us enter arm in arm. His jaw dropped.

"Dad, this is Davis. Davis, Dad." They shook hands and settled into a conversation like old friends.

He and Dad talked football while I returned a few texts from Nicholas. My ends were tied up, and Nicholas and I had plans for Skype and a movie when I got to my new room. I thanked Davis a hundred times for being happy and constant for me when I'd needed him. Even if he hadn't known he was doing it, it had meant more than I could explain.

"Nice meeting you, Mr. Smith." Davis extended his hand once more to my dad.

"Well, did you get to do everything you wanted?"

I looked around. "Yep. Ready."

"Davis is a nice boy. Headed to play lacrosse at Yale next year. Wants to be a teacher. Nice safe occupation, teaching." He nodded as we crossed the street to his rental car.

"He's wonderful, but he's not my Marshal."

Dad rolled his eyes in a clear imitation of me. "Stop calling him that. He's not *your* Marshal, and anyway, the FBI is way better."

"Uh-huh." I tapped the car roof, eager to get a shower and check my e-mail.

Dad unlocked the door and narrowed his eyes my way. "You know, if you hadn't unpacked those boxes at Thanksgiving, I'd have a lot less work to do in Texas."

"No worries. The Austins will be there to meet the movers when they get to your new place. The rest won't keep you away for long."

"Long enough."

We slid into the cold car and shivered together for a minute.

"I haven't lived in D.C. since . . . "

"I know. Me either." But it was time we both lived our lives. Dad loved D.C. Moving home was perfect. In five months, I'd be there, too.

He wrapped one strong hand around mine on the seat between us. "I love you, kid." My phone buzzed, and Dad rolled his eyes, this time for real.

"Tell your dad he's got about twenty-four Austins waiting for him." –Nicholas.

"He's dropping me off now." –Me

"Can't wait to see you." –Nicholas

"I'm on my way." –Me.

Dad pulled away from the curb and I smiled into the sun.

My real life was finally beginning.

Acknowledgments

Heartfelt thank-yous to: Jackie Mitchard, for pulling my story from the pile and giving it life. My agent and friend, Dawn Dowdle, who believes in me. Kristin Ostby, living proof that this industry really is about books, not numbers. My beta readers, critique partner, and friends who sacrificed their precious time to read my troubled pages: Nikki Brandyberry, you are wonderful wrapped in awesome. Jennifer Anderson, my fellow "Creeker" and partner in literary shenanigans, Valerie Haight, my cosmic soul sister and Wendy Delfosse, my sweet friend. Also, an enormous, face-to-the-floor, thank-you to Matt Petrunak, Brittany Blair, Cynthia Preston, and the amazing KSU students who brought my story to life in the most incredible book trailer ever made. Finally, most importantly: Massive adoration to Bryan, my husband, sidekick, utter enabler and BFF who has never doubted for one second that I can change the world. Silly man.